Always Kiss the Corpse
ON WHIDBEY ISLAND

Sandy Frances Duncan & George Szanto

TouchWood
Editions

TouchWood Editions
www.touchwoodeditions.com

Library and Archives Canada Cataloguing in Publication
Duncan, Sandy Frances, (date)
Always kiss the corpse on Whidbey Island /
Sandy Frances Duncan & George Szanto.
(An Islands Investigations International mystery ; 2)

Print format: ISBN 978-1-926741-05-5 (bound). – ISBN 978-1-926741-13-0 (pbk.)
Electronic monograph in PDF format: ISBN 978-1-926741-68-0
Electronic monograph in HTML format: ISBN 978-1-926741-69-7

I. Szanto, George, (date) II. Title. III. Series: Duncan, Sandy
Frances, (date) . Islands Investigations International mystery ; 2.

PS8557.U5375A75 2010   C813'.54   C2010-902099-5

Editor: Rhonda Bailey
Cover image: Denis J. Tangney, istockphoto.com

We gratefully acknowledge the financial support for our publishing
activities from the Government of Canada through the Canada Book Fund,
Canada Council for the Arts, and the province of British Columbia through
the British Columbia Arts Council and the Book Publishing Tax Credit.

Mixed Sources
Cert no. SW-COC-001271
© 1996 FSC
FSC

The interior pages of this book have been printed on 100% post-consumer
recycled paper, processed chlorine free, and printed with vegetable-based inks.

1 2 3 4 5 13 12 11 10

PRINTED IN CANADA

For June and Jerry Underwood

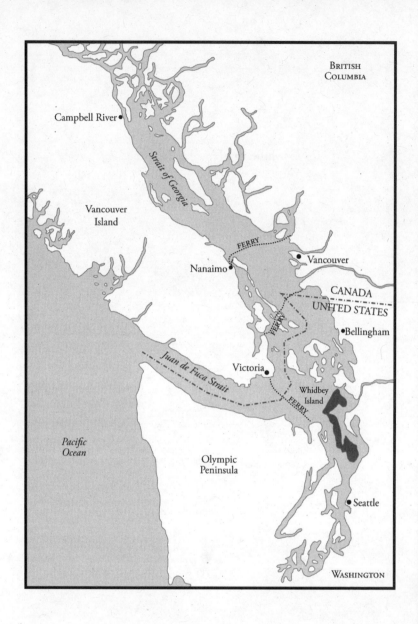

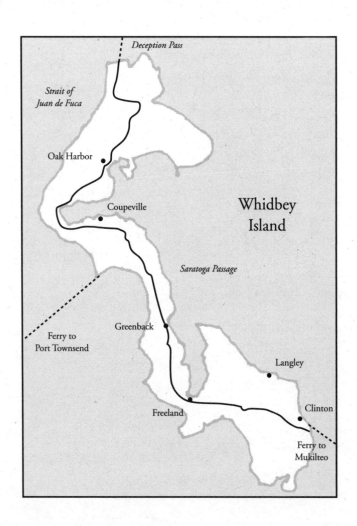

Deception Pass

Strait of
Juan de Fuca

Oak Harbor

Coupeville

Whidbey
Island

Saratoga Passage

Greenback

Ferry to
Port Townsend

Langley

Clinton

Freeland

Ferry to
Mukilteo

THESE PEOPLE WHO pay their respect to the dead, who are they? What had these ten—eleven now—mourners to do with Sandro?

The men and women in the room, likely they lived on this island. Why Sandro had chosen to move here to Whidbey made no sense. The rest of the family, the community—except poor Maria—we all live in Seattle. That's where Sandro should have come, home. Not onto an island, separated by time and water from those who care the most.

Andrei again scanned the room. No Maria yet. The space, wood-paneled, was decorated into nothing, two painless seascapes to the right, one flowered landscape beside him, medium quality carpeting. Not even a crucifix. The all-purpose chapel. No solace to soothe the soul.

Set against the long wall stood a table draped in white. On the table the coffin, burnished oak, gave off a fine lustre. At the head and the foot, vases of red roses. Yes, the funeral home had assured him, Sandro's body would be laid out according to custom.

At the far end of the room sat a young woman with green hair. How would Sandro have met such a person? In the corner stood two women, one tall, dark-haired, the other a blonde, animated, looked competent enough. The tall one, attractive, seemed late twenties—slender, a straight dress too blue for the occasion but full red lips and pretty eyes. The blonde, shorter, a few years older, talked with a portly man in a double-breasted suit, either a man of substance or trying to pass himself off as important, sucking in his belly to give an appearance of a broader chest.

A small wiry man wearing a navy blazer over a shirt and tie caught Andrei's eye, walked over, reached out his hand and introduced himself; the name went out of Andrei's brain the instant it entered. "Friend of Sandro's. You family?"

Andrei must stand out, different in this group. He gripped the man's hand. "Andrei Vasiliadis. Sandro's uncle."

"Terrible thing, just terrible. I liked Sandro a lot."

Andrei nodded. "You were close friends."

The man shrugged. "Not real close, no. We bowled together, same team. Once a week. Had a beer after."

"Ah." Not close, but the man had come here this wet afternoon.

The man smiled. "We kinda carried the team. We were the best, both lefties."

Andrei's brow twitched. Had Sandro been political?

The man caught the confusion. "Left-handed."

"Oh. I see." The competent blonde and the portly man were approaching, and Andrei felt an uneasiness. In one way, satisfaction; these people dealt him respect. In another, failure; he had not, in the moment of arriving, taken on the role of welcomer.

The blonde reached out her hand to Andrei. Another introduction, another name gone. "I worked with Sandro at the hospital. We were good friends." She smiled, her eyes red. "And this is Dr. Jones."

A doctor?

He too shook Andrei's hand. "My deep sympathies."

"Thank you."

"So upsetting, so sad." The doctor scowled.

The blonde agreed. "I just don't understand."

"No," said Andrei, "neither do we."

"He'd been in such a good mood lately, real upbeat."

"I hadn't seen Sandro for a couple of years." Andrei dropped his head. "Not since his father's funeral. My brother."

"That's very sad too." The blonde dabbed her eyes. "And for his mother."

Andrei shook his head. "She and Sandro talked every week. He wasn't sick, he'd have told her. And she says the same about his mood, always up."

"Will she be here this afternoon?"

"Yes. She wants to see Sandro a last time."

The blonde and the doctor glanced over at the coffin. She said, "You mean you'll open the coffin?" She shivered a little.

"Yes. My sister-in-law requested it."

"Won't that be hard for her?" The doctor crunched his eyebrows.

"Of course." Had it been up to him he'd have insisted the coffin stay closed, despite custom. He'd prefer no repeat of Maria's collapse when she'd viewed her husband's body. Since that funeral she'd taken his, Andrei's, advice. Mostly. Still, there'd been no arguing with her about an open coffin.

"I work at the hospital, I see how people die," the blonde said. "The dead should be allowed a final dignity. Away from the eyes of others."

The doctor said, "I agree."

"A mother has the right to kiss her son goodbye." Andrei felt a need to defend his brother's widow: an open coffin was normal. Still—"Any relative, or even a close friend, has that right. If they want to take it."

Through the doorway came a woman in her early thirties, pale makeup, black dress; behind her an older woman, also in black, on the arm of a tall man about the first woman's age, he in a dark jacket, slacks, no tie.

"Excuse me," Andrei said, and joined the new arrivals. He kissed the older woman on the cheek, embraced her for a moment, stood back. "Hello, Maria."

She tried to speak. Words wouldn't come. The tall man took her arm again, led her to a chair, sat her down. The young woman took the seat beside Maria. The man said to Andrei, "Mr. Vasiliadis, we met a long time ago." He mentioned his name. "I'm very sorry. I've known Sandro since fourth grade."

Sandro's old friend introduced his wife, who now held Maria's hand. One by one people introduced themselves to Maria, including the green-haired one. Maria nodded thanks to each for coming.

A smooth-cheeked, tall, slim man in a black suit and blacker tie appeared silently at Andrei's side. "Sir, if you're ready?"

Andrei glanced at his sister-in-law. Her face had taken on a quality of uncertainty, as if she had forgotten where she was. Even, possibly, who she was; what she had been she was no longer, not a wife, not a mother. Was she strong enough to gaze at the face of a son whose soul now dwelled with both his earthly father and his heavenly Father? "Maria? If you can't do this, I'll do it for you."

Hearing the words brought Maria back to the room. She stood, stiff and straight. "No. I must kiss Sandro."

Andrei glanced at the funeral director, and nodded. The man, his black shoes glowing with high polish, removed the roses from each end of the coffin, and raised the lid. Red velvet lined the underside. The body had been wrapped in a white shroud, proper for death. Andrei took Maria by the arm and led her across the room.

When she reached the coffin, she slowly lowered her head and wiped her eyes. When she opened them again her lips were inches from the body's face. She paused, then drew back, mouth agape. Shaky sound came from her throat.

Andrei put his arm around her waist. "What?"

She breathed harshly and stood straight, staring down. "That's—" a hoarse whisper, "that's not Sandro!" She started to fall.

PART I

ONE

"NO, DETECTIVE WORK isn't half so glamorous as movies like *Marlowe* make it seem." Kyra Rachel stood up from the sofa, found the remote and ejected the DVD.

Jerome Benson poured more red wine. "You don't solve murders and find missing persons?" Jerome, tall and slim, had thinning ruddy hair and, Kyra thought, the warmest pair of deep brown eyes she'd ever seen. She and he raised their glasses and sipped.

"We mainly deal with delinquent spouses, false insurance claims and, let me see—" She changed the topic. "The best thing about being a snoop is working for yourself and you know about that."

"Come on, the pharmacy—"

"Your own business."

"So no guns or bad guys all over the place?"

Kyra looked at him with a smile, her head shaking. "It's anything but romantic."

"I'm relieved." Jerome's tone teased. He was intrigued with Kyra. She and her associate ran a detective agency, working on both sides of the US–Canada border, specializing in islands.

Kyra lowered herself to the sofa, now close enough to Jerome so that if she turned to face him—or he to face her—their legs would touch. "No need for relief." In January, she had started an art history course at Western Washington University; among her fellow students, Jerome Benson. Till now, the first week of March, they'd spent a few Sundays exploring Bellingham, visiting funky art galleries, a couple of times walking Jerome's dog, Nelson. Kyra and Nelson had taken an instant dislike to each other. So Nelson was not invited to her place this evening for takeout Thai and a movie. "I don't get involved in danger."

Jerome let his arm slide along the top of the sofa. "How'd you and your associate get started in the first place?" He sipped his wine.

"Oh, I was already doing some investigating for an insurance company here. And I knew Noel from before, we'd been good friends for a long time. Then Noel's partner died, and he was devastated. Worse, at real loose ends. Till he got involved in an investigative project and asked me to help him. The agency developed from there."

Three possibilities. Relax onto Jerome's arm maybe now, or maybe later, or maybe not at all. She got up without making a conscious decision. This was Jerome's first evening at Kyra's. She'd have to decide how intimate she wanted to be with him: friend? lover? Jerome, she thought, was a nice man. "Care for a tour of the condo?" She'd carefully not offered before the movie. Now they could end up in the bedroom. She felt her neck grow warm.

Jerome stood, glanced again around the living, dining, kitchen area, and stepped over to the sliding glass door. Beyond it a small deck hovered above the lights of downtown Bellingham. "In the daytime, can you see the bay?"

"Ships in the harbor, and over there Lummi and Portage Islands." Kyra followed his glance. Jerome stood a comfortable few inches taller than her five-six. "I'm glad I sprang for the place." For a moment she took it all in through Jerome's eyes, a condo filled with new furniture. The only remnant from her previous life was a Hepplewhite chair, a present from her father. A rich indigo sofa and matching loveseat, plum-and-cream-striped armchair, wicker and glass coffee table, dining table and six mahogany chairs. All on her credit card. A teak wall unit housed new china, a sound system, some books. She wondered when the place would stop feeling like a showroom in a furniture store. "You like the window over the kitchen sink? I think it makes the place feel homey." She finished her wine. "And here's the guest bedroom-cum-office. All I've got is a pullout couch and my desk." The desk, a door blank on two filing cabinets, held computer, printer and two phones, Kyra's private one and the agency's business line. She led the way through the living area and down the hall, pointing out a spacious bathroom, the washer/dryer/linen closet, a large storage cupboard. The hall ended at her bedroom with its attached bath.

"Very nice." Jerome's eyes swept across a red floral duvet on the queen-size bed. He hesitated, then slowly backed away.

"I'm waiting to see what Noel thinks."

"Ah, your partner. And very *very* good friend?" Jerome arched one handsome eyebrow.

Kyra laughed. "Not in that way." She returned to the living room, sat on the sofa again and divided the remaining wine between their glasses. "Though I had a wicked crush on him when I was between twelve and fifteen. God, over twenty years ago. No, I told you, Noel's gay."

"Always?"

"Oh yes. Long as I've known him. Brendan was his partner."

"Who just died, you said." Jerome sipped his wine.

"Last June." Kyra caught herself. Jerome's wife too had died, last January, over a year ago now. Metastasised breast cancer. In her early forties, he'd said. His son, the giver of Nelson, the dog, to his mother, was away at college in the East. Noel's Brendan had been in his fifties; non-lymphocytic leukemia. The many ways to die. "Noel and I see each other mainly when we're on a case, and sometimes not even then. He's up in BC. In Nanaimo. On Vancouver Island. He does a lot of work on-line." Jerome's arm had again wandered along the back of the sofa. Kyra, so slightly, leaned into it. "I'm thinking of having a housewarming potluck. Can you come? I'll get some friends in, and maybe Noel can pop down. How's Thursday?"

"Sounds great." Jerome let his hand slide onto her shoulder. "I can't remember my last potluck. What should I bring? I do a lot of things in one pot."

"Whatever. My only rule is dishes can't be specified. If everybody brings dessert, that's that."

"I won't let that happen." Jerome's smile softened his authoritative tone.

She turned her face to his smile. Well, let's find out—

The phone rang. Amazing timing, that phone. Would not-answering make too strong a statement? She glanced at her watch. Five after nine. She gave him a rueful smile. "I'd better get it." She walked quickly from Jerome's arm to the den, and picked up. "Islands Investigations International, Kyra Rachel."

Jerome watched Kyra listen to the phone. He tried to keep himself from realizing he'd almost kissed a woman again. Was he prepared for such a— What? Just a kiss, right? Okay, he was clearly attracted to her. So more than a kiss? It wasn't as if Bev somehow hovered above his head, watching and admiring, or condemning. Bev had been ill for too long a time. But still. And then this friend, this Noel. Supposedly gay.

But gay isn't enough, is it? Jerome had a cousin in Omaha who was bisexual, he just passed himself off as gay, but he played around with a lot of friends' wives. Anyway, they say very few people are absolutely one sex or another. Intriguing new material in the pharmacological journals in the last few years.

He heard Kyra disconnect. The caller had done most of the talking. He turned toward her, no, not ready. Looked now like she'd punched in a pre-coded number.

Her words came through clearly: "Noel? . . . Yeah, I know, but a worried man just phoned me. Says a woman friend of his claims it wasn't her supposedly dead son in the casket at a viewing today, so where is he and who's in the casket . . . Yeah, good question. I said I'd see her tomorrow, both of us if you can make it . . . She's in Bellingham but her son lived—or lives—on Whidbey Island . . . Can you take that Raven flight down? . . . Yes, about nine-thirty . . . I'll pick you up . . . Okay, good . . . See you." She set the phone on its base and returned to the living room.

"I couldn't help overhearing."

She smiled. "Well. You'll definitely meet my business associate at the potluck."

Both stood without moving. Jerome stared at the DVD on the coffee table, and picked it up. "I'll return this. Thank you for a very pleasant evening." He kissed her lightly on the cheek.

"Thank you," she echoed, the ghost of his kiss tingling on her skin. But she made no attempt to kiss him back.

He shrugged into his windbreaker. "I'll read recipes for Thursday night. I guess you'll be busy with this case. It sounds strange."

"I'm available by phone. Here or cell."

Jerome's smile glowed. "I'll call." He left.

Oh dear, thought Kyra. Dear oh dear. Should she take a long hot bath? Her body needed soothing. Jerome was unlike many men she'd met, no heavy attempt to come on to her. Something wrong with her? Clearly he'd been prepared to kiss her. Prepared? Was that good enough? Why didn't he desire her, and passionately? Maybe he was just the nice man he appeared. And did she want to become involved with just a nice man? Or maybe lots of passion, waiting to be unlocked?

She'd take her bath in the morning. In the bedroom she undressed, black slacks back in the closet, white shirt in the clothes hamper. Standing in her bikini underpants—There. She'd undressed herself. Vance, Simon, Sam, all three of her ex-husbands had enjoyed undressing her, in various ways.

From a shelf in her closet she took a small leather case. She opened it. Six padded pockets lined with blue velvet, each containing a red ball an inch and seven-eighths in diameter. She picked up one and squeezed it tight in her palm. She released it and it rolled into its pocket. No way of figuring how to juggle Jerome. To juggle, you needed options. Could she seriously become involved with a pharmacist?

Dr. Stockman Jones adored his house. Others were allowed to admire it, but only he felt its caress each time he came home. That its seventeen rooms and two barns, one now a triple garage, were built 103 years ago by a Seattle ironmonger, grown rich by supplying miners off in search of Yukon gold, mattered little to Stockman. That it had been revamped in postwar plastics as a summer cottage for an aircraft czar was a concern that had been overcome by the decorating genius of his wife, professionally known as Bonnie O'Hara. But that a shingle might be loose, the cream paint on the crenellated supports of the mock fascia might be chipped, the glass on his front door might be smudged, this pained him. His house had been his reward from God, and Stockman Jones must care for it.

The house, its lawn smooth as a golf course green, stood two hundred feet back from the road up the hill from downtown Coupeville. The view encompassed the harbor, Penn Cove, and the Whidbey Island Naval Air Station Seaplane Base across the water.

When they'd taken off the plastic siding and found the old wood shingles beneath, still in good repair, Bonnie had suggested they paint them a creamy orange, the window frames highlighted in maroon, and the trim white. Stockman had been aghast. Houses should be all white. This was not a merry-go-round. She'd shown him books of turn-of-the-century wood frame houses painted a rich array of hues. He gave in. And now the colors pleased his eye. Passersby might admire the house for its nobility but could see nothing inside. Respect, like grandeur, like privacy, was indispensable in Stockman Jones' life.

All the virtues of his house were necessary this morning because Dr. Jones had slept badly. As he showered, his mind refused to give shape, much less order, to the new situation.

He dried himself and patted the soft roundness of his belly. Bonnie was right, time to lose some pounds. A thought took him: maybe direct action was the wrong way to go, maybe planned inaction should be their tactic. Not Stockman's preferred way of coping, he wasn't a passive person, not in the clinic, not at the hospital nor with his church. But in this instance, maybe. Because certainly it had been Sandro Vasiliadis in the coffin.

That poor woman, his mother. May God have mercy. Well, nothing to be done. History can't run backwards. Nothing to be done, so do nothing.

He'd try that out on the others, doing nothing. He was pretty sure of their reactions:

Lorna would agree with him. She was pragmatic and sensible about the conditions of their clients and the importance of the work.

Richard would continue to take Sandro's death hard, that was inevitable. Richard brooded about their clients, and often his brooding paid off. It was as if he placed his thoughts in some oozing cauldron and stirred them, witch-like, until he distilled a clear solution to a specific concern. The results had often brought answers, considerable credit, and research money to WISDOM.

Gary would be the most complicated. Gary, like Stockman himself, was an activist. This too had served the clinic well. It had been Gary's brilliant paper, then his politicking, that had brought in the handsome contract from Bendwell Pharmaceuticals. But Gary could also be a loose-cannon kind of activist.

Stockman dressed casually, comfortable flannels and a soft cotton shirt. After the morning's surgery he had an ethical guidance meeting at his Church, and as an elder he had noticed it was easier for the others to converse with him when he appeared informally. He smiled. And there'd be more of the casual life for him in the months and years to come, time to pay back to his community and his Church the lessons he had learned. So yes, the more he thought about it, the better he liked the idea of inaction.

Bonnie had finished her breakfast when he came downstairs. She kissed his cheek and patted his belly, raised her eyebrows and grinned.

He stroked her short brown hair, graying in front but dark still on top and in back. "I've decided inaction is the best way to go."

"Does that include not eating?" She tilted her head to the right, a kind of flirting that always warmed him.

He laughed a little. "We'll see."

"You sound better than last night."

"Inaction. Just let go, that's the way. That's what I'll suggest."

"The Zen of WISDOM?"

"Zen?" He chuckled. "You been spending time with the granola crowd?" He poured himself some coffee, started to add sugar, stopped himself. He saw Bonnie's wry smile.

"The Zen of control," she said, "like your Zen of management. You're getting to be quite the Zen master."

He shook his head, ending their banter. "And what have you got going today?"

"Back to the cedar coastal by the Rhododendron Gardens, the owners aren't happy with the colors of the billiard room. Then up to the base, the new admiral's been given a house that's too small for his six kids so they have to re-do the basement."

"Doesn't sound like much fun."

"I know. So I tripled my fee. They didn't bat an eye."

"Government's paying."

"I guess. Anyway, we can use the money. Franny called while you were in the shower. They've found a house, could we lend them eighty thousand for a down payment please."

Stockman laughed. "Those kids've figured it out. Money does grow on the parent tree."

She grabbed her jacket, "Got to run," pecking his mouth as she passed.

He phoned the clinic to leave a message for Dawn but she was already there. Such a conscientious girl! Yes, she'd call the others for a meeting. She checked their calendars. Had to be late afternoon. Stockman would have preferred a morning meeting. No, Richard and Gary had appointments till four.

He cut two slices of bread and made toast. He buttered them and spread a little marmalade. No, a lot of marmalade, he'd need the energy before the day ended. He chomped it down. He stuffed a file into his briefcase. Jacket, new snap-brim fedora just back in style. Out the back way, past a million crocuses, purple and yellow against new young green, to the barn Bonnie had turned into a place of comfort for their vehicles, and a separate apartment on the second floor designed with the kids in mind and whatever babies would come along.

He'd take the Jag today. He drove down his driveway and glanced back at the house. He had wrought all this. After medical school he'd been in deep debt. Twenty-one years of surgery had brought him what he had. He pulled into the street.

TWO

NOEL FRANKLIN WAS looking forward to working with Kyra again. Only three weeks since their last case, someone sabotaging generators on Lasqueti Island. A collective of islanders had hired them, and what fascinated Noel was not so much solving the case, which they had, but that the islanders were unanimous in wanting their services in the first place. Unanimous islanders? Unheard of.

He glanced through the float plane's window, so tiny it seemed as if he had to view the constricted panorama with only one eye at a time. Below him the south end of Gabriola Island gave way to Valdez. Off its southwestern edge the green lumps of Reid, Ruxton and DeCourcy, then Thetis and Kuper Islands. This has to be one of the most beautiful parts of the world, these jade-like islands rimmed with white where green-blue waves broke on their rocks. He'd lived on this coast all his life, had never wanted to live elsewhere.

The morning sun was shining as if it were May, not early March. Maybe it'd burn the last of the clouds away. If the wind didn't scatter them; it was buffeting the plane hard enough. No matter, he loved float planes, trusted them in a way he never trusted jets. Something goes wrong, just glide on down to the chuck and skitter along on pontoons.

Another nice thing about float planes, they were so noisy you didn't have to feign sleep or read a book to avoid conversation with a seatmate. This one was hogging the shared armrest. Okay, he silently told the log boom beneath him, that's a big man and he can't help it, it must be really uncomfortable. But still Noel felt irritated. Only six passengers in this twelve-seater, and Biggo didn't have to sit next to him.

Convenient of Raven Air to start this service, Campbell River, Comox, Nanaimo, Bellingham, Everett, Seattle, just when he and Kyra were getting Islands Investigations International off the ground. The case on Gabriola Island had been their first and, he'd vowed, it would be the last time he'd join her in anything physically dangerous. But what he'd appreciated about Kyra then, she'd just shrugged, agreed break-ins didn't suit some people, lots of investigation could be done on computers and telephones, and dropped the topic. When Brendan passed away, Kyra became his only friend. He needed her.

Passed away? Gone to meet his Maker? Shuffled off this mortal coil? Each worse than the previous. He'd lost Brendan, that's all there was to it. Passed away? All Noel knew was his single love was gone forever.

Brendan had Died. Nearly ten months ago. Brendan was Dead. Noel turned his head even more to the window, moving away from the pressure of his seatmate's arm; now hanging over his side of the armrest! Dead. No euphemism worked. Dead was Dead. Noel blinked fast. He would not cry.

Down below, a big BC ferry chugged through Active Pass. Up here, just a hop across the Strait to Bellingham. He began mentally collecting himself. Just for the hell of it, nudged against his seatmate's elbow till it dropped off the armrest.

He was looking forward to staying with Kyra in her new condo. A surprise, she'd actually bought something.

⁓

Kyra watched the float plane send up spray as it glided to the end of the wharf. Ten-thirty, nearly on time. She zipped up her Gore-Tex against the stiff breeze and pulled the collar high. Her hair, a mass of long dark brown curls, helped keep the back of her neck warm. The first sun in over a week had burned a few of the clouds away. A land crew person sauntered along to tie a line from the dock to the plane's strut, then a small door opened and a uniformed man crawled out. Three women climbed down, a young man in fashionably baggy pants, a large man, then Noel, carrying a black leather jacket. Kyra waved. A customs official checked him through. He picked up his overnight bag and his computer and joined her.

She hugged him. "Good flight?" She took his bag.

"Bumpy. Tight cabin." But he was smiling.

She smiled back and led him up the pier to the adjacent Hotel Bellwether parking lot. "I phoned to tell you I was down here waiting, but you didn't answer."

He put his arm around her shoulders. "You can't leave a cellphone on in a plane."

She unlocked her car, a Tracker.

He took his arm back and pulled his cell out of his pocket. "Besides, if I leave it on someone might actually find me."

"Exactly the idea, Noel." She'd hoped he would love his Christmas present. Guess not.

He set his computer on the back seat, covered it with his coat. He gave her a hug, and a peck on the cheek. "Hiya partner."

"Hi yourself. Hop in. We've got twenty minutes to get to Lake Whatcom." He looked trim and fit, his thinning blond hair newly cut short. He wore a black turtleneck, black jeans and his favorite polished black loafers. At forty-three a handsome man of delicate build, four inches taller than herself.

He folded himself into the passenger seat. "So what do we know?"

"Nothing I didn't tell you last night: Garth Schultz's phone call and Maria Vasiliadis' whispered words, *That's not Sandro*."

"Who's Schultz?"

"I'm not sure. I had company so I got just the barest details."

They sped down State Street. "Do we know what he died of?"

"No."

"Name sounds Greek."

"Schultz?"

Noel grinned. "Don't be obtuse." Her cheeks were flushed and as usual her lipstick had disappeared.

"All we know is name, address, eleven o'clock appointment, and it wasn't her son in the coffin." Kyra turned onto Alabama Street and began the climb up the straight steep hill. She gunned the engine. She didn't much like this car but it had good acceleration. Sam had given it to her when she started her snooping career. He'd thought its name was a good joke.

Under the I-5, Alabama all the way to Whatcom, Kyra talked about her new condo. Noel stared ahead, out the window. He appreciated few things as much as the return of the sun in late winter. This year more than ever.

Kyra shifted to a half-teasing tone. "How's Talbot?"

"I haven't been pushing."

"No?" She glanced his way and gave him a wry smile.

"Brendan's not going to happen again."

"I thought Talbot had this crush on you." Kyra pulled out to pass a cement truck.

"What crush? I want dinner with somebody sometimes. That's about all I can handle. And," he squinted at her, "who was your company last night?"

"A nice guy from my Art History course. Jerome. You'll meet him Thursday. I've invited him and some others for a potluck."

"Nice? What's nice?"

"Hmm, dunno. Maybe too nice. The bad thing about him is his dog."

Now Noel raised an inquiring eyebrow.

"Big slobbery thing. We walk along, he gets between me and Jerome and growls."

Noel barked a laugh.

"I take it as a personal insult." At the shore of Lake Whatcom, its grays and thin blues reflecting the sky, they turned left along Northshore Drive. Kyra dug in her purse for a notebook and thrust it at Noel. "I wrote the address on the last page. Dulcey Lane."

Noel read out street names. "There it is."

The house, a trim white bungalow on the north side with a view of the lake between the houses across the street, sat between two mid-size blue spruce. They got out, locked their doors and tramped toward the house. Kyra rang the doorbell, bing bong.

The door opened slowly, with an Inner Sanctum screak. A woman's head appeared from behind the half-open door.

"Mrs. Vasiliadis?" Kyra inquired.

"Yes?" The door opened more.

Kyra introduced herself and Noel. "We're Islands Investigations International. Sandro's friend Garth Schultz asked us to come over."

"Oh. Garth."

"May we come in?"

She opened the door fully.

A solid woman in maybe her late sixties, black dress and stockings, comfy beat-up leather slippers, shortish hair on end as if she'd been pulling it. A dark line of mustache on her upper lip. Not sixty yet, Noel thought, but she looks so weary. Heavy lines on her forehead, puffy eyes, cheeks hung to jowls and her shoulders into her upper arms.

"Come in." She took charge as if she knew she had to, and closed the door. She smiled. At least her mouth did. She turned and they followed through an arch into a living room.

An impression of blue: chesterfield, two armchairs, carpet, curtains, and a painting of hills and valleys on the wooden fireplace mantel.

Mrs. Vasiliadis dropped onto the chesterfield. "Excuse me," she said. "The doctor gave me something to help me sleep and it's left me exhausted."

Kyra sat in an overstuffed chair.

Mrs. Vasiliadis said, with effort. "So you're a friend of Garth Schultz?"

"He phoned me." Kyra glanced at her with a frown of inquiry. "But I'm afraid I can't immediately place him. I'm better with faces than names."

Noel took a chair—wooden arms, faded brocade seat and back.

"Garth used to be Alessandro's best friend." She rubbed the tissue she was holding between her palms, and frowned at it. "I thought he said he knew you personally."

"I've undoubtedly met him," Kyra soothed, "and I'll remember when I see him."

"When they were little Garth always stood up for Sandro."

"If you give us his address, we'll talk with him," Noel said. "What can we do for you?"

"Find my son." Her eyes filled with tears and she blotted them with the tissue. "I leaned down to kiss—" she faltered.

Noel pulled out a notebook. "We know this is hard. We'll try to help. Can you tell us what happened?"

She did, and ended in tears. "It wasn't Alessandro."

"You're certain?" Noel spoke gently.

"Oh yes." She pulled herself together. "Since it's not Sandro who's dead, he must be alive. I've called and called his house, and no one's there. So where is he?"

"We'll try to find out and—"

"And what mother's son is in the casket? It's not Sandro so we can't bury him. When Sandro dies, he'll be buried in our Orthodox tradition. But he can't be buried if he isn't dead."

"Why do you believe he's not?"

"Alessandro has a very dark thick beard. He shaves again in the afternoon if he goes out in the evening. That face had hardly any hair." Maria's eyes welled up again. "This man's skin was smooth, his hair far too long, he looked—"

"Yes?"

"—not like Sandro. The person in the coffin had the wrong lips. The wrong face. No, it's all wrong." She sniffed. They waited while she composed herself. "Whose is the body?"

"Garth Schultz said the funeral was on Whidbey Island?" Kyra asked.

"It wasn't a funeral, it was a viewing for Sandro's friends. To pay their last respects." Her voice broke, and she cleared her throat. "Sandro moved to Whidbey a couple of years ago. He works at the hospital, he's an LPN, licensed practical nurse."

"Have you talked to the police?" Noel asked.

"A State Patrol officer. The one who told me Sandro was dead."

Noel leaned toward her. "What's the person in the coffin supposed to have died of?"

"They say he was a drug addict. They say he overdosed." Maria took a fresh tissue from the box on the coffee table. "Which again proves it wasn't Sandro. He had no use for drugs."

"Do you know Sandro's friends on Whidbey?" Kyra asked.

"No."

Noel asked, "Who was at the viewing?"

Mrs. Vasiliadis shrugged. "My brother-in-law came. Andrei Vasiliadis. He might remember some names. Sandro's taking courses at Skagit Valley College."

Noel said, "What we can do is explore the situation on Whidbey. Could you give us Sandro's home address?"

Mrs. Vasiliadis pointed to a little black book on the phone table. Noel got up and brought it to her. She thumbed through and read an address.

Noel wrote it down. "Did you try going to his house?"

She looked stricken. "I couldn't." She dropped her face to her hands. "When they said he was dead, I couldn't. Yesterday, Andrei—My brother-in-law went. The house was locked and silent."

"Have the police been there?" An easier question.

She lifted her head but didn't look at him. "I don't know."

"Do you have Mr. Schultz's address?"

"And your brother-in-law's," Kyra prompted.

She read from her book.

"A woman at the viewing told Andrei she had his house key to feed his cats," Mrs. Vasiliadis remembered. "And that she was a nurse too."

"We'll talk to them all," Kyra reassured her as she stood. She gave Mrs. Vasiliadis a pamphlet explaining Triple-I's fee structure.

She glanced at it, and set it aside. "Andrei will take care of that."

"We'll be back to you very soon."

"Don't get up," Noel said. "We can see ourselves out."

—— ——

Dr. Lorna Albright could feel that the day would test her elasticity. Some mornings she woke with a sense of the hours ahead; other mornings while still half-asleep she'd already solved a couple of upcoming problems. The night gone by had been of the second sort.

She dressed. She lined her eyebrows, her only concession to the cosmetics industry. A plump person in her early fifties doesn't need makeup. But she did have very thin eyebrows. She chose the small silver clamshell brooch and pinned it to her suit jacket. She poured a glass of orange juice. The telephone rang. Dawn, from the clinic: Stockman had asked for a meeting. Gary and Richard were busy till three o'clock and four o'clock respectively, was late afternoon possible for Lorna? She checked her daybook. Nothing at four. Still, irritating. Luckily Tuesday was her day at WISDOM anyway, not at the lab. She ate a bowl of cereal.

On Tuesdays she didn't see Terry Paquette, her research team partner and Richard Trevelyan's wife. Terry, who ran WISDOM's lab, was as close a friend as Lorna Albright had. Often when Lorna was at the lab they went out for lunch.

She hoped the meeting wasn't about the Vasiliadis death. A shame that, but they had to move on. She locked her front door, started her car, headed onto the island highway. Ten minutes later she parked in her space. WISDOM's home was a low cedar-sided building fronted by grass, a bushed-in garden in back, and shrubs that flowered in their seasons. From behind the counter in the reception area Dawn greeted Lorna. Dawn Deane, now in her late thirties, had been part of WISDOM, the Whidbey Island Sexual Definition Management clinic, for twelve years, and was definitely a team member. They'd hired her as a redhead. Three years later she became a blonde, then shifted to ebony. Now she was blonde again. Her vivacity made her attractive to men and women, older people and kids, and whatever she did to her hair or her face suited. She handed Lorna a printed list of her day's appointments, the first at 11:00. The 4:00 PM meeting was inked in. "Coffee?"

Lorna's office was the smallest because these days she consulted less often with clients. She'd agreed to it; her real place of work was the lab. She was trained as a gynecologist, but most of her work had shifted from clinical to research. Dr. Gary Haines had set up the contract with Bendwell Pharmaceuticals, he was their schmoozer, but Dr. Lorna Albright ran the lab. Terry was in charge of day by day functioning, but Lorna organized, directed and evaluated the work. Tuesdays at the clinic she met the occasional client, consulted with Stockman, Gary and Richard, read the journals, and spent a chunk of time online, checking in with distant colleague-friends, reading through the circumlocutions of other sexual definition centers around the world.

Dawn brought Lorna a steaming cup of coffee. Lorna settled in to a week's worth of paper mail. She glanced at her watch; past ten. Then she gave herself over to the pleasure of checking abstracts of the articles she'd later choose to read. At four o'clock Dawn knocked on her open door. "They're ready in the board room."

Around the long table, eight chairs. Lorna used to argue for a smaller table but the others believed a client should be allowed a physical distance from the three men and the woman who might transform his or her life. Stockman Jones, the urologist and surgeon of the team, now sat at the head, looking downright casual. To his right, Gary Haines, their psychiatrist. From the start Gary had specialized in human sexuality in large part because he himself loved sex and saw no need to hide this. Lorna couldn't understand why women flocked to him considering he normally wore a pungent-pine aftershave that would work better as mosquito repellent. Across from Gary sat Richard Trevelyan, their endocrinologist and the most recent member of the team, with them for twelve years now.

It was Richard who, thank goodness, had brought the clinic to the island. At sixty he was also the eldest team member. His comfortable face was handsomely craggy under a lot of white hair. Lorna smiled, said "Gentlemen," her usual opening statement at such meetings, sat beside Richard and tried not to inhale Gary's cologne.

Stockman folded his hands and leaned toward the others. "Thank you all for making the time. Yesterday I went to the viewing for Vasiliadis. I'm afraid the event became a bit of a botch-up. The mother didn't believe it was her son in the coffin." He glanced from Lorna to Richard to Gary.

"Shit," said Gary.

Richard's head was shaking. "They had the coffin open?"

"Apparently that's usual in Greek Orthodoxy," Stockman said.

"Damn it," said Gary, "why couldn't—"

"Hang on," Lorna broke in. She turned to Stockman. "Is there a problem here?"

"I'm not sure. I don't think so."

"Course there's a problem," Gary said. "We sure don't need negative publicity."

You should know, Gary, thought Lorna; the mess he'd left at the Seattle clinic—She addressed Stockman again. "But didn't that nurse say it was definitely Vasiliadis?"

"Of course. And everybody else who got a glance agreed. It's a minor thing."

Richard sighed. "It's a terrible thing. And I take full responsibility."

Lorna lay her hand on his arm. "Stop it, Richard."

"It was my fault. If I'd administered the dosage over a longer time, three-four weeks maybe—"

"Richard, Richard," Stockman interrupted, "you were brilliant with the others. Johnson is perfect, and so is Gustavson. We all agreed on Vasiliadis' course of treatment."

Richard said, "I should have re-analyzed the tests."

"That's my job! And Terry's!" Lorna's hands were clenched tightly on the table.

"We'll learn from Vasiliadis," said Stockman. "We already have."

"We have to do something, Stock," said Gary.

"Why? What?" Gary in active mode: Stockman felt wary.

"No we don't," Lorna said. "We were his physicians. We did what we thought best. The only thing is to continue our work." She glanced around the table. Gary's right hand clamped itself into a fist, then he stretched his fingers. Richard stared at the table. In Stockman's eyes she saw agreement. "Okay?"

Stockman said, "I think yes. If we could bring Vasiliadis back, we'd all do everything we could for him. But he killed himself."

"With a hormonal stew tearing up his brain and his body," Richard muttered.

Stockman turned to him. "What would you like to do about it, Richard?"

Richard Trevelyan stared at the backs of his hands. He shrugged. "It's too late for Vasiliadis." He glanced from one to the other, his eyes damp. "The work has to go on, that's the important thing."

"Shit," said Gary. "I really thought he was calmed out."

"We are none of us perfect." said Stockman.

"But we try to get there," said Lorna. And knew she meant it.

Stockman nodded, as did Richard. Gary raised both arms, hands palms out, his I-give-up gesture, and stood. "I've got a patient. Anything else?"

"Nothing. Thank you, Gary."

Richard too stood. "Yeah," he said, and walked from the room. Gary followed him out.

"And thank you too," Stockman said to Lorna.

Lorna nodded. Back in the office she read an article by a colleague in South Africa. Baldini had followed up some groundbreaking work on mating patterns of a fish called *Serranus fasciatus*. He detailed the transformation of *S. fasciatus* from its hermaphroditic birth stage to a pure male stage by the reabsorption of ovarian tissue. This process, he'd shown, occurs in only one male of a group, who then becomes dominant. The remaining hermaphrodites comprise his harem. His role was to mate daily with each of them. Easy as pie. For a fish.

From Kyra's balcony Noel stared out across roofs below, the bay and islands. She'd taken his advice, Buy a place with a vista, it's relaxing on the eyes and the spirit. He turned back to face her. "Great location."

"Thanks. You like the space, too?"

He took in the living room, dining room, kitchen, and glanced down the hall at the closed bedroom doors. "It's very good."

"And?"

"And what?"

"My question precisely."

"I'm taking it in."

"Okay. Want a drink to take it in with?"

He checked his watch. "In a bit."

She opened a door. "My office. Your bedroom."

Just the makeshift desk, phones, electronics. A reading lamp on the edge of the desk. He hoped the pullout couch made into a firm bed. "Great. No distractions while working or sleeping."

She mock-scowled. "I've just moved in, Noel." She picked up the business phone and tapped out Maria Vasiliadis' number for Garth Schultz. Not there. Not even a machine.

"It'd be good to see him today." Noel looked at his watch. "What do you want to do about supper?"

"Out. Lebanese. With the potluck in a couple of days, I've got to conserve my energy."

"Right. And it's important to keep the kitchen clean." He caught her small smile. "I'll unpack." He headed for the office and opened his case. Nowhere to hang anything. He draped his gray slacks over the back of the chair. Ah well. She'd caught his reservation about the condo and was going to ask him to elaborate. Long ago he'd learned that when someone has a new toy she likes a lot, don't criticize its imperfections. But the living room made him uncomfortable— something inharmonious about it. He picked up the phone, pressed Redial. Still no answer.

Kyra, arms folded, was waiting. "I don't think you're impressed with the place."

"I am. It's a great space."

"I don't hear a lot of enthusiasm."

"No, I like it a lot. Just . . ."

"What?"

"I guess, the furniture. I mean—"

"All top of the line."

"I don't mean that. I mean it feels, well, a little out of balance."

"What's that mean?"

An edge now to her voice. Nowhere to back off. "That wall? It's too short for the sofa. And the loveseat, I think it should be across from the sofa, not at right angles. Also, your dad's chair, if you had it by the window, it'd be sort of relaxing to sit there and stare out."

She squinted. "I thought this was the most natural arrangement."

"Nothing's natural except when we make it so. Right?"

"Maybe."

They spent the next fifteen minutes rearranging furniture, Noel's mood forced light, Kyra's from irked to neutral. Okay, the new layout didn't look bad. And he was right about the chair.

At five-thirty Noel tried Garth Schultz again. A woman's voice came on, raised over a baby's wail. "Garth Schultz, please."

The woman yelled, "Garth, phone!"

"Sounds like a madhouse," Noel whispered to Kyra.

Yes, Garth agreed, seven-thirty, supper would be over by then.

———

Andrei Vasiliadis stared out the large window of his fourteenth-floor office. Late afternoon sun glittered off Lake Washington. His arguments against the new headquarters for Cascade Freightways had nothing to do with the view from the floor-to-ceiling windows looking east and south. Just, he didn't belong on Sand Point Way, and he didn't like the fact that the head of the company had to be called a CEO and had to have an office in some ritzy building far from where the job got done. For thirty-six years he'd worked out of the warehouse down by the docks, just as his father had for nearly five decades. Down where the ships came in and the trucks got loaded. Even today, this minute.

He still used that phrase, getting them loaded, but it was all containers now. Far from the old docks, the longshoremen strikes, the union halls, the fights. He'd weathered those times, had the scars, to the ego and some sewn-up cuts as well. He'd even weathered the container battle. First he was opposed, containers would kill the dockside jobs. Then, when he recognized the inevitability of it—a ship arrives with containers pre-loaded, crane them down, set them on trailers and they zip off on x-teen wheels—he bought in and did his best to placate those redundant longshoremen who were his friends, getting some of them jobs with Cascade.

That's what he was good at, helping people. And why Cascade had outlasted most of the competition. If you take care of your people they end up caring for you. As true for business as for the family. Your neighborhood, your Church.

Sure, he knew the kids had to find their way. But where he could help, he did. Brought them into Cascade if they wanted, nieces, nephews, whoever. Didn't have to become truckers, truckers have a hard life, some guys like it, some don't. Vasily, his nephew, was strong, but Andrei wouldn't put that kid on the road. Vasily had a different kind of strength, troubleshooting strength; Andrei could relax a bit knowing Vasily was around. His other sister Delia, her husband had converted, Chuck Livingston the lawyer, he'd taken on Cascade as half his practice. Chuck didn't come cheap but he'd saved Cascade's hide a few times. Andrei could trust Chuck. And Andrei's kid brother Dom's wife Marina, Marina the looker—Marina's brother, Dr. Philip Deriades, was a wonder. Andrei had convinced Philip to take a two-year residency in industrial medicine and paid him full salary while he was in school. Now Philip was a national leader in the field. Great for Philip, and good too for the company except when he was off to some conference. Just back from one last Friday. Now due in ten minutes. Philip would be more comfortable here than down in the old refurbished ratty office with the white-painted windows where everything smelled of harbor. Where Andrei would much rather be.

It felt good to reflect on success. And right now, because he wanted to keep yesterday's image of Sandro out of his memory. Andrei had given Sandro his first job. Sandro was a good driver, not big but tough, the kid had acted tough even when he didn't have to. Never could figure out why Sandro hadn't lasted. Kid needed the job, baby on the way, and that shouldn't have happened either. Carla must be, what, ten, eleven by now. And Sandro had divorced Diana. Poor little Carla had been barely four. Did it without consulting anyone. Didn't talk with his father or his mother, how can a man divorce his wife without talking to his parents?

Soon as Sandro's death was confirmed, he'd see Diana and tell her.

If Sandro had wanted it, Andrei would have been there to listen, to help. Sandro didn't even murmur about a problem. There are very few problems in the world that can't be worked out. Not if there's a bit of good will. Relationships aren't all that difficult. A lot of listening, sometimes giving in, a little niceness, what's so hard about that? Poor Diana had told her mother-in-law that Sandro hadn't even told her, his very own wife, his intentions! Just announced at breakfast: I'm leaving. It had do with sex, Andrei had learned that much. He'd called Sandro in, closed the door, demanded to know what this divorce idea was all about. Sandro didn't talk much, didn't answer Andrei's questions, some platitudes about starting over, wanting a career, medicine maybe— Medicine! The kid had finished high school, but that was it! And you don't walk away from the mother of your children. For a couple of minutes Andrei felt he'd broken through, Sandro admitting Diana wanted more kids, Sandro saying he wasn't interested in sex with her— What a dumb idea. Gorgeous girl like Diana. Anyway, you don't need a lot of sex with your wife to get kids, choose your time, suddenly she's in the family way, she doesn't care about you for the duration of the pregnancy and long after. Break up a family because your wife doesn't turn you on? Crazy.

Yes, Sandro looked weird in the coffin. But Andrei had seen his share of the departed and a good undertaker can make the face look healthy. Maybe the Whidbey funeral home didn't have a good undertaker, maybe the Protestants and the Catholics don't have open coffins. Ridiculous, should've brought him down right away to Sporo's place. It all started years back when Maria and Kostas moved up to Bellingham, away from the community. Andrei knew Maria didn't want to leave Seattle but Kostas was a rebel, always had been. Part of why Maria loved him, Andrei figured, Maria always wanted to rebel but she never dared.

A knock on the door startled him. "Come in!"

A man in his mid-forties entered, bald pate gleaming, three-quarters of a circle of thick black hair ear to ear around the back of his head. A bushy black mustache. Suit and tie. "Andrei. Good to see you."

"Hello Philip. How was the trip?"

"Fine, fine." They sat in the two big chairs and watched dying light stroke water. An exchange about the paper he'd given, the three kinds of industrial rehabilitation, outgrowth of Dr. Deriades' experimental treatments for potential repetitive stress among Cascade workers. "Some disagreement but I think I convinced my colleagues prevention is what it's about."

Andrei sighed. "Philip, I need your help."

"Of course."

"Sandro."

"Ah."

"You've heard?"

"Just a bit. Maria thinks it's not Sandro's body?"

Andrei described Sandro's face, and Maria's reaction. They should bury him quickly, but with Maria's doubts, she was wrong but—

"I suppose you've started with the assumption this wasn't Sandro. Tried to locate him? Call him?"

"I'm sure I saw Sandro's body. But still I drove by his house on my way to the ferry. Locked, no one there. No answer on his phone. No car. I spoke to the police in Coupeville this morning. His body was identified by a co-worker, a nurse. I called her, she confirmed what she'd told the police. But Maria doesn't believe it."

"The police say he overdosed. Heroin?"

The shame the boy had brought on them. He expelled a loud breath. "Yes. But maybe worse. If he did it deliberately—"

Philip finished, "—he can't be buried in hallowed ground. The protopresbyter and the community will not be pleased."

"The family will not be pleased. I am not pleased."

"Surely Sandro wouldn't commit suicide. He knew the disgrace for us."

"An accident. Overdose is shameful enough."

Philip scowled. "I could look at the body."

Andrei nodded. "If you would, Philip."

A wry smile. "Not my idea of pleasure, of course. And I'm not a pathologist. But I'll do what I can."

"Thank you."

"I'll go right away." Philip left.

The two best things about Andrei's office were, first, his private bathroom, and second, the cabinetry on the wall across from the window. The middle door, right side, hid a collection of fine bottles. Assorted brands of ouzo, as well as the drinks of many other nations. Right now Andrei chose a thirty-year-old Scotch and poured two fingers of it, neat.

Andrei himself had not always been the perfect member of his community. He'd been a rough kid, at twenty-three arrested for pot possession. The fact that everyone smoked pot in those days didn't help. In the community, one was not everyone. The protopresbyter had convinced the authorities to drop the charges, and Andrei promised before his parents and priest never to touch pot again. And he hadn't. The hot glow of shame grew less bright, till it faded into a distant past. He was never caught for the acid he dropped on occasional weekends with friends, well outside the community. Then he reached twenty-seven and something turned in him. He rejected small private pleasures and became a man responsible to those he cared for.

Now, not much warmed by the good Scotch, Andrei feared Sandro had brought shame on them all.

THREE

TWILIGHT THICKENED INTO dark. The Schultzes lived on a quiet
street of two-storey fifties clapboards; lights on in many houses, curtains undrawn. Poignant, Kyra thought, looking in on families from
empty streets.

The door swung open as Kyra and Noel climbed the three steps
to the stoop. A man stood in the entry, hand on the doorknob. Maybe
thirty, longish curly hair, a sloppy-muscled look that would run to
flab as he aged, a thin attractive face overlaid with worry. Kyra wanted
to trust him instantly but remained wary. He looked familiar but she
couldn't place him. Just a familiar type?

"Noel Franklin." Noel handed him his card. "Mr. Schultz?"

"Yes," Schultz acknowledged, taking it.

"And I'm Kyra Rachel." Kyra stuck her hand out.

Schultz took it with a frown. "Mrs. McDermott? I'm Garth
Schultz. I work for your husband. Site prep, backhoe?"

"Sam's my ex-husband," Kyra corrected, then smiled. "Right! That's
why you're familiar! Christmas parties and picnics! How's your wife,"
she searched for a name, "and your child?"

"They're fine, thanks. Sorry, I didn't know Sam and you split up.
He never talks personal at work. I did know you'd gone into detecting
so I told Sandro's mom to hire you. And call me Garth," he said to
Noel. "Come in."

"Is it them?" A voice from the living room, then the clatter of child
in the hall. A small face peered around Garth's thigh, small hands
clutching his pant leg.

"Yes!" He lowered his voice. "Mackenzie, let me back up." Garth
swung the girl to his shoulder and opened the door wide. Kyra and
Noel entered. Garth shut the door. "Poor Mrs. V. Her husband died
not long ago. And now her only kid." He shook his head. "We took
her home last night and Debbie called the doctor, she gave Mrs. V. a
sedative. In here." He gestured through an archway.

Noel wondered, take his shoes off? But Garth was wearing his.

They followed him into the living room. A small-faced pretty woman nursed a baby on the sofa. "Hello, Debbie." Kyra, glad of Garth's prompt. "I remember Mackenzie, but not the baby."

"Ralphie. He's nine months. I missed last Fourth of July," Debbie chuckled, "and you weren't at the Christmas party." A polite question in her tone.

"Sam and I separated a year ago February. I'm Kyra Rachel now." Damn Sam, she thought. Telling no one, not taking their separation as permanent?

"That's too bad," said Debbie, all domestic contentment. She tucked her breast back in her shirt and sat the baby up to burp him. He obliged. The floor was cluttered with bright toys. Mackenzie kicked at them, systematically.

"Won't you sit down?" Garth looked around for an unoccupied chair. One held a package of diapers, another the unfolded laundry. Half the sofa was taken by Debbie and the baby.

"Perhaps the kitchen?" Noel suggested.

"Okay." Garth led them down a short hall. Mackenzie trailed along. The table contained supper remains. Garth set plates and bowls by the sink.

"Read me a story, Daddy."

"In a while, kiddo. I have to talk to these people."

"Read to me!"

"You went to the funeral home on Whidbey Island yesterday?" Kyra asked.

"Yes. I drove Mrs. V. down."

Mackenzie piped up, "Justin said a word today, at daycare—"

"Did you think the body was Sandro's?" If she ignored the child, Kyra thought, the child would get the message. She accepted the fact she didn't like children. Certainly not this one.

"Shit! Justin said shit! What's shit, Daddy?"

Garth rolled his eyes.

Kyra thought: Get that kid outta here.

"You have any paper?" Noel asked Mackenzie. She nodded. "And crayons?" Nod. "Can you go into the living room and draw me a picture? I'd like your drawing to take home to put on my fridge."

Mackenzie climbed up on the chair next to him. "I can draw it here."

"I especially want a picture that's been drawn in the living room," said Noel. "That's the only sort I put on my fridge." He smiled down at her.

Mackenzie considered. "Okay." She climbed down and thudded off.

A side of Noel Kyra had forgotten—Noel taking her fishing when she was ten.

Garth ran a dishcloth over the table.

"Mrs.Vasiliadis said you were Sandro's best friend. You sort of looked after him?" Kyra set her notebook down.

"He did a lot for me too, taught me things. Yeah, I protected him. He was a small quiet kid, liked reading and music, so the rough guys went for him."

"What did he do for you?"

"Stuff like—" Garth pulled out a chair, thinking. "Pointing out things. How people do the opposite of what they mean sometimes, how to figure that. Like in junior high we had a teacher who was always sucking up to the smartasses in the back row and I got mad 'cause I figured he should pay attention to the guys that cared about school, like Sandro. But Sandro said the teacher really wanted to murder the smartasses so he had to undermine them. I'd never thought about that, but he was right. Like I mean, Sandro understood people. Like Debbie does." Garth frowned. "I sure don't. Like I don't see Debbie's getting mad till she blows. Sandro knew that stuff. He knew plants and insects too, he loved studying those. He shoulda gone into biology, I always said."

Kyra rephrased her earlier question. "Was that Sandro in the coffin yesterday?"

"Well," Garth looked at his hands, big hands, close-cut nails. He picked at a cuticle on his index finger. "My thought was, if Sandro was still in junior high, that would've been him. But yeah, I never really doubted it was Sandro. He just looked different somehow. We haven't seen each other since he moved to Whidbey." Another cuticle. "You just can't keep up with friends when you have children and both Deb and me work. So it's kinda exhausting." He glanced at them. "You have children?"

They both shook their heads.

"Deb and me haven't been out anywhere in two years. We could hire a sitter but we'd be too tired to enjoy it."

"You went to the viewing on Whidbey Island without the children," Noel noted.

"Oh yeah. First time we left them with anyone other than the daycare."

Kyra said, "Mrs. Vasiliadis said 'they,' I assume she meant the police or coroner, think the dead man had been a drug user, and he'd overdosed."

Garth's head snapped up. "You get through high school without drugs, you get to thirty without, then you do drugs? No way!"

"You know who he hung out with on Whidbey?"

"He had friends at the hospital. A nurse from there identified his body, I think she was at the viewing. And he was on a bowling team, I remember."

"His mom said he was taking courses."

"Oh yeah? Good. He was smart."

"Anything else about him that'd help us?" Noel asked.

Garth thought hard. "Nope. Just things. Like the tadpoles. Where we lived? By the lake? Bunch of tadpoles we went out to see every day after school, watch them develop and things. So one day these guys we know, they're scooping tadpoles out and pulling their new legs off and leaving them on the grass and the tadpoles aren't dead, they're flopping without their new legs, and Sandro belts on the guys and scoops the tadpoles back in the water and starts to cry. The guys woulda murdered him but we were both so mad, I dunno where Sandro got the strength, it was like maybe God wanted the tadpole destroyers punished, but we lit into those guys, they were a grade ahead of us, and they cleared off. Then both Sandro and me cried."

As he was doing now, Kyra noted. They waited. The little girl burst into the kitchen waving a piece of crayoned paper. She looked only at Noel. "Here! I did it in the living room all by myself, Mommy's bathing Ralphie!"

Noel took the piece of paper she slapped down. "Can you tell me its story?"

Kyra craned for a look and Noel tilted it her way. An uneven blue circle with lines, a squarish brown thing, a red blob.

"It's a dog," Mackenzie announced, her tone saying anyone would know that. "A boy dog. He's Shit. That's Shit's house and that's Shit's dish. He's a happy dog and that's the sun."

Kyra, Noel and Garth stared at the picture.

Noel said, "That's a fine drawing. It'll look good on my fridge. Thank you."

Garth said, "It's bedtime, kiddo." He showed them out. "It was Sandro in the coffin, but he sure looked different."

Back in the car Kyra refrained from starting the engine. "Everyone," she said softly, "should have a Garth for a friend."

Noel nodded. "I thought, in there, one of the advantages of being out in the field, you get to see the real insides of houses. And you meet real people. Fortunate kids, Mackenzie and Ralphie, having him for a father."

"Yep."

Philip Deriades had some notions about what he'd learn on Whidbey Island concerning Sandro but he wouldn't speculate. He would drive up to the north end of the island and take the bridge over Deception Pass down to Coupeville. A longer route but, because of ferry line-ups and the trip across Possession Sound, maybe faster. If he got his inquiries done in time he'd return on the *Kittitas* from Clinton. Ferry lineups and crossings were good times for mulling. He might be dealing with some hefty stuff on the way back.

Andrei had brought Philip in during the middle stages of Maria's husband's cancer. Too late, Philip saw at first glance. Eldest of the five Vasiliadis sibs, Kostas should have been head of the family from the moment of the death of his own father. But Kostas at twenty-two had impetuously moved with Maria to Bellingham, to sire his own stock. Only one offspring, Sandro. And Sandro never became the leader Kostas had wanted his son to be.

After Dom, who was married to his sister Marina, Philip knew and liked Andrei best—Andrei, by default head of the Vasiliadis family. Andrei had shown himself over the years to be the force that bound them to each other. It was appropriate that Andrei should now, after Maria's outburst, insist, for the family and its place in the community, that Sandro's body be laid to rest with full decorum and low profile.

Philip had been to Whidbey Island several times, though never on business. As he drove through Oak Harbor, and now into Coupeville, his eye caught the institutions of his profession—hospital, medical center, labs. His secretary had called ahead to make an appointment at Oceanside Funeral Home. He'd examine the body and speak with whomever was in charge.

Lights on inside the funeral home, no apparent activity. A sign on the closed door said Enter, but he rang the bell. A man in black opened the door. Philip introduced himself. The man in black invited him in. He stepped in. He saw several closed white doors and a white staircase with a varnished wood balustrade.

"I'm Claude Martin. This," the man's hand swept a hundred-eighty degrees, "is Oceanside."

"So I gathered from your sign."

Martin opened the first door on the right. "My office." He walked in.

Philip followed. Again, stark white walls, several Shaker cabinets—pine, Philip guessed—and some certificates hanging behind a six-foot wooden desk that held only a telephone and a blotter. Claude Martin gestured to two black captain's chairs with white cushions. Philip sat. Martin pulled on the cuffs of his black suit jacket. It matched his trousers, tie and shoes, as well as his black hair slicked back firmly. Martin's shirt, white, made it appear to Philip that the man's chest was drawn back, beyond the body. Martin lowered himself into the chair behind the desk.

"How can I help you?" Martin's mouth edges curved up a little but no smile appeared.

"It's about the Alessandro Vasiliadis viewing."

The curve dropped away. "An awful moment for Oceanside."

"Tell me, did the body come directly from the morgue?"

Claude Martin's brow knotted in the middle. "Of course."

"The necessary papers came with it?"

The knot tightened. "Of course."

"And these papers bore the name Vasiliadis."

"That's correct."

"The body would have been identified at the morgue, then?"

"Dr. Deriades, we do not accept unidentified bodies."

"I have here," he took an envelope from his shirt pocket, "a letter to you from Andrei Vasiliadis, Sandro's uncle. It says you are to let me see the body."

Martin's eyes widened. "That's not possible."

Philip contained his irritation. "Why not?"

"Because I don't have the body."

"What?"

Martin shrugged. "As I said. The body's gone. Back to the morgue."

Philip stifled his anger. "Why?"

"I told you. We don't take unidentified bodies."

"But you also said the body arrived with the proper papers."

"Until the lady who should know her son announced this wasn't him."

"Wait a minute. Didn't Mr. Vasiliadis tell you to do nothing till he contacted you?"

"He may have. In the meantime, I was holding a body and its identity was in dispute. Oceanside is not a place for derelicts."

"Did you embalm him?"

"Of course."

Philip folded his fingers together and stared at them. "At the morgue, you say." He watched Martin nod as he pulled out his cellphone. "Do you have the number?"

"Use my phone, press two."

Philip did, wondering whom he'd get if he pushed one. From a pleasant but unbudging bureaucratic voice at the other end he learned it was impossible for a citizen to see a corpse without the approval of Burt Vanderhoek, Sheriff of Island County. And where could Sheriff Vanderhoek be found? Check out his office. Which Philip tried, to be told the sheriff would be on duty this evening. If Dr. Deriades arrived at the office at seven-thirty, the sheriff, barring emergencies, would see him. Philip got the address.

He turned to Claude Martin. "Mr. Vasiliadis won't be happy you returned his nephew's body to the morgue."

"I'm not certain this was the nephew—" the curved lip non-smile, "after the mother's repudiation."

"Your responsibility was to—"

Martin held one hand up, limp fingers curved toward Philip. "I will apologize when the matter is settled."

When—that is, if—Andrei pays you, you mean, Philip thought as he stood. "Thank you for your time." He turned, opened the door, walked through the white hall and out to his car.

Dinner. He remembered restaurants along the waterfront. He found a red false-fronted place, Toby's; looked like a pub. Inside, most tables were full. He was given a place near the door, ate mussels and fries, drank some draft ale, and was finished by 7:20. He drove uphill to the sheriff's office.

The door was locked. As he turned around, a truck pulled into the parking lot, two dogs on the bed. They growled at Philip. The driver's door opened. Philip noted a rifle hanging on a rack inside the rear window. A man unwound himself and stepped out. Tall and corpulent. Khaki uniform.

"Sheriff Vanderhoek?"

"Who wants to know?" Philip introduced himself. "Well, come in then."

In the office, desk and tables cluttered with files, many open and enmeshed with each other. He showed Vanderhoek the letter from Andrei and explained his need to see the corpse.

"Stupid case," said the sheriff.

Why stupid? What cases were less stupid? "Can I get your okay to take a look?"

"Tonight?"

"I'd prefer not to have to come back."

"Not supposed to get morgue entrance 'cept during the day."

"Why not?"

"Nobody official there."

"Isn't the morgue part of your jurisdiction?"

The sheriff considered this. "Probably. Just as soon get rid of this one."

Philip couldn't help himself. "Why?"

"Bodies complicate things."

That they do, Philip thought; alive or dead. "Possible to speak with the coroner?"

"Tomorrow."

"May I see the report?"

The sheriff searched through a precarious pile of papers on the table behind him. He handed Philip a thin file.

Labeled Vasiliadis, Alessandro. Little information. Description of the body, but Philip would do his own exam. Cause of death, respiratory arrest. Puncture marks in left arm, noted as intravenous administration of heroin. Overdose? Found in the blockhouse at the cemetery. Sloppy report. And an embalmed body can't tell much of a story. He handed the file back to the sheriff.

Philip followed the sheriff's truck up two streets to the hospital. The sheriff parked and told the dogs to be good guys.

The hospital was a neat one-floor facility; sixty-eight beds, in double and single rooms, the sheriff told Philip, and two operating theaters. In the basement, storage. And the morgue, with an attendant, reading a small-format *Archie and Veronica* comic book, seated near the door. "Billy, you want to show the doctor here the corpse? I got to get back to the office."

Philip said, "Only one corpse?"

"Coupeville's a quiet town."

The sheriff left. Billy wheeled a gurney to the far end of the room. Philip followed. Billy opened a small door, slid a slab holding a sheet-covered mass onto the flat bed, unveiled the face.

Drained, the face suggested what Sandro might have looked like without a beard: narrow cheeks, small chin, full lips. The rest of the face showed some likeness to the Sandro whom Philip had seen over the years at Vasiliadis parties—brow, cheekbones, eye-hollows, nose, ears. "I'm going to examine the body, Billy."

Billy shrugged. "Sure." He returned to his chair and comic book.

This was Philip's least favorite medical role. Here was a major cause for his interest in preventive medicine. He should have brought Herb Feverel along. Not only was Herb a fine endocrinologist, it'd be good to react out loud right now. Herb did owe him a couple of favors. Gloved, gowned, and masked, Philip found his mind returning to medical school days when they'd each had their own cadaver. Okay, here goes.

Face, devoid of facial hair. Dark hair on top of the head, looking black but technically a dark brown, before always short, now long and arranged along the brow, behind the cheeks, along the sides of the neck; Claude Martin's doing, Philip assumed. He didn't recognize the chin line, and couldn't say for certain if the lips were fuller, as a mustache had always drooped there. He reached over and with some difficulty raised one of the eyelids; the pupil was clouded, but dilated. He drew the sheet further down and was struck by the heavy breast tissue. Not huge, a fat man's breasts. But the corpse was slender. Nipples normal size. A bluish tinge to the skin. No chest hair. He'd never seen Sandro in a bathing suit so had no image to compare. He examined the arms. Again, almost no hair. On the inside of the left upper arm, nine puncture marks, small red spots irregularly placed, tissues surrounding injection sites variously bruised. Had Sandro sold his blood to buy dope? Wrong place. What kind of needle marks? Best guess was heroin tracks, don't try to force conclusions. He pulled the sheet down to show Sandro's genitals. Penis normal. Testes enormous, size of a couple of small grapefruit. Strange. Who was Sandro's physician? Legs normal. Again, very little hair.

He covered the corpse, de-gloved, de-gowned, made preliminary notes. "Thanks, Billy."

He got to the last ferry for Mukilteo with twenty minutes to spare. From the car he called Herb in Seattle for an instant consult, describing the body. It sounded to Herb as if Sandro had been undergoing substantial hormone treatment. For what? Impossible to tell without examining the corpse. Maybe some kind of sexual readjustment, some hormone combination that had increased both the man's masculinity and his femininity. With the facial hair gone and the enlarged breast tissue, the best guess was he'd been treated with a range of female hormones. Hormonal shifts that powerful could lead to strong mood shifts, possibly contributing to suicide. Philip should definitely locate Sandro's doctor.

Would Herb be willing to look at the body? Herb was pretty busy—Philip would appreciate it *very* much. Well, Herb could take a quick trip up early tomorrow.

On the ferry Philip mulled over what he'd learned. A new level of confusion.

Noel and Kyra returned to her condo around nine. The answering machine flashed. She pressed Play. Jerome's voice, asking her to call. Background voice of Nelson, bark, bark.

Kyra, hand on the phone, said to Noel, "Vodka's in the freezer." She glanced at the sofa. "Oh, I haven't done your bed."

"Make you a drink?"

Yes, she wanted to say, but thought better of it. "I'll see what Jerome wants first."

She'd look up Jerome's number—Oh, here it was, memorized already. Hmm.

He answered on the second ring. "Hello? Shut up, Nelson!"

"Hi. What's up?"

"Any idea how many vegetarians you're having on Thursday?"

"Not me, not Noel." Oh dear, Kyra thought, she still hadn't reached Jacquie and Margery—oops. Sarah and Mike were set.

"I was going to bring Oysters Rockefeller."

"Oh my."

"And Crab Cardinale."

"Yum. But that's a lot for a potluck. And neither of those are one-potters."

"They're one-dishers."

"If you say so."

"I'm looking forward to Thursday." His voice had softened.

"Me too." She realized she wanted to continue talking with him, just for the pleasure of it. But she'd better phone the others before it got too late.

"How's it going with the woman whose son it wasn't?" Jerome, moving into relaxed.

Jerome, the potluck, the case. Her brain felt a little jerked. She got up, waved from the doorway to get Noel's attention, made drink-pouring motions. "It's all still confusing, Jerome. We might have to go to Whidbey Island tomorrow."

"You be careful," he said.

"Sure."

"Take my phone numbers with you."

"They're in my book."

He hesitated. "Kyra? Please take care."

41

"Always."

Noel handed her a vodka and tonic water. She drank. Her ice clinked. A nice, lingering hang-up. Kyra fast-dialed Margery, apologies for the lateness—yes, she could come, and may she bring her sister's friend Bettina, just moved to Bellingham? Sure. Jacquie declined, an evening with her mother. Kyra collapsed on the sofa with Noel's TV news and sipped her nightcap. Did the rearranged room actually feel more comfortable?

FOUR

WEDNESDAY MORNING KYRA and Noel were on the road shortly after nine. Yesterday's wind had blown the clouds away, and uncommon March sunlight soaked the greening earth. The Tracker bounced along. Noel gloried in crocuses, hyacinths, flowering cherries, plums, and magnolias. Miraculous spring! Hard, on a sopping winter day, to believe spring will someday return. The sun warmed his face.

Before leaving, Kyra had handed him a key. "Here."

"What?"

"Yours. To the US office of Triple-I."

"Your place?"

"I have the Triple-I Canada key. Your place."

"Thanks." He smiled and pocketed it.

"Coupeville's about an hour. Time for coffee." She hesitated. "Uhmm—our appointments are at ten-thirty."

"The same time?"

Kyra flicked him a glance.

"The only morning time for both the sheriff and the funeral guy." She sensed his irritation.

"Sweetheart. We're partners, right? Partners consult, right? As you have frequently pointed out." Noel closed his eyes against the sun.

She caught a muscle jumping by the corner of his mouth. "You were shaving and all that. I thought it'd be okay."

He clicked his tongue in exasperation.

"Which do you want, the law or the funeral parlor?"

"Doesn't matter." But it did.

"Toss, then."

Noel dug a quarter out of his pocket—Canadian, should've raided his American change jar back in Nanaimo, hoped he wouldn't need to feed a parking meter—and flipped. "You call."

"Heads."

"The Queen it is." Noel put the quarter away.

"I'll take the sheriff."

He'd known which she'd choose. He would have to walk into a mortuary. Again. "You know where these places are?" He saw Brendan in the small, silent room, lying still and white. He—No, not now.

"Coupeville's not big. We'll find them." Kyra's voice softened. "And, sorry, I should've yelled louder than your ablutions."

"Doesn't matter." Though it did. He rubbed his nose. "So. What do we know?"

"We know Garth believes the body is Sandro. Maria doesn't. Why not? Because it isn't, or because she's denying her son's dead? Whoever it is, he died of a heroin overdose."

"I'll make a note." Noel opened his laptop. "We know Sandro had good friends and hated sports."

"Two people remarked on the absence of his heavy beard."

"Actually," Noel recalled, "no facial hair at all. Different from not having a beard. What makes facial hair disappear?"

"Chemotherapy? You mean, did he have cancer?"

"Hair on his head. Maybe electrolysis?"

"Would one take heroin for pain relief?

"Maybe marijuana?"

"Marijuana's more for nausea and poor appetite," Kyra stated. "Anyway, not in this US of A. Canada can legislate marijuana for medical purposes, but not us. Marijuana's the Official Weed of the Devil."

"Some states have done so."

"It's not federal."

Noel nodded. "Are we sure he was on heroin?"

"That's what the report says, apparently."

"Are we sure he was an addict?"

Kyra thought for a moment. "Both his mother and Garth insisted, no way would Sandro take drugs."

"Which could mean it isn't Sandro. Which is what we have to focus on. We're hired to find out if he's dead or not, that's all." Noel stared through the windshield. They were entering the Skagit Valley, an alluvial plain given over to farms. Fields were brown and fallow, dotted with large puddles the strengthening sun tried to dry. Some showed the light green of early growth.

"Except Garth hadn't heard from Sandro recently. Maybe he started shooting up last year." An eye out for the Anacortes turn-off.

"We don't need to find out precisely how he died, just if it's Sandro who's dead." She mulled. "What else makes facial hair disappear?"

"Hormones?"

"Maybe just trying to have less beard?"

"Or," Noel told a herd of cattle, "he had prostate cancer and was taking estrogen for it?"

"I don't think he'd be old enough. You know, if we could get access to DNA testing—" She spotted the sign: Anacortes–Whidbey Island. She pulled into the right lane and slowed. "And we better talk to Sandro's colleagues—find out how he looked and acted recently."

They drove west along a two-lane highway, the sun now behind them. Noel said, "There's Mrs. Vasiliadis' comment, 'A mother should recognize her own son.' How do you recognize someone?"

"Hmm," Kyra murmured, thinking she'd recognize any of her three ex-husbands if they popped up in that field among the cows. "It's the whole picture, the gestalt."

"But suppose all you have is appearance, no motion, no gesture, no slouch or stiffness."

"Like the corpse for Mrs. Vasiliadis?"

"Once I was Christmas shopping at a mall in Nanaimo, figuring what to get my parents. I kept seeing bits of them in half the seventy-year-old couples around. Then my parents really did appear. Looking like a seventy-year-old couple, but I instantly knew it was them. Now how did I know that? And not the other couples I'd been turning into them?"

Good question. "You'll recognize your parents in their coffins because you'll have gone through their deaths with them. Like I will with mine. But this mother didn't, the death was sudden. Nobody in Sandro's family, or his oldest friend, had seen him for what, months? Years? Why? Just busy?"

Now trees loomed ahead. The flat farmland fell away, the road curved and they swept across a narrow two-lane bridge. Below, maybe a hundred feet down, the waters swirled, ignorant of direction. "Deception Pass," said Kyra. "This bridge was a 1930s make-work project."

"Well now." Noel examined it. "How much is an island a real island if the island is connected to the mainland by a bridge?"

"You mean," said Kyra, "a bridge can keep an island from being a real island? And if so, maybe Islands Investigations International shouldn't be on this case in the first place?"

"Just wondering."

"That logic's hard on Prince Edward Island with its new Confederation Bridge."

Claude Martin's office was spare: two wooden chairs, a bare wooden desk with another chair. No computer, no family pictures, just a phone and blotter. Noel hadn't seen a blotter in years. Impressive-looking certificates hung on the wall. The receptionist had showed him in. Now Martin the mortician was taking his time. Noel sniffed hard. No embalming or other funereal odors. Despite their absence, he shuddered.

He should have insisted: the sheriff! Not that he particularly wanted to chat with some local sheriff, but he didn't want to be in a funeral home. He shifted in the chair. Now his stomach was clenching. They had taken Brendan to Brentwood Gardens in Nanaimo—the package that had been Brendan, the shell. A bald old gentleman had told Noel he could see Brendan just as long as Noel wanted. Brendan's body lay in the chapel. Noel entered the chapel. The backs of twelve rows of benches faced him, all empty; an aisle between them, a small raised platform ahead. At the end of the aisle, the coffin. A recorded organ, barely audible, had dirged through the thick chilled air.

Enough. The matter at hand was Claude Martin. Where the hell was he.

Who would decide to become a mortician? Noel could grasp garbage collecting and septic tank cleaning, jobs you needed virtually no training for. Get desperate enough, you can work on a tank-truck that sucks shit out of concrete septics. Going to school for dozens of years to become, say, a dentist, and spend the rest of your life manipulating broken teeth and patching up rotten gums, even that he could figure. But learning to clean a corpse, drain the fluids or whatever, smear makeup on dead skin? In keeping with the man's flat phone voice, yes. He wondered how Kyra was doing with the sheriff.

He preferred Kyra and himself interviewing people as a team.

They functioned well together, not in any good-slash-bad cop way but with differing tactics. They heard different details and stances in the answers people gave. Besides, when they worked together they weren't working separately. Obvious but important too, because Noel worried about Kyra when she was left to her own devices. She got herself into serious trouble easily, and sometimes into danger. She didn't know when to stop pushing. Not that an interview with a local sheriff could be dangerous, but still.

The door opened and the receptionist, a round woman of pre-served middle age, smiled at him. "Mr. Martin apologizes. He'll be just a couple more minutes." She closed the door.

"Thanks," Noel said to the doorknob. He wondered if Claude Martin liked to put visitors off their stride, keeping them waiting. No one, no one, then suddenly Martin appears: And this morning, will you have a burial or a cremation? Or, flashing open a catalogue: We could stuff you like this tiger?

No, morticians didn't have tactics. Investigators did. Like domi-nance in questioning. Noel usually maintained dominance, over both women and men. Begin dominant, stay dominant. Few out-managed Noel. As a young journalist he'd learned to pounce. With Brendan neither had tried to dominate, not in situations nor with each other; balance was part of how their love fitted together. Between Kyra and him, dominance often went back and forth; their kind of balance lay in the to-and-froing itself.

The door opened again. A man came in, tall, black hair, black mus-tache, black suit and tie, brilliantly shined black shoes. "Mr. Franklin, Claude Martin. So sorry to keep you waiting." He reached out his hand.

Noel stood and took it. Soft, not quite limp. "Good of you to see me, Mr. Martin."

"This is about the Vasiliadis viewing?"

"That's right." Flat like on the phone, no sense of what Martin was thinking, feeling. "I've been retained by Sandro's mother. You met her the other evening."

"Yes. Terrible thing. For the family. For us as well."

"I can see it might be a nuisance for you, but why terrible?"

"Won't you sit?" He gestured to the chair Noel had risen from.

Noel sat. Sometimes dominance required letting others take the lead.

Martin sat behind the desk and leaned across the blotter. "For the body of the departed, the Oceanside Funeral Home comes as close to hallowed ground as any space not sanctified by churches and temples. If the body of an unknown lies here, it compromises the legitimacy of our other clients. There is something," he sat straight and his eyes glowed but his voice remained unchanged, horizontal, "sacred here. It emanates from the walls, the floors. The air is filled with holiness. You must sense it?" His eyes were now on Noel's face, scanning it.

"A special place? I guess. Were you present the whole time the mourners were around?"

"Yes. I oversee every detail at Oceanside."

"Do you know who was here?"

He shook his head. "Many people pass through Oceanside." A flicker of his lips, a smile that never arrived. "However, if they signed, their names will be in the guest book." He picked up the phone, pressed a button, waited. "Would you bring in the Vasiliadis guest book? Thank you." He put the phone down. "We shall see."

"Of the people who were here, whom do you remember?"

"The mother of course, she began this difficulty when she denied the body. I can say little about her, she was here so briefly. And the young man and woman who brought her, they seemed kind but they looked exhausted."

"Who else?"

"The uncle, Vasiliadis. He took charge."

"Your sense of him—?"

"A man who's used to being in charge. Everything had to be done his way. Instantly."

"And who else?"

Martin stared at the ceiling as if searching for a film of the Vasiliadis viewing. "A young woman with items dangling from her ears and her nose. The ear ones were apparent because she had a very short crew-cut. Which was dyed green." He faced Noel again. "I don't remember the name, but I'll recognize it. She had large handwriting."

Noel nodded. No negative reaction, no reaction of any sort, from Claude Martin. "Go on."

"Also a large man, he said very little. I've seen him around. I think he's a physician."

The tiniest hint of disgust, or superiority, in Martin's tone. "Anything else about him?"

"Well, let me try. You're taxing my memory."

Again the flat lips tried to twitch up. Was Martin simply incapable of smiling? Some frozen muscle? Noel chuckled for both of them.

"He seemed taken by a fetching young woman, maybe thirty years old, dark hair. But she was clearly with—and I do mean *with*, if you take my meaning—another woman, shorter."

"Hmm," said Noel.

Martin sat in silence. "That's all I can remember, I'm afraid."

A knock at the door. It opened. On a forty-five-degree angle, a head and smile thrust themselves through the opening. "Guest book?"

"Thank you."

She handed the book across the desk to Martin, beamed her smile at Noel, and left.

"Could you match the names with those people you've been describing?"

Claude Martin glanced at the names. "I welcomed them, that's all." He handed the guest book, open, to Noel.

Noel read: Rudy Longelli, Cora Lipton-Norton, Andrei Vasiliadis, Brady Adam, Ursula Bunche, Dr. Stockman Jones. "Only six people here?" He copied the names into his notebook.

"More. And the mother, and the two who came with her. Clearly the others didn't sign in. It was early, of course. Four or five people came after the family left. There was to be a funeral in Seattle, the uncle told me."

"Maybe there still will be. If it's decided the body you have here is Sandro's."

"*Had*, Mr. Franklin. When the mother denied it, we shipped it back to the morgue."

Noel blinked. "Where's the morgue?"

"The hospital." Martin shook his head. "I've thought about what happened, you know. The mother's reaction. Maybe I'm to blame."

"How?"

"I may have made the body look, uhhm—too good. I take pride in my work. But sometimes the result is too perfect."

"I don't understand."

"In my profession one must establish the essence of the departed. One must—recreate."

In Martin's voice a sudden tinge of—was it awe?

Recreate: what Brentwood Gardens had done to Brendan. At the head of the aisle, the coffin, its lid open. Brendan's body. His black turtleneck, gray flannels, gray running shoes, as he'd wanted. A waxen face, his hands bare. Noel had reached out to touch Brendan's right hand, a so-familiar gesture. A cold right hand, inflexible. Noel didn't want to touch Brendan, yet couldn't not. Noel didn't want to kiss Brendan. On the forehead. One last time. But he did. Against his lips, rubber cooler than the room. Not Brendan.

"One tries," Martin said. "To return to the departed whatever it was that made him a quintessential individual. No one else could look this way. In life, we see in others only a piece of what they are. One piece, you understand. I try to bring back the whole person."

A weird kind of humility in Martin's voice. Noel nodded again.

"I've done my best work with automobile accidents. Sometimes the body is so charred, or dismembered—This body was difficult. I worked on him for a long time."

"Difficult how?"

"With suicide, it's always difficult."

"You know it was a suicide?"

"Yes."

"Has the sheriff's office called it a suicide?"

"I don't know."

"What does the coroner's report say?"

"It doesn't matter."

"I beg your pardon?"

"This man killed himself."

"How do you know?"

"I saw his face when he arrived here. This was not a happy corpse."

"I'm sorry?"

"A man who overdoses isn't happy."

"You have many overdoses on Whidbey?"

"This was my first. But I could see his unhappiness. I could see as well, this had not always been an unhappy man." He sighed. "I needed to recreate his essence."

"And because you succeeded, you think his mother didn't recognize him."

"Possibly." He rubbed his right palm against his left. "If it was in fact her son."

Noel stood. "We'll try to find out."

"I wish you luck." Claude Martin stood quickly, marched to the door, held it for Noel.

Noel said, "Thanks for your help."

After dropping Noel at the funeral home, Kyra had navigated the two empty blocks to the County seat.

The Sheriff's Office was the first room after the main door. The receptionist, identified by a plastic nameplate on her desk as Miss Brady Adam, informed an intercom that a Ms. Rachel was "—here to see you, Sheriff."

Mutter, the intercom replied.

"You can go in," Miss Brady Adam allowed brightly. She had rich dark brown hair styled in a short pageboy, black eyelashes nearly as thick as Kyra's, and 1930s rosebud lips.

Kyra knocked on the door indicated and opened it. Sheriff Burt Vanderhoek sat behind a desk. He'd started to rise but when she appeared he sat again. She wondered what was wrong with her appearance— clean, fairly new jeans, a blue-striped shirt under a designer—well, rip-off designer—sweatshirt in stonewashed mauve, and her only one-year-old navy and maroon Gore-Tex jacket. She'd showered and washed her hair this morning, even applied lipstick. She figured she was okay and everything else was his problem. She closed the door and proceeded to the chair on her side of the desk. "Sheriff—"

"Vanderhoek," he barked.

Kyra smiled. She didn't feel like smiling at this fat, officious asshole. "I'm hired by Maria Vasiliadis, the woman who didn't recognize—"

"I know who she is."

"I need to determine whether the body is or isn't her son." Pictures of German Shepherds covered the walls.

"Crazy business."

Kyra provided her most winsome smile. "A mother should be able to identify her son."

"Darn right," said the sheriff. "The woman who ID'd the body did, without doubt."

"Who was that?"

The sheriff breathed in, largely, and out, largely.

"A friend?"

"How should I know?" The sheriff looked as if he were searching his memory bank for a good reason not to give the name. Reluctantly he said, "Bunche. Works in X-ray at the hospital."

"Thank you." Kyra wrote it down. "How did Vasiliadis die?"

"OD'd."

"On what?"

"Heroin."

"Yeah?"

"What the report says."

The man believed in authority. And had photos of fifteen German Shepherds on the wall. Or fifteen photos of one. "Was he a known user?"

"Not on the list. Needle tracks up his left arm, though. Too many damn drugs on this island, all the Navy guys—" He clamped his lips shut.

What, from their tours of duty? She smiled as if agreeing. Question: What's worse than smiling your teeth out to get information? Answer: Scowling and staying stupid. Vanderhoek seemed to thaw, slightly. A big man. Not fat, but burly. Tall. A vote-getter description for a county sheriff. On his desk stood pictures of a prettyish woman, a prettier girl in graduation robe and mortar board, a pimply youth with a basketball. "You're satisfied it's suicide?"

The sheriff shrugged. "Anyone who overdoses is a suicidal type. Suicidal stupidity or active suicide, it's all the same to me."

"Where did Vasiliadis die?"

Silence for several seconds. "Where the body was found. The blockhouse at the cemetery."

"What's a blockhouse?"

"Small shelter, open doorways and windows. Just barely a shelter."

"Who found the body?"

"A kid. Twelve." The sheriff rubbed his nose. "Not much fun for him."

True, thought Kyra.

Vanderhoek thawed another degree and leaned back.

"How'd he get to the blockhouse?"

"Drove. His car was right close by."

"Is that how you identified him?"

"Name on registration. But we had the positive ID from the X-ray lady."

"Did you check out his house?"

"Nope."

"Why not?"

"No need. He lived alone."

"But isn't it important to—"

"Look, Miss, this is a suicide. The next of kin was the mother. We informed her, okay?"

"But his house could've—"

"We're not talking investigation here, okay?"

"Yes. Sure. Um—Sandro's mother particularly noted his lack of facial hair. The coroner or whoever handled the autopsy, did he comment?"

"Not that I recall."

"Was the autopsy thorough?"

"Why wouldn't it be?"

"You tell me."

The sheriff bristled. "Thorough as necessary."

"To establish suicide, you mean?"

He nodded. "Our coroner is always thorough."

"Once it's decided it's suicide, that's enough autopsy?"

He nodded.

She needed to push. The phone rang. He lunged. "Vanderhoek." Pause. "Uh-huh." Pause. "Right away. Bye." He slammed the receiver down and stood up. "Got to go out, Miss, ahh—"

Kyra stood too. "Rachel. Here you are." She laid a Triple-I card on his desk. "We'll complete our investigation and let you know what we've learned."

The sheriff's mouth opened. No words came out.

Kyra doubted he knew the phrase, *such effrontery*. But he was searching for some version of it. And did he have Miss Brady Adam phone him ten minutes into an interview?

———

"Say I was only listening to Martin. I mean, like I'd had my eyes closed. I'd have had no sense of him at all, he was that flat." Noel sipped his latte.

"Flat how?"

"Practically no timbre, almost no inflection, close to total mid-range. Would've been hard to tell if this was man or woman if I hadn't been sitting right there. Or if I hadn't read his name."

"Most people talk like that."

"Not like Claude Martin."

"Most men and women intone their words within a range of three or four notes on the scale, around middle C."

"Come on."

She added the contents of a packet of sugar to her latte. "That small range is about all you need. Except, when somebody's talking, there's more going on than just what's audible."

"Yeah?"

"It's what we were talking about before, affect. It conveys what the speaker's feeling. And it creates a mood in whoever's listening. What you're saying is Claude Martin's voice held little emotional tone."

"I guess." So Kyra's voice must be filled with affect since he got her mood from whatever she said. "Maybe morticianing takes away your affect."

Kyra raised one eyebrow. "Or maybe you become a mortician because you have none in the first place."

Noel took out his notebook. "Anyway, I got a list of those who signed the guest book."

"Good."

"A doctor, Stockman Jones. Two women who, as Claude conveyed, seem to be a unit. Brady Adam and—"

"I just met her."

"You did? How?"

"She's the sheriff's receptionist. Very pretty."

"She seems to be with a certain Ursula Bunche."

"That simplifies things. She officially identified Sandro. She works at the hospital." Ursula Bunche. Kyra suddenly giggled. "This is too silly."

"What?"

"If Ursula and Brady are lesbians, if they get married, if Brady takes Ursula's last name—"

"What?" He glanced at his list. He laughed. "Oh god."

"Okay, who else?"

A man, Rudy Longelli. A woman with green hair, Cora Lipton-Norton." He closed his notebook. "A few others, but they didn't sign in." He finished his latte. "Talk to Brady Adam?"

"I'm not ready to meet up with Vanderhoek again."

Noel grinned. "Didn't hit it off?"

"I hate pandering for information." She described her interview. "He made my skin crawl." She got up, leaving half her latte. "Plenty of affect there, the sheriff of Island County."

FIVE

KYRA PULLED OFF North Main into the Whidbey General Hospital's lot and parked. They followed the sidewalk through emerald lawn to the front door. It opened automatically.

Noel flinched.

Kyra quirked an eyebrow.

"The smell. Those trips to the hospital with Brendan."

"Yeah." Kyra touched his arm. "Hushed and busy. Some kind of disinfectant."

Funeral home, thought Noel. Now hospital. Order reversed.

At the information desk Kyra asked for Ursula Bunche.

The receptionist tapped on her computer keyboard, glanced up at the screen. "X-ray. Down that corridor to the right."

They walked along the hall to another receptionist. Bunche was on her break, maybe the cafeteria, should be back any minute. They sat on a brown plastic sofa.

"We should check out the morgue while we're here," Noel said.

"Why? We wouldn't recognize Sandro. Better to talk to the woman who ID'd him."

"That too. But let's be thorough."

Three uniformed women appeared in the hall. Kyra stood and said to a petite, blonde, competent-looking woman in a white pantsuit, "Ursula Bunche?"

"Yes?" The other uniforms continued down the hall.

Kyra let Noel patter their explanation and hand Bunche a Triple-I card.

"Poor Sandro." Ursula glanced at the card and stuck it in her pocket. "Look, my break's over but I'm off at three. Can you come back?"

Noel held out his notebook. "Can you just tell us who these people are and where we might find them?"

She looked. "Rudy, he's on Sandro's bowling team. He's a plumber. Alice at the liquor store's his wife. She'll know where he's working. Brady works for the sheriff."

"Yes, I've just met her," Kyra smiled.

Ursula squinted at Kyra but didn't respond. "Cora, I think she's a student Sandro was friendly with at the college. She was at the viewing, green crewcut. Sorry, they're waiting for me in X-ray."

"Thanks. See you at three. The front door?"

A nod from Bunche. Kyra said, "Liquor store to find Rudy." Alice, plump and motherly, said he was plumbing some new condos in Oak Harbor. Out by the Golf Club, Swanton and Monticello area.

Twenty minutes of highway north, fifteen minutes of wrong turns and they drew up to a muddy construction site. In the middle sat an L shape of two-storey condos, framed, undersided with pressboard, empty window holes. Kyra parked near a collection of trucks and vans. Noel made his way across a planked walkway over the mud and stuck his head in the nearest door. "Rudy Longelli work here?"

A man in a hard hat and coveralls slipped between two wall frames. "Who wants him?"

Noel handed him a card. "May we take a minute of his time?"

"Far's I'm concerned you can, he's on lunch break." The guy, maybe the foreman, handed Noel back his card.

Kyra looked around. "Where'd he be eating?"

"Probably Aztec Tacos. Down in the Mall."

"How do we recognize him?"

The man shrugged and started to turn. "Skinny. Wearing a blue and black flannel shirt, Mariner's hat."

"Thanks."

Back in the car, Kyra wheeled out. "Remember a mall?"

"No. But even island towns have malls. Full of Ye Olde Shoppes."

"So if he's eating we can multi-task too."

They spied a twenty-store mall on the right complete with Aztec Tacos. Inside the café's turquoise plastic decor a couple of dozen people munched and slurped. Noel spotted a blue and black flannel shirt. "Rudy Longelli?"

The man looked up. "Yeah?"

"We'd like to talk about Sandro Vasiliadis." Rudy's hands were full of burrito. Noel put a Triple I card on the table. Kyra explained, hired by Sandro's mother, and so on.

"Yeah, I was there. Sad thing. He was a good guy." Rudy took a bite.

They slid into the other side of the booth. Kyra saw from a wall board that Aztec Tacos offered chimichangas. Her order was ready.

"We bowled together," Rudy mumbled, still eating. He was extremely thin, Noel noted—asset for a plumber, crawling under floors? "For Krawcyk and Sons Garage. Him and me, we were the best of the team." He waved his burrito in his left hand. "Lefties."

Lefties. Kyra smiled. "An advantage in baseball but I didn't know about bowling."

"Yeah. Sandro was maybe even better than me." He slurped something dark up a straw. "He played badminton too."

"We've heard he didn't play sports growing up."

"Dunno about before. Just those two now."

"Was he seeing someone? Living with someone?"

"Not that I know of." Rudy started on the second burrito.

A cautious friend, Kyra decided. A server arrived. Kyra ordered a chimichanga and Noel two soft chicken tacos.

"Did he have many friends? A partner?"

"No partner, no." Rudy mumbled, mouth full. He swallowed, then said, "He used to be married. Has a kid, she's about ten or eleven. Used to bring her bowling sometimes, nice kid. Come to think, I haven't seen her for a while." He ate more burrito. "But usually we just bowled and had a beer after. Never took him home to meet the wife." He sighed. "Too bad now. The wife said I shoulda, our kids might've got along with his."

"He seem depressed recently?"

"Nope."

"Anything different that you noticed about him?"

"Like what?"

"Well, his face, say."

Rudy munched and thought. "When I first met him he had a beard. When he shaved it off he still looked like he needed a shave. But recently he didn't. I was kinda wondering if he had that new laser treatment. I coulda asked but figured it was none of my business."

"Did you see him in the coffin?"

"Quickly."

"You're sure it was Sandro?"

"Yep."

"What about friends?"

"Yeah, I guess. I saw him with a green-haired girl a couple of times, maybe she was his girlfriend, he just grinned when I asked him."

"Any others?"

"Mmm." Rudy finished his burrito and drink. "You know, I just don't know." He looked at his watch. "I gotta go. Gotta rough in five more this afternoon."

"Keep our card," Noel said. "In case anything comes up."

Rudy took it, said, "See ya," and walked away without looking back.

A couple of hours till their conversation with Ursula Bunche. Kyra found a phone book, looked up Cora Lipton-Norton, dialed the number. A machine. Okay, head over to Skagit Valley College and track her down.

Oak Harbor had some fine-looking fast-food places, seemed to be frequented by young families from the Naval Air Station. "Too bad we've just eaten," Kyra mourned, "we could've grabbed a souvlaki at that Greek takeout."

"Too messy to eat while driving. You need a picnic table and eight minutes to chomp down any serious souvlaki."

They headed to Pioneer Way. The college campus was several buildings on nearly treeless land overlooking the Oak Harbor Marina. It took four askings, people of all ages, to find the registrar's office. Three women at four desks. Six computers, forty or fifty file cabinets four drawers high, over a dozen shelves filled with catalogues and loose-leaf binders: the record-keeping branch of the college. Noel approached the woman at the nearest desk, forties, blondish-grayish curled hair, a matronly bosom.

An instant smile. "May I help you?"

Noel introduced himself and Kyra and handed her a Triple-I card. When he explained they were private detectives, the two other women tuned in. He and Ms. Rachel needed to locate a student here, Cora Lipton-Norton. "Does she have any classes today, Ms.—?"

"I'm not sure I can help you, we—" She glanced over her shoulder. "Sheila, this gentleman wants to know about a student here?"

Sheila looked up from her keyboard. "What would this be about?"

Triple-I's tactics normally called for Kyra to begin when they dealt with men, Noel with women. But maybe this time, Kyra thought, she should've started the interview. Oh well.

Noel said, "It's important we talk with Ms. Lipton-Norton."

"It's the college's responsibility to protect the students from outside intrusion. While they're here on campus, I mean. What do you want her for?" Sheila, a woman in her fifties, gray eyes that looked hard through lightly tinted glasses, glanced from Noel to Kyra.

Kyra, recognized, decided to step in. "We need to talk to her about another student. Well, possibly ex-student, as you may know. Sandro Vasiliadis."

"Ex, you say? Did he graduate?"

"No," and Kyra made full eye contact with Sheila, "we have reason to believe he may have died. Last week."

"One of our students? Was he in the Navy?"

"No, he lived on the south end. Used to work at the hospital."

"Oh dear, no, we hadn't heard." Sheila's hardness dropped away. "The poor man."

Noel asked, "Did you know him?" and caught Kyra's glance: Let me play it. Okay, she was right on this.

"No, I didn't. We have many students." She turned to the others. "Did you know him?"

"No," and "Nope." Sheila said, "But what do you want from—?"

"Cora Lipton-Norton," said Kyra. Triple-I protected client confidentiality as much as possible, but in this case Kyra could see no way of doing so. In the hope that at least one of these women was a mother, she told the sad story of Sandro's mother's doubts, despite other identifications. "Mrs. Vasiliadis is clinging to the hope it's not her son who died. But certainly someone's son is dead."

"Oh, that's terrible," said Sheila. The others' heads nodded, agreeing.

"We can help you track down Cora," Sheila continued. "Would it help to talk to any of the professors of the student, Sandro was it?"

"Sandro Vasiliadis, yes. We'd appreciate that."

She sat at her computer. "That was V-a-s—?"

Kyra spelled the name. "Likely registered as Alessandro."

Sheila entered the information. She squinted at the screen. "You did say Alessandro?"

"That's right."

"We seem to have a mis-entry here. We don't have any Alessandro Vasiliadis."

Kyra squinted. "No?"

"Mistakes happen, it's rare, but sometimes. We have a Vasiliadis. But it's Alessandra." She stressed the final *a*.

"Typos, yes." But, Kyra thought, Mrs. Vasiliadis had said, Rudy had said: no beard, no five o'clock shadow.

"It must be the same person. Alessandra, or dro, Vasiliadis is, was?—oh, the poor dear—taking two courses. Professor Atkinson in American History, that would be the US between the World Wars course. Atkinson's popular, a large lecture course, he might not know his students well. And a course in Sociology, gender politics, cross-listed in Women's Studies."

"Who's teaching that one?" Kyra asked.

"That would be," Sheila pecked at the keyboard, "Harriet St. Clair. The names are in the catalogue." She strode toward a shelf, took down a book and handed it to Kyra.

"Is either professor on campus today?"

Sheila gazed at Kyra, and sighed. "This is all—quite terrible. When a student dies. I can look." She moused her way through several computer windows. "Professor Atkinson doesn't have classes or office hours today. Professor St. Clair teaches at three, so she's likely in her office now." Sheila told them the office number.

Kyra bulldogged on. "We need to speak with Ms. Lipton-Norton as well."

Sheila, back to the computer. "She should be leaving a science methods course in ten minutes. Elementary education, third floor, down the hall, room 349."

"Thank you."

In the hallway Kyra started to speak but Noel took her by the elbow. "Outside." They sat on a low cement wall. "Okay. What have we got here."

"If you're thinking what I'm thinking, we know what we're thinking. But we need to talk to a friend. Like Lipton-Norton." She glanced at her watch. "Who'll be leaving class in about five minutes. Come on."

Through a glass slit in the 349 door they could see students shuffling, standing, collecting notebooks and jackets. The door opened to release a young man in a hurry. Others followed. A thin young woman wearing heavy eye makeup and thick brown lipstick, a tough face, came out. Her short hair was emerald green.

Kyra stepped toward her. "Excuse me, are you Cora?"

"Huh?" But suddenly she smiled and her face was transformed to lovely. "Oh, no. You want her," she pointed into the room, "that's Cora."

A while since he'd seen such a finely formed face, thought Noel. Kyra thanked the girl. They waited for a second woman with short green hair. As she passed, Kyra again asked, "Cora?"

"Yes?" Hesitation. Taller, also thin, ears with rings as Claude Martin had mentioned, and the green hair. Maybe an inch of it, but the fuzz held a lot of color. She wore jeans and a short-waisted pullover which revealed three rings in her navel. Her thumb hooked a sweatshirt over one shoulder, the other hand grasped two books and a notebook.

"May we speak with you? It's about your friend Vasiliadis."

"Oh. Oh. Okay, yeah."

Noel asked, "You want a coffee?"

"Uh, okay. The cafeteria? Tea, maybe." She led the way down two flights into a large space with a stage at one end. The dominant sound, students' voices at a hundred tables. Cora led them to the drinks section, a vending machine. She chose tea, Kyra coffee, Noel nothing. They found an empty table. "Like, what do you want to know?"

Kyra slid Cora a Triple-I card. "You were at the viewing of the body?"

"Oh, it was awful. When the mother came."

"What was awful?" Noel spoke his gentlest.

"Her face. She, like, didn't know."

"What?"

Tears now at the corners of Cora's eyes. "About her child. Trying to deal with herself."

"How?" Noel asked, just as Kyra echoed, "Herself?"

Cora answered Noel. "Sandra was my friend. I tried to, like, help."

"By?"

"Telling her things. She was confused."

"About?"

"How to live like a woman. Much as she could. Outside herself she'd always been a man, except like inside she wasn't. Now at last she could live like a woman. Dress like a woman, think out loud like a woman. She did a lot of that already. She was pretty much a woman really."

Kyra said, "Sandro was a transvestite, then?"

"I guess you could say that. But it was like much more complicated. Jeez."

"Did she wear women's clothes at the college?"

"Well, yeah, sorta. You know how it is, what's women's clothes anyway. Like, jeans, T-shirts, everybody wears those. But Sandra liked wearing dresses, pantyhose, heels, all that. And makeup too, jewelry." Cora giggled, and wiped away a tear streak. "But she wore, like, jeans, too."

"Did she have friends at the college? Who'd she hang out with?"

Cora sighed. "See, this was like her first semester. She was just like starting. She was getting to know herself. She didn't have time, right, to meet a lot of people?"

Noel said, "How'd you get to be friends?"

A small blush from Cora, and she rubbed her cheek. She paused and blinked before she said, "Oh what the hell. I, like, picked her up." She laughed lightly, forced.

Kyra said, "That sounds complicated."

"No big deal for me, before I figured it out. Well, I'd just about figured it out when Sandra told me. But it was like a real big deal for Sandra."

"I bet," said Kyra.

"We were already at my place. She was wearing like a black silk blouse and she smelled great, and we kissed for a while. Then she like says to me, 'I got to tell you something.' And she does. For a couple of seconds it blew my mind. And then I thought, like, this is really interesting. And we started talking. We talked a lot after that. And hugged a lot. I really do think I helped Sandra." Cora stared at her undrunk tea. "Then she died." The tears came back. "I think I loved her. Or him."

Kyra said, "It's awful." Meaning his—or her—death. Noel nodded in agreement.

"She was like so—so brave. And so beautiful. Already."

For a few seconds no one spoke. Then Noel said, "Cora, you've helped us a lot. And what you've told us will help Sandro's—Sandra's mother too. Maybe not right away, but soon. May I ask you another question?"

"Sure," said Cora.

"You say Sandra was beautiful, and brave. Was she—happy, too? Or upset?"

"Oh no, it was great, she was really happy. Well, till about a week ago, I mean a week before she died. I didn't see her that week. We like talked on the phone a couple of times."

"Did she—talk at all about suicide?"

Cora turned to stare at Noel. "Sandra? Hell no! Sandra had like everything to live for. She could act how she wanted, dress how she wanted. At last. Why would she like want to kill what she loved most, being Sandra?"

"I don't know. But thank you for telling us about her. You've been very generous." Noel spoke the words as a kind of apology. He got up slowly.

Kyra stood too. "You've been really helpful."

Cora looked from Kyra to Noel, and back. "Yeah." She stared at the table.

They thanked her again and left. Outside, Noel said, "Well, there's a shocker."

"Like, yeah. Sure explains a lot."

"Think we need to talk to the gender politics prof?"

"I think we maybe, like, really need to, like, yeah," said Kyra.

"Okay, sweetheart. Enough."

"Why didn't Ursula Bunche tell us any of this. Too rushed?"

"Maybe. Maybe."

They found the gender professor. But she barely knew Vasiliadis who always sat in back, rarely spoke.

They drove back to Coupeville saying very little. By San de Fuca's lagoon Noel turned to Kyra. "Do we tell Maria Vasiliadis directly that her son had become a transvestite?"

"Or?"

"Don't know. Something to take away the sting."

"Like?"

Noel shrugged. "You know, there's so much I don't get." He rubbed his palms on his thighs. "I've been openly out for a long time, right?" He considered that. "Nearly twenty-five years. I think I know a lot about the gay community. I'm comfortable there, just as I am in most communities. But with Sandro there's something else. It all sounds too different. I've spent a little time with some cross-dressers. I don't know, they just leave me uncomfortable." He shrugged. "Could it be Sandro was physically altering his sex? Not just dressing?"

"Must've been taking something to get rid of the hair. We better find out."

"We don't have to. We're only hired to find out if the body was Sandro's."

"How would he have gotten rid of the beard?"

"I don't know." And right now Noel didn't care. The case was over. It was Sandro in the coffin. "But I'm glad we're done with this one."

"Why?"

He shrugged. "Sandro-Sandra gives me the creeps."

———

The Tracker pulled up at the hospital. Ursula Bunche, wearing a black and red mackinaw, waited in front. Her blonde hair hung free. Noel opened the back door. She got in, said, "Let's talk somewhere else. Drive to the water. There's Toby's."

Kyra drove downhill. At Toby's they sat and ordered beers. "Okay." Kyra turned to Ursula. "Some questions. Did you know Sandro was a transvestite?"

Ursula looked from Kyra to Noel. "She wasn't."

"Come on, we just spoke with his friend Cora at the college. And to the registrar. He's even registered as Sandra."

"That's right. And does Cora believe Sandro was a transvestite? Did you speak with Rudy Longelli?"

"Yes."

"And?"

"Sandro was a buddy and a good bowler."

Ursula nodded. "With Rudy, Sandra wore men's bowling clothes. But other than that, for the last five months she dressed as what she believed she was, a woman. So she wasn't a transvestite."

Noel let out his breath as if he'd been holding it for the last hour. Which maybe he had. "He thought of himself as a woman? Not just playing a female role?"

"Right. Female to the core. Except for a few male body parts and how they were messing him up."

Noel feared he knew what was coming.

"Why bowling?" Kyra asked. The beers arrived.

"She didn't want to give it up. She loved bowling, she loved being part of that team, with Rudy and the others. Probably because she was so good, and the team needed her." Ursula smiled at Kyra. "She told us she was going to enjoy bowling as a woman, too. But she couldn't be in the men's league if she was a woman. Makes sense, right?" She laughed a little.

"Okay," Kyra said. "Sometimes he-she wore men's clothing, but mostly women's clothing. Wouldn't you say that makes Sandro a transvestite?"

"Don't think in such narrow categories. Sandro was learning to be Sandra, small steps at a time. Five months ago she crossed the line for good. With occasional exceptions. Cora helped Sandra a lot. Brady and I did too. We laughed a lot. We'd laughed together from when I first met him, when he worked at the hospital. He'd wonder what it'd be like, being a woman. The bearded lady in the circus, he'd say, and laugh. Lots of laughing." Ursula sipped her beer. "They'd have destroyed him, his family I mean, if they'd known what he was thinking. He was scared."

Kyra said, "Back when she—uh, he—was married too, you figure?"

"Pretty sure. He said about being married, that he used to wish he was the wife and she was the husband. What finally caused the split was sex. It was so no good for either."

Kyra said, "This verbal he-she stuff is hard to deal with."

"I know," said Ursula. "I thought of Sandro as *he* till that line those months ago. When he got to the other side, I could begin to think of Sandra as *she*."

Noel said, "Do you think, before, with his wife, he felt gay?"

Ursula thought about that. "Not from what he told us. He let himself be picked up a few times at gay bars. This was while he was still married, he figured he had to try. But he said, the way he was, sex with men was no good either. He figured if he and his mom had ever been able to talk about it, they'd have agreed, sex should be between a woman and a man."

Noel, despite himself, found he was sympathetic to Sandro.

"Which," Ursula turned to Kyra, "is why I said Sandra wasn't a transvestite. She was in the midst of an SRP, a sexual reassignment procedure."

"A sex-change operation," said Kyra. "Wow."

"A big step," Ursula agreed. "She'd been thinking about it for years. But there was no way she'd go through all that while her father was still alive. When she took a new step forward, like when she started wearing nylon panties regularly, sometimes she'd say to me or Brady, 'My dad would kill me.' Sandra'd laugh. But from other things she said, I think she feared her father literally would've killed him. Her."

"Then when his father died?"

"Right. Then she started acting on what she was feeling, getting information. Thinking about and wanting and needing something doesn't get it for you. An SRP costs. Sure, he was saving a bit from his salary." She laughed. "He used to say, One day I'll be transgendered into a very old lady. But then last year his grandmother died. She left each of the grandkids about fifty thousand. And Sandro started the process of metamorphosing into Sandra. It was slow. It should be slow."

"Amazing," said Kyra.

"Yeah," said Ursula. "Some people are born different,"

"Why didn't you tell us all this this morning?"

"First of all, there wasn't any time." Ursula sniffed, and wiped her nose. "And secondly I promised Sandra I'd never talk about any of this, without her permission. Unless it was already public knowledge. So you had to find out differently. I couldn't break my word."

"Well," said Noel, "I guess that's it."

"Pretty much."

No one spoke.

"You're trying to figure what to say to Sandra's mother."

"Something like that. Be right back." Noel got up and headed to the men's room.

Ursula sipped beer in silence, and stared out to sea. At last she said, "I have to go to Sandra's place. To feed the cats. I went Sunday after I identified him, after I spoke to the police. Want to come along?"

Kyra said, "Sure," before realizing how much she did.

Ursula went to the washroom. When Noel came back Kyra explained about the cats. Noel said, "We have to go?"

"I'd kinda like to see how Sandra lived."

"This isn't what we were hired for. We've done what Mrs. V. wanted."

"Sure, but aren't you curious too?"

"Not particularly."

"Okay, you stay here and drink beer. I'll pick you up on the way back."

He thought about that. "I guess I am a little curious about the house." Drinking beer alone wasn't why he'd flown down to Bellingham.

SIX

PHILIP HAD CALLED Andrei first thing in the morning. Andrei's secretary told Philip that Mr. Vasiliadis was not available until the end of the afternoon. No, not even for Dr. Deriades. This surprised Philip. He'd been sure Andrei would make time no matter how busy he was. Then Philip guessed Andrei wanted to get a day's work done before hearing the report. Andrei, Philip figured, feared his worst suspicions would be confirmed. Bad news comes easier late in the day, you have a drink or three to numb the pain. And a sleeping pill for overnight.

Just as well to wait. Maybe Herb would report by this PM on his examination of Sandro's body.

Philip arrived at the executive offices of Cascade Freightways at four minutes before five, armed with Herb Feverel's analysis. Philip waited only two minutes. Andrei stuck his head out. Philip went in, Andrei closed the door. No, it wasn't too early, he'd take a bourbon. Andrei poured the liquid into two crystal glasses and handed one to Philip. They sat on the deep chairs.

"So," said Andrei. "Tell me."

Like Andrei, Philip Deriades preferred to keep blemishes incurred by members of the community within the community, or better, within a tiny part of the community. But he couldn't guarantee certain information could be contained. It took a man like Andrei to arrange for that restraint. For this Andrei needed all surrounding information. Therefore Philip set out most of what he'd learned: the body at the viewing was Sandro; Sandro died of a heroin overdose; still unclear if Sandro was a long-term and regular user or if he'd overdosed early in his drug life; equally unclear if this was an accident or if Sandro had intended to kill himself.

"I see," said Andrei. "Go on."

Philip took a deep breath. "I consulted with a colleague, an endocrinologist at Virginia Mason. He likes to say, Dead men tell no lies. He diagnosed with some certainty what was going on with Sandro. He judges Sandro's body was in chronic sexual imbalance, just in what way not even Sandro could have told us, and he—"

"Wait a minute." Andrei sipped his bourbon. "Sexual imbalance. I don't want to guess what that means. Medically."

"Medically we can reconstruct a situation. But not psychologically. Medically it means there were some elements, genetic materials, hormones, that were more female than male in Sandro."

"You mean, Sandro was part woman?"

"Something like that."

"So he was a faggot." Andrei spoke with contempt.

"We have no evidence of that."

"Then I don't get it."

"You've seen versions of things like this." Philip spoke slowly. "You know how some men, at least on the outside, are heavily masculine, muscles, hairy, tough, aggressive. And some guys aren't, they're gentle or sentimental, pussy-whipped or whatever. And some women are strong and tough, some are feminine and compliant—"

Andrei glared at Philip. "Is that what they teach you in industrial medicine?"

"Medical school. And that's what a different medical school taught my endocrinologist friend." Philip looked at his empty glass. "I'd like another drink."

Andrei waved his hand in the direction of the liquor shelf.

Philip took Andrei's glass, filled both to half, and brought them back. "There's lots of forms of sexual distribution. We're pretty certain that Sandro was getting some heavy hormone treatments."

"Hormones? To make himself more of a man?"

"We don't think so." Philip took a swallow of bourbon.

Andrei whispered, "More of a woman?"

Philip nodded. "Yes."

"Oh my god!"

"We think he was having himself transgendered. That's the word these days."

Andrei focused on the table. Both hands rose to his face and he rubbed it, up and down. "Oh, Philip . . ."

"I'm sorry. Maybe I shouldn't have told you—"

Andrei dropped his hands, his mouth a straight line. "You had to. What else?"

"That's about it." Tell Andrei who might have been doing the work on Sandro? He'd find this out whatever Philip said now. "There are five major clinics in the northwest that do this kind of work. And two in British Columbia. The closest is on Whidbey Island. It's the logical place Sandro would have gone to."

Andrei stood. "I'll be right back." He walked slowly to an unobtrusive door, opened, stepped inside, and closed it.

Philip took his glass, got up, strolled to the window. Outside, lights bristled in the dulling distance. All kinds of homes, all kinds of people. All those different sexualities. Poor Andrei. He took too many responsibilities onto himself. Philip sipped. Sandro would have been in desperate straits to inject enough heroin to kill himself. Poor son of a bitch. Maybe, if Philip had known and been able to talk to Sandro, he could've done something.

The door opened. Andrei reappeared. A major transformation: a beaten man had gone into the bathroom, a superman had come out. Andrei looked a foot taller and fifteen years younger. "I need your ongoing help."

"Of course."

"Learn for me all you can about this clinic on Whidbey."

"I'll get on it right away."

"With discretion. I don't want anyone to know what you're doing. The sooner we know more, the better. And this is between you and me. The present level of disgrace is plenty."

"I agree."

"Also, it mustn't be suicide. He'd be buried in unhallowed ground. Everyone would know. The most important person to not hear of this is Maria."

"Of course. But she'll want to know why Sandro didn't look like Sandro."

"Blame it on the heroin. Something that sounds good medically. You'll make her miserable. But not as miserable as the truth. Let her remember her son as her son. Not her daughter."

Philip placed his glass on the table. "Right."

Andrei strode to his desk and sat down. "The information on that clinic as soon as you can. Who the doctors are, just exactly what they do. I'll make sure they keep their mouths shut."

"I'll call you."

"Thanks."

Andrei watched Philip leave. The protection of respectability was essential. He now had to talk to two people. The protopresbyter, Father Peter, his church's spiritual leader, who would not be told the full truth. And Andrei's nephew, Vasily. Vasily the troubleshooter. Andrei needed some troubles shot away.

—

Noel, Ursula and Kyra sat in the Tracker outside the sheriff's office waiting for Brady to emerge. She finished work at four. Noel added his notes onto his laptop.

He twisted to face the back seat. "Where was Sandro supposed to have the surgery?"

Ursula squinted in thought. "Her doctors were all at WISDOM. That's the Whidbey Island Sexual Definition Management clinic. But he never actually said if—" She thought some more. "You know, I don't remember Sandra talking about surgery." Another thought. "Mostly she seemed content moving ahead slowly."

"You have to have surgery, don't you?" Kyra asked. "Lop off the penis and all that?"

Noel shrivelled a little.

"As far as I know," Ursula agreed. "But surgery usually comes well after the hormones."

"Where's this clinic?"

"Oh right here in town. Just up the hill, in fact." She spotted Brady. "Over here!"

Brady crossed Sixth with a puzzled expression.

"Get in." Ursula opened the door. "We're going to feed Sandra's cats."

"Hi," Kyra said. "We met this morning."

"Oh?" Sudden recognition. "Right." She grinned. "Hi."

"My partner, Noel Franklin." Check out this WISDOM clinic? In fact, no need. As Noel had noted, they'd done their job.

"Hi." Noel smiled.

Brady smiled in return, climbed in beside Ursula and closed the door. "A drive in the country, how nice." Brady and Ursula kissed hello.

Noel, noting the kiss, felt a chill loneliness shake him. It passed.

Kyra headed out toward highway 20.

"We're going down the Island nearly to Clinton," Ursula, head navigator, said. "How was work, lovey?" This to Brady.

"Another day, another dollar."

"Is the sheriff always that cranky?" Kyra asked.

"You should see him when he really gets a bee in his bonnet."

Does Brady need to talk in clichés? Noel unfolded the map of Whidbey Island.

After a few miles—God, how Noel hated miles, they were so much longer than kilometers—highway 20 morphed into 525. It was a pretty island, gently rolling land cleared for farming. Many fields were muddy, as suited March; some were bright green, also appropriate for March. Kyra asked the two women how they liked Whidbey.

"A lot," said Ursula. "Every time we go away we can't wait to get back."

"Do you usually take the ferry off?"

"Depends where we're going," Brady said. "If it's Seattle we take the ferry, if it's north we take the bridge."

Impeccable logic, thought Noel.

"What's best about the island?" Kyra continued.

"Well, the size," Ursula replied. "It's big enough so we can get most of what we need, and small enough to be laid back and friendly and still sort of countrified."

"How'd you get here?" Kyra asked.

Ursula grew up in Seattle, really liked it. "But it just got too frantic, and the prices?"

"The Microsoft effect?" posited Noel.

"Boeing, Microsoft, all of them."

"And me," Brady chipped in, "I met Ursula at a friend's party and it was love at first sight. Head over heels. We moved here quick as a flash."

"We concentrate our investigations on islands," Kyra offered as explanation for her questions. "How would you compare Whidbey to the other San Juans?"

"No idea," said Brady, and simultaneously, "Don't know," from Ursula.

"We've never lived on another island," Brady added.

"And we're really not curious, 'cause Whidbey is wonderful," Ursula finished.

"Feels like a big island." Noel glanced from the map to his watch. "We've been driving for twenty minutes. Why did Sandro live so far away? Working at the hospital, courses in Oak Harbor?"

"She moved after she took leave from the hospital," Ursula said. "The house belongs to one of the nurses, he's in Rwanda for a year. Sandra got cheap rent by caretaking."

"I think—" Brady paused. In the rear-view mirror, Kyra caught her glance at Ursula.

Who said, "Oh. It's all right, hon, they know about the sex change."

"Did you tell them?"

"They found out by themselves."

"Oh, okay then." Brady continued, "She wanted privacy so she wouldn't run into somebody she knew. Till the change was finished."

"That makes sense," Noel admitted. "You liked her, eh?"

"Oh yes! We did a bunch of things together, movies and we had lunches. And sometimes we'd go shopping and we'd have the time of our lives. Like last October. The first time Sandra," Brady's tone emphasized the name, "had gone out in public, you know, dressed as a woman. Some clothes I'd given her, and she looked pretty good. But she wanted her own stuff, and she was really nervous when she picked me up, like she was going to play with fire. She even asked me to drive."

"Where'd you go, Oak Harbor?"

"Oh no. We went to Bellingham. To the big mall. Bellis Fair?"

"Of course." Kyra disliked it well.

"She worried somebody from Bellingham would see her, her mother's friends." Brady giggled. "But when we got into the clothes, she relaxed. She took to them like a duck to water."

"What did, uh, she buy?" Hard to make that mental switch, Kyra thought.

"Oh, she had to have everything, underthings first. Lingerie, she called them. We had a great time. Masses of lace and frills. And some cute dresses, and skirts and tops. High heels, she must have tried on a dozen pairs for every one she bought, and she walked really well in heels, cool as a cucumber. All kinds of dangly earrings, and lots of makeup too. If I hadn't been along she'd have looked like a tart from a B movie!" Brady and Ursula laughed. A sadness tingled in their voices.

"Did she wear normal things? Jeans, T-shirts?" Kyra asked.

"Oh sure, but tight T-shirts, especially as her boobs swelled." Brady stared out the window. "We went again. The January sales, before classes started. Sandra needed school things. That was real neat too."

"Turn here," Ursula ordered. Noel checked his map to find out where they were. Langley Road. Soon she said, "Turn here." Log Cabin Road. And, "Here." Storrs View Drive. They were just south-west of Clinton, near the bottom of Whidbey Island. Kyra pulled into a long driveway that wound past a ramshackle garage and a stretch of bushes. She stopped in front of a small cedar cabin. They got out.

A covered veranda ran along the front and down one side of the low house. They climbed two steps. Ursula unlocked the door. The veranda's roof cut the light to the windows so it was dim in the room they entered, only four-thirty. Two cats unravelled themselves from the sofa and attacked various legs, meowing about how dread-fully they'd been neglected. "It's just been two days," Ursula informed them. "You're not so badly off." She glanced across to the kitchen area. "Look. You still have food." The cats, one orange, the other gray, wound around her legs as she filled the dishes with dry food from a bag under the sink. Then unfilled the litter box.

Noel stared at an aquarium against the far wall. He switched on the light. Various water animals glowed. He made out some brightly colored fish and two dull sea slugs. Snails clung to the glass. The room also featured a sofa, two armchairs, coffee table, two end tables and a desk holding a computer and printer.

Kyra opened a door to a bedroom. Neat, bed made, no clothes flung on surfaces, the pictures on the walls straight. In the closet she found a number of dresses and light suits, skirts and blouses. And a man's bowling shirt and pants, proclaiming sponsorship by Krawcyk and Sons Garage. High heels lined up on the floor beside a pair of sandals, two pairs of low heels, sneakers and bowling shoes. She rifled through again: no further male clothing.

The dresser, a standard man's highboy, held a vanity mirror. Garage sale issue, Kyra thought. In front of the mirror, a large silver tray contained more cosmetics than she'd owned in her whole life. She unscrewed a vial of cologne. Not bad.

Noel and Brady appeared. Brady opened a dresser drawer. "Here, feast your eyes, it's the lingerie Sandra bought when we went shopping."

Kyra and Noel glanced in. Lacy, flimsy panties and bras, the sort that, the less fabric, the more they cost. Kyra smiled ruefully now at Brady's *B-movie tart* comment. What was Sandro wearing when the kid found his body?

Ursula appeared. "All that soft clothing. Sandro, before Sandra, kept saying how important it was for him to go the other way. He did everything he could to move himself the other way."

Sandro owned more lacy little things than Kyra did. He must have felt mighty different from what his male image had projected.

Noel said, "Rudy Longelli mentioned that Sandro had a daughter. Do you know if he'd made a will?"

"No, I don't," Ursula said.

"Very few thirty-year-olds make wills," Brady observed. "I'm twenty-nine and I don't know anyone who has one. You haven't, have you, babe?"

"No. And," she added, "I'm thirty-seven,"

Kyra thought, I haven't either, and looked at Noel.

"I made one when my partner got sick. We both did. But mine leaves everything to him and he's dead." He grimaced. And Brendan had left everything to Noel, so Noel never had to find gainful employment again. "But we'd better look. Where did Sandro keep his papers?"

Ursula and Brady shrugged.

They trooped back into the large room. The no-longer-complaining cats were grooming themselves. Noel opened the desk's top right drawer. Paper, disk-holder, a few pens.

"Sandro was left-handed," Kyra reminded him.

In the top left drawer a cardboard folder with a Velcro flap held Sandro's documents: birth certificate, graduation from high school, nursing license, vaccination certificate, medical plan, address book. No will. Papers back, the lower drawer. A photo album. Pictures of

Sandro, the first with a beard and wearing only jockey shorts, the second with no beard but still in men's undershorts, then the rest— Noel riffled through—Sandra in lacy lingerie. A record of how his skin was smoothing, facial hair disappearing, breasts swelling. "Have you seen these?" he asked Ursula and Brady.

"No," Ursula said.

Brady thumbed through. "All the photos have the same background." She looked around, "Like that wall there."

"He's in the same position in each photo," Kyra ob-served.

"It would be like Sandra to keep a record of her changes," said Ursula. "She was fastidious and methodical."

"Who took the photos?" Noel wondered.

"Maybe she did," Kyra said. "Maybe there's a Delay button on the camera. If the camera stood on that bookcase up against the wall, that'd work."

"That'd work," Brady repeated.

"May we take them to show Mrs. Vasiliadis?" Noel asked Ursula. "To convince her it was her son in the coffin."

Ursula shrugged. "I guess so."

"Good." To Ursula and Brady: "We'll be responsible for the photos. We'll leave the album with Mrs. Vasiliadis or get it back to you." Noel realized he was explaining his actions to the keeper of the house key; Ursula wasn't in charge here. Should they really show Sandro's mother these pictures? Could she handle the images? Would Sandro/Sandra have wanted Maria to see them?

Noel and Kyra glanced into the bathroom and the other bedroom. Both neat. In the closet Noel located a camera. It did have a self-timing device. He turned it on and flashed through the memory. No images.

Kyra went back to the bathroom. A sink. On the right a hairbrush and comb, on the left a glass, toothbrush and paste. You learn a lot about people from their medicine cabinets, she believed. Here the usual nail files and clippers, tweezers, scissors, Band-Aids, antiseptic cream. And three little bottles of medications, two prescribed by Richard Trevelyan, M.D. She called Ursula in. "What are these?"

Ursula glanced at the labels. "Strong painkillers. New." She read: "'As needed.' Hmm." Another vial. "Hipoperc. Never heard of it.

Which doesn't mean much. 'Five drops twice daily.' Interesting. Not dispensed by a pharmacy. Come on, we better go."

Noel turned off the aquarium light and scratched the orange cat's head. The gray one slept.

———

Terry Paquette clicked the light switches. The lab went dark. But not black. The fish tanks glowed with green or blue or yellow lights, according to the needs of their inhabitants. Her last function every evening was to walk the four sides of the room, one final glance at each of the eighteen tanks. She didn't need to do this, the kiddies would be fine until morning, but she enjoyed the stroll. Peace hovered here. Among her kiddies she preferred, because they moved with such grace, the caridean shrimp. Though she'd never breathe such a preference in front of the midshipman tank or close to her sixspot gobies or the parrotfish. Her second favorite were the saddleback wrasses from Hawaii, and as she passed their tank she whispered their Hawaiian name, *hinalea lau-wili*. The syllables humming from her lips, she felt the kiss of warm breezes and soft lapping water. No matter how raw the Whidbey weather, her mood would be smiling all the way home. It was nonsense to prefer one or another species—aesthetic choice made no difference in the work. In the long run, likely the molluscs would prove most valuable and they had no personality whatsoever. But the wrasses gave her stability.

She'd need balance this evening. Richard, on the phone, had sounded shaky. He was taking Vasiliadis' death hard. As if he were questioning his career. Well, she was sad about the death too. She hadn't known the man, let alone the woman he was becoming, but she'd followed his progress over the last months through the team's reports. It was the medical part that bothered her most—he'd overdosed and died so no way of following through on what seemed to be evolving into a successful reassignment. Overdosing: an absurd accident. Richard had wondered if Vasiliadis had purposely killed himself. If any of the team could be faulted it was not knowing Vasiliadis had been shooting heroin. If anyone was to blame, really—she avoided such notions in scientific matters—it would be Gary. Gary had done the psychological analysis and declared the client a good subject. If he was unbalanced, Gary should have caught that. Still, she wasn't about to blame Gary. Vasiliadis couldn't be brought back, the clinic had to move on.

Except Richard wasn't moving on. Yesterday he seemed to be controlling his so-called guilt, but this afternoon he sounded anguished. She said she'd be home by six. She rolled her chair to the shrimp tank and watched the kiddies flick themselves through the simulated seagrass meadows as the water's slow waves gave the grasses a smooth undulation. Pretty little beasts. Too bad they all had to die.

She sat for five minutes. Okay, get along now, Richard needed her. As she needed Richard. They'd been everything for each other since they married, over twenty years ago. He'd been a man given to dramatic guilt then, and he hadn't changed. They met when, at Johns Hopkins, he'd heard a paper she was giving; he was impressed, they talked, discovered they had research concerns in common, and stayed in contact.

Best be gone. Again she wondered about the lab, why it comforted her so. Three rooms of the large space had been transformed into individual offices, hers, Lorna's, and the other that the lab technicians used. On contracts the lab was known as The WISDOM Laboratory, but someone had taken a lead from that acronym and called the lab WIRED, Whidbey Island Research in Endocrinal Development.

Terry locked the inner door, opened the alarm panel, activated it, and locked the outer door. Before WISDOM acquired the building it had been a Navy laboratory, but its security wasn't as state-of-the-art as even her own computer. The locks were okay and the alarm adequate, but the six-foot iron mesh fence with eighteen inches of cantilevered-out barbed wire was a joke. Even she, at fifty-three, could find a ladder, climb up, cut the wire—not electrified—and scramble over. Now she unlocked the gate, got in her car, headed out, locked, drove away. She worried sometimes that their sham security gave people the wrong idea—it looked so impressive surely some national secret had to be hidden inside.

The drive north to Coupeville took fifteen minutes. Richard's black Prius sat on his side of the driveway. She found him behind the house, contemplating the early miniature irises. He held an elegant martini glass, half full. She kissed his cheek. "You're ahead of me."

He smiled at her. "By two."

"That bad?" She took his arm. "Want to go inside?"

"Okay."

They walked up to the deck. Richard slid open the floor-to-ceiling door. The living room glowed with warmth. "Nice fire. You've been home a while?"

He poured her a martini from the shaker and refreshed his own. "Since just after we talked. I couldn't stand being there any more. I cancelled my patients."

They sat in two floral-covered, overstuffed armchairs, facing the fire. Terry leaned forward. "You didn't kill the patient. Okay?"

"Technically." He took a swallow of ice-cold martini. "Technically Sandro killed himself either accidentally or on purpose. But I gave him the hormones that must have tripped his brain."

"Gary diagnosed his brain and didn't catch a tripping point, and Stockman agreed with Gary. Anyway, it was Lorna and I who balanced and tested those interrelated hormones. The same series that worked perfectly for two others. To both of them you're a hero." She got up, leaving her martini, knelt beside him and took his hand. Limp and sweaty. "Something in Sandro's chemistry was different. We'll find out what."

"That's what the others say, too—Stock's pious We go on, Gary's furious We go on, Lorna's soothing We go on." He rubbed her hand. "I don't know if I can. Not if I don't know what I'm doing. And from now on, how can I know?"

"How could you ever know? On any of them?"

"True. I've been careless for too long."

"No." She knelt up higher, and brought her face close to his. "You are probably the most careful physician I've ever met. And don't you dare contradict me. You know I'm right." She kissed his cheek.

"I didn't tell you." Richard stared into the fire. "Vasiliadis came to see me that morning. The day he died. He was fuming."

"But he'd been fuming all week, you told me he was really fuming the day before. When he confronted the four of you."

"Not like this. When he talked, ranted, Lorna at least could quiet him down." Richard leaned toward Terry. "When he came in he was practically frothing. At first he couldn't speak. He'd burst past Dawn, she couldn't stop him. He was wearing a dress with a loose skirt and low heels and his makeup was all askew. For Sandro, very bad signs."

Terry nodded. Sandro was turning into a strongly feminine woman. This recognition had been, at first, a positive symptom. Where had they gone wrong?

"He sat and tried to calm himself. I wanted to help but he kept waving me away and shaking his head. Finally he said, 'Want to see what you've done?' I said I could see, and we'd solve the problem, but he interrupted me, he said, 'I mean really see!' I asked him what he meant.

"He stood, and lifted up his skirt." Richard stared into his martini, raised the glass and downed it all. "God, Terry." He got up, filled his tumbler, no ice, no water, and drank half.

"Richard, please."

Richard spoke evenly, solemnly: "I tried to examine him but he pulled the skirt between his legs and sat and he said, suddenly deathly calm, 'Dr. Trevelyan, it hurts like hell. You've turned me into a monster.' He started to cry. I gave him water and Demerol. I got him to lie down and told him to wait, and said that I'd be right back. I needed to consult with Stockman, or Gary. But not even Lorna was there."

"Why didn't you call me?"

"I don't know. I just didn't."

"What else did you give him?"

"Nothing. When I got back to my office he was gone. I went outside but he wasn't anywhere. I left messages for the others and finally found Stockman, and I told him what happened. We tried to figure out what to do. Gary came in, and then Lorna. We tried to contact Sandro, bring him back, but he didn't go home all day."

No, thought Terry, he went and found himself some heroin to kill his pain. Or maybe he already had some. And shot it all into himself. Awful.

Richard's gaze held hers. "The four of us agreed we wouldn't tell anyone."

Yes, they had always been a team, despite their differences. Richard had, all his career, wanted to be part of a true team. "Let's take some time off. Maybe we could go somewhere. A few weeks."

"Maybe," said Richard. "Maybe."

SEVEN

KYRA AND NOEL dropped Ursula and Brady in Coupeville at Ursula's car. Noel almost gave the plastic bag containing Sandro's photo album back to them to return to the house, but finally held on to it. But the nearer they got to Bellingham, and Kyra drove with her foot heavy on the gas, the larger grew the package lying on the floor at his feet. It felt inappropriate, even wrong, to have taken this private chronicle of transformation.

Noel had known, early in puberty, that his sexuality was somehow different from that of his friends. It took him a little longer to figure out why, when he fantasized, his objects of desire weren't lean blonde Carline or busty Lettie or sweet gentle Sue. They were attractive, he could see that, but not in *that* way. Instead he was drawn to Burt, and Peter. They didn't look particularly strong, robust or stylish, in fact Burt usually had a zit or two going, but it would've been with them he'd have tried to explore his fantasies. If he'd dared.

He hadn't been attracted to his best friend, Jason. He could talk to Jason about practically anything, but not this—not till nearly the end of their last year in high school. A warm spring afternoon, a long walk in Stanley Park, Jason going on about Roberta, after a month of dating he'd worked up the courage to ask her to think about maybe considering the possibility of their having sex together, and she'd just whispered, Yes, as if for the last month nothing else had been on her mind. Jason talked to Noel about sex for half an hour. Noel spoke less and less till finally Jason said, You know, Claire's real hot for you, bet you could make it with her, and Noel blurted, I can't, Jason, I'm gay. Which brought their conversation and the walk to a standstill. You can't be, Jason kept saying.

Over the summer, when Noel would call, Jason was always busy; with Roberta, who else? Noel left for the University of Victoria and Jason went to Simon Fraser, so during the academic year they hardly saw each other. Noel never had a close buddy again, except for William and then Brendan, and Brendan was so much more. When Noel turned nineteen he explained himself to his older brother

Seth, who said he'd guessed a long time back, making Noel cringe and tell Seth he wished they'd had this conversation years ago. The next evening Noel told his parents. His mother's face whitened, she said nothing, she stared at him. His father cried. After some minutes they hugged him, told him they would always love him, and went to bed. It took two years before they came to accept their son as a gay man.

But Sandro, dead, wouldn't be telling his mother anything about his own differences. Mrs. Vasiliadis soon would be devastated, doubly—Sandro's death confirmed, and Sandro well on his way to becoming Sandra. At least Noel had remained a son, pretty much unchanged in either appearance or action. But Sandra . . . How would a mother receive a son who had transformed himself into a daughter? He stared at the highway ahead. A large green and white sign proclaimed: Bellingham 6. "Kyra. We've got to talk about this."

She glanced at him. "About what?"

"Our meeting with Maria Vasiliadis. How much to tell her."

"Just what she hired us to find out. That everyone agrees it was Sandro in the casket. No it wasn't some other mother's son in the casket, yes it was her son."

"And if she keeps probing?"

"Why would she?"

"About his face, no beard, all that."

"We say we have positive identification from people who knew Sandro in the months before he died, and that's it. All we have to do is tell her what she asked us to find out."

"You don't think she has the right to know about his last months?"

"Maybe you're right. Maybe she does."

"Good. And you can tell her."

"No, you should."

"Why?"

Kyra exited the highway, popped onto city streets. "If you think she should know, then you talk to her. You'll get closer to giving her a sense of what Sandro was going through."

"What, you think a queer can know why somebody wants to change his sex? Well just whoa up!"

"Huh? What?"

"I don't know a damn thing about transgendering, okay? I've never given a thought to it, okay? And even if I had, that's not me. Okay, Kyra?"

"I just meant, Sandro was a man—"

"And I'm a man, and dammit I'm staying a man. And a man who was in a constant relationship for thirteen years, okay? I knew where I was and where Brendan was, okay? No uncertainty there, okay? Which, if I dare say, cannot be said of both of us."

"What's that got to do with this case?" Now Kyra wanted to seal her lips and pull back behind them everything she'd said since this conversation started. Three husbands. One divorce, one widowhood, and now a separation. Not memories she wanted to deal with today. Or maybe ever. Unfair of Noel to bring this up. Okay, maybe she wasn't being fair either. "Not a thing to do with this case, right?"

Noel relaxed. A bit. "Right, no insight by virtue of my sexuality. But if you want to think in those terms, okay, you better do the talking. You're a woman, Maria Vasiliadis is a woman, Sandro was turning into a woman. You're the obvious choice."

"All we have to do is tell her what she asked us to find out." Kyra pulled into the condo's garage. They called in Chinese food, ate it with beers, and carefully avoided the case. She felt a strain between them but thought better of mentioning it. It'd be all gone in the morning. She hugged him goodnight.

With Noel's door closed, still only 9:45, Kyra called Jerome. She filled him in on their case, the unpleasant job the morning would bring, and her disagreement with Noel about how much to tell the mother.

"Well," Jerome spoke slowly, "congratulations. You're very good at what you do."

"We try to be."

"Actually, I meant you."

"No no, we each do our part."

"But now you say Noel doesn't want to play his part."

Just what she'd been thinking, but Jerome shouldn't say it. She winced with disloyalty to Noel "Depends, I suppose, on what each of us thinks our parts are."

"Hmm," said Jerome.

"What's that mean?" It felt a little okay, Jerome taking her side.

"That your sense of what to tell the mother is right. Does she need to know everything?"

"Well mostly I agree. But then—"

"You'll decide. But if it were me, I wouldn't want to know all that. Especially since it no longer makes any difference."

Kyra wondered how much she'd want to know. Would she be a different person if she hadn't known that Simon, her second husband, killed himself? Did it mean Jerome would want the truth watered down? Or want it at all? "Maybe you should know as much as you can handle. But how do you know how much that is?"

Jerome said, "That poor woman has a life ahead of her. To know all that was in her son's mind, that'd be terrible."

Kyra nodded—and remembered Jerome couldn't see her. "Yes," she said. They talked a few minutes more, potluck plans, and she promised a report tomorrow evening.

In her room she sat for a few minutes, still dressed. Such a reasonable man, Jerome. Pragmatic and intelligent. And nice to her, trying to defend her before an absent Noel. *Nice*; there it was again. How much did she need *nice* in her life?

Not the question for tonight. From the shelf in her closet she took the leather case and opened it. She removed two of the six juggling balls: tell nothing to Maria Vasiliadis, tell part to Maria Vasiliadis. Up from her left hand went the first ball, up went the second, she caught the first in her right and up again, the second. A minute, two. Good exercise, but juggling two balls was easy. She caught the two, reached for two more, one up, two up, three, catch one—tell all to Mrs. Vasiliadis—and re-toss, catch two and up again, three and one and two, and kept them going. Higher arcs and she grabbed the fourth ball, up high, hands catching, reaching, tossing, till only rhythm held sway and her mind, fully relaxed, knew she was juggling Maria-all, Maria-part, Noel-no, Jerome-yes, a smooth oval. Three minutes, four, five. Now all that had seemed clear when speaking with Jerome had gone unclear. She caught the balls, one-two-three-four, squeezed them, set them back in their case. Usually juggling satisfied her, clarified her thinking. Tonight, nothing.

At 8:03 Thursday morning Andrei Vasiliadis looked up from his newspaper to see Vasily walk toward him, past other booths, to their usual space in the back of the Pancake House. An eerie feeling came over Andrei, watching Vasily—it could've been him, Andrei, thirty years ago coming toward the sixty-one-year-old him now. He wondered if Vasily felt as if he were approaching his older self. Aging with each stride.

They did look alike, big muscular men, black haired—well, Andrei a touch gray-slicked. His nephew even sported the same thick mustache. The family always commented on the look-alikes.

"Hi." Vasily slipped onto the bench opposite his uncle.

The server approached with coffee and menus, and poured at Andrei's nod. Vasily ordered the full stack of pancakes with blueberry syrup, Andrei the bacon and eggs special. They talked for a while about Vasily's parents, their big trip to Greece next week. Finally Vasily said, "What's up with you?"

"Sandro." Andrei glanced around. No one could overhear but he lowered his voice anyway. He told his nephew about Maria denying Sandro's body, the lack of facial hair, the sex change theory.

"Sex change? Jeeeesus."

"None of this must become known. And especially not by Maria."

Vasily, two years older than his cousin, had never much liked Sandro, from toddlerhood considered him a wimp who tried to act tough. "Yeah, right. Who does know?"

"Find out. Go to Whidbey, look around, see who's saying what and keep them quiet. There's a clinic in Coupeville that does sex business. Here only me, you and Philip know."

"Think Philip's trustworthy on this?"

Andrei considered the question long enough to let Vasily know he'd settled this for himself. "Yes."

"You know any names on Whidbey?" The server arrived with their orders. The two men remained silent while she arranged the plates and left.

"There's a nurse worked with Sandro, name's Ursula something. Do your stuff."

Vasily rolled his shoulders under windbreaker and blue cashmere as if already doing his stuff. He poured syrup on his pancake stack and cut an enormous forkful.

Andrei inhaled eggs, bacon and hash browns, disdaining the orange slice and parsley garnish. "Official cause of death is a heroin overdose, that's bad enough, but if this other business gets about you can pretty much figure what the community'll think. Say."

The community supported its people through anything—well, any God-created disaster. Human variations from the norm were shunned. Sandro's family would be cut off. Vasily changed the subject. "How's Nikki?"

"Fine. Just fine."

Andrei's tone had gone hearty. He got hearty when things weren't fine. Vasily's cousin Nikki, middle child of Uncle Andrei and Aunt Petra, was "an artist." Last time he'd seen her she'd been dressed in black jeans, black sweater, black nail polish, black lipstick. Her hair was jet black already.

"She's doing triptychs. Overlaying prints of traditional church images with modern advertisements." Andrei shook his head. "Awful. Maybe blasphemous. Now she wants to go to Greece for a year. How's your, uh, Helena?"

Vasily looked up. "Cynthia's fine." He winked. "Couldn't be better. Much better than Helena."

Andrei gave him a stern look. "You're what? Thirty-two? Start thinking family thoughts."

"Yeah." Vasily dropped his head to consider his last forkful of pancake. He lifted it up, put it in his mouth, chewed, swallowed. He blotted his lips. "Life's okay right now, though."

Showered and breakfasted, the album in its plastic bag on the floor at Noel's feet, Kyra drove them to Dulcey Lane, spotted the two blue spruce, and parked. "Well?"

"Here's my notion," said Noel "I'll tell Maria it was definitely Sandro, and we'll see how she reacts."

"Fair enough. And the album?"

"We'll take it with us." He put it in his briefcase. They got out. He rang the bell.

Maria Vasiliadis opened the door, same black dress? Face still drawn. "Oh hello."

Noel smiled. "May we come in?"

"Yes, of course. You didn't call."

"No." They both preferred not to alert a client that they had news; the client could easily imagine something worse than whatever Kyra or Noel might tell her. Noel, Kyra following, crossed the threshold into the living room.

"Please, sit. Will you have some coffee?"

"No thank you. Kyra?" His look to her said, *Don't*.

"Not for me either, thank you."

Noel sat. The others did too, Kyra on a chair, Maria Vasiliadis on the couch. Both kept their gaze on Noel. He said, "Mrs. Vasiliadis, we're very sorry to have to offer our condolences on the death of your son."

Her stare stayed on him for another moment, then her head dropped, her hand rose to her face. She sat in silence. Her other hand found a tissue, she transferred it to the right and dabbed her eyes. "Tell me."

Noel explained, mentioned the attestations of Ursula Bunche and Brady Adam, of Rudy Longelli and Cora Lipton-Norton.

"I can't believe it." Maria glanced to Kyra. "I know what my Sandro looks like."

Kyra leaned toward her. "Mrs. Vasiliadis—maybe—since you hadn't seen him for quite a while without a beard—"

"Sandro is my son, Miss Rachel. He was born from me. He had no beard when he was born. I know Sandro's face. A strong face, good looking. That wasn't his face."

"His friends—"

"They must be lying."

"Why would they lie?"

"I don't know."

"We believe they're simply telling us what they know, and believe." Kyra spoke softly.

The tears came again. Maria squeezed her lids tight. She wiped her cheeks with her fingers. "Then what are you not telling me?"

"We're telling you what we know and—"

"Did he have cancer?"

"Mrs. Vasi—"

"Was he getting radiation treatment?"

"We don't know anything about cancer."

"Then what? Why?"

Kyra glanced toward Noel. He nodded. Kyra said, "We know very little. We weren't certain we should tell you—"

Maria looked directly at Kyra, hands clasped in her lap. "You have to."

"I think you must have been a wonderful mother to Sandro." Kyra moved to sit on the couch beside her. "Yes, he was having treatment."

Maria's brow furrowed. "For what?"

"We've learned Sandro was a very divided man."

Maria nodded, in question rather than agreement.

"Maybe in his hormones, his sense of himself, he was not always a man."

Maria stared at Kyra.

"Mrs. Vasiliadis. We learned that Sandro had begun to respond to the more feminine part of himself. We learned—" Maria sat very still. "He was undergoing what's called an SRP. It's a standard treatment, more and more men go through it—"

"SRP?"

"Sexual reassignment procedure." No response. As if Maria had stopped breathing. "It's fairly common, there are other men like Sandro, it happens." Shut up, stop the prattle. "His friends say Sandro had wanted this for—a while."

"This SRP?"

"That—inside him lived the woman he'd always wanted to be." There. Spoken. Now Maria knew. And would always know.

"The woman."

"He was changing himself. He told his friends he had to change himself."

Maria spoke slowly. "He changed himself to a dead person. My son—changed himself to—a dead person." She shook her head. "No," she whispered, and louder, "No." Silence, then she shrieked, "No! No no no!!"

Kyra reached out for Maria's hand, then pulled back. Maria stared dead ahead. No one spoke.

Till Noel said, "Mrs. Vasiliadis? May I bring you anything?" No answer. "Some water?"

She turned to him. "What else must I know about Sandro?"

"You know everything now." No, no need for her to see the photos.

"He had a lot of very close friends who loved him," Kyra said, hearing it ring lame in her head.

More silence. At last Maria said, "Good." And some seconds later, "Thank you." Still she hadn't moved.

"Can we call someone for you?"

"No," she said, "there's no one." She stood slowly, as if uncertain her legs would keep her upright. Then she walked carefully to the door, and turned. Noel and Kyra stood now. "Please," Maria said. "I want to be by myself." She opened the door.

Kyra spoke gently. "Are you sure—?"

"Please."

Kyra and Noel left. The door closed behind them.

EIGHT

IN WISDOM'S CONFERENCE room, Richard Trevelyan sat at the head of the table. He had called the meeting. An emergency, he'd said. Gary Haines hated it when Richard chaired—five minutes of agenda could stretch into an hour. Richard was terrific in his medicine, but Gary wished Richard would save his orderly tendencies for that. Dawn had phoned everyone at eight this morning. Very unlike Richard. No agenda supplied in advance. Maybe this was the beginning of a new Richard. Damn unlikely, Gary smirked. He'd spend the next hour—god, let it be no more than that—with his mind roaming through the details of his latest case.

Gary sat at Richard's right, Stockman across the table to Richard's left. The five other chairs stood empty. Almost simultaneously Gary and Stockman checked their watches. Lorna, late as ever. Usually three or four minutes. As if on cue, the door opened and Lorna came in. She said "Gentlemen," and sniffed the air. She glared at Gary, marched to the window behind him, and cranked it open forty-five degrees. The thin venetian blind clacked lightly in the breeze. She sat on Stockman's side, one empty chair between them.

"Hey," said Gary. "That's a raw wind."

"Gary, I've asked you and asked you! That damn cologne. Leave it off when we're meeting!"

"Sorry. By the time Dawn called—" Lorna was right, she had asked him. But Lorna was getting weird. Menopausal? As expensive a cologne as the market offered. Women loved his cologne.

"It smells like dying eucalyptus. Offends my olfactory sense."

Your dress offends my visual sense, Gary nearly retorted. A hideous olive green that emphasized her plump frame. He clenched his teeth.

"Please," Richard's whisper, hoarse but firm, "don't squabble. We need to talk. Calmly."

"Okay," Gary said, "what's this about?"

Stockman added, "Can we make it short? I have a luncheon."

Lorna turned to Stockman. "Richard believes there's an emergency. Let's hear him out."

"Thank you, Lorna," Richard said. "We're under a lot of strain, but we mustn't take it out on each other."

"Strain?" It irked Gary when Richard played pseudo-shrink. In questions of the mind, WISDOM belonged to Gary. "What strain?"

"Indeed," Stockman said. "Even under strain we behave like professionals." He frowned at Richard, then at Gary. "Go on."

Staring for the first time directly at Richard, Gary realized the man looked awful. Like he'd aged ten years in a week, his face nearly as white as his hair, new lines from cheeks to jaw. A tremor in his hands? More of this and Richard could become a resident in that hospice he consulted at. He'd be sixty this year. Gary, at forty-eight the youngest of the team, took pride in the illustrious career he'd put together in so short a time.

Richard cleared his throat. "I've decided I should go to the police and explain my part in Sandro's death."

"Are you crazy?"

Richard turned to Gary. "If they know what we've done here, they'll have a motive for his suicide and can close the case."

"As far as they're concerned, the case is closed." Gary glanced from Stockman to Lorna. "Tell him. I mean, again." To Richard he said, "There is no case. Death from drugs is routine. And," he leaned on his forearms and brought his face nearly to Richard's, "we had nothing to do with Vasiliadis' decision to kill himself. Okay?"

"Not we. Just me. I want to go to the police. I need to explain my role in Sandro's state of mind."

"No way!" Gary couldn't believe Richard's stupidity.

"It's not just your role," Stockman spoke gently. "It's WISDOM's research. We should do nothing without consulting."

"That's what I'm doing," Richard said. "Consulting."

Lorna finally spoke. Stalling had let her brain get into gear. "I understand what you're getting at, Richard. When did you decide this?"

"Firmly, yesterday. But I've been back and forth with it all week." He crossed his arms. "I feel completely responsible. The hormone mix, or one of them, clearly set him off. You didn't see his testes. I can't get the image out of my mind. His pain was terrible."

"We could have done more for the pain, you're right," Stockman said. "And over time you'd have adjusted the hormones."

"We don't know why it didn't work. But the fault lies with me." Richard's lips tightened.

Lorna said, "It's not your hormone mix, it's all of ours. Terry and I developed it."

"Yeah, but I'm the endocrinologist. I'm the one administering it."

He'd gone even paler, Gary realized. Get him a tranquilizer?

Stockman leaned forward and spoke, still gently. "Richard, I understand your sense of responsibility. And when one feels he doesn't live up to his highest standards, there's often a strong desire to confess." He smiled, conciliatory, like in his counseling at the church. "But speaking to the police, that's not confession. WISDOM didn't cause Vasiliadis' death. Going to the police would just open up sluice gates to water that's already well settled. You could go to your religious leader—"

Richard shook his head.

"If you want I could make you an appointment with my pastor. He could meet with you. That's the place for confession."

Not the place for Richard, Gary thought. Richard needs to be kept away from talking to anyone. Except maybe to him, Dr. G. Haines. "Richard, we could talk for a few minutes after this meeting."

Richard held his glance for a second, then looked down at the table.

Lorna said, "The work, Richard. With police attention turned our way—All those people we'd have to hold off helping."

"We're cutting edge, Richard, you know that." Gary took delight at Lorna's shudder; with the breeze behind him, wafts of aftershave must have wisped her way. "Our responsibility is far greater than to a single person. Especially if that person is dead." Gary couldn't figure out why Richard didn't see that; it followed logically.

"Yes." Lorna said. "The client is dead. There's nothing to do for him. But we can do lots for the living. We have to move on. Look, it's Thursday. Let's think it over for the weekend, all of us, and reconvene on Monday. If you still want to go to the police, we'll figure the best way."

Gary watched Richard turn to the blinds clacking in the breeze. He looked at his colleagues. What was Richard seeing? Three respected physicians, members of their communities? Gary hoped they'd convinced Richard.

Richard said, "I guess waiting out the weekend won't change much for Sandro."

Stockman stood, and clapped him on the shoulder. "Good man!"

Gary reached out his hand to Richard, who took it, smiled a little, and shrugged. Lorna gave Richard a hug.

Monday was only three days off. Not likely, Gary thought, Richard's little guilt problem would go away.

Andrei Vasiliadis drove his pearl-gray Monte Carlo north on the I-5, cruise control set to a mile under speed limit. No rush to get to Bellingham. He'd prefer not to go at all. But his responsibility stood clear. Maria would listen, she would thank him. Then he would meet with Father Peter, explain to him as to Maria, and discuss the details of the funeral. He had been to many non-Orthodox funerals and each time felt blessed his religion had its rituals and patterns for life's large passages. For Sandro, Andrei would organize the few final details. The protopresbyter need know nothing more than the rest of the community. Definitely Sandro's death was an accident.

Unexpectedly complicated had been his conversation yesterday evening with Diana, Sandro's ex-wife. He'd waited till he had Philip's report; with the certainty the body was indeed Sandro, he brought Diana the news. They met at ten-thirty in the evening, Diana having assured him Carla would be in bed. Stuart, Diana's second husband, was out of town; Stuart, it turned out, couldn't father children himself and had long wanted to adopt Carla. Now, with Sandro's death, he probably would.

Diana had offered Andrei coffee. Too late at night. A drink? He took a Scotch. She was very attractive, barely thirty, black hair cut short, her eyeglasses ever low on her nose, dark eyes accentuated above the upper rim. At Sandro and Diana's wedding he'd suggested to her that she take off the glasses—she would be an even more splendid bride. She refused. Andrei came to believe that without the glasses as highlight, her face would have been plainer. "I must tell you this," he began. "It's about Sandro."

"Yes?" She studied his face.

He knew they'd parted bitterly. He knew that after the divorce Sandro had Carla with him every second weekend, from when she was four. "Diana, I'm sorry. Sandro died a few days ago."

For a few seconds she said nothing, then sighed sharply. "Maria phoned me. But she didn't give me any details. What happened?"

"He overdosed."

Her brow wrinkled. "Drugs?"

"Heroin."

A tight head-shake. "Sandro? No."

He explained: undoubtedly an accident.

"He had no reason to take drugs. He was happy with himself."

Andrei regarded her carefully. "When were you last in touch?"

"Couple of weeks ago." She smiled. "On the phone."

"What did you talk about?"

"His life. His work."

"Diana—" What was she avoiding? "It doesn't matter. I'm sorry."

"We'd begun to talk again. In the last year or so."

"Why?"

She laughed lightly. "Whatever else, he was Carla's father."

"Did he still have her every other weekend?"

"Till last October. Then it stopped."

"Oh?" Andrei, not sure why, felt a shiver. Leave this conversation? Except it was his responsibility to go on. "Why?"

Diana linked her hands, leaned forward and supported her chin on her knuckles. "When did you last see Sandro?"

Oh dear god. "Before he died? Possibly, two years—"

"Did you see him in his coffin?"

Andrei nodded.

"Did he die as a man or as a woman?"

Andrei rubbed his brow with his palms. "You knew this." He dropped his hands and stared at her.

"I am the mother of his child." She looked straight at him, hazel eyes through her glasses, and her tone announced: of course he would tell me anything important.

"It's why he couldn't be with Carla, not for the time being. She believes he went away. To Greece, we say. They e-mailed each other. And Sandro and I talked, every week when Carla was at school. He wanted to know about her, how she felt, did she miss him. She didn't write about personal stuff in her e-mail."

"And did she miss him?"

"At first. But she's nearly eleven. She has her friends. And even a father, at home every day. Well, most days." Diana smiled. "Sandro explained how he'd always felt like the wrong person in the wrong body. That it wasn't my fault our marriage ended. He liked me well enough, he said, even loved me. But—it became more and more difficult for him to touch me. And he hated it when I became tender with him. It became impossible."

Andrei thought he understood. He could sympathize with Diana. Sandro, however, he found increasingly disgusting. "Does your new husband know about Sandro?"

"His transformation? No. Sandro asked for my secrecy."

"Have you told anyone else?"

"Of course not. I promised."

Andrei held her gaze. "May I ask for your continuing secrecy? For the sake of Maria and the community?"

"For the community? I don't care. But for Sandro's sake, yes, and for Carla's sake, of course!"

"Will you tell Carla? One day?"

"Tell her what? Her father changed his sex?" Diana's gaze fixed on the far corner or the room, but her hands were working independently. "That didn't happen. Tell her he was happy as a man?" Diana shrugged and looked down at her fingers intertwined, white-knuckled. "I don't know."

Andrei saw Sandro's chalky face in the coffin, no beard, the breasts Philip had mentioned.

Now in the morning Andrei found himself in front of Maria's house. He pulled into the curb, sat, and reflected. The open wounds were being cauterized. Diana's silence. Now Maria's ignorance. It'd be okay. Maria's door opened. A man and a woman came out. The woman followed the man down the sidewalk. Who were they? What did they want? Maria knew he, Andrei, was coming and had to talk to her. The man and woman got into a small white box-like car, the woman behind the wheel. She drove speedily down the street. Andrei pulled the key from the ignition and got out.

Inside the house he followed Maria to the living room. They sat on the sofa. "There's no easy way to say this," Andrei said. "I'm afraid it was Sandro there, on Whidbey Island." He took her hands.

"Yes, I know."

Andrei had feared she would again break down. Instead she had accepted Sandro's death, had in fact done Andrei's work for him. "Good."

"It's awful."

"Yes."

"I'd been thinking I didn't understand why. But perhaps I do understand."

"Some things are beyond understanding."

"Some things just are." She gazed at him.

"Yes."

"That's how the detectives saw it, too."

Andrei jerked away. "What detectives?"

"The detectives. They just left."

He grabbed her forearms. "The police?"

"No, of course not. The ones we hired."

"The ones we hired!?"

"Of course. The police never worried about Sandro. I was so sure it wasn't Sandro."

"But I told you I'd take care of that."

She sighed. "Yes, and I said you'd pay them."

Andrei sighed too, wearily. Detectives to deal with, on top of everything else. "Of course I'll pay them. Who are they?" And what had they told Maria?

She gave Andrei their names and address. "They were very kind. They'd found a lot of information, about how it had to be Sandro."

"Good. Good. What did they tell you?"

"They told me—" She thought about this. "They didn't tell me how he died."

"But I told you that. Remember? The day before we went to that place on Whidbey Island. An accident."

"Yes. But afterwards I was sure it wasn't Sandro so I had to find out where he was."

Oh dear, poor Maria. "But it was Sandro, as we now know. And he died of poisoning, with the drugs he took."

"An overdose," she said. "Heroin."

Andrei nodded. "Heroin."

"My son. Who was becoming my daughter."

Oh shit, thought Andrei, oh shit shit. "Dear Maria—" He gripped her hands tighter.

Her lips tried to smile but her jaw wouldn't let them. "They said this was happening to Sandro. I believe them."

"But—why?"

"They told me what I knew. But I didn't know I knew."

"But—what?"

"They said, Sandro was always divided. I knew that."

"How?"

She pulled back. "You know, at times I think Kostas knew as well."

"Did you ever talk about this?"

"No. We didn't have anything to talk about."

"Then you didn't talk to anyone else, either?"

Maria shook her head.

"Now, you won't say anything to anyone?"

"Probably not."

"Thank you." He squeezed her hands and released them. "It's much better that we say nothing."

"Is it maybe better, too, that Sandro is dead?"

"A terrible thing to say!" But Andrei knew damn well Sandro dead was better.

"Would he have been happier as Sandra?"

"My dear, you mustn't talk like that."

"I think I will one day accept that Sandro is dead. I've accepted that Kostas is dead. We learn ways to deal with death. But how would I deal with my son who is suddenly my daughter? Would I rather have Sandro as Sandra than not at all?" She closed her eyes. "I don't know."

He patted her shoulder. She would probably remain silent. But a new leak had opened, and it must be plugged. Vasily couldn't handle this. Andrei would deal with the detectives himself.

PART II

NINE

KYRA UNLOCKED THE Tracker doors. "Two and a half days. Prepare a bill and we're done."

"A fast and simple case." Unfortunately over.

"Yep. That poor woman."

They sat in silence till Noel said, "Nothing we can do."

"You're right." She started the engine. "Time to shift gears. Get in the mood for our carefree party tonight. Go shopping so I can figure out what to cook." She pulled away from the curb. "Isn't Crab Cardinale done in individual shells? Jerome's bringing it."

"Hell of a lot of work. What are the others bringing?"

"Haven't a clue." Kyra turned onto Alabama, leaving the lake behind. Minutes later she took the ramp onto the I-5 and they bumped along the freeway's concrete. "You know, I think I'll do aroundments for tonight."

"You'll do what?"

"Aroundments. Whatever goes around the main dishes."

"I've never heard the word."

"Just made it up."

Noel laughed. "Okay, I'll see what inspires me." He was now looking forward to the potluck. Well, preparing for it with Kyra. "Maybe some beforements."

"They're hors d'oeuvres," Kyra retorted without humor. *Beforements* made her *aroundments* sound pretentious.

The tires click-clicked to the Fairhaven exit and into Albertsons half-empty parking lot. She turned off the engine, got out and locked. Noel followed her.

Not as windy as yesterday. Tattered clouds filtered the sunshine. Puddles on the cement. Must have rained last night. Good detecting, guy, Noel thought.

Kyra collected a cart and started down an aisle, a model of domestic efficiency.

Noel looked around for inspiration. Pasta? Meat? Fish? A large selection of Mexican foods. Maybe he'd make something more substantial than beforements.

He found a basket. When Brendan was still eating normally, he and Noel had experimented with recipes. Once they'd made a great Turkish thing, primarily lamb and apricots; could he remember the seasonings? Served with couscous. If Kyra had told him before he left Nanaimo about her housewarming he'd have brought recipes. Housewarming— Better get her a gift. In the meat section he noticed a special on lamb chops; that decided it.

Kyra cruised by at top speed, baguettes in the child carrier. "You decide yet?"

"No, but—"

"Good, 'cause I'd rather get the hors d'oeuvres, okay?"

He grinned. "Very okay." He mentioned Turkish lamb but didn't think she heard him. Kyra would have herbs, right? He located couscous in the bulk food section. Wine? He didn't know American wines and tracked Kyra down in canned goods debating artichokes. Two bottles of red and two of white in her cart. He read the labels, retraced his route and collected one of each.

A housewarming plant? He wasn't pleased with the balcony of plants he'd inherited. Brendan had become obsessed with container plants shortly before his diagnosis. Noel had hoped the plants would die over the winter; he couldn't just kill them. They lived on.

Candles? He picked out a box of six, metallic blue. He noticed a corkscrew. It looked like a moon rocket. He loved corkscrews and he'd never seen this design before. If she didn't like it she could give it to him for his birthday.

He spotted her at the checkout, waiting. "You have herbs? Thyme, oregano, marjoram?"

"Uh, no."

He couldn't believe it. Well, she'd just moved in. He found the herb section. After paying he put his bag in the cart with Kyra's three and wheeled it out to the car. "Should hold the hordes for a bit," he said. The puddles reflected bright light. He squinted until a cloud-tatter found the sun. Kyra opened the back. "Did you notice that store's open twenty-four hours a day? Who shops at 3:00 AM?"

"Shift workers. Snoops." She smiled. "I did once when I was on surveillance and hoped my guy was deep asleep. It feels safe and there're no children running around."

"What's wrong with children?" Noel fastened his seat belt.

"Oh, I didn't congratulate you," Kyra started the engine, backed out and shifted into Drive, "on getting the Schultz kid out of our hair. Brilliant ploy, asking her for a picture."

"Thanks. But children aren't difficult. No more than most people." He wondered if he should ask, then just said, "You never wanted kids?"

She paused for a moment. "Sam and I talked about it. Good thing we never decided."

They would've been attractive kids too, Noel thought, wild curls unavoidable with parents like that, and solidly built like Sam. If Brendan had lived . . . About ten years ago they'd investigated adoption, an extremely difficult option for gays back then. But the times they were a-changing and now or soon it might be possible. Noel felt a bite of wistfulness for his Brendan-less life, for never the chance of being a parent.

Kyra turned off the Old Fairhaven Parkway onto Fourteenth Street. "Did you say your brother was coming?"

"Next month. With Jan. And Alana."

"Alana must be, what, twelve by now?"

"Turning seventeen."

"God. That must make Keith— You mean he's in college?"

"Stanford. Second year. He's got scholarships." Watch the uncle-pride. "Alana's in the silent stage. I thought only boys did that."

Kyra smiled. Fifteen had been her worst summer on Bowen Island. Noel had brought William to his parents' cottage. They'd started living together. They sat on the verandah, their arms around each other. They included Kyra in walks and a couple of trips to Horseshoe Bay for fish and chips, but it was a crushing realization to learn Noel wasn't waiting for her to grow up so they could marry. That summer she'd had huge reasons to be silent.

"Plan to come up while they're on the Island," Noel was saying. "We can have a big meal. Or at the parents' in Qualicum."

"Love to. Is Seth still working for the space program?"

"Yes. I've never figured out exactly what he does. Just Astrophysics, he says."

"And Jan?"

"New job with autistic children."

"Oooh. Hard." Kyra pulled into the lane behind her condo and flicked her remote. She parked. They collected the groceries.

Upstairs, while Kyra put the groceries away, Noel opened his laptop and wrote up the Triple-I bill: 2.25 days @ $500/day X 2 = $2250. A short report: definitely Alessandro Vasiliadis in the coffin. Death certificate available upon request; requests from the family only.

"What do you think?" he yelled at Kyra. "Is Maria an *A* or a *B*?" He meant their categories for billings. *A* got the full bill, *B* some dispensation.

Kyra appeared in the doorway. "Her house would indicate *B*."

"That's what I think. I'll half it."

"But she said send the bill to Andrei."

"Oh, right. He has a transport company, doesn't he. I won't half it then." Noel turned on the printer and produced the report and the bill. He located Andrei Vasiliadis' fax number in his address book, and sent off the printout.

When he came out of the study, Kyra had made them each a grilled cheese sandwich. Then she buzzed about tidying, setting the table, cleaning the bathroom. Noel busied himself with lamb and apricots. Then nothing but waiting till six.

The light was fading over the harbor beyond Kyra's window. A minute after six and the phone beeped: the downstairs entry. Kyra spoke, pressed nine, headed for the door, opened it.

"Your friends are on time."

"Sarah the Prompt."

Elevator door opening, footsteps muffled by hall carpet, appearance of a tall, thin, dark-haired woman holding a casserole dish before her and large petit-point bag over her shoulder. Kyra took the casserole, Sarah fished in her bag and produced a wine bottle. Greetings and introductions, and Noel Franklin met Sarah Millbank. Kyra took the casserole into the kitchen.

Noel said, "Like some of your wine?"

"Thanks." Sarah reached into her bag again, "Indoor shoes," produced one, the other.

Is she Canadian? To Kyra he shouted, "Coats in your bedroom?"

"Couch in the study, please!"

His bedroom. Oh well.

Sarah, re-shod, shrugged out of her coat. Noel carried it away. She advanced to the living room and looked around. "Oh, it's stunning." She walked to the sliding glass door. "What a gorgeous view!"

"The couple of cubic feet right where you're standing? They're actually mine." Kyra's smile contradicted her solemn tone. "The rest is the bank's."

"But the bank lets you live here."

"For a hefty monthly fee." The phone beeped again. Kyra went to attend.

Noel filled a glass and handed it to Sarah. Reaching for it she moved like a willowy model. Then she slouched, and the willow became a stick. A commotion in the foyer. "Kyra tells me you're a recreation therapist."

"Yes. And you're her detective partner."

Several pots and three bags headed through to the kitchen. Noel caught flashes of two small blondes and a stocky man. Kyra and an armful of coats made their way to the couch. Chatter, dither, clatter. Noel glanced at Sarah, who smiled complicitly: let's stay out of there. Noel nodded.

"Recreation therapy sounds challenging," he threw out.

"It can be. You get the body moving and things shift in the psyche."

"Sounds complicated. How did you meet Kyra?"

"The juggling club." Sarah slouched further and sipped wine. "A pretty informal group." She smiled.

The kitchen area calmed into organization and instructions. Dishes clanked into oven or fridge. People emerged, shepherded by Kyra. He'd best open more wine. He liked his new corkscrew present disguised as a hollow rocket. Should've bought two.

Kyra introduced Sarah and Noel.

"Ah, the other detective," the man said, sticking his hand out. "I'm Mike Ferris."

Noel shook it. "Hello." Kyra's lock-pick teacher. A red tinge to his close-cropped hair. His freckled face seemed relaxed and open. Forty-two, forty-five, around his own age.

"This is Margery." Kyra touched the shoulder of the taller small blonde. Noel remembered: she ran the investigation department for Puget Sound Life and had brought Kyra into detecting. About his age also, Noel guessed, incipient plumpness held in check. She looked commonsensical.

"And this is Bettina—"

"Lawrence," Bettina offered quickly. "Bettina Lawrence."

"She's just moved to Bellingham."

"This week."

"Where from?" Sarah asked.

"Spokane. I wanted the coast, but not Seattle." The descriptor that came to Noel was: *pert*. No taller than five-one. Margery, beside her, looked huge at maybe five-four.

"My sister's neighbor," Margery explained to all.

"Wine, everyone?" Noel asked.

"Indeed." Pert Bettina directed a conspiratorial smile directly at Noel. Her nose turned up slightly at the tip. She stepped forward, picked up a glass, held it out. Blonde hair, professionally streaked. Noel poured.

"We're missing Jerome." Kyra glanced at the clock. Twenty past six. Maybe something horrendous had happened to Nelson the Dog. She should be so lucky.

Kyra set crackers, cream cheese, smoked salmon on the buffet. Sarah took the plate and passed it around. Kyra left, returned with oyster-stuffed artichokes, a baked brie, Melba toast. Noel the sommelier relaxed—all glasses were filled.

"Margery says you're detectives," chirped Bettina. "Tell us about your cases!"

Noel looked at Kyra, Kyra at Noel. Both knew the other's reaction: *Oh fuck*. But Bettina had voiced what all wanted to know and the group was primed.

Noel became responsible. "After a case, we respect our client's privacy."

"Oh, sure." Bettina laughed. "Margery said you specialize in islands. Which island was your last one on? I'm really looking forward to visiting all the islands!"

"At Puget Sound," Margery cut in, "we never name names or

locations. But maybe Kyra can mention some details."

Kyra cocked her head, shrugged, and said slowly, "We recently had a case that involved transgendering."

Damn, Noel thought. Come on, Kyra, act professionally and keep quiet.

"Oh, which way?" Bettina sipped, giving him her full attention.

She shouldn't have started on this. Sidestep. "Male to female is the most common."

"Most common," repeated Bettina. "But the power imbalance goes the other way."

"Huh?" Mike grunted.

"Like tomboys?" Sarah looked at Kyra. "Girls and women have less power so they're freer to ape male roles. In rec therapy I get a lot of tomboys."

"Well," Mike acceded, "maybe some lucky girls get to be tomboys. But what about the boy who dresses up in his mother's dress and high heels and she scolds him. Or he needs to cry and he's told little men don't cry."

"Hah." Noel leaned back. Shift. Now. "We had an interesting case a few weeks ago. Everybody on that island has a generator, and a saboteur was messing with them—"

"I think," Bettina sat forward on the sofa. "It's wrong to surgically alter your body. You only have to alter your mind. If you go in deep you'll find your true inner sexual self."

They looked at her. Three people drained their glasses.

Margery passed hummus, pita, olives. Kyra glanced at Noel. Where was Jerome? She'd figured him for greater punctuality.

Kyra excused herself. In the kitchen she checked the progress of food warming and chilling.

"The thing about the generators—"

Margery broke in: "Had your client had the surgery?"

One more answer, then *Enough*. "No, still at the hormone stage." And clearly enough about generators. Noel got up, brought out and opened bottles of white and red, and set them on the table. "Serve yourselves." The transgendering talk lived on.

Bettina cut a chunk of brie, slabbed it on a cracker, and took off on another tack. "I'm going to change careers, I'm tired of aesthetics."

She spoke directly to Noel. "Did I say I'm in the middle of getting divorced?"

"No," said Noel.

"And I'm going into grief counseling."

"I see."

She smiled sweetly. "So if you have any bereaved clients—?"

"That too has to be confidential." Noel spoke firmly.

"I've been researching and can tell them where their loved one can be buried."

Sarah said, "Doesn't a funeral director do that?"

"Did you know," Bettina said, "that suicides can't be buried in sanctified cemeteries? That's the way I can help people. I'll get some cards made and you can give them to people who hire you."

"I don't think that'd be appropriate," said Kyra. But *sanctified cemeteries* was good.

Margery said, "Puget Life had a policy holder, this heavy guy who drove an excavator, and one day on a steep slope the machine rolled down the hill. Well, the company didn't want to pay the claim because we'd insured him as a woman. Which he'd been. It was all quite startling. In the end, though, we did have to pay."

"Didn't she tell the company she'd switched?" asked Bettina.

Margery shrugged. "No."

"It'd be more interesting if he'd stayed an excavator woman," said Sarah.

"Society has to tolerate a greater variety of behavior," Bettina advanced. "Everybody should stay what they are and not have to switch. Or not break up marriages just 'cause you want variety. My husband left me after twenty-two years for a twenty-year-old bimbo."

Assorted mutters of sympathy.

"You seem to be doing pretty well," Margery observed of Bettina.

"I'm going to make it hard for her. And him."

"You have children?" Mike inquired.

"No." Bettina paused. "I did. She had cystic fibrosis. She died at eleven."

Intakes of breath. "How sad," said Sarah. "I'm sorry."

Bettina inclined her head. "It was dreadful."

"God, to lose a child—" Mike said.

Margery nodded. "You have children, Mike?"

He laughed. "Not that I know of."

Simpatico, Noel thought. Not gay.

"You married?" Bettina smiled innocently.

"Nope." Mike turned to Margery. "Nearly, a couple of times."

Nice shifting away from Bettina, Noel thought.

But the woman persisted. "What do you do, Mike?"

Now he gave her his full attention. "Recently I spent some time in a male institution."

"Oh? A boys' school? I don't approve of segregated education."

"A different kind of academy. Courtesy of the State of Washington." He winked, and Noel laughed. "Of course I was wrongly convicted."

"Oh?" inquired Sarah, just as Bettina pronounced: "Prison." She paused for a single breath. "If a man has a sex change, would they put him in a men's or women's prison?"

Kyra headed for the office phone. She picked it up and dialed Jerome's number.

"Maybe it depends how far along you are." Mike slid away from Bettina's question. "All I know is male prison. But some inmates get turned into chickens."

"Aha!" Bettina so near to physically lunged that Mike backed up in his chair. "That upholds my theory of bisexuality. Men with men are homosexual, but once out they choose women! And besides—"

"I think it's more complicated than that," Noel interrupted. Sarah nodded.

Kyra listened to Jerome's phone ring ten times. She set hers down. Where was he? A sharp ring, she jumped, then picked it up. A dial tone. Ring! The other phone, the business line. Should she answer? Ring!

Of course there'd be no answer at seven in the evening, Andrei thought after the third ring.

Then someone picked up. "Islands Investigations International."

"Yes. Ms. Rachel or Mr. Franklin, please."

"This is Kyra Rachel."

"Ah. Ms. Rachel. This is Andrei Vasiliadis, Maria Vasiliadis' brother-in-law. I believe she hired you regarding my nephew Sandro."

"Yes."

"And you reported to her that the body in the coffin was indeed Sandro. It's quite terrible and Maria is in considerable despair."

"I'm sorry, but we were taken on to—"

"I understand. But, and correct me if I'm misstating this, she did not hire you to discover that Sandro was transgendering his body."

"No, but—"

"It's unfortunate you passed on this information to her, Ms. Rachel."

"In our line of work we decide what someone who hires us needs to know. Given the circumstances, we figured Mrs. Vasiliadis needed this information."

"We in the family feel you've made a grave mistake."

"Sorry about that, but you in the family didn't hire Triple-I."

Okay, it didn't sound like he could guilt her. Andrei sighed, audibly. "In a real sense, Ms. Rachel, I did, since I'm paying your fee. But never mind. May I speak with you in confidence?"

"If you speak quickly. I'm in the middle of a meeting."

"Our great concern now is to bury Sandro in the correct fashion, according to his community and his religion. With as little distraction as possible. We are letting the community and the family know he died accidentally of a drug reaction. Some might learn heroin was involved. But no one must discover that Sandro was transforming himself. The shame to the family, and especially to poor Maria, would be overwhelming. So I urge you, Ms. Rachel, in the strongest possible manner, to seal your file about Sandro. And, if I may add, your lips as well."

A second's silence; then, "In all Triple-I's cases, there is total confidentiality between ourselves and our clients. We'd never reveal their identities, that wouldn't be ethical. And while Sandro wasn't exactly our client, his identity in that sense now belongs to his mother. We discuss details of a case only with clients."

"I have your word as to that?"

"You have my word. And my partner's. Our word is our bond."

"Thank you, Ms. Rachel. And a note of warning. Make sure the seal is airtight. You understand me? You'll have my check in a few days."

"Goodbye." The line at the other end clicked.

Andrei poured himself a small Glenmorangie, no ice. He believed he could trust her. An irritant, but he'd smoothed it away. He sipped. He checked his watch. Time to head home. Only since the last couple of years did he actually look forward to going home. In the old days he'd be in the office till ten, eleven. Always a problem to solve, always a difficulty to overcome. He put on his scarf and coat, and headed for the elevator.

He had faced many difficulties with regard to the company—labor, technology, executive personalities. Relatively few crises in the family; because it was his practice to become aware early of small issues and keep them from growing larger. He should have been aware of Sandro's crisis. He should have put a stop to it sooner. Could it be, he thought, that I'm growing old? He smiled. Older, anyway. Like everybody else.

You understand me? You understand me?!!! The son of a bitch. She sighed, and banged her fist into her palm. She glared back at the receiver: pompous autocrat, good thing you didn't really hire us, you— No, back to the party. Shit, we shouldn't have even begun talking about the case. But we didn't really, did we. No identifiers. Bloody Bettina. With a glance out the window at the city lights, Kyra returned to the living room.

"—so she applied to counsel women at a feminist crisis center," Sarah was saying, "but they turned her down, she'd grown up as a man and didn't have a woman's cultural awareness."

"How you grow up is important, all those years of being a little girl or a little boy."

Bettina still sharing her opinion. Maybe, Noel thought, it's her reason for being.

Mike asked, "How old was he when he switched?"

"Twenties, I guess."

"So she had no experience of her first period." Bettina looked around. "If you sex-change to a woman, do you menstruate?"

"Without a uterus?" God, Kyra thought, was this woman dumb or what.

Bettina turned to Noel, but said nothing. He spoke to Kyra. "How long are we waiting for Jerome?" This conversation was becoming too female.

"Ten more minutes?"

A touch of worry? "Good." He smiled at her with sympathy. She grinned back.

The entry phone beeped and Kyra took it. "Hello?" Jerome. She buzzed him in.

Noel caught Bettina still staring at him. Dimwit.

The minimum time from the building's front door to suite 507 was three minutes. She took a sip, opened the door, waited. Jerome appeared down the hall. He looked frazzled. "What happened?" He carried two glass pots, and a bag over his shoulder. She took the pots.

"I'm sorry I'm so late. My son phoned."

"I was getting worried."

"Sorry."

He took off his coat, dropped it on a chair, took the wine bottles from the bag and left it with his coat. They headed to the kitchen and deposited the pots. He hugged her lightly and kissed her cheek. "I'd have phoned you, but I had to get things out of the oven and get here."

"Glad you did." She smiled.

"Any room in the oven for these?" He gestured at the pots.

Kyra looked. "No. Microwavable?"

"Yes."

In the living room, Kyra introduced him.

Noel handed him a glass of wine. Pleasant open face, small scar on right cheekbone, thinning chestnut hair. Slender, maybe six feet. Tan cashmere cardigan over a striped shirt, tailored fawn trousers.

"Good thing you arrived." Bettina stated. "I wasn't sure we'd get dinner tonight."

"Sorry." Jerome raised his glass. "Cheers."

"We've been talking about sex changes," Margery told Jerome.

"Oh?" Kyra had said most of these people wouldn't have met before. Had one of them changed sex? An intimate topic for the unacquainted.

"What would it be like being the child of a transgendered person?" Mike puzzled.

"They'd need grief counseling." Bettina elaborated: "They'd grieve for the lost parent." A couple of frowns. She simplified: "The old one the new parent had killed."

"Maybe it'd depend on how old the child was," said Sarah.

"And," Bettina declared, "if the child has two mothers or two fathers it's like gay parents. Those kids need grief counseling because they've never had the opposite-sex parent."

"One doesn't grieve for what one doesn't know." Noel spoke sharply.

Sarah said, "I know a number of gay couples with kids and they're all well-adjusted. Adjustment comes from love and honesty and trust."

She sounded as acerbic as Noel felt. Lesbian? Time to eat. He left to help in the kitchen. Kyra raised an eyebrow his way. He raised both back.

They ferried food to the table. Jerome was talking, gamely, about a drug salesman who one month turned up looking as if his sister had replaced him. Except no, a transvestite. Well turned out, so hard to recognize. Not transgendered. Jerome was glad for that, any kind of surgery sent shivers up his spine.

"Yeah." Noel nodded.

Bettina leapt in, "Oh you're so right. My theory is—"

Kyra cut her off. "Come, time to warm my new table. Hope you're all starved."

The group stood, re-sorted itself and sat. Noel's Turkish lamb, apricots and couscous. Jerome's crab in a single pottery casserole, not in shells, and his oysters. Bettina's moussaka. Keep it from my lamb, Noel thought, fear of war between Turks and Greeks. He chuckled silently. Oops, slow down on the wine. Salads from Sarah and Margery. Mike's marinated clams.

They toasted Kyra's new condo. She thanked everyone for coming. They dug in with much Please pass the this, Some more of that, please. Noel kept his eye on the emptying bottles, slowed his consumption briefly, then thought, Hell, I'm not driving.

Sarah turned to him. "How did you and Kyra decide to go into business together?"

"Did she never tell you?"

"Only that she had an associate now."

"Last fall she came up to Nanaimo just as someone asked me to investigate a situation on Gabriola Island, so I asked her to help. She'd been doing jobs for Margery's company, I'd been an investigative journalist. Things carried on from there." He smiled at Kyra. She returned it, thinking, a good version for present company.

"What were you in jail for?" Bettina asked Mike.

"Bettina!" Margery snapped.

"What?"

Mike said, "Burglary. But remember, I was wrongly convicted." He gave her an ironic smile.

"Did you appeal?"

"Nope."

"Why not?"

"Lousy lawyer."

Wouldn't take him for a criminal, Noel thought. Hmm. He filed the stereotype, *criminal*, for later examination. First burglar I've met. That I know of.

Kyra could hear Bettina's wheels turning: a real burglar or a pawn in the correctional system? Deciding, she looked charmed. "Really! Were you a top-storey man? A cat burglar?"

"A wrongly convicted run-of-the-mill burglar," Mike said.

"What was your biggest heist?"

"Your dinner's getting cold," said Margery to Bettina.

Talk broke into smaller groups. Gradually they finished eating. Mike announced his specialty for dessert was Irish coffee, which they could have in the living room. Bettina thrust her package at Kyra even before they'd all sat down. "For your new apartment."

"Oh," said Kyra, "you shouldn't have." And wished Bettina hadn't.

"Oh yes," Bettina beamed. "I just know any of Margery's girlfriends will like it."

Girlfriend. How quaint.

Noel, head buzzing, helped Mike pass tall thin blue-green pottery mugs. The coffee lay hidden beneath steam rising around a dollop of whipped cream. Both mugs and content were his gift. His last present to her had been her lock picks. When she "graduated" from his tutelage.

Kyra opened housewarming presents. A potted plant appeared, an aspidistra from Margery. "Houses need at least one plant."

Bettina's present was a case of makeup samples, myriad little tubes: lipsticks, mascaras, blushers, rouge, eyeshadow, vanishing cream. "It's top-line," Bettina announced, "and that's the advantage of being in aesthetics. These will really improve your looks."

Kyra smiled a Mona Lisa. "Thank you," she said kindly. As to a small child.

Bettina purred.

Sarah gave her a dream catcher. Noel brought the rocket-ship corkscrew from the buffet and handed it to Kyra. "If you don't like it," he placed his hand on his heart, "I've fallen in love."

"Oh, who with?" asked Bettina.

Noel looked at her. "The corkscrew, the corkscrew."

"It looks great, thanks." Kyra blew him a kiss. "Only a little used."

Much chat and examining of presents. Jerome found his bag and returned with a wrapped package. Kyra opened it. A red object, maybe eight inches long, with what looked like handgrips. "Is this what I think it is?"

"Yep," said Mike.

Kyra said, "A can of Mace."

Several people shrank back. Jerome said, "Don't worry. There's a safety cap. You have to lift it before anything can happen." And to Kyra, "Does it fit your hand okay?"

She squeezed it. Her index finger fell naturally into place on the grip dispenser.

"It's pretty powerful. Mace Triple Action, they call it. Pepper spray that makes the eyes slam shut, tear gas, and an ultraviolet marking dye. Light enough to carry in your purse. And you should, Kyra."

Bettina said, "My theory, too." Her words a touch blurred.

Kyra stood slowly. "Thank you, Jerome. Thank you, everyone."

TEN

IN THE OLD days—say, two years ago—Andrei would have found the conversation with the protopresbyter comfortable, even easy. He and Father Leo had understood each other well, they'd worked together on countless projects. But Father Leo had driven himself too hard. And eaten and drunk too well. Philip's surgeon friend had been optimistic, quadruple bypass was commonplace these days, 90 percent successful. But the other 10 percent were real people too; one of them was Father Leo. Myocardial infarction on the table and he died at 59. Andrei's age, that year.

The new protopresbyter, Father Peter, had come from Sacramento. He was just half as old as Father Leo. The teenagers liked him, which was important, and he dampened some of their wilder ways. The young professionals got on well with him; he talked their language. Vasily and Father Peter played poker together. And many older members had come to trust him. Father Peter understood quickly enough, once everything was spelled out, but there was none of the instant rapport that Andrei and Father Leo had had.

Andrei pulled his Monte Carlo to the curb next to Saint Demetrius, and turned off the windshield wipers and engine. He glanced at the clock on the dashboard: 9:58. He got out, locked, shivered lightly in the drizzly air and pushed open the iron-slat gate leading to the church's courtyard. He walked through, drew open the church's door and stepped into the foyer. Ahead lay the hall, wooden pews, aisle to the grand altar with its gilt facade, the apostles staring down.

Father Peter waited in his office. Still working at 10:00 PM, earliest he'd been available; even for Andrei. So different from Father Leo. A knock on the office door, a voice calling, "Come in." He stepped into a small space, cluttered, papers in piles and books on the floor. Indecent how this office had been transformed. "Good evening," said Andrei.

Father Peter, seated behind the messy desk, was a tall man, well-defined forehead, nose and cheeks, mustache and small beard around lips that tended to smile often. His plaid shirt lay open at the collar. "Andrei. Good to see you. Just toss your coat over there." He pointed to three bare hooks on the wall. "I hope this isn't too late."

"Not at all. Father Leo and I would often meet at this hour." But at Father Leo's home, on a night like this in front of a warm fire, a glass of cognac or port.

"Have a seat."

Andrei sat in the only chair free of files. "I won't take a lot of your time. It's about Sandro."

"Yes, I visited Maria again yesterday. She was still hoping. So hard."

"Today everything is clear. We're prepared to go ahead."

They talked about announcements, flowers, timing. Andrei said, "I think I should give the eulogy."

Father Peter nodded slowly. "Yes."

But Andrei sensed doubt. "I'll make it short. I've known Sandro all his life, he worked for Cascade, I'm both his uncle and his ex-employer."

"Of course."

"There will be some talk. In the community, I mean. Have you heard any comments?"

"Comments?"

"About Sandro. How he died."

"I've heard very little. Mostly from Maria. But until today she still doubted the dead man was Sandro, so—" he shrugged.

"You should know something else. We hope this won't become common knowledge." The phrases Andrei had composed came with difficulty. "Sandro died of a complicated drug reaction."

"An overdose?"

Andrei shrugged. "A reaction."

"Is there any question of suicide?"

"No, no," Andrei cut him off. "No question. A dreadful accident."

"I'm sorry."

No shock or real sorrow there. What had Maria told him? "Yes. We're all upset."

"And," Father Peter's eyebrows tightened, "if I may ask, had Sandro been under treatment for a while?"

117

If yes, then why hadn't Andrei found help for Sandro? if no, then why now, why an overdose? "I don't know."

Father Peter repeated: "You're certain his death wasn't suicide."

Hadn't the man heard him? "No reason to assume so. No note was found and his friends report he had everything to live for."

"Ahh." A few seconds of silence. "Was there a new person in his life, then?"

"I believe, yes, you could say that."

"Then my sadness goes out to her as well."

Did the priest know? Was the man playing with him? "Thank you," was all Andrei could say. He found himself standing. "Very much." He reached for his coat.

"Thank you for confiding in me, Andrei. If there's anything else you'd like to speak about, you have my ear. You can count on me." Father Peter stood.

He was wearing jeans, for god's sake!

"No, I think that's all. Thank you." Coat in hand he backed toward the door, glancing over his shoulder for fear of creating an avalanche of files and books. Out the door, back to the car. A sense of safety. Unreal safety. Was that just young priest language, You can count on me, whatever you want to tell me?

He drove away. He had to speak with Vasily. Ten-fifteen. He drew out his cell and pressed Vasily's coded number. Answering service. Off with his Cynthia or whoever. Andrei left a message, Call when you get in. He tried Vasily's cellphone. No response.

The conversation with the priest wandered through Andrei's memory, and drew to an abrupt halt at the priest's words: Mostly from Maria. He had heard very little. Mostly from Maria. Who else had he heard from then? Andrei hadn't asked. He got home and slept badly.

He woke, and got out of bed. A gray 7:15 AM. Vasily had never called last night. Hadn't gone home, hadn't checked for messages. Andrei reached for the phone.

Kyra loaded the dishwasher. Noel scrubbed casseroles in the sink. She told him about Andrei Vasiliadis' call last night. "He particularly stressed he didn't want anyone in the family or the community to know about Sandro's transgendering."

"Hmm."

The phone rang. Kyra glanced at her watch: quarter past eight. She lifted the receiver. "Hello?"

"Hi, it's Margery. Thanks for the party. It was lovely, great food, fascinating talk."

"Yeah, it was."

"It would've been perfect except for—Kyra, I'm sorry. I'd only met Bettina once on the fly for about fifteen minutes. She's not really my sister's friend, I just phoned her, my sister, she was a neighbor, their husbands golfed together, she's never—"

"It's okay." Kyra laughed. "Bettina added a certain spice. Suicide and sanctified cemeteries, how alliterative. She's, uh, unique. And what did you think of Jerome?"

"He's nice! And he stood up nobly under Bettina. She's a litmus test. Thanks for being understanding."

"No prob." She glanced at the slanting rain beyond the aspidistra. "Thanks again for the plant."

Noel had started the dishwasher, which churned enthusiastically. Kyra poured more coffee, cut oranges into slices, made toast, brought everything to the table.

Noel sat back. Jerome was different from Sam, in physique and temperament. Different too from her other husbands, Vance the wife-beater, Simon who killed himself? He'd met neither.

The guests had started leaving about ten. Margery, pleading a headache, likely a ploy, took Bettina away. Sarah left soon after, then Mike. Jerome stayed for another Irish coffee. About eleven he recalled work the next morning.

Kyra and Jerome said goodbye at the condo door. They kissed lips lightly. "Thank you for the Mace."

"I hope you never need it."

When he got home, Jerome had phoned Kyra. "Hi. I'm back. Thank you for tonight. Very nice party. I enjoyed your friends . . . I should've stayed, helped you clean up . . . I agree, more energy in the morning . . . Well, good night . . . I'll try."

He put the phone down and stared at it. Nelson came to stand beside him, head raised as for a pat. Jerome scratched the back of his neck. A kind of certainty to a dog, you know what he wants, what he can give. But about Kyra, no certainty. Only questions. He liked her well enough. How much? Hard to say. Did he want to get emotionally involved with her? He wasn't sure. Did she appeal to him, did she arouse him? Pretty sure that right now he himself was keeping that from happening. She was tough and smart. Could he handle that? And, well, what would Bev say? He had often not known what to think about people and situations till he had talked it through with his wife. Too late.

He wanted to go to bed. He still needed to take Nelson out for his evening walk.

Kyra's sofa bed was lumpy on the right side. Noel had fallen asleep thinking about Kyra and Jerome, the kiss between them that wasn't much of a kiss; but a kiss it was. He slept badly and awoke with a sore hip. He got up, washed, started breakfast for the two of them. Kyra joined him. They drank coffee, munched toast. Noel said, "How long have you known your beau?"

"Come on, Jerome's hardly my beau. He feels more like an older cousin than a possible lover."

"Kissing cousin?"

She mused. "The sort of cousin I'd think twice about getting involved with."

"Thinking twice is always good. Anyway, he's not your type. Your physical type, I mean."

"True, he doesn't look like solid Sam."

"How about like Vance? Or Simon?"

"Nope."

"But it is, after all, possible to enjoy both vanilla and pistachio ice cream."

"Depends on—" The business line rang. "Who now?" She got up. "Islands Investigations International."

"Hi, this is Ursula Bunche on Whidbey, Sandro's friend. Is this Kyra?"

"Yes, hi."

"Listen, Brady and I've been talking, and we're upset that people might think Sandra could have killed herself." Ursula spewed the words, as if she'd rehearsed the speech. "She just wouldn't, she was so looking forward to life, trying out ideas. Open a flower shop or a lingerie store, ideas like that." Ursula sounded both troubled and fervent.

"You think it was an accident?"

"If so, an extreme fluke. Sandra taking heroin doesn't compute, not even an experiment. She didn't even drink by herself." Ursula faltered, then went on. "See, Brady and I sometimes have a joint in the evening but Sandra wouldn't join us, she didn't like the effect. She drank maybe a glass of wine, a couple of beers, no hard liquor, she liked to control her head. We can't believe she'd try heroin."

"Something else?"

Ursula hesitated. "Unlikely. But she was having an extreme reaction. See, just before she died— Look, it's kind of hard to tell you this."

Kyra said, "A bit at a time is easiest."

"Okay. Her—well his—testes had become all swollen. She didn't know what was wrong."

"What do you mean, swollen?"

"Three or four times in diameter from what they'd been, Sandra said. Swollen with semen. It hurt like hell."

Kyra winced. "What did he do?"

Silence on the line. Then, "The only thing she could think of. She masturbated."

"And that helped?"

"For a while. But a couple of hours later they filled up again." Ursula sighed. "She couldn't sleep, and it hurt like hell to walk."

"For how long?"

"Just a few days before she died. The last time we talked she was in real despair. She said something like, This is what I get for going the other way."

"Oh god," said Kyra. Noel turned to her, a silent What? on his lips, but she ignored him. "Had she maybe gotten some painkiller? And had that reaction?"

"I don't know." Ursula sounded weary.

"Do you know who was in charge of her medically? The specific doctor?"

"She said all the physicians dealt with all the patients." Ursula paused. "Dr. Jones was at the viewing."

"So." Kyra waited a moment. "What are you thinking?"

A longer pause. "In the light of day I think it must have been a weird accident." A self-deprecating laugh. "In the depths of night, I wonder if someone could've done Sandra in."

"I see." Kyra waited.

"Either she died by accident, thinking she could control the pain, or she—"

"By shooting herself full of heroin?"

"I know, I know. But if the pain was so great she had to end it?"

"That'd be a lot like an accident."

"Yeah, none of this makes much sense. So we're thinking, is it possible maybe somebody killed her?"

"Any ideas?"

"Not a one. Nobody close to her that—at least I can't imagine that."

"Then?"

"It probably was an accident. But we'd like to be sure. Could you and Noel think about this while you're investigating?"

"We're off the case. The family's satisfied that the body was Sandro's."

"Oh." Ursula paused, then, "Brady and I don't have much money but we could hire you for a bit."

Sounded like Ursula would be a B category client. "Three hundred a day plus expenses." Noel at the door looked at her quizzically.

"Yeah, we can afford that. For a couple of days. Want to meet up and talk? I'm going down to Sandra's today to pick up the cats."

Kyra was writing Ursula Bunche on the pad. Noel glanced at it and nodded.

"Can you wait? We'll join you and check out her place again."

"I was heading down this morning. I do a half-shift today, twelve to four."

"See you at the hospital at four." Kyra set the phone down. "We're re-hired," she informed Noel. "To find out if maybe Sandro's death wasn't an accident." She reported Ursula's hypothesis, the swollen testes, the need to masturbate.

"Poor son of a bitch." Noel shuddered. "At least I haven't headed home."

"Ursula wondered if maybe somebody disliked Sandro enough to kill him."

"Are they scaring themselves? Or—?"

Kyra shrugged.

Noel said, "And you ran a mental means test?"

"I made a flying leap and cut our fee for hard-working nurses and receptionists."

"Individual decision forgiven. But you're playing havoc with our consultative model."

"Sorry." She paused. "But we're still curious, aren't we?"

For a moment Noel said nothing. He felt only a curious discomfort. "Kyra, sometimes you're too macho for me."

"But we're going to work on this, aren't we. Each of us with our own expertise."

"Expertise? Last night showed me how little I know about transgendering. Would a newly made woman menstruate? Now I'd say, only if ovaries and uterus were implanted, so no."

"So maybe silly Bettina's question wasn't so dumb. So we have to figure out these things. And that's what you're so good at. Like, why would anyone want a sex-change in the first place? Why not just cross-dress?"

"How would I know? It's not a topic I'd considered until the day before yesterday."

"I need a shower. Can you get on-line, see what's there about sex changes? And whatever you can find about that WISDOM clinic."

"How long a shower are you going to have?"

"And let's take overnight bags, in case we stay on Whidbey."

Noel thought. "You know, if it might be a question of foul play, we'll need to meet up with our sheriff friend."

"Your turn."

"What happened to our joint interviews?"

"I just don't want to see that guy again."

"Kyra, I don't like this."

"You want to go to the clinic?"

Noel shook his head. "You can."

"Fine." She headed off to ablute. In the shower the thought hit her that Jerome and Noel were alike in some ways: precise, methodical, quiet, good senses of humor. And in some ways not at all similar.

Noel called Brady at Sheriff Vanderhoek's office. "Hello Boss, can I get an appointment with your boss?"

By the time Kyra returned, he had saved thumbnail bios of the WISDOM doctors, of the clinic itself, and a couple of dozen other pages. She read the bios while he packed his bag, removing his memory stick and putting it in his pocket.

The Whidbey Island Sexual Definition Management clinic and its work with the sexually uncomfortable of all sorts, impotent men, dysorgasmic women, the sexually conflicted due to childhood problems, those who had been abused, the oversexed—The site did go to great length to assure people there is no such thing as oversexed, there were only mismatched partners or medical conditions WISDOM could treat.

WISDOM held a contract with Bendwell Pharmaceuticals and a grant to pursue an unspecified project. Four physicians, links to their own websites, and hundreds of entries about their work:

Lorna Albright, M.D. Harvard 1972, residency in gynecology at McGill and the Jewish General, Montreal, until 1976. The search engine showed numerous papers, most recent ones on hormones of hermaphrodites.

"I read a couple of the abstracts but couldn't understand a word," said Noel when he saw where she was.

Gary Haines, M.D. UC San Diego 1987, psychiatric residency, UCLA. Mainly articles in his field, reports of conferences. Surrounding entries, his papers, shrink-speak easier to grasp than bio-speak. Wait, something different, a hit on a newspaper article, Seattle *Post-Intelligencer*, June 1997, a patient upset, too much in the way of hands-on, he made her have intercourse.

"What's this, Noel?"

He came over. "I tried to follow up but I couldn't find anything right away so I left it for later. Haines and the woman must have settled off the page."

"The woman dropped the charges?"

"Or Haines compensated."

"Diddled his patients, did he?" She continued reading.

Stockman Jones, M.D. U. Penn, 1973, urological and surgical residency at the Menninger Clinic, 1979, articles about the variance of surgical process in transgendering, male to female and vice versa. Also a number of publications on the importance of religion when making life-shaping decisions, all very delicately phrased.

"A born-again?"

Noel shrugged.

Richard Trevelyan, Ph.D. Northwestern 1972, thesis on "Significance of Esophageal Varices in Carcinoma of the Liver," abridged and published in *Science* in 1973, much academic chatter back and forth. Then a post-doc at Temple U., Research Associate. 72-79, M.D. U. Chicago, 1983, residency in endocrinology and internal medicine at Johns Hopkins. Looked like Trevelyan had ejected from the academic system later in his career than Albright and Jones. Many published papers on liver and blood, such as "Significance of Estrogen Levels in Obstructive Liver Disease." Also on the diseases of sex trade workers.

"These guys did home in on sex," Kyra noted.

"There's also a history of 'The Team.' Sort of self-hype."

"Oh good. Tell me." She combed her hair, tangled strand by strand.

Albright, Jones and Haines met at a conference on treatment of sexual definition in Phoenix. They were all Brilliant Young Things. Each presented a paper. They liked and respected each other, they covered a large spectrum of medical knowledge. They consulted each other and decided to set up a clinic together. Where? Seattle looked like a great possibility.

They collected Trevelyan in 1997, soon moved the clinic to Whidbey and renamed it WISDOM, coinciding with the Bendwell grant. Noel read to her, "In a rural atmosphere, bathed in the mellow breezes off the Japanese current, those in sexual discomfort can release themselves from their bonds, let them waft away as gently as rain-forest fog."

She laughed. "Wonder how much it costs for bonds to waft away."

"No idea. My bonds never waft away when fog settles in."

"What did you learn about the sex change process?"

"I'll dig around. Do your nails or something."

Kyra pulled the Tracker out from between two cars parked very close on each side, swung toward the exit and fumbled on the dashboard for the garage door remote. The door slid up. Outside, all the promise of spring was being washed away by a misplaced November storm. Rain slanted from a low-slung pearl sky, splashing mud. She glanced at her watch. "I better step on it." She did.

"Watch the road, it's slippery."

She touched the brake pedal. "What did you learn about transgendering?"

"Mostly I confirmed my ignorance. I know almost nothing."

"Till you got on-line?"

"Not really. There's a lot of info. I just barely scratched the surface." Noel pulled his laptop from its case and opened his Word files. "Like from a site called the Transgender Café, sort of an info/chat room." He searched about. "The stats vary immensely. Some estimates of twenty thousand transgendered people in North America, some saying two-tenths of a percent of the population, which would make it half a million. There's a report that argues one in thirty thousand males, one in one hundred thousand females. Huge differences, but more than just the occasional oddball."

Kyra zipped up the ramp onto the I-5. The heater spewed warmth and she turned it down. However irritating her Tracker, it warmed up quickly. Why did she dislike it so?

"It seems a kind of new frontier of consciousness. Trans is the touchiest category of sexual existence. You remember when bisexuals used to be vilified by the gay community?"

"Not really."

"Well, that's what's happening to trans folk now."

"You keep saying 'trans.'"

Noel shrugged. "It's one of the terms that keep coming up. Some prefer 'intersex.' Some don't like transgender, they prefer transsexual. And the other way around. Here's the best definition I could find: 'when a person's emotional and psychological and intellectual identity is different from what their physical body and sexuality would otherwise predict to be the case.'"

"That's pretty clear."

Noel sighed. "Actually, it's not. Because the definition is based on the whole idea of being different, which would make a politically outspoken trans or intersexed person really angry. Because for them it's not a matter of being different. They aren't different from themselves."

"Huh?"

"It's as if all your mental and spiritual and physical bits are lined up in a way that the larger world sees as odd. Some trans people feel like women in men's bodies. Some feel like lesbians in straight women's bodies. A woman I read about calls herself trans, physically she's a woman, likes that, likes being feminine, and is attracted to female-to-male transsexuals."

"Complicated. Do we have a politically correct term?"

"I don't know." He paused. "And what you get on the Internet can only be an abstraction of what it really feels like. I love the web, but it ain't real life."

Kyra drove in silence, absorbing. Just plain being a woman was hard enough.

"Then there's the rest of it," Noel went on, "all the science. Masses of work in sexuality and embryology, neurology, endocrinology in the last twenty years. Nobody knew this stuff when I was in school." He glanced at another report. "So, in relation to when you confused homosexuality with transgendering—"

"I didn't."

"When you thought I could explain Sandro better to Maria than you could." He opened another file. "Completely different. The homosexual, male or female, feels he or she is in the right body and has no desire to trade it in. But the transgender candidate knows his or her external sex characteristics don't fit the internal gender state." He scrolled down. "Some studies figure there's a disconnect between the way the brain and the sex organs develop. Female is the embryonic default position— Don't grin!"

"Can't help it." Kyra grinned more. "Sure, all embryos start out as female and need huge doses of androgen to switch to male. But we've had thousands of years of being told male is the dominant position, or the default. So I'm allowed to grin. Years of blaming women for not producing sons when it's actually the man's department to supply the Y chromosome."

"Mmm," mumbled Noel. "Here's something else, and I agree with it. The most important site of gender identity is between the ears, not the legs. Got that?" More finger-moving. "There's a gene called the Testicular Determining Factor. It's in charge of one's sex and fetal gonadal development. Oh. The first recorded sex change was in Roman times."

"Surgery? Then?" She shuddered. "Is surgery part of all transgendering cases?"

"Seems so." Noel clicked another file open. "Costs anywhere from five thousand to twenty-five thousand per. And things can go wrong, but that doesn't get advertised a lot. I saved a long entry about the procedure." More tracking. "Six to eight days in the hospital, then bed rest for however long it takes. Of course that's in the States. Wonder how long they let you stay in hospital in Canada."

"What?"

"The overhaul of the health care system."

"Oh, right."

Noel clicked some more. "The surgeon fashions a vagina out of the penis. A longer penis means a deeper vagina. Tissue from a short penis can be augmented—"

"What do they do, just turn the penis inside out?"

Noel felt his scrotum shrivel. He'd scrolled through this on screen as clinically as he could, but now, reading it again, he twinged from thighs to gut. Out the window, blurry trees, farms, a herd of wet cows. He didn't want to know how fast Kyra was driving.

"How do they make a penis in a woman-to-man procedure?"

Now he feared his balls would withdraw completely. "Don't have anything on that. I imagine from the vaginal lining." Noel glanced at Kyra. Tight mouth and raised lip. Her innards withering too?

"I can't imagine wanting to be the other sex." A double-trailer cargo van swayed by, spraying them faster than the wipers could cope. For a moment it blinded her and she slowed.

"As I was telling you," Noel scrambled around on his computer, "one can't say that."

"What?"

"The other sex. There aren't only two. All sorts of variations. Sex as continuum. You also can't think of nature versus nurture

128

any more, it's all interwoven." He read: "'To show how potent a small change at the molecular level can be, boys are sometimes born with uterus, fallopian tubes and internal vagina, but with cryptor-chid testes where the ovaries should be and normal male external genitalia. They have hysterectomies and grow up as male and male-identified. Then there are genetic males with normal androgen levels but female external genitalia and undescended testes.' And so on. Fascinating." He continued scrolling and reading silently.

Kyra felt grateful. Necessary detail. Armor for her WISDOM visit. The Tracker sped along, regularly passed by whooshes of large trucks. A calmer highway across the flatland lay ahead. Now the wind swept them head on.

"Here's a bit about so-called girls who changed to boys at puberty," Noel announced. "Their undescended testes flooded them with testosterone, the testes descended, the labia fused as scrotum and the clitoris enlarged into penis."

"Holy shit," said Kyra.

"It says the boys adapted and became well-adjusted men with families. They were raised as girls but always felt like boys. Amazing."

"Natural transgendering?"

"I guess." A couple of minutes later: "Hermaphroditism is natu-ral in some species."

"Yeah. In certain fish and molluscs. I did a course on that in oceanography."

"When you were a kid, did you belong to a secret club? Everyone with special names?"

"Yeah." She laughed. "When I was eleven. And if you forgot anybody's name the penalties were dire. God, it was hard enough to remember my own name. You?"

"We had a complicated handshake. One hand backward. Same fear, ostracism. You want so much to belong. Not be different. Or just a little, and have others to be different with. To belong with."

"And being sexually different?"

"Yeah, well, that's always the big one." For Sandro, he suddenly realized, the motivation might have been to belong with himself.

"You said there's a transgender e-café?"

"Yeah." A rise of trees loomed out of the distant gray. "Lots of people need to talk to people like themselves." A minute later they crossed the Deception Pass bridge. He looked down. Water blended with mist, all below drifting, obscure. So it should be, crossing to an island, Noel thought with satisfaction—their car as on a ferry, its prow hidden in the proximate fog. A fine metaphor.

ELEVEN

THE MOKAS MORTUARY hearse drove so smoothly the wheels might have been riding on air. Only a Cadillac, but maybe they'd customized the springs and shocks to give each of their corpses an even ride. Vasily didn't feel like talking this morning so just as well Nico had a hangover; that and driving took all his attention. A great evening and amazing night with Cynthia but at 8:03, the moment he'd switched on his cellphone, there was Andrei. Vasily's explanation of using a bit of benevolent persuasion yesterday to get the hearse arranged had undercut Andrei's annoyance, but something remained in his tone, maybe worry. Vasily promised to have the body in Seattle later today. Andrei said he'd talk to the docs at the clinic and seal off that spigot.

Vasily and Nico left the highway and drove down to Mukilteo along the Sound. The hearse clock said 9:34 as they lined up for the ferry. Their only conversation this morning was to choose between the ferry and the bridge at Deception Pass—more miles across the bridge but the ferry was slow and you had to line up early. Nico wanted to drive to Whidbey. Vasily saw Nico's red eyes and made the decision: Nico needed sea air. Nico objected to the hearse on the ferry, salt spray bad for the paint. Vasily said he'd spring for a wash when they got back. Vasily reminded Nico that Andrei was paying so they'd do it Vasily's way. End of conversation.

The twenty-five-minute crossing over the choppy waters of Possession Sound was rougher than Vasily liked, and foam did leap up to spray the hearse. He spent the time organizing the contents of his satchel. In Clinton they drove up the hill and away from the water.

In his early twenties he'd come across to Whidbey first with Miriam, then with Lisa. A ferry made a girl feel freed from her parents and on the island nobody would spot her walking into a motel. Some good times on Whidbey, Vasily remembered. Nico drove past Useless Bay Road. Vasily smiled. It'd been there ten years ago. Soon as Lisa read it she'd said they had to drive down, so he did. Now I'm free, she said, and started to cry. They'd had a good time. Back in Seattle, Vasily had dropped her pretty quick.

Now Nico drove north past one small church after another, Trinity Lutheran, All-Saints Confessional, This and That. Vasily wondered about those communities. For sure their kids would marry out. Cynthia was great in bed and even to talk to, but he'd never marry her. He was Greek after all. If he wasn't Greek maybe he'd marry Cynthia. Was Andrei right, time to settle down? That meant getting married, having kids, it didn't really mean settling down. Maybe after being married for a while he'd settle down.

They passed the road to Langley, then Holmes Harbor in Freeland, by Greenbank and a sign for the Naval Air Station Hancock Target Range. On the left a road headed to Fort Casey, now abandoned but with World War II battlements still in place. He remembered spooky relics, gun emplacements on the ramparts and cavernous storage rooms below. One evening in late summer he and Miriam hadn't been able to hold off any longer, no way would they make it back to the motel, so in one of the lower rooms they'd found a mid-sized cannon, great turn-on for Mir, and they'd screwed standing against its lower barrel . . .

The hearse turned right toward Coupeville. Nico said, "Which way now?"

Vasily pulled himself out of his memories and found the map. "Should be down off this road." Past a hospital, a school, couple more streets. "Turn here." He pointed right.

They found the offices of the County Seat. Nico pulled the hearse into a small lot at the side. Vasily said, "This won't take long." He got out, headed for the main door, went in. Inner door to the sheriff's office and Vasily opened it. A few tired chairs, magazines on a coffee table—godawful place to work. The receptionist behind a desk turned to him, gave him a dazzling smile as her lovely thick hair settled on her shoulders. Too much eyebrow but the most gorgeous mouth. Maybe he'd come back to Whidbey when this Sandro business was settled. Her smile told him his chances with her would be pretty good. "Hello."

"May I help you?"

The sign on her desk said Miss Brady Adam. "I need to speak with the sheriff."

"You have an appointment?"

Damn, had Andrei made that call? Better assume so. "Yep."

"Oh, you phoned him directly? This morning?"

"Yeah. Just to be sure."

"I'll let him know you're here." She got up. At the inner door, she knocked.

With appreciation Vasily noted the great hips and damn good ass held tight by that skirt—

She turned to him. "You may go in."

As he passed he brushed his elbow against her upper arm. She didn't seem to notice.

Behind a desk sat the sheriff, a big man. "Come in. Sit down," he waited as Vasily did, "what d'ya want to know about now?"

"Now?"

"About your goddamn mountains out of molehills case."

"Look, I think you're confusing me—"

"Isn't that why you called?"

"What case?"

"The one your partner got so nosy about, the overdosed dead kid case, the mother doesn't know her own son case, the why you made an appointment with me case. That case."

Vasily forced a smile. "Well that's what I'm here for—"

"You detectives have your nerve. I'm a municipal employee, for Coupeville, see? And I don't have hours and hours to hang around my office while you—what'd you say?—interview me."

Not good. Andrei had said the detectives were done. Vasily's smile remained. "I think you've made a mistake. I'm not a detective. I'm a cousin of the dead man. I've brought a hearse, I'm here to take his body back to Seattle for the funeral."

"Oh." The sheriff stared at Vasily. "I see."

Did he? "So if we can—"

"Not so fast. There's a right way and a wrong way to do things. Procedures."

"So we finish the procedures quickly—"

"Nothing quick about procedures. Why they exist. Make sure everything's done proper."

"Then let's get started." Vasily smile was slipping quickly.

"I need to check some things out here. First of all, last I heard, the mother claimed the corpse was somebody else's."

"That's all settled. It is Sandro Vasiliadis."

"You got the certificate that says that?"

"His mother knows her son. She—"

"Didn't last time. Just denied it. I need an explanation for all that."

"Sheriff, Sandro is Andrei Vasiliadis nephew."

"I don't care whose nephew or great uncle the corpse is, I can't release it without proper papers. From what I see you don't have the papers."

"I've got the hearse and the driver from the mortuary right outside."

"Does he have the papers?"

"He's the mortuary official, for god's sake!"

"Won't do no good. I need papers to release a body."

Vasily sighed, to control himself. "And where do I get these papers?"

The sheriff shrugged. "Anyway it don't matter whether you got papers or not, 'cause it's too late in the day and I can't release the body now till Monday morning."

"Eleven AM is too late?"

"I got a busy day."

A greater crime to beat the shit out of a sheriff than out of an average citizen? The desire was nearly overwhelming. "Where do I get these papers?"

"Municipal office, third door on the right." The sheriff explained carefully, door by door, certificate by certificate, seal by embossed seal. "Come back Monday."

Vasily got up. "This'll cause you trouble, Sheriff."

The sheriff smiled. "Son, nothing causes me trouble."

Vasily turned and left because he couldn't do anything else. He passed through the outer office but barely heard the lilting voice say, "Bye."

Anger and concern, tightly packed together, cramped the sheriff's gut the moment the door closed. Nobody threatened Burt Vanderhoek. If Brady hadn't been outside he might've softened the greaseball up some. But she didn't like that kind of stuff. Even if she did he wouldn't have bashed the guy around. Not here in the office anyway.

But the greaser had to follow the rules. Trouble was, Burt couldn't exactly say what the rules were. They'd know at the Municipal offices.

Damn Greek family to blame for all this, the red tape they caused, specially if it really was their corpse. Just like everybody else, either breaking the law or thinking about doing so. Better call Carl.

Carl Assounian, the State Patrol officer overseeing the Vasiliadis case out of Oak Harbor, answered on the second ring. "Oh Burt. What's up?"

Burt laid out the visit from the Greek guy.

"You did it right on the button, buddy. Nothing I can help you with anyway, we're in the middle of a crackdown in Seattle. Tell you about it when I see you."

Okay, Burt was off any hook he maybe hadn't noticed. He worried about Carl, though. The guy sounded under a strain, likely because he'd given up cigarettes. Or had he started again? Yeah, something weird about that body, mother not recognizing her own son. Maybe not her son? Bet she's lying about something, most people usually are.

A knock on the door. "Come in!" Brady, to say his other appointment had arrived, the detective from Islands Investigations International, a Mr. Franklin.

"Jesus," said Burt.

———

Brady, chatting with Noel before announcing his arrival to Sheriff Vanderhoek, let Noel know the man sounded out of sorts today, just been talking with someone who'd upset him, if Noel wouldn't mind waiting five minutes before going in? And if he could make the meeting quick—? Noel pretended to read a *Field and Stream* magazine while he waited. He glanced at Brady, engrossed by her computer screen. A traditionally attractive woman. On the web he'd found a phrase for her version of things sexual—terrible to generalize, but people do—a lipstick lesbian. Female-pretty in any man's eyes, and attracted to other women. He understood very little about who attracted whom. He had loved Brendan and that was that. He'd never love again.

Brady said, "I think he's ready to see you now," got up, "as short as you can make it," knocked on the door, and announced Noel.

Noel went in. Big man, like Kyra had said. Lots of dog pictures. He didn't stand, gestured Noel to a chair, and barked, "Okay, what now?"

"Just a few minutes of your time, couple of questions—"

"Your partner asked all the questions."

"A follow-up. How do you know Sandro Vasiliadis was a heroin addict?"

"He died of it."

"Yes, but—"

"Arm full of needle marks. That screams *addict* to me."

"Was the syringe with the body?"

"Nope."

"Any equipment?"

"Nope."

"Do you keep tabs on the addicts in Coupeville?"

"Tabs?"

"Lists, or whatever. On who's using."

"Nope. Anyway we don't have addicts in town. And the corpse wasn't from here."

"Right." No addicts in Coupeville? "I'd like to see the autopsy report."

The Sheriff grimaced. "Gotta talk to Doc Ferrero about that."

"You mentioned Vasiliadis' car. Where is it?"

"State Patrol's yard."

"I'd like to see it. It's been fingerprinted and so on?"

He picked up a brass German Shepherd paperweight. "It's not been fingerprinted and so on."

Noel sighed, and stood. Brady would be pleased at how quick he'd been. He wasn't pleased with himself; Vanderhoek was a bastion of non-information. "Thank you." He headed for the door. He was pretty sure he heard the sheriff mutter, "Goddamn civilians."

Brady turned out to be more relieved than pleased. "He's been in a foul mood for the past few days."

"Thanks for the insight. See you." Noel headed for the outer door. A thick gray rain beat against the glass. He turned back. "Too wet out there. May I wait here? Kyra should be by soon."

"No prob." Brady smiled prettily.

He checked that his cell was on; Kyra would phone when she finished.

Vasily, sweating lightly, dialed Andrei's private line. He heard, "Yes?"

"I'm on Whidbey. Two things. Bad news."

136

"Tell me."

"The detectives are still on the case. The sheriff was expecting one of them when I came in. He thought I was the guy."

"Then the woman detective lied to me last night."

"Looks that way."

"But Maria didn't hire them again. This makes no sense."

"Maybe they're poking around on their own."

"No. People don't work without pay."

"Maybe island people do?"

Silence while Andrei thought. "No. I don't think so."

"Then someone else hired them."

"Could be."

"Who?"

"Someone concerned. A friend of Sandro's."

"Garth?"

A moment, then: "Not against Maria's wishes. Maria is done with detectives."

"Then who?"

"Go to the funeral home. Read the guest book, see who was at the viewing. Maybe one of them. Find out who and convince them to fire the detectives."

"Okay."

"And the other bad news?"

"The Sheriff won't release Sandro's body till Monday. I have to fill out a bunch of papers."

"Bring them here. I didn't want to involve anyone else but now I have to get Chuck. He'll deal with the legalities."

"Chuck's good." Vasily hesitated. "Andrei, I'm sorry about not getting Sandro back."

"The body can wait. Just so long as the casket stays closed."

A gatekeeper, Kyra thought. If Triple-I grows, will we too need a gatekeeper?

Question: What's worse than a gatekeeper at the door?

Answer: Having no gatekeeper, which would mean we have nothing to hide.

This blonde one, about her own age, was called Dawn Deane

according to the nameplate, but her tone shouted that sunset had arrived for Kyra's quest: "No, today isn't possible."

Something about the reception room made it difficult for Kyra to come on hard. "I need very little time, it's for the benefit of one of your ex-patients, a few questions—"

"I can make an appointment for you early next week."

"If you just explain to whoever's in that I—"

Ms. Dawn Deane, glancing at Kyra's card, spoke gently. "Ms. Rachel, each day the workload of the clinic is set up in advance. If you tell me when you can come back?"

As gatekeeper, the woman was good. Soothing voice, a match to this attractive room. Dawn Deane sounded as if she truly wanted to help. Yet behind the velvet desk sat a will of steel.

"Next week might be too late to help Sandro's friends. Time's important here."

A wrinkle appeared on Dawn Deane's forehead. "Who did you say?"

"Sandro Vasiliadis."

Dawn Deane looked sad. "Tragic." She thought for a moment. "Excuse me. I'll see." She headed down the hall to the right, knocked on a door, and disappeared. Kyra wondered if she should follow Dawn Deane and open the door. But the harmony of the waiting room insisted that any show of discord would work against her. This room knew how to keep people in their place. Offset lighting, soft carpet, serene seascape lithographs on the walls—each of them, she noted, numbered: 23/80, 17/30, and so on. No simple prints for the WISDOM clinic.

"Ms. Rachel, Dr. Jones can give you a few minutes."

Kyra turned quickly. "Thank you." A clever reception room. She'd been drawn from her mission.

"This way."

Dawn Deane opened the door she'd disappeared behind earlier and gestured for Kyra to go in. The office felt even more comfortable than the reception room, not so much in appearance as in demeanor, as if the office had good deportment. With erudite tomes on dark wood bookshelves filling two walls, it felt like an intelligent place as well. The third wall was all window, a March garden outside, crocuses nearly finished, little blue and yellow iris spikes, the grass emerald through the rain. On the fourth wall, more lithographs.

The man behind the desk stood, came around, reached his hand. "Dr. Stockman Jones."

She shook it. "Kyra Rachel, Islands Investigations International."

Jones, about Kyra's height, near-spherical face, chubby, white shirt and silk maroon tie, said, "Please have a seat." He returned to his desk's protection. His suit jacket hung on a coat rack. "You represent a friend of Sandro Vasiliadis?"

Kyra sat in a narrow, brown leather chair that seemed to embrace her. "Yes. My client is concerned about Mr. Vasiliadis' death."

The circle face nodded itself into a globe of a head. "A tragedy. We at WISDOM had gotten to know him well."

"Was he acting strangely in the last days of his life?"

"Why do you ask that?"

"My client has trouble believing Sandro wanted to kill himself."

"Is that your client's assumption? That he killed himself?"

"No."

Jones prayed his hands, leaned his chin on them. "We assume it was a complete accident. He overdosed himself. No grounds to suggest suicide, no note, no word to others."

"Did you know Sandro was a heroin user?"

"We wouldn't have taken Sandro as a client if we'd believed he was addicted."

"Maybe a recreational user?"

"Not that we knew."

"Yet Sheriff Vanderhoek says there was a row of needle marks in the corpse's arm."

"I know nothing of that."

"Wouldn't you have checked, examined him regularly?"

"We have our procedures and we follow them carefully."

"But specifically here, in Sandro's case?"

Dr. Jones' eyes narrowed. "Ms. Rachel, who is your client?"

Kyra answered automatically, "I'm afraid that's confidential." The words spoken, she knew what was coming.

"Just so. Therefore you can appreciate that we cannot divulge information to you about Sandro Vasiliadis. I've already told you more than I should. I'm sure you understand."

"I'd just like to know if he was acting strangely before he died."

"I'm sorry. That would fall into the category of confidential." He glanced at his watch. "And that's all the time I can give you. I ask your pardon but I can't help you further."

Such a serene tone to Dr. Jones' words. How polite it would be to smile, to thank Dr. Jones and walk quietly away. Out of Jones' sight she clenched her fists—and mentioned Ursula's fear. "Maybe someone else doped him."

"Nonsense." Jones stared at her, his round face shiny. "It was an accident." Kyra stared at him. For eight seconds, complete silence. "Who would want him dead? And why do you think such a thing?"

Kyra shrugged. "It's a hypothesis. When the facts of his death are badly answered by the suicide or the accident hypothesis, we try to come up with others."

Slowly Jones nodded. The flat line of his mouth made him appear grave. "You posit that someone killed him. You find that a better hypothesis than accidental death?"

What the hell, be honest. "Can't say I do, actually. But our client would like to be sure."

"We were all shaken here, perhaps that's why we prefer to think that it was an accident and not suicide. But—"

Jones was wrestling with himself. About what? "But?"

"There was no reason for him to kill himself. He was about to release the person who had been imprisoned inside his body."

"Is that what you do, Dr. Jones, release the imprisoned person?"

Jones smiled. "One of the many things." He stood. "I do apologize, Ms. Rachel, I'm already late for my appointment." He reached for his suit jacket and slipped it on. "Perhaps my partner Dr. Haines can give you a few minutes for an overview of what we do here?"

"Sure. Thanks." What choice.

Back in the reception room Dawn Deane smiled at them both. Dr. Jones marched down the opposite hall, knocked, opened a door and entered. The reception space again soothed her. Dr. Jones would now be explaining to Dr. Haines— Wait, the doctor who prescribed those pain pills, the name of the doctor on the vials, the endocrinologist— And that chilling fact about Sandro before he died, Kyra had tucked it out of mind, his balls so flooded with semen he had to jerk off who knew how many times a day. Hormone problem? The endocrinologist's name?

Suddenly Dr. Jones stood beside her. "Dr. Haines can give you five minutes. I'll take you over." He led her along the hallway and ushered her into his colleague's office.

A cooler and more Spartan version of Jones' own. As many lithos, another garden view, two bookcase walls equally impressive. But the paint was dead white, the carpet thinner and paler. Some kind of scent hanging in the air. Gary Haines, maybe ten years younger than Stockman Jones, the gray at his temples creating a distinguished border to a handsome jagged face above blue shirt, bird of paradise tie and black suspenders, got up from his teak desk. Jones introduced them. Haines nodded. No handshake. "Ms. Rachel is working on a strange hypothesis about Sandro Vasiliadis, that perhaps someone killed him."

Kyra wished he hadn't mentioned that.

Haines' eyebrows knotted into a single line. "Why do you think that, Ms. Rachel?"

"Precisely what I asked her. Excuse me, I have an appointment. Nice meeting you, Ms. Rachel." He turned and left.

"Sit down." Kyra did, again a comfortable leather chair. Dr. Haines sat, right buttock on the edge of his desk, left leg crossing at the knee, forcing Kyra to look up at him. "Dr. Jones asked me to tell you about the clinic. But what's this about someone killing Sandro?"

Kyra forced a smile. "Dr. Jones exaggerated. I told him I'm trying to find a possible alternative hypothesis for Sandro's death. If you doubt suicide, and accident seems improbable, it may be something else."

"Why not an accident?"

"Was Sandro a regular heroin user?"

Dr. Haines folded his arms and stared at Kyra.

He's going to break Jones' record of silence. Well, damned if she'd speak before he did. Or smile. Or look away. She waited for a quarter minute of torturous restraint.

He shifted his hips to sit on both buttocks. He glanced down at Kyra as if about to dismiss her. "I'll speak to you briefly about this if I can have your word that you'll take it as confidential."

"Of course." She forced herself to lean back, increasing Dr. Haines height above her.

"I'm sure he wasn't a regular user, but I believe he used heroin occasionally. We wouldn't have treated a regular user. Whatever, it wasn't getting in the way of his transformation, so— Honestly, I don't know. I suppose it's possible . . ." Haines blinked. "Perhaps his use had increased recently, but I'm dubious. Occasionally?" He shrugged. "Regularly, no."

"I see." She didn't.

"Which is why his death was accidental. Injecting too much, never coming back."

"And you don't believe it was suicide."

Dr. Haines smiled, without humor. "No reason. He was about to become the woman he wanted to be. Everything was progressing wonderfully."

She squinted up at him. "A happy person taking heroin."

"Well. Occasionally."

"Why does a happy person take heroin?"

Haines dropped his feet to the floor and stood. "I've seen it in a number of patients, Ms. Rachel."

A waft of sweet, acrid cologne suddenly socked her in the nostrils.

"The euphoria of achieving the desired transgendered state comes in waves. On the crest, the fact of the process itself creates great happiness. In the trough, doubt sets in. We have medicines which can blot that doubt, and we monitor our patients carefully. Sometimes the doubt is greater than the patient can stand, even with medication. So the patient turns to an artificial process for bringing the euphoria back. Some use alcohol, others marijuana or cocaine. One or two have tried heroin. With Sandro," he shrugged. "I wouldn't have been able to tell, not with certainty, before he died. But the evidence of his body— It speaks for itself."

That made sense. Or did while he was speaking. She got up. "Thank you for your analysis."

"You're welcome. And if there's anything else?"

"One more question. What about his swollen testes? Is that the result of these treatments?"

Haines' eyebrows knotted into a single line. "I know nothing about Sandro Vasiliadis' genitals, Ms. Rachel. I'm a psychiatrist."

"He never spoke with you about it?"

"Now you're into doctor-patient confidentiality." A warning smile came to his lips.

"Thank you." She reached out her hand. He brought his forward slowly. It felt soft and cool. "Goodbye." She headed for the door.

From Haines a quiet, "Goodbye."

In the pleasant reception room, the tension from Dr. Gary Haines' office draining, she smiled at Dawn Deane, who smiled back for a moment before picking up the phone. "WISDOM Clinic, good afternoon."

Kyra let herself out into gray light. She glanced at four names on the door, gilt outlined in black. The two she'd just met, plus Dr. Richard Trevelyan, Endocrinology. Dr. Lorna Albright, Gynecology. She went back inside.

Dawn Deane raised a single index finger, one minute. She set the phone down, and smiled at Kyra. "Yes?"

"Could I speak with Dr. Trevelyan as well?"

"He's gone for the day. Would you like to make an appointment?"

"When?"

Dawn Deane glanced through her appointment book. "Wednesday would be the earliest. Two o'clock?"

"Sure," said Kyra. Damn.

In his office, Stockman Jones picked up the phone. "Yes, Mr. Vasiliadis. What can I do for you?"

"We met at the viewing of my nephew, Sandro Vasiliadis."

"I remember."

"You were his doctor."

"Several of us at the clinic were his doctors."

"I speak of this to ask for your help."

"If I can, Mr. Vasiliadis."

"I rarely ask for help, Doctor."

"Yes?"

"You must understand. Sandro, his parents, I and my brothers and sisters and their families, we are part of a community. Much of our life revolves around our Church. Our good acts and our good names are our greatest riches."

"I do understand. My own Church is very much part of my life. I'm an elder. My responsibility is ethical counseling."

"This makes it easier for me, Doctor. We're concerned, Sandro's mother and I, that the procedure Sandro was undergoing not become public. This isn't information the community needs to know."

"Yes, I fully agree."

A moment of silence, then: "Thank you."

"I am not doing you a favor here, Mr. Vasiliadis. It's our policy at WISDOM to be completely discreet about all our clients. For their protection and for ours."

"I understand. I thank you. And Sandro's mother thanks you."

"I hope she's begun to recover."

"It will take time."

Should he tell Vasiliadis? He glanced at Kyra's card. "Did you know, sir, that a detective is trying to find out more about Sandro's death? A Kyra Rachel of Islands Investigations International."

A sigh. "Two of them, I think. You've met the woman?"

"She was here fifteen minutes ago, asking questions."

"And you told her—?"

"Nothing. Discretion and confidentiality are essential to our work."

"Very good."

"Then could I ask you to do all in your power to keep these detectives from pushing harder?"

"I'm doing everything I can. So it won't be a favor at all."

"Thank you."

"And I thank you."

TWELVE

AT TOBY'S, KYRA ordered the hamburger platter, Noel fish and chips. They sipped mugs of foamy beer.

Kyra said, "So it was better, right?"

"I don't see—"

She interrupted him: "Without your cellphone I'd've had to get out of the car and come to get you, then back through the rain to the car. Or you'd have had to stand in the rain."

"It's practically not raining anymore."

"Getting very wet. This way you only got a little wet and I stayed dry."

"Okay, I'm glad you didn't get wet."

"It's an economy of comfort. That's what these phones are good for."

"I guess so," Noel conceded. "Okay, what do we know?"

Kyra described her visit with Drs. Stockman Jones and Gary Haines, that both were guarded but did concede Sandro might have been upset. Haines suspected Sandro used heroin occasionally.

"Against anybody else's sense of Sandro." Noel had even less to report. They should get to the hospital early to meet with the coroner, Ferrero. Noel had called from Brady's office for an appointment. The man was out, back by mid-afternoon. Some woman's voice had set a meeting for three-thirty.

"At the hospital," Kyra said, "we should take a look at the pharmacy, check security."

"Why?"

"Maybe Sandro got the heroin there."

"Except Ursula already told us hospital pharmacies don't keep heroin."

"Ursula does X-rays so how would she know. Maybe they use heroin for detoxing."

"More likely methadone."

"We have to follow the heroin trail. That's what killed him, however it happened, accident, suicide or murder. So what do we know we don't know about heroin?"

"You mean, was he high when he left home? Or did he buy the heroin later?" Noel frowned. "The sheriff implied that Sandro OD'd, got in his car, drove to cemetery and died. When you say it flat like that it doesn't make sense."

"Yeah. And where did the heroin come from? A dealer on the street? A bar? Maybe the hospital. I'm not ruling that out yet, Noel."

"Maybe the Navy base."

"Maybe."

"His friends keep saying they can't see him with heroin."

"Maybe they know something they don't know they know."

The waiter, a man with a bulldog face who might have been Toby himself, plunked down a thick hamburger open on a big bun, red onions and sliced tomatoes on the side, surrounded by a four-inch heap of fries; and two pieces of crisp golden-battered halibut on fries. Noel and Kyra paused for first bites. Very good.

Kyra wiped sauce off her lip. Noel stared through the window. In the mist, only the near water was visible. He said, "You think he bought the heroin dressed as Sandra?"

Kyra shrugged.

"What was he wearing when he was found?"

"Good question." Kyra caught Noel's eye. "Oh no. No way. You should've asked when you were in his office. You go back."

"Okay, okay."

"Was Sandro a threat to someone? Did someone hate him?"

"No sense of hatred."

"A threat? To his family? Possibly. To a lover? Male, female, or as we've learned some other kind of other? Or a threat to a so-called friend?"

"Far as we can tell, not to Ursula or Brady. Or Cora or Rudy for that matter. Not Garth."

"Okay, why did Sandro move to Whidbey? Did he decide on transgendering and move nearer the clinic? Or did he get to the island and the clinic was there?

"Worthwhile questions. Answer? I dunno." They ate in silence for a while, looking out at the mist. The kind of moment Noel loved, the calm before collaboration. "So let's find out."

They left, drove up the hill, sat in front of the sheriff's office. "We could track down the kid who found Sandro," Kyra said. "Then we wouldn't have to meet up with the sheriff again."

"True. But the sheriff is right through that door," he gestured, "and we don't have the first idea where to find the kid."

"His name would be in Sandro's file."

"Which is sitting in the sheriff's office."

"Okay." She opened the Tracker door and slipped down. The mist had lightened, the clouds beginning to crack. Noel caught up with her. In the office she said to Brady, "Hi, we're back. We need to see the sheriff again, one very quick question."

Brady, worry holding her bright lips low, said, "You really do? He's in the dumps."

"It's important."

"Gee, maybe we should just let Sandra be."

"We can't, not yet. And we need information only the sheriff can give us."

"Can I help? I keep my ear to the ground."

Kyra glanced at Noel. He shrugged. Kyra said, "Okay. What was Sandro wearing when he was found?"

Brady closed her eyes. "I can see the file on his desk," she muttered. Her eyes opened. "I've got a head like a sieve. Sorry. I'll tell him you're here." She got up. "You'll be quick?"

"Even quicker than last time." Noel grinned. "Say the civilians are here."

Brady frowned. "You want to see that file or not?"

"Sorry, Boss." Noel dropped his head pseudo-contritely.

Brady rapped on the inner door, opened, entered and closed it. Behind the door they heard large muffled sounds.

Noel said, "We'll locate Rudy again and talk to Ursula when we pick her up. Cora too?"

"Okay."

"First to the cemetery."

Brady came out. "He can give you a moment." She gestured to the open door.

Sheriff Vanderhoek stood behind his desk, leaning forward on his knuckles, staring down at a file between his hands. "Blue T-shirt, blank on both sides. Old sweatpants, baggy, dirty at the knees. Three unused tissues in the right pocket. White socks and loafers." He looked up at them, an irritated stare. "Body sitting on the ground of the blockhouse, leaning against the south wall."

"Underwear?" Noel asked.

"Nope."

"No underwear? Or the report doesn't say?" Kyra's irritation bristled.

The sheriff glowered. "No underwear."

Noel asked, "Coat? Jacket? Hat?"

"Nope. Anything else?"

"How'd Sandro get to the cemetery?"

"His car." To Kyra: "Didn't I tell you?" Vanderhoek thawed a fraction. "Ninety-eight Ford Fairlane."

"Any prints other than Sandro's?"

"That's four or five."

"What?"

"Questions."

"Sheriff—"

"Okay, okay. No other prints."

"Well. Thanks."

As Kyra passed through the doorway the sheriff growled, "Close the door."

In the waiting room Noel said, "Thanks, Brady."

Kyra asked, "Are you coming with us to Sandro's place?"

"Sandra's. Yes."

"A question for you too, okay?"

"Sure."

"I know you don't believe Sandra would take heroin. But it was heroin that killed her. Can you think of anyone who might've been her connection?"

Brady thought hard, this time not closing her eyes. "No." Her head shook. "Nobody."

"How do we get to the cemetery? It's not on our map."

"Easy as pie." Brady gave them her heart-shaped smile.

Her directions wound them directly to the cemetery on the side of a hill. They drove up a dirt road. No parking area, so at the crest they pulled over and got out. Nobody around, lonely and misty.

Gravestones dotted the slope below. Ahead on the left lay a pike-fenced space containing a stone pillar, some kind of memorial. Fifty feet to the right stood a small square structure with a doorless entry. They approached, checking the ground for anything the police might have missed. But they spotted only low daisies among grass and weeds.

The blockhouse, built of heavy timbers, the floor dirt, the space roofed but with open doorways on both sides and two windows without glass, was empty, not even trash or leaves blown in. Noel said, "We know he was found here. Did he die here?"

"He wasn't about to walk here dead. Or drive here dead."

"Right. So either he died here or somebody brought him here."

"As in, he came here to shoot up and happened to die? Then why no dope paraphernalia?"

Noel said, "The official theory is he got the dope from somewhere, was either using regularly or was so depressed he figured he had to kill himself. Why here?"

Kyra snorted. "So he could be buried close by."

"Come on, we have to think as he would. He's depressed, the hope of becoming a woman fading fast. He needs to leave the physical pain behind, blow his mind so the psychic pain goes away. What would you do?"

"I'd go home, have two or three stiff drinks, maybe get into bed, get cozy, take a hundred sleeping pills and go quietly. Or if I was really brave, the drinks, a nice hot bath, and a razor blade to my wrists."

"Yeah," Noel folded his arms against the cold, "and keep warm."

"So was he thinking he couldn't be a woman? It's a fairly standard procedure, right?"

Noel stared out across the rain-bleak landscape. "A man who wants to be a sexy pretty woman. He'd have given anything to look like Brady. Killing himself, wouldn't he try to look female-sexy in his last moment?"

"Hmm." Kyra paused. "Except suicide would be an admission of defeat."

"But dirty baggy sweats. No jockey shorts. Not even panties."

"Maybe because of his bloated testes?"

"All the more reason for support."

"I guess," said Kyra.

"Mostly he dressed as Sandra. Why sweats, of all things?"

"And loafers. Look how muddy the path is. Was there dirt on his shoes? Mud?"

Noel said, "We could ask Sheriff Vanderhoek."

"Maybe Brady could find out."

"Give her a call."

Kyra squinted at him. "Something wrong with your phone?"

"You like these toys."

She rolled her eyes, found the phone in her purse resting on the Mace can, consulted her electronic address book and poked in the number. Brady agreed to check about the loafers. As Kyra broke the connection she said, "I've got messages." She pressed number codes and listened. For a second she smiled. Then scowled, and closed up the phone.

"What?"

"Thanks from Mike for the potluck and greetings to you. And Sarah wants her and me to spend a few hours juggling together. And a less jolly one, Cora Lipton-Norton. She said she'd been threatened. A man telling her to keep her mouth shut about Sandro's sex-change operation. If she talks about it, she'll get hurt."

"What did she do? Say?"

"First that she'd talk to whoever the fuck she wanted to."

"And?"

"So he told her he'd burn her green hair out with lye. And a couple of other things she didn't want to repeat."

"So she called you?"

"She didn't know what else to do."

"Who was it?"

———

Just before noon Nico had driven Vasily to a car rental in Oak Harbor; way too conspicuous driving a hearse. Nico would drive it back to Seattle by the bridge. Whatever, said Vasily.

Vasily didn't like Oak Harbor. An offensive place, the small-townness plus all the Navy types. Women, kids, all of them blobby. Waiting at home while their husbands went to war, watching TV or coming off base into Oak Harbor and stuffing themselves at one of these millions of fast food joints. But who the hell wants to live a whole lifetime on an island. Islands were great to take a girl to but settling down on one? No life on islands, no clubs, not a lot of unattached women, no great food.

Four people on his agenda, Sandro's buddies. Best find them unaware, then make them real aware. The green-haired one came first; he'd called the home numbers on Andrei's list and she was the only one who'd answered.

Amazing, that Andrei. Vasily had gotten the list of mourners from the creepy undertaker. One was the lovely Miss Adam, the sheriff's secretary, and that information made Vasily's afternoon. He'd read the list to Andrei. Andrei said only four names mattered, the man, Longelli, and the three women, Bunche, Lipton-Norton, and Adam. Vasily didn't need Adam's address, he knew where to locate her. It then took Andrei—actually the communications guys on the ninth floor—just minutes to find where the other three lived and worked.

Vasily couldn't figure why these people kept on being friends of Sandro. For the women, some kind of sexist stuff like they were pleased they were getting one more for their side? But the guy, Longelli, he made no sense. Unless he was weird in some other way. All fuckin' confusing.

Well, whatever. Vasily had figured on being straightforward with them, just as Andrei would—polite, but let the inner strength show. Except it hadn't worked so well with the green-haired one, her filthy mouth rattled him. So he showed more of the inner strength than he meant, he made his point and she damn well understood it. No big deal anyway. She didn't have to do something, just keep from doing something.

With Rudy Longelli he needed a casual conversation, enough tone so the guy would get Vasily's intent. For half an hour he'd watched Longelli shift back and forth, construction site to van, getting some tool or piping from the back. Always other workers around. So Vasily was taking too much time for this guy, had to get back to Coupeville to take care of Nurse Urse. Miss Adam would finish at four-thirty or five. Okay, the plumber. Here he came again, over to his van, opening the back door, in, out again, a small package.

Make it happen. Vasily stepped out of his rented Taurus sedan and crossed the road. He kept the van, parked on oozy mire, between himself and the carpenter. He opened the van's rear door, stepped up and in, closed it behind him. No room to stand. He crouched in the corner behind the passenger seat. Not much light, but enough. A regular warehouse, pipes and fittings and do-hickeys.

Maybe ten minutes, and the door opened. Longelli stepped in. Vasily said, "Longelli."

Longelli, startled, stood and bashed his head on the ceiling. "Shit! Who're you?"

"I represent the interests of the Vasiliadis family. The family of your friend Sandro."

"What're you doing in my van?" He pressed hard on his head. "Damn!"

"Taking a few minutes of your time."

Longelli squinted at him. "What for?"

"It's about Sandro." This guy, Vasily figured, was pretty dim. "Like I said."

"What about Sandro?"

"We're concerned, Sandro's mother, his uncle, all of us, that Sandro's good name and reputation stay unblemished."

"Well sure, me too."

"Rudy. Did you just hire detectives to investigate Sandro's death?"

"Are you crazy?"

"Okay. Just make sure you don't talk with anyone about his procedure."

"His what?"

"The process he was going through."

"What're you talking about?"

Dim wasn't the word, just plain slow. "You know what I'm talking about."

"Honest, I don't have any idea."

"His procedure. You get me? You don't talk to anybody about any of it."

"I can't not talk about something when I don't know what it is."

"Don't play games with me, Longelli. You could get hurt."

"This is ridiculous. Get out of my truck." He stepped backward.

Vasily reached forward and grabbed Longelli's forearm. "Listen, Rudy. You like your fingers? You need fingers for your plumbing, Rudy?"

"Let go—"

"Sure, Rudy." He squeezed Longelli's arm hard. "As soon as I get your word, man to man—you get my meaning, Rudy?—that you shut your mouth forever about Sandro's procedure."

"Ow! Stop it—Sure, I won't say anything."

"Not to anybody."

"Yeah, not to anybody."

"That's good, Rudy, that's very good." He relaxed his grip but didn't let go. "Because if you do, I hope you've got good insurance. Get what I'm saying here, Rudy?"

"Yeah. Yeah."

"Excellent. Now go enjoy what you're doing. Be real pleased with your hands, Rudy."

"Yeah."

"I'll be watching. Listening." Vasily grabbed Longelli's elbow, eased him from the van and stepped down after him.

"Okay, Rudy, back to work."

"Sure. Right."

Vasily watched as Longelli rounded the edge of the truck and walked away. He sat for a minute in his Taurus. Dumb plumber. Vasily drove away. But better than Green-hair. Now the nurse, then Miss Adam. Invite her for a drink, talk about the family's hope for respect and—what was that word?—closure, on behalf of Sandro. She'd be sympathetic, she'd smile pretty with those luscious lips, they'd have dinner together, and after dinner—well, take it one thing at a time. Miss Brady Adam would be his present to himself.

<hr>

Kyra stopped the Tracker by a van with a side plate: Rudy's Plumbing. "Looks like he's here." Noel opened his door, glanced down. "Pull up a little? Or do I swim to shore?"

She drove on ten feet. "Happier?"

"Much. See you in there." He tracked his way through yellow mud to a foot-wide plank and walked along it to the front entry. Kyra found a longer, less mucky way around. Inside was dry but windows hadn't been installed yet, and gusts of wind whooshed through. She inhaled the smell of a new construction site: wet sand, fresh concrete, and especially the pungent sawmilled conifers. She loved these smells.

A man wearing fingerless gloves ripped an inch off a two-by-six board. When his saw had whined into silence, Noel asked, "Where do we find Rudy Longelli?"

"The plumber? In the basement."

"Thanks." Noel found a hole in the floor, a ladder leading down. Kyra caught up with him. He pointed: "Supposed to be down here." He didn't care for precipices. He shouted, "Rudy?" No answer. Oh well, for the good of the case. He grabbed the top of the ladder, his foot found the rung, he tested it, it held his weight, he swung on and stepped down. It's true, the first step is the hardest. His foot touched solid ground. Above him Kyra swung onto the ladder and ran down backwards.

Beyond an open partition they found Rudy. Noel said, "Hi again."

Rudy swung around. In his right hand an acetylene torch blasted four inches of flame. In his left, a wrench. "Jesus, you scared me."

"Sorry," said Kyra. "We need to ask you more questions about Sandro Vasiliadis."

"You and everybody's brother. What's the matter with Sandro?" He lay the wrench on a crossbeam, turned off his torch and set it on the ground. "Can't all of you just leave him dead?"

"All of you?" Noel glanced quickly at Rudy's face. It looked mottled red as if the blood had drained from it and was coming back unevenly. "Us and who else?"

"You and that big mother— A Greek guy."

Noel felt Kyra's silent demand: proceed with caution. "Greek? Who?"

"He said he represented the Vasiliadis family and he threatened to break my fingers if I talked about Sandro."

Kyra said, "What happened?"

Rudy told them. "I still don't know what he doesn't want me to talk about."

"Maybe for now," Kyra said, "don't talk about Sandro at all. He's right, you will be safer."

"But what's this procedure business about?"

Kyra glanced at Noel. He nodded.

"What are you guys saying?"

"Nothing, really."

"Hey, it's my fingers."

"It's complicated," Kyra said. "Sandro was in the process of having himself transgendered. He was becoming a woman."

"Sandro?"

"Yes."

"No way."

"It's what was happening. His beard hair was gone, his face was softer, you didn't notice he was getting a bit rounder, breasts starting?"

"Sandro with breasts? Come off it."

"This guy who threatened you, he must've thought you knew. And now that you do, you can keep quiet about it."

"I woulda kept quiet anyway. He scared me." He glanced from Kyra to Noel and back again. "You're serious?" They both nodded. "Jesus Christ." Rudy clanked the windshield down on his welding mask. Up again. "Is that why I thought Sandro was using one of those hair solvents on his beard? Dilapatory or whatever?"

"You were thinking that?"

"I wasn't really thinking that, but I was thinking I was going to be thinking that, if you get my meaning."

Both Noel and Kyra nodded.

Kyra drew in a big breath of moist construction smells and said, "We don't know this guy who threatened you. But we think he's serious."

"Damn right." Rudy banged his helmet faceplate again.

Noel leaned in. "Our question about Sandro—"

"Shit," Rudy whispered, "I can't believe it. I bowled with him, for chrissake." He stared at the cement floor. "In the men's league."

"There's something you can maybe help us with."

Rudy released a balloon of air. "Yeah?"

"You have any idea where Sandro could've bought heroin?"

"No. I don't know those things." He glanced beyond Noel and Kyra. "And I would've thought Sandro didn't know either. I thought I knew Sandro. A little. I guess I didn't at all. Shit." His bit his lip.

Kyra patted his elbow. "Thanks. If you don't talk about Sandro, the Greek guy won't be back." She started across to the ladder.

"Okay." He looked around. He seemed dazed, but found his wrench. He grabbed it tight. Then he said, "Oh shit."

Noel turned. "What?"

"I just been talking to you about Sandro."

Noel shrugged in acknowledgement. "You can talk to us anytime. We're safe. But we'll shut up too. Not a word to anybody."

Did that relieve Rudy? They left him banging his wrench into his other palm.

Back in the Tracker they sat in silence. Finally Kyra laughed a little and said, "You know what we're doing?"

"What?" The windows began to fog.

"Exactly what this guy's warning others not to. He isn't going to like us."

"The least of our worries."

"Yeah?" Kyra turned on the engine to blast air onto the windshield. "What else?"

"Our Greek charmer isn't on his own. He keeps saying, on behalf of the family. Sandro's family. Who're they?"

"Maria? His uncle what's his name?"

"Andrei Vasiliadis. I faxed the report and bill yesterday, remember?"

"Yeah. The—" she stuffed the words back down—"who phoned last night. Represented the family at that funeral home."

"Maybe we should pay him a visit."

"What're you thinking?"

"Maybe he figured he could get rid of the embarrassing Sandro problem by getting rid of Sandro."

"Pumping him with heroin?" Kyra shook her head. "There are easier ways."

"Maybe it's not sex change. Maybe it's basically heroin. Maybe Sandro learned his uncle was moving heroin around. Uncle gets rid of him, heroin as some kind of ironic justice."

"Maybe maybe maybe. We better talk with Andrei."

"Seattle tomorrow?"

"Looks like our friend's got the viewing list too. Let's see if he's met up with Ursula, and Brady, and the doctor from that clinic. But remember Ursula saying Sandro thought his father could actually kill him? This Andrei is the father's brother."

"Hmm," said Noel.

In the fifteen-minute drive from Oak Harbor to Coupeville the rain stopped and started up again three times. They parked in the hospital lot. "Okay," said Noel, "we go to the coroner and the pharmacy."

"Yes." She turned to him. "But first you get to use your cellphone."

"What for?"

"To check with Dr. Stockman Jones."

"You know him. He'll talk to you."

"It's just a phone, Noel. Go on, call."

Noel folded his arms. "You said he was hard to get to. Come on, use your connection."

Dawn Deane buzzed Dr. Jones' office, told him Kyra Rachel was on the line, it was important. Stockman took the call. The detective asked if he had been threatened by a Greek-looking man, telling him not to speak of the Sandro Vasiliadis case to anyone. Dr. Jones assured her he had not been threatened by anyone. As she knew, the Vasiliadis case like all WISDOM's cases were confidential. Ms. Rachel thanked him. He thanked her for the warning, he set the phone down.

Damn! What the hell were those Vasiliadises doing? He'd better tell the others— Tell them what? He thought for a moment, then picked up the phone again and asked Dawn to track down Andrei Vasiliadis in Seattle.

Kyra glanced at her watch: 3:10. Fifty minutes till Ursula's half-shift ended. "We have time."

The pharmacy was a simple high counter with a lower shelf to drop off prescriptions, another to pick them up. No obvious entryway, must be a door at the back. Of course you could leap over the counter— Not Sandro's kind of thing, they agreed. Each time a patient put in his order, one of three pharmacists would walk through a safe-like door at the side and disappear; the dispensing room had to be back there. They tried to walk around but the rear was an outer wall. Kyra volunteered to go out into the thin rain. She found a door, well locked. Easily break-into-able with lock picks, but likely not part of Sandro's training. Dubious Sandro found his heroin here—if the pharmacy even had any.

The coroner's office was in the morgue. And that would be where? In the basement. The coroner was Dr. Ferrero. They walked down a flight of stairs to a hallway and many half-glass doors. Noel tried a couple of handles; locked. At the far end a sign said, Morgue. Kyra knocked. No answer. She listened. Music? She tried the handle. It turned. They went in. Chill pervaded the space. The inside light revealed a man at a desk, and a radio.

The man saw them. He opened a half-glass door. "Yes?" He wore a sweatshirt and jeans.

Noel said, "Are you Dr. Ferrero?"

"No."

Noel waited. "Is Dr. Ferrero around?"

"No."

"When will he be back?"

"Maybe tomorrow. If they need him."

"Who, the corpses?"

"The hospital."

Noel took a card from his shirt pocket. "We were supposed to meet Dr. Ferrero here this afternoon. Get him to call us back, okay?"

"Okay." He took the card and started to close the door.

"Will you do that this afternoon?"

"No."

Noel was disliking this young man. "Why not?"

"He's sailing."

"In this weather?"

"Sure."

"It's very wet out there."

"So's the ocean."

Noel chuckled. "When can you get him my message?"

"Tomorrow. Maybe."

"Thank you."

THIRTEEN

NOEL AND KYRA headed back through the rain, heavy again, and climbed into the Tracker. Two more hours of this aqueous twilight before it would be completely dark. Four or five other vehicles in the parking lot dimmed as the windshield steamed up. After a few minutes Ursula tapped on the passenger window. Noel unlocked the back door. She climbed in. She looked pale, and worried or scared. "What's up?"

She sat and closed the door. "Oh jeez, you wouldn't believe—I was accosted and—threatened."

Kyra half-turned. "Who by?"

"I don't know." Ursula was struggling to hold herself together. "A man, a big young guy, dark hair, mustache, well enough dressed—"

"When did this happen? And where?" Kyra asked.

"He was waiting outside X-ray just after my break. He asked if I'd hired two detectives and when I said, 'Who wants to know?' he ordered me to unhire them. You."

"Why?" asked Noel.

"He said too much information was floating about, the family just wants to get Sandro buried and remembered properly. They don't want any detectives picking over Sandro's bones."

Kyra mused. "How much do you know about Sandro's family?"

"Just that he wanted to stay as far away from them as possible. Sandro had a fair mass of cousins." Ursula drew a tentative deep breath. "He said he'd be excommunicated from his family if they found out about the sex change."

"How," Noel inquired, "was he going to keep it secret?"

"Yeah, well—I guess when it was a *fait accompli*, they'd have to like it or lump it."

"If it's any comfort, Sandro's friends Rudy and Cora had visits from this guy today. He's going through the viewing guest book."

Kyra turned to face Ursula. "What did you say when he ordered you to unhire us?"

"Just that Sandro was my good friend and we had to find out why he died. He looked like he was going to haul off and sock me but my supervisor passed by just then and the guy scrammed. He did say, 'Watch it, you're walking close to the edge.'"

"So," Kyra said. "Do we continue or quit?"

Some color was returning to Ursula's cheeks. "My call says you continue. It's not even been a day yet. Oh! Maybe he got to Brady! Come on!"

"What?"

"If he's threatened her—"

Kyra turned on the ignition. "Sheriff's office?"

"She's due out in minutes."

Two blocks down to the municipal offices. Ursula with her new worry seemed to pull herself together. Kyra parked again and peered at the front door through whipping rain. Ursula got out, her umbrella exploded wide, she galloped to the sheriff's office. Kyra and Noel waited. After a couple of minutes Brady came out, followed by Ursula. A man in a gray Taurus in front of them opened the door and put a leg out, then pulled it back. Brady and Ursula walked to the Tracker, each with an arm about the other, talking earnestly.

———

Vasily saw it all. Miss Brady Adam kissed the other woman on the mouth. Totally fucking disgusting. An island full of perverts. Usually he could tell the queers, Seattle had more than its share. But on this island everybody was either a faggot or had a crewcut. Or green hair. And some, like Sandro, didn't know what they were.

But that Brady Adam, what a waste. She should know better. Had to know better. With a body like that she probably did know better. Maybe this was a tryout thing with her. Because she was a man's woman. Vasily knew about these things. When this Sandro stuff was settled he'd come back here and remind Brady Adam that deep inside she was meant for other things.

Damn! Not when he was done with Sandro, but right now. Tell her to keep her mouth shut. Stupid telling Andrei he didn't need her home address. Too clever by half. So follow them, get her when she was alone.

———

In the car, Noel turned toward Ursula. "What's the story?"

"No," said Ursula, "Brady hasn't seen him."

Brady said to Ursula, "What happened to you?"

Ursula told her what she'd said to the detectives but played down the threats. Brady digested Ursula's tale, took her hand, and assured herself Ursula was okay. "I wonder if your thug was the guy who had an appointment with the sheriff this morning. Big, dark-haired, a mustache. Wearing a leather windbreaker?"

Kyra in the rear-view mirror noted Ursula's nod. "Ready to go?" She started the car and headed up toward route 20, Noel as map-reader.

"He let his elbow touch me," Brady said, "and he thought I didn't notice. Coming on to me in the sheriff's office." Her tone became wistful. "I wish these guys could figure out I like girls." She grinned at Ursula. "One in particular."

Kyra said, "Oh well. The front seat of this car likes guys so we're 50 percent for each." They all chuckled.

Ursula, squinting through the rain, said, "Oh. There's one of the docs from WISDOM."

"Which one?" Kyra screeched to a halt.

"There with the umbrella. Dr. Trevelyan."

"The endocrinologist?" Kyra flung the gearshift into park. "Justasec." She leapt out.

Noel, Brady and Ursula watched Kyra wave, shout, flag him down. He stopped. He listened. Great head of white hair, Noel thought. The doc said something, smiled, continued on his wet way. Kyra ran back to the car and leapt in. "Eight-thirty tomorrow at the harbor. He's getting his boat ready." Way to get around the clinic gatekeeper!

With the Tracker rolling, Noel asked Brady, "Did you find out about Sandro's loafers?"

"Yeah, when I re-filed the file. Clean."

"No mud?"

"Nope. Shiny."

"So," Kyra mused, "how did he get to the blockhouse? Without picking up mud or grass."

"No suppositions in the sheriff's files," Brady said.

Kyra stopped at the light on Route 20. "How do you put up with that Sheriff, Brady?" On green, she turned south.

"Shall I tell them?" Brady asked Ursula in an arch tone.

"Why not?"

"Gun culture," said Brady.

Kyra guffawed.

"Pardon?" said Noel.

"Burt and I talk guns. Especially antique guns that still work."

"What do you do with guns?" Noel felt his jaw loosen and consciously clamped it up.

"Well, now I shoot skeet."

"She's scores well." Ursula, the proud partner. "Last week she hit fifty consecutive birds."

"I've just seen an 1890 Greener of Birmingham in mint condition. It's got a varnished walnut stock and they're holding it for me, but I know I can't afford it. It's gorgeous, the bee's knees. We had the sheriff over once to see my guns and we've been to his house. For guns, he doesn't even mind my babe." She prodded her partner's ribs.

"Do you do dogs too?" asked Kyra. "He sure has a lot of pictures."

"We don't do dogs," Brady said firmly. "Cats are okay."

"What did you shoot before skeets?"

"Skeet. It's singular."

Noel said, "What is a skeet, anyway?"

Ursula said, "It's two clay birds, and she shot trap before. Which is also a clay bird, but it's propelled from a different house. Skeet comes from a left house and right house, but a trap's let go from a single house right in front."

More than he wanted to know, Noel thought.

Brady elaborated: "My dad hunted. We had a ranch in Wyoming until I was fifteen, then things happened." Her tone shrugged. "My brothers and I used to go out with my dad and hunt deer and ducks and elk for the freezer. We ate all the meat we shot." She sounded both proud and defensive. "Last time we were there, even my sweetie took up arms." Noel saw, in the rear-view mirror, Ursula put her arm around her lover.

"What sort of guns do you have?" Brady asked Kyra and Noel.

"We don't," Noel said.

"Detectives without guns?" Brady's voice squeaked with surprise.

"We haven't needed them."

"You might."

Half of Kyra's mind had stayed with Sandro's loafers. Why were they clean? Did he have some shoe fetish and wipe the mud off? "By the way, what do you think of the clothes Sandro was wearing when he was found?"

"Oh yeah," said Brady, "I re-read that when I filed the file."

"What clothes?" Ursula asked.

"Blue T-shirt, worn dirty sweats, white socks and loafers," recited Brady.

"There weren't any clothes like that in Sandra's closet when we looked," Ursula observed.

"They wouldn't be there if they were on her," said Brady, the sheriff's assistant.

"One set of men's clothes," Noel said. "His bowling outfit. If he wanted to kill himself—herself—would he have dressed in men's clothes, or women's?"

Brady said, "Since Christmas she most often wore women's. I told you about the lingerie buying trip."

"No underwear," said Noel.

"Weird," said Ursula. "Maybe more conflicted than we knew."

For perhaps the first time since Sandro Vasiliadis' suicide, Dr. Richard Trevelyan was thinking clearly. He had two questions: What happened? and, What should I do about it? But there simplicity ended. The second question could wait till Sunday, on the boat. The ocean always helped. He poured himself a beer. Tacking was a lot like mulling, a back and forth kind of progress. He had to be clear. For that detective, too. He shouldn't be talking to her. Luckily he'd been quick to suggest they meet early at the marina by the *Panacea*. With luck it'd be raining and she'd make it short. Or not show.

He had to understand what had happened to Sandro. He didn't dare go further with another patient till he could work out where their mistake lay. The process the two before Sandro had gone through was an elegant correction of a developmental error.

Sandro, like every embryo, had started out female. Sufficient fetal androgens such as testosterone helped transform the embryo to male. In Sandro and many of those who came to WISDOM for transgendering, that process had derailed. The sex of a fetus is initiated by a single gene, the Testicular Determining Factor; TDF sets loose a cascade of determining genes. For reasons still not clear, the fetus that became Sandro was only partially subjected to such a gene shower. With a range of hormonal treatment, much of the transformation could be either completed, in female to male transgendering, or reduced, for male to female. Then only the cosmetic transformation remained. But such transformation involved surgery and pain, always physical and, because not gradual, often psychological.

The WISDOM team understood that obviating either kind of pain would require breaking new ground. Such a discovery would bring immense renown and a great deal of money to the clinic and to its funder, Bendwell Pharmaceuticals. Four years ago the incredible breakthrough had happened.

For the first two patients, everything worked as predicted. Then something went wrong with Sandro. What? Richard sipped his beer. He felt pretty sure that the problem lay not in some recent mistake, but in a misunderstanding going back months, even years.

In the beginning the team had agreed the way to go was to find a hormone made according to instructions from a gene that would initiate the complex job of making genitalia. They needed, specifically, a hormone that said, make female genitalia.

For nine years Lorna, with Terry's help, conducted research into hermaphroditic fish families. The successful results came from the protandrial and the bi-directional groups. WISDOM's partners had therefore agreed that for the next years the clinic's primary research would be devoted to male to female transgendering. The work had gone well, and remarkably quickly. Lorna and Terry, with Richard's input, had been able to isolate a neurohormone, which they called percuprone, secreted by the cerebral ganglion that stimulated the hermaphroditic gonad. When injected into a male mouse, in seven cases out of ten it became functionally and morphologically female. It didn't work the other way around, no female to male results, but they had to try.

Their second success was with the black hamlet, which practiced egg trading. Prior to a sunset simulated in the lab, two black hamlets met by the reef in the aquarium. Through some mechanism none of the researchers could understand, the hamlets agreed to trade; they each showed agreement with a head-snap. The WISDOM team gathered to witness this, and they were amazed. Suddenly one hamlet was female, and she gave her eggs to be fertilized by the other. In exchange, the hamlet that did the fertilizing, now also turned female, dropped her own eggs, which were then fertilized by her partner, who for this purpose had become male.

From the black hamlet they had isolated a norepinephrine-like hormone which they called hipophrine, or hipop. Hipop activated the initiation and the termination of sex-reversal. And hipop, when received by a male mouse, also turned it into a female six times in ten.

But, remarkably, when doses of the two were given simultaneously, a ratio of 1.2 parts hipop to 1 part percuprone, almost every mouse transformation was a triumph. They tried rabbits. A 98 percent success rate. Then came an obvious mistake, too obvious now. Bendwell could've helped them fast-track it through FDA. They'd argued; Richard should have argued harder. Stock, Gary and Lorna were clear: skip the monkeys, a mass of research now showed that mammals shared so much DNA, mice and rabbits were close enough: worth the risk. And it had worked! Two men had become the complete woman each had always felt himself to be. Or rather, nearly complete; neither developed a uterus. But reproducing as women was of no interest to them.

Something had gone wrong with Sandro. How? The huge testes Sandro had shown him— Dreadful. Richard pored through journals, consulted dozens of books, tracked down hundreds of sites on-line. Nothing. He remembered an early bit of research at the lab. Couldn't place it. Terry would know. He finished his beer, and poured another.

Terry came home at six. "Hi." She hung up her wet coat.

"Glad you're home." She looked tired. Lines from cheekbones to mouth, more gray in her short curly black hair. Just fifty-three, but she refused to touch it up. Aging naturally, she called it.

"How're you doing?"

"Approaching adequate." He raised his glass. "Want one?"

"Love one." He poured her a beer. "Why adequate?"

"I still haven't figured out whether to go to the police."

She clinked her glass to his. "Not much to be gained."

"Not for Sandro, no, or even for the clinic. But for me? I'm not sure." He sipped. "Listen, I'm going to take *Panacea* out."

"Oh?"

"Yeah. Sunday morning. Think this all through on the water."

"Most important is figuring what went wrong. The police can't help you there."

"Remember, six or seven years ago you were working on something where the male had huge gonads?"

Terry smiled. "The guys in the lab loved it. But it was a dead end."

"Can you find it?

She thought. "Is it important?"

"Probably not."

"I may have transferred it from my old computer." She went to her study. It took her eight minutes. "Here it is," she called. He came in. His glass was full again, she noted.

He said, "Maybe I should forget about the boat, just see the police tomorrow."

She stood, took his drink, set it down and hugged him. He hugged her back. She said, "The police can't help, Richard. But you're right, take *Panacea* out. It'll do you both good."

They held each other for a minute, then she pulled back. "Want to read this?"

On the screen, the lab's research on the midshipman, a fish found off the west coast of North America. Two kinds of males. The Type Ones matured slowly but got to be larger, and their vocal systems, which they used for courting, developed great strength. Their gonads made up 1 percent of their weight. They built careful nests, and hummed to attract females. Type Twos matured quickly, 9 percent of their body weight was taken up by their gonads. They didn't hum. They stole nests and females from Type One males.

Terry said, "What do you weigh these days, Richard?"

"Maybe one-sixty."

"If you were a midshipman your equipment would weigh over fourteen pounds."

Richard shuddered. "Like Sandro." He reached for his beer. "I'll be in the garden."

"Take a raincoat." Terry smiled.

He left. She picked up the phone and called Lorna. "Hi. Can we meet? Richard's still pretty upset . . . Okay, the lab . . . Eight's fine."

<hr/>

Where the hell were they going? Right after Miss Brady's sickening kiss with that woman, they'd driven out to route 20 and turned south. Just drop Miss Brady and go your stupid way! He held a couple of hundred yards back, though with the rain it wasn't likely they'd notice. He followed the Tracker, which, given a woman driver and the wet road, roared along pretty fast. She slowed through Greenbank. He had to brake. Women drivers.

He drove into Freeland and out. The Tracker ignored the turn-off to Langley. Heading to the ferry? But then the Tracker turned right. The sign said, Cultus Bay Road. Another turn, and Vasily followed behind. He checked the road names as he went, have to retrace his steps, damn few houses around, nobody to ask, and he'd be fucked if he got himself lost on this island after dark. Another turn, onto Logchurch Road— Shit, he knew exactly where they were headed. Which meant the man and the woman in the Tracker were the detectives. Shitcrapfuck.

The Tracker pulled into a driveway. Vasily slowed and glanced down it. Long and curvy, he couldn't see a house or the Tracker. He pulled past, U-turned, parked on a shoulder fifty feet away. Gray and wet. He marched back to the drive and headed down. Around a curve and there stood a house, the Tracker parked in front. Everything underfoot was soaking, puddles and mud owned the driveway, his shoes soggier than at the Longelli construction site and the bottom of his pant legs soaked wet into his socks. Driveways should be paved. Fuck, he hated the country.

<hr/>

It had only been forty-eight hours, Wednesday evening, since anyone had been here, but the charming little house felt unlived-in and unloved. Houses do that quickly, Noel thought and wondered about his condo in Nanaimo. "Anybody notified the owner that his tenant died?"

Ursula looked at Brady, who shrugged. "I think the State Patrol would have, they usually take the bull by the horns. I'll get the sheriff to check on Monday."

"The owner's away, you said?"

The two cats wound themselves plaintively around their ankles. The food dishes sat empty, the litter box full. At least the aquarium fish coped by themselves. Mostly. Brady found fish food on a kitchen shelf.

Ursula said, "Yeah. On a year's leave, doing good deeds in Rwanda."

"Hard to get hold of?" asked Kyra.

"Don't know." Ursula, to the excitement of the cats, opened the cupboard under the sink. "Okay guys, I'm hurrying. Out of my way, Sapphire." This to the gray one. "Tawny, you too." She pulled out the food, started to close the door, opened it again. "Holy shit! Look!"

Tucked in behind where the bag of food had been lay two syringes in sterile plastic, and rubber tubing.

"Those weren't there on Wednesday," declared Ursula.

The cats wound in and out of legs, pleading starvation.

Kyra stood. "You sure?"

"Yes."

"Any dope with them?"

"No." Ursula stared into the cupboard. "Somebody's been here."

"Who?" Brady's voice had gone thin.

A question no one could answer.

The cats' meows were increasingly assertive. Ursula unrolled the bag and poured food into their dishes. Complaining stopped, crunching began.

Noel took the photo album from his shoulder bag and put it in the left-hand desk drawer where they'd found it. That felt better. He rejoined the others in the kitchen.

"Someone making the case for Sandra as a heavy-duty user?" Brady's lips had thinned to a stern line. "I don't buy it."

"Yeah," said Kyra. "Pretty dubious."

Brady shook some food into the aquarium. Four small bright fish with orange and white stripes, lines of black and orange heads, whirled on the surface. "We can take the cats home, but what about the fish?"

"Technically it's up to Sandro's mother," Kyra said.

Ursula looked at her. "Back to the will problem?"

Noel clicked his tongue. "That can take forever. Know a fish lover who'd take them?"

"I'll ask," Ursula said.

Noel sat down at the computer and flicked it on. As it loaded he noted a sticky tab on the side of the monitor: Diana, and a phone number. "Ursula? Who's Diana?"

"Diana? Diana who?"

"I don't know. Just Diana."

"Sandro's ex-wife was Diana. She's remarried, I think. Husband's name is— Wait, I'll remember."

Noel copied the phone number and waited for the icons to show.

"What're you doing?" asked Kyra.

"Seeing what's on here."

Ursula took the litter tray outside and emptied it into a compost bin beside the carport. Brady searched for a cat carrier.

Noel tried to connect to the Internet. Password? Only a moment's thought: Sandra. People are so obvious. Bookmarked were a series of sites highlighting the words transgendered and transgendering. He copied web addresses for later searching. On the hard drive under My Documents, a directory called "Trans-g," a sub-directory, "Letters," with a number of sub-sub-directories; those containing the largest number of files were labeled "Nikki," "Chelsea" and "Martine." He thought about privacy, then glanced through them. Helpful and supportive; were he in Sandro/Sandra's position, Noel would appreciate e-mails of this tone. Nikki lived in San Francisco, Martine in Omaha, and—Ha! Chelsea in Seattle, including, in her third letter, a phone number.

If an Andrei Vasiliadis meeting was on, they could talk to Chelsea tomorrow; two birds. He'd phone her later. Or? Okay, go outside for privacy, use his cellphone. He wrote down Chelsea's number and turned the computer off. He located a side door into the carport. Pouring again. He dialed Chelsea's number.

Someone picked up. "Hello?" Dulcet contralto tones.

"Chelsea?" Noel asked. Affirmative. "I'm a detective, Noel Franklin, Islands Investigations International."

"Yes?" More wary.

"I'm investigating the death of someone you may know, Sandro Vasiliadis, and—"

"What!?"

"Sandro Vasiliadis."

"Yes, I heard. But you say he's dead?"

"I'm afraid so."

"But when? How? What happened?"

"We're not actually sure. My partner and I wonder if one of us may talk with you tomorrow?" A sudden formality to his grammar. Was Chelsea herself/himself transgendered? Was Noel not completely comfortable in this area? Do birds fly?

"Certainly. Come by. About eleven? But how dreadful!"

"It is," said Noel. "His friends here are deeply distressed." *Distressed.* What a word. Were Sandro and Chelsea lovers? He had to start thinking about Sandro as Sandra. Hard.

"I'm completely—completely shaken," said Chelsea. "Thank you for telling me." She gave him the address.

Back in the house he said to Brady, "Sandro's car's in the State Patrol compound. Where's that?"

"Oak Harbor."

Kyra, who'd joined them, asked, "Was there anything in the car?"

"I can't look at the file till Monday morning." Brady had had enough.

So, come to think of it, had Noel. Onward to dinner.

Ursula wrestled Sapphire and Tawny into a traveling cage Brady had found; the cats protested fiercely. She turned out the lights and locked the door, then slid onto the Tracker's back seat. Brady passed her the cage, got in, and they balanced the traveling cats across their laps.

Vasily had seen the man come out to use his cell just in time, a close call. He'd heard him talking to someone named Chelsea, an appointment tomorrow. Too many detectives and queers around. And all just walking into Sandro's house? Miss Brady, he'd get her later. Leave, make tracks, all four of you!

Finally the Tracker started up and faded down the driveway. Silence descended. Vasily tried the door from the carport in case the man hadn't locked it; no such luck. Around to the front, jimmy the easiest window. None were easy. The tool shed. A chisel and hammer. Armed, back to the verandah. Three judicious blows to the chisel butt and the window slid open. He worked himself through. Then he wandered from room to room, looked through closets. Whole bunch of women's clothes, god. Medicine cabinet, shelves. Desk. Photo album—

Shit. Disgusting. Sandro with a beard, and pretty soon without, and with breasts needing a bra. Jeeesus, how the hell did they make that happen? Vasily set the album down. At the open window he breathed in deep. Holy fuck, what the hell was he supposed to do with this? Show it to Andrei? It'd kill him. Little faggot Sandro. Must've jerked off to pictures of himself.

Vasily let himself out the carport door. That burn barrel around back— He stripped out the photos, set them alight and dropped them in the barrel. Thin smoke twisted up and hung in the moist air. There. For the family. Just what Andrei would have done. But no need for Andrei to know. The last photo smoldered. He bundled all the female clothing into trash bags he found in a kitchen drawer. Better report, see what Andrei thought he should do. He got out his cellphone.

FOURTEEN

"HOWLER MONKEYS OKAY, but howler cats?" Noel spoke above the wailing from the back seat.

"There, there, cats," soothed Brady. "Shut up."

Heavy rain had returned. Noel asked, "Ursula, do you know what happens when one dies of a heroin overdose?"

"You mean, did Sandra suffer?" Brady asked.

"I mean more, what's the clinical process?"

Ursula folded her hands under her part of the cat cage. "We see ODs at the hospital every so often. And a few years ago my neighbor called me over when her boyfriend OD'd." Brady stroked Ursula's arm. "All opiates kill by depressing respiration. Heroin cuts down the number of messages the brain sends to the muscles in the chest. Breathing becomes slower and slower, then you get the Cheyne-Stokes effect—"

"Refresh me on that," Noel said.

"Irregular breathing, a rising crescendo of shallow breaths, followed by an extremely long pause when you can think the person's already died, then a sharp uptake of breath again."

"Yeah, now I remember. What else happens?"

"Cyanosis—a blue tinge starting at the extremities, low blood pressure, slowing heartbeat, apnea—"

"Is that part of the Cheyne-Stokes breathing or a longer pause?"

"Longer pauses in the Cheyne-Stokes pattern. With heroin you have tiny pinpoint pupils. Then when you're near death your pupils expand. And when you're dead your pupils get really large."

For a moment all were silent. Even the cats, briefly. Suddenly Ursula said, "McRae!"

Why such excitement? Noel turned. "Sorry?"

"Diana McRae. Sandro's ex-wife's remarried name. And their daughter is Carla."

"Ah." Noel wrote both names beside Diana's phone number.

Kyra mused, "How, where and why would Sandro have got heroin, that's the question."

"The sheriff claims there are no addicts in Coupeville," Noel added.

"He's wishing." Brady laughed. "There probably aren't many suppliers though, they'd be in Oak Harbor. The minute a new one surfaces here he locks him up or runs him out of town."

The cats found second wind and headed up the scale again.

Brady said, "I'll report the planted syringes tomorrow."

"To the sheriff?" assumed Noel.

"Wouldn't be his jurisdiction. State Patrol."

"Oh yeah," Noel muttered. The ubiquitous Royal Canadian Mounted Police and the occasional urban force were easier to figure out than the many divisions of American policing.

"Who, how and why put the syringes under the sink?" mulled Kyra some more.

"If they'd been there on Wednesday," Ursula said, "I might be one percent convinced Sandra did. But they weren't, so I'm a hundred-ten percent convinced she didn't."

"On the nose," said Brady.

"Tell me something," Kyra said suddenly. "Did Sandro want to be Sandra with a woman or with a man? A lesbian or a het?"

"We never got that far." Brady laughed "We were too busy with underwear."

"First she wanted to be Sandra," said Ursula.

"Kyra." Noel touched her arm. "Let's stay focused on his—her death."

A few miles of silence. Kyra stopped at the Coupeville light. "How do I get to your place?"

"Turn right. Down to the shore."

Except for some misty streetlights the evening was dark. A car came toward them, and another. Most people were home, tucked in for the night. Which is where Kyra wanted to be. They needed an early start tomorrow. "Is there a reasonable hotel or bed and breakfast?"

Brady said, "There's one where my parents stay. Oh, our place is left in two blocks."

"The Inn," said Ursula. "It's close." She laughed. "Everything in Coupeville's only a few blocks. We'd invite you to stay with us but our place is really small."

"That's fine." Noel wanted only to put his feet up and have a drink, then a good meal. Five more minutes with these cats—

The Coupeville Inn, a two-storey gray clapboard heritage building, its front cheerily lit. Kyra slowed, then turned and headed to Ursula and Brady's. Through the rain the house did look tiny.

Back at the Inn, Kyra parked. Noel found the manager, so militarily upright and wizened he could have fought in the War of 1812. A cigarette dangled from his lips and yes, he had a suite. "Don't rent by the hour," he said, cigarette bobbing.

Noel glared. "My business partner and I need to be in Coupeville overnight." His voice had sunk to baritone.

"Oh well, business." The manager waved him off as if dismissing a whole regiment.

Kyra arrived with the bags. Some finicky key-jiggling and the room's heritage lock opened. A quaint rabbit warren. Living room with pullout sofa. Large windows, the view black, flanked a gas fireplace. A bedroom and kitchen, bathroom and squished separate lav.

Noel sank onto the sofa, toed off his loafers and propped his feet on the coffee table. "Ahh," he sighed. "One more cat yowl and I'd have given them a vocalcordectomy."

Kyra prowled. "You want the bedroom?"

"No, you take it, I'm okay here." He got up and flicked a switch he'd deduced controlled the gas fire. It did.

Kyra set her bag on the bed, drew out a bottle and headed for the kitchen. Clatter, clatter, and she handed Noel a vodka on ice. And one in hand for her.

"With your usual foresight." He smiled and toasted.

"You have a clever partner." She kicked off her shoes and flopped into a chair, curled her feet under her. "Okay, nothing's fitting. No mud on his shoes so likely he was carried there."

"Right. And the syringes. And how could he walk there with all that shit in him?""

"Brady and Ursula's doubts get more solid."

Noel sipped, and studied the flames. The simulation of burning logs in gas fireplaces was becoming realistic. "We need a major What Do We Know. After we solve the dinner problem."

"We're a block from where we had lunch."

"It's pouring. Let's hire a cook."

"This is not a real hotel." She waved her arm. "No restaurant."

"Takeout? Delivery? Go out?"

Kyra got up and prowled. Rotary dial phone on top of a phone book: mildly heritage. "By the address, across from Toby's there's a gourmet-sounding seafood place."

"See if they deliver."

Kyra looked at him. "Gourmet places don't deliver."

"Pick up? We can toss."

"I've got this far. You call." She sipped vodka, pulled out and sucked an ice cube.

Noel sighed and lurched up. Damned if he'd use his Alice In Wonderland Drink-Me phone. He thrust out his vodka-less glass. She sighed and took it.

He dialed, talked. She handed him his glass. "With some agony," Noel said, "they might deign to let us pick up one of their minor dishes but even a fifty-yard dash would do the dish much injustice and it is Friday evening, and so on."

Kyra smiled. "So we go?"

"If we stay there to eat, Samson's will treat us to a gourmet wonder that will extinguish the pain of traveling the Lewis-Clark Trail through the virulent blizzard."

"Then, refortified, we will figure out the weirdnesses in this case."

"At least put them in some order."

Vasily approached the WISDOM clinic. A couple of lights in the parking lot but no cars. The rest of the area lay in darkness. He drove a block down the hill, turned left onto a residential street and parked in front of a pickup. Just another citizen of Washington State, said Vasily's license plate.

He slipped a tool belt from his satchel and clipped it around his waist. He closed the car door quietly and locked it. He walked back to the clinic, hugging the hedges, avoiding streetlights. A car approached from behind and Vasily moved slowly into the shadow till it passed. The worst space lay ahead, the forty feet of empty lawn between sidewalk and the WISDOM building itself. WISDOM, how fuckin' pretentious. Vasily glanced east and west, and behind, and listened. No cars, no people, no dogs. He walked quickly to the front door. Two ways of getting in, he figured, door or window. He pulled on a pair of plastic gloves and tried the front door handle. Course not, that'd be too easy. Though one time it had worked, just been left open. No security sticker. No lights on an alarm panel. Some folks're so sloppy. Or maybe there's no real security here for two reasons: nothing worth stealing, and the cops patrol regularly. Better worry about that. He walked on grass around the east side to the back. A door, then stairs going below ground to another door. He tried the lawn-level door; locked. He checked four floor-to-ceiling sliding windows; all locked. He walked down the stairwell and turned the door handle. Locked too, but the door itself felt loose. A pencil flash from the tool belt, a beam on the door molding. Weatherproofing on the sides and top, except at the hinges on the right. He grinned. Outside hinges. And these people found insurance?

With a padded hammer and round file he tapped at the pins, rusty but he oozed oil into the slits, one by one removed the pins, top hinge, bottom, middle. With a chisel he inched the hinge side of the doorway from the frame, the bottom, the top. Loose, but held in place on the left by a deadbolt. He drew the door to the right. The deadbolt slid from its jamb hollow. He leaned the door against the far side of the well and dropped the hinge pins into his pocket. He played his flash into a hallway, cardboard file boxes stacked on both sides.

No way was he going to look through all these boxes for Sandro's file. Anyway, stuff down here likely wasn't current. Was Sandro still current? He searched for a small light on a box that would tell him a security system existed. He didn't see any, and walked down to a T. On the left an open space, a normal basement with piping, heaters, pumps, a washer and dryer, a freezer, two refrigerators. Three padlocked metal cabinets, floor to ceiling. Drugs? All doctors had drugs. On the wall to his side, more boxes, maybe a couple of hundred.

Left and right, a closed door. He tried the right one, it opened. He played the light around the room. Three large tables, each with a sink and cabinets underneath. Each with a computer, and lab equipment laid out and ready to use. Small high-up windows on the side where the ground sloped down. Just a small lab. He closed the door.

The left side. A fully equipped, least as far as he could tell, operating room. Beyond it, two single hospital bedrooms. Changing your sex must cost a lot.

Between the lab and hospital walls, a staircase. He climbed to a landing, and a door. He opened it. Reception area behind a desk—the secretary's, he guessed. More comfortable chairs to wait in. Ahead, the front door he'd tried from outside. Again he looked for a security device. Nope. Through the window, all lay still and silent.

A hallway to the right, another to the left, likely the doctors' offices. If he knew which doctor was Sandro's—Jones maybe, he'd been at the viewing. He tried the right hallway. A door, Dr. Lorna Albright, Gynecology. Vasily opened it. He flashed his light about. Desk, computer, printer, pictures, bookshelves, couple of file cabinets. Okay, he could come back. Next door, Dr. Richard Trevelyan, Endocrinology. His door too opened. Trusting each other, these people. Inside, the same layout. He closed the door, passed through reception and walked along the far hallway. There: Dr. Stockman Jones, Surgery. Another unlocked door. Similar set-up, except for a dozen photographs on the desk. Vasily checked them out with the flash; a woman and three kids, different ages but they all looked like the same woman and kids. No picture of Miss Sandro. Too bad. The file cabinet. Three drawers. Many files in each. But labeled with weird names, not people's names. Shit. He closed the last drawer.

Wait a minute. Maybe all four doctors dealt with Sandro. So his file would be a general file. Where? Back downstairs? He returned to the reception area. Outside the front door, on the street, lights— He dropped to the floor. A car drove by and disappeared into the dark. He flashed his light to the secretary's desk, and behind it. More file cabinets. The door to the basement divided two ranges of cabinets so he hadn't seen them coming up. And, real neat, the drawers went alphabetically. V is for Vasiliadis, right side, middle drawer. He opened it. Thompson, Truman, Underwood, Ursell. And Vasiliadis. Vasily plucked it from its folder. Thick. He opened it— Another car coming by. Not important. Still, he crouched a little. Suddenly a beam of extreme light swept the lawn to the right. Vasily's legs folded as he fell behind the desk a half second before light penetrated the glass facade and for a very long time lit the room as bright as day. If he breathed they'd see the air move. Finally the light swept the lawn to the left. Then darkness. When Vasily allowed himself to look over the top of the desk, the car had disappeared.

No big deal, local cops making their rounds. But if they'd walked around back he'd've been sunk.

He sat in the secretary's chair and looked through the file. Notes and charts. He couldn't figure out what they said. A fat envelope. He opened it. Pictures. Oh god, how gross!

Sandro. At various stages of his transformation. Same transformation as the pictures Vasily had burned, except— He supposed the word was, clinical. Sandro without clothes, not even undershorts, for crapsake. How could he let them?! Poor fuckin' asshole. They must've threatened him. Jeeeesus.

Okay, the file *would* go to Andrei. Vasily got up slowly and glanced out the front. Silence and darkness. He took the file, including the pictures downstairs, out the doorway. Door in place, deadbolt in place. Pins in hinges, a light tap and they dropped into the rounds.

No, the pictures weren't for Andrei. They'd follow the others into a fire.

Back in his car Vasily set the file and tool belt in his satchel, the pictures in his pocket and drove north at two miles above the speed limit toward Deception Pass. He crossed the bridge. He was off Whidbey Island. What a fuckin' weird place.

⁓

Dr. Lorna Albright needed no intuition to know WISDOM had a big problem. Maybe Terry would have some idea what to do. Terry understood Richard; she should, after all these years. Lorna stopped at the lab gate, got out, unlocked and drove in, parking in her space. She got out again, returned to the gate, locked it. Her legs felt tired. Her sneakers crunched across gravel to the cement pathway. Invest in a remote for the gate? She'd bring that up.

She took the building keys from her shoulder bag, shone the light at the door handle, unlocked and stepped into the foyer, closing the door. The inside motion-detecting light flooded on. And invest in outdoor detecting lights too. She deactivated the alarm.

Another key opened the right-hand side of the double doors to the lab. They should get cards for opening doors. One card for the whole building. Mental note: call a security company. She stepped inside quickly to keep bright light from interrupting the sleep cycles of the fish, no early dawn for them. She stopped as usual, and let her glance range the tanks, each with its muted night lighting. Everything looked normal.

She walked to her office, one of three. Terry worked next to her. The two technicians shared the large office across the hall. Last week she had given them all her revised research paper. She needed their reactions before she sent it back to the editor for renewed peer review.

Lorna's office had enough room for a couch. She flicked on the light and closed the door, the usual pattern even in daytime. Like the rest of the lab, her room had a window only in the door; no daylight allowed in the building, a holdover from its Navy days, essential now. She picked up a couple of newsletters, lay on the couch, tried to read. Words floated in bright light as it reflected off glossy paper. Really tired after the stress of this week.

Bendwell, delighted with WISDOM's work, had responded to last year's third-and fourth-quarter reports with compliments, enthusiasm and the promise of increased funding. WISDOM and Bendwell were on the way to bringing non-surgical reconstruction onto the list of procedures available worldwide, and the hipop and percuprone patents had been applied for. Their own wealth and the well-being of others would grow from past successes, but the excitement of this research was fading; time to move on.

There was also something sadly sexist about the clinic helping to transform men only. Dr. Albright had a plan. Around mid-year, in the quiet days of summer, she would recommend they expand into protogynist transgendering. Research in protogyny was the way to go. Bendwell would provide the funding to help women become men.

Between tonight and then, however, a cauldron of stress was burbling away. Would Richard still want to go to the police on Monday? That'd be a busy day for him, what with his evening consult at the hospice. Had they convinced him yesterday? An investigation of the clinic would tie them up in red tape and they'd lose valuable time. More dangerously, details of their work could leak out, maybe get picked up by one of the several other labs engaged in similar research. WISDOM didn't need that. She closed her eyes. After a while she heard movement at her shoulder and the whisper of her name. She opened her eyes. Terry.

"Hi." She sat up.

"Hi," said Terry. "Thanks for coming."

"What's up with Richard?" Lorna pointed to her desk chair. "Have a seat."

Terry did. "Still wants to speak with the police. He was talking about going this evening. I think I convinced him to wait, at least."

Lorna leaned toward her. "We haven't discussed this, but how are you feeling? Sandro's death, Richard's guilt—it must be hard on you, too."

Terry sighed. "Poor Sandro. I never met him, but I think I know him. All he wanted—and it went awry."

Lorna waited.

"And Richard. I feel for him. He's been so close to those men, and so pleased with the women they've become, so proud of WISDOM's work. I understand why he thinks he has to do something." She shrugged. "But going to the police makes no sense at all."

Lorna nodded. "You sure he's home?"

Terry nodded.

"He didn't leave after you went out?"

"I don't think so. But I don't know."

Lorna pointed to the phone. "You want to call him? See if he's there?"

Terry stared at Lorna, then went to the phone. She spoke for a couple of minutes, then hung up. "He's watching tennis on TV."

"So he's okay."

"I'm not sure. He's taking the boat out Sunday. To get some air, and think."

"He'll calm himself down."

"I don't know who Richard means by 'the police'? The sheriff?"

Lorna shrugged. Good question.

"You know the sheriff?"

"No."

"He hunts with a friend of ours who says the sheriff's a good shot, but slow upstairs." Terry leaned forward. "Maybe, if Richard talked to him, he could vent, and be okay."

Lorna considered this. Slowly she shook her head. "Still not a good idea."

"Nothing might come of it. Richard could explain how bad he felt and the sheriff could do something official and that'd be it. He doesn't want a mess. Our friend says the sheriff finds his job difficult enough."

Lorna stayed silent, reflecting.

"He's so upset."

"For god's sake, I know he's upset! We're all upset. Just get him to sit tight."

"I said that to him yesterday, 'Wait a little.' And he turned on me, he said, 'We should have waited earlier. Now it's too late.'"

Lorna sighed. "You wanted to wait, too."

Terry shrugged.

Lorna placed her hand on Terry's arm. "If you can rein him in till Monday . . ."

Terry looked at Lorna's hand. Lorna removed it. "I'll try," Terry said. "I'm going home."

"I'll read some." Lorna nodded at her desk.

Terry walked to the door. "See you Monday."

Lorna forced herself to smile. "I hope not before." Damn!

"Definitely worth a two-block dash," Noel conceded.

"Four blocks," corrected Kyra. "We have to go back to the Inn." She was replete with Seafood Wellington—scallops, shrimp, morsels of salmon in a phenomenal sauce, hint of tarragon?—encased in melt-in-her-mouth pastry. All accompanied by plain rice and a green salad, balsamic vinaigrette.

Noel picked at a few last tidbits of salmon steak, baked potato and first of the season asparagus. They'd shared a bottle of a smooth Washington State Sauvignon Blanc. Samson's was indeed best appreciated by eating on the premises.

Kyra asked, "Do you know anything about guns?"

"No, do you?"

"No. And no desire to learn."

"Okay, we stay away from cases involving guns."

"How do we know what a case involves before we're on it?"

"Yeah." Noel looked around for the server. Three minutes later he'd paid the bill and filed the receipt in his wallet.

Kyra put on her Gore-Tex and they dashed the two blocks through the rain. Back and dry, she asked, "Do you think Sandro was a threat to anyone?"

"Don't know enough to think." Noel flicked on the gas fire. Then he sat down and opened his laptop. "First fact: Likely Sandro confided in only three people that he was becoming a woman, Ursula, Brady, Cora. Not Rudy or Garth or any of his family."

"Women, not men. Less threatening, more sympathetic."

"The Greek enforcer figured, wrongly, that Sandro had told Rudy."

"Right. Three who signed the guest book get told to keep quiet or else."

"Why only three?"

"Maybe he overlooked the doc. Could he know Brady and Ursula were a unit?"

Noel typed.

Kyra got up and paced. There wasn't much room. "Early March. A rain forest. Walking to the blockhouse, his shoes stay clean?"

"He didn't fly."

"Carried."

"By whom?"

"Someone he knew. Someone he didn't know."

"He parked away from the door. No mud tracks."

"Oh, I nearly forgot. Those women Sandro corresponded with on e-mail? One lives in Seattle and she's got a website. Chelsea. I set up a meeting time with her."

"Who's Chelsea?"

"Someone with a soothing voice."

"When?"

"Tomorrow at eleven."

"No, when did you make it?"

"At Sandro's. When you were in the bathroom."

"When I went back to get the name of the medicine in the cabinet. The liquid one."

"I don't remember—"

"Hipoperc. No pharmacy or physician mentioned on the label."

"Oh." Noel typed.

"Hey, maybe Jerome can figure the medicine out. What did this Chelsea's site tell you?"

"She has a women's boutique."

"Is she transgendered?"

"No idea."

"What's her market?"

"Probably anybody who wants to buy. Whatever she is sexually, on her website she looks like a capitalist."

Kyra thought about that. "What else did you find out?"

"The site's also meant for people who're thinking about or are in the process of or have already been transgendered. A chat group, questions and advice."

"Like?"

"I didn't have a lot of time to look through."

"How many people is she dealing with?"

"I'm not sure. Some could be the same people writing under different names."

"What kind of questions?"

"Lots of stuff about dating and sex. Other than that, anything from the early scary—'I feel like I'm a woman inside but I'm not sure and do I have to be castrated to find out if I was right and for god's sake what if I was wrong?' From that to someone who'd already become a woman, should she wear padded bras or get breast implants or find one of those bras that just pushed a lot of fatty flesh around so it looked like she was small chested but still had her own tits."

"God." A small shudder from Kyra. "You learned a lot in a short time. Freaks me out."

"It doesn't take long." Yeah, it'd be best for him to meet Chelsea alone without Kyra. He turned back to his computer notes.

Kyra shifted ground. "No underwear." She fiddled with a curl of hair, stretched it out, let it snap back. "Bloated testes. Wouldn't he want more support than from sweatpants?"

"Maybe he liked roominess."

"On another subject. Remember in the Gabriola case? How it's hard to distinguish between opiates without certain tests. When we hear from the coroner we have to find out if it was heroin for sure. Opium or, say, morphine. They'd each mean something different."

Noel listed the clothes Sandro's body was dressed in; lack of mud on shoes; returning photo album; syringes, no dope; Chelsea and her address; hungry cats.

Kyra fished out her cellphone. "Chelsea at eleven? I'll try to see Vasiliadis after that."

"No. Try for the same time. You'll be better one on one with him."

She squinted at him. What about their working together preference? Did he want to meet Chelsea by himself?

Noel added Rudy's, Cora's and Ursula's being threatened to his list.

Kyra dialed, waited, asked for him, got him. "Mr. Vasiliadis? This is Kyra Rachel . . . Yes, that's right, the detective you tried to intimidate . . . I know, I know, but I'd like to meet with you tomorrow morning around eleven . . . Yes, about Sandro . . . I'll tell you when I get there . . . Eleven-thirty is fine . . . I have your address." She broke the connection.

"Let's leave the accident-suicide theories for a minute." She dropped the phone into her purse. "Could someone in Sandro's family have felt threatened enough to kill him?"

Noel raised both eyebrows. "You could ask Uncle Andrei."

Lorna's mind refused to concentrate on anything other than Terry at home, with Richard maybe getting ready for a guilt-ridden talk with Sheriff Burt Vanderhoek. All Lorna knew about the sheriff was he kept getting re-elected. He might not be entirely stupid.

Call Stockman, tell him about her chat. He'd been as concerned over Sandro, and then for Richard, as the rest of them. No, Stockman had a right to a quiet evening. Still, Lorna had to talk with someone. At eight she decided, and called. Answering service. She started to leave a message, then didn't.

Call Gary? He'd gone mercurial over the last week, his mood swings needing a shrink of their own. If she caught him on a high he'd talk her ear off. She tried to read some more. No good. She called Stockman again. Still no one home.

Okay. Gary. Probably wasn't there either. He picked up after three rings. "Gary? It's Lorna."

"Oh. Hi."

"Didn't expect you to be home."

"Might go out soon. What's up?"

Nine-fifteen. Her colleague the swinger. "Look, I just had a heart-to-heart with Terry. She's very upset about Richard."

"Still wants to talk to the cops?"

"She's convinced him to take his boat out Sunday and think it all through."

"Yeah. Good."

No high for Gary tonight, rarely so monosyllabic. "She thinks if Richard goes and spills his beans to our local guy, the sheriff, nothing'll come of it. She hears the sheriff's none too bright."

"No. No good."

"Might cauterize Richard's sense of being wounded."

"I don't like it."

Lorna waited. Silence. "Any other really superior ideas?"

More silence. At last he said, "I'll try to think of something."

Talking to Gary was worse than talking to no one. "Okay, think of something."

"I will." Silence for maybe fifteen seconds. "See you." The line went dead.

Lorna set the phone down too. Time to go home. She'd take a sleeping pill.

FIFTEEN

YES, RICHARD HAD promised Terry, if he did any diving he'd be careful. It was still dark as he carried fins, mask and wetsuit below deck. *Panacea*, a 28-foot Carver Riviera, had gone into the water only two weeks ago, a warm, sunny February weekend. She was running sweetly—after a $1780 tune-up. Then for five days it rained, then all that business with Sandro, and Richard hadn't been out since. Raining again now. Tomorrow better be a great day. Damn Sandro.

When Richard and Terry had first come to Seattle, a colleague at the hospital and her husband took them out onto the Sound overnight. Richard became an instant motor-yacht person. He bought a used six-year-old Bayliner Ciera and turned himself into a nautical mechanic. But sailing out of Seattle every time he wanted to be on the water was a drag; too far from solitude. So he docked the Ciera at Coupeville's marina and they drove out most Friday afternoons. Then to overcome the miserable traffic on the I-5 he and Terry both managed to change their schedules to work weekends and be off a couple of days mid-week. Still not good enough. They needed a house on Whidbey itself. It was while they were buying the place that Stockman Jones approached him. Dr. Jones and his colleagues, Dr. Albright and Dr. Haines, were impressed with his work. Would Dr. Trevelyan consider preliminary discussions about coming in to WISDOM as a full partner? Their previous endocrinologist had taken a position in Kansas City. Richard and Terry discussed this. He explained to Stockman and the others that, seeing himself nearly into his sixth decade, he was giving more of his life over to enjoying as many non-professional days as possible—his house on the island, his boat, the open water. No problem, they responded, anything could be worked around.

So Richard joined WISDOM. It took less than a year for him to convince the others that their work would fare better on Whidbey Island: cheaper, larger properties, lower wages for staff, and with the clinic's reputation the clientele would flock to it. And Gary needed to get out of Seattle for his own reasons. Lorna realized she'd get about six times as much research space. Bonnie, Stockman's wife, took a little convincing, but on seeing the possibilities for revamping pieces of the island's Victorian architecture, she was won over. WISDOM came to Whidbey.

It had been good from the start. The four of them made a true team, an organism working towards a single end. Though in the last few days he'd felt less part of the team.

Panacea had arrived in Richard and Terry's life the same month as the relocation of the clinic. No children or pets so they came to love the boat as their baby, joking that if they'd brought up three kids, their college educations would have cost less than what they poured into the boat.

Richard glanced at his watch. 8:24. A grim gray morning, damn misty rain. The detective had six minutes to get here.

<hr />

Kyra followed Dr. Trevelyan's directions to wharf #4, halfway down on the right. Crazy place to meet a doctor, in the rain. Why not over breakfast, talk while sipping hot coffee? She pulled her anorak high. Noel did the same. They marched down the wharf to a building at the end; a large sign promoted a huge shark skeleton inside. She turned left to the floating wooden branch wharves and counted because they weren't numbered. Dark and slippery. She shivered. At four she turned right. Halfway along, a man in jeans and weatherproof jacket stood on the rear deck of a solid-looking power boat. Yes, *Panacea*, printed across the boat's stern, and she recognized the man from yesterday. "Dr. Trevelyan. Kyra Rachel, and my partner Noel Franklin. Did I say that we are Islands Investigations International?"

"Yes, you did."

He hadn't invited them onto the boat. "I'd like to talk with you about Sandro Vasiliadis."

"Yes, you mentioned that."

"Dr. Trevelyan, you saw him before he died. Possibly you were the last person to see him alive."

"I saw him at four o'clock."

"What was he wearing?" Kyra was asking the questions, Noel noted down the answers.

"A skirt and blouse, pantyhose." He paused. "I couldn't tell you the color."

"And he was upset?"

"Yes."

"About?"

"His condition."

"The state of his testes?"

Richard squinted at her. "What do you mean?"

Oh, he knew exactly what she meant. "Who might have supplied Sandro with the heroin that killed him?"

"I have no idea. None."

Man standing on boat. Detectives standing on wharf. Oddly divided. She could barely see Trevalyn through the misty rain. "He was your patient."

"He was, actually, the clinic's patient."

"Can you tell me what kind of drugs was he taking?"

"I'm sorry, Ms. Rachel, I'm afraid that information is confidential."

Noel glanced at his notebook, protecting the page from the wet. "Was he taking beta-GD and Percocet? Prescribed by you?"

Trevelyan scowled. A few drops of rain cascaded from his forehead down his nose. "How did you find that out? Have you been sneaking into his private life?"

"That information would be privileged, too." Then Noel smiled. "But you could help us by explaining what those drugs do."

"Also, he had one other drug, hipoperc, a liquid, no prescribing name, no dispensing information. Where did that come from?" Kyra punched. "And what is it?"

Richard sighed. "The poor man—"

"The drugs, Dr. Trevelyan?"

"Beta-GD is an artificial version of a hormone that occurs naturally in the human body. Percocet is a powerful pain reliever."

"Sandro was in pain, then?"

"I've said so. At least the day he died." He looked pointedly at his watch.

"Do you believe it was an accident?" Noel asked. "Or that he killed himself? Or—"

"I'm assuming suicide. But it doesn't matter, he's dead."

"And the other drug—" Noel glanced again at his notebook, "hipoperc? The liquid Ms. Rachel has mentioned?"

Trevelyan squinted, then blinked a few times. "I don't know what that is."

"Are you sure?"

"Is my name on the label?"

"No. But we found it with the other bottles. As my associate said" —clear the man was hiding something—"no prescribing or dispensing information. Just the word *hipoperc*."

"Probably some over the counter acetylsalicylic acid variant. People should throw those things away."

"But you did prescribe the others."

Trevelyan stared down at the deck. "I've spoken enough about Sandro. He's dead. Leave him his privacy." He stepped through the wheelhouse down into a below-deck galley.

"Thanks for your time," Kyra called.

<hr>

Four minutes later Richard glanced out. They were gone. Damn! Hipoperc just lying around at Sandro's house. How did she know? Damn!

Maybe it really was time to go to the cops. The State Patrol. Terry said she doubted the suicide was important enough for anyone outside Coupeville to care.

These detectives cared. And how did they find out about Sandro's swollen testes?

<hr>

As the Tracker drove down Route 525 from Coupeville to the Mukilteo ferry, the sky cleared. Whidbey looked very much like southern Vancouver Island, Noel thought. A rain-washed spring-harbinger morning on the West Coast—or the Pacific Northwest, depending on which country you were in—glimmered with the sparkle of innocence. Each tree branch stood in sharp outline against a near-touchable blue sky, fences glowed an unmarred white, and a pasture presented a knee-high wealth of green to a small herd of Herefords. Too often Noel took his environs for granted, but this morning he recalled the trip he and Brendan had made about this time of year to Montreal and Boston: slippery frozen slush in Canada, melting slush and the smell of a winter's worth of dogshit decongealing in the US. He said little, the occasional small smile on Kyra's lips telling him, as that deer scurried into the woods, or a few minutes ago an eagle swooped across a clover-thick field, that she too was taking a mental respite from the case. Even if she did drive too fast.

Their interview with Dr. Richard Trevelyan had been so brief they made it to the southern end of the island and the nine-thirty ferry with six minutes to spare. Speeding down, they had only one conversation:

Kyra said, "Sandro changed clothes between Trevelyan and dying. Why?"

"We've been thinking he'd want support for his genitals. Maybe he didn't want any contact and the sweats were roomier."

"Than a skirt?"

Noel said, "That guy was lying. Or at least hiding something."

"Yeah."

On the ferry they spoke little: Want to get out, stand up front? Why not? Great morning. Yep. Noel used the men's room then got caught up in the ferry's bulletin board: by actual count, sixteen advertised concerts scheduled on Whidbey in the next week; house for sale, not cheap; transport needed for a hundred chickens from Coupeville to Orcas Island; two dozen young goats for sale; land clearing, firewood for sale, chimney sweeping.

Kyra and Noel agreed to meet at the Pike Place Market entry around one. "If it's going to be much later, I'll call. Or you can call me."

They drove up the hill from the Mukilteo dock. Kyra brought them back to Sandro. "What'll you say to this Chelsea?"

A woman possibly transgendered from a man. For a moment Noel wished Kyra were talking to her instead of him. "See what she knows about Sandro. Follow up on what she says."

"What did she sound like?"

"Like a man or like a woman?"

"Yeah, or whatever else."

He thought, then shrugged. "Actually, I couldn't tell."

"Hmm." She passed a truck weighed down with rebar.

"I gave you the gist of her site last night. You want the agonizing or the titillating stuff, you can get on-line yourself."

Kyra shot him a sharp glance, more concerned than angry.

"You okay?"

"Course I'm okay."

She hesitated. "Are you?"

"Yeah. Just fine. Nothing like a case of possible murder to make me feel great." And he'd handle this chat with Chelsea in his usual professional manner. It was only, he had to admit, that the idea of someone wanting to be transgendered reduced his sense of himself. Nothing, at least nothing sexual, had thrown him so much since he'd gone through the process of coming out. But this Sandro business was just another case of dealing with people who weren't like him, right? Just as most people weren't, right? No big thing, right? "Yeah, basically okay. But it's still *terra incognita* to me."

"Me too."

They left the I-5 near the city center, passed Pike Place Market, turned a couple of corners. Noel saw the street. "There." Kyra stopped in front of an understated fashion boutique, though a little too naked steel and glass for Noel's taste. In the window, four attractive dresses.

Kyra considered them. "I could wear that black and white one, no problem."

Noel checked his watch. "Twenty minutes early."

"Oh well. Poke around."

"Yeah." He got out, waved Kyra goodbye, and faced the boutique. The sign above the window read, in simple caps, CHELSEA. Beneath, modestly, it said: Seattle Portland San Francisco. He opened the door and went in.

A thin, tall young woman with long dark hair greeted him. "Hi there." She smiled.

"Hello," Noel answered quickly enough. But it took him a second to realize the pleasant baritone came from the red-dressed woman.

"I'm Charly. Can I help you?" The smile remained, muted red lips forming a narrow mouth. The face was pleasant, brow and ears mostly hidden under the rich hair, a thin nose, brown eyes with a hint of shadow, narrow chin.

From the way she said Charly, Noel could tell the name had a deleted *e*. "I have an appointment with Chelsea." Noel heard his own voice a couple of notes higher than normal. "Noel Franklin."

Charly nodded. "I'll see if she's free."

Charly turned. Transgendered. Not so much the voice, but the profile. In his research he'd learned that most men have an obvious

Adam's apple, most women don't. Sometimes the final step in trans-gendering is its surgical removal. Charly hadn't had this done. But from behind, Charly, skinny at first sight, walked willowy, with the cool grace of a high-fashion model.

He looked about. The boutique seemed little different from many he'd been in. Not that his experience was broad, but he'd been dragged along by women friends who wanted his opinion on clothing or shoes. The walls, eggshell beige, were draped with dresses and skirt-blouse combos. Three mannequins faced the entryway, one wearing a smart tight white dress, one a black silk suit with white blouse, one low-cut tight purple sateen pants, bare midriff, short purple top showing a lot of cleavage. Behind the mannequins stood racks of outerwear and underwear. At the center, a square of mirrors—the boutique, multi-plying itself. It felt uncluttered, at the same time insisting: you'll find what you want, we have a little of everything, all the very best.

"Mr. Franklin."

Noel turned. A solid woman of perhaps forty faced him, Charly's antithesis, and he guessed the two images were part of the boutique's marketing. "You're Chelsea?"

"That's right. Shall we talk in my office?"

"Good."

She turned, Noel followed. For such a substantial person, she had a remarkably slender waist outlined by a narrow cord belt. She wore a three-quarter sleeve, straight, royal blue dress to just above her knees, her three-inch pumps supporting elegant legs. The cut of her hair, a glossy auburn, showed the lower half of a graceful neck, and elongated ears, each set off by one small diamond earring. Her broad shoulders reminded Noel of a picture he'd seen years ago of the young Raquel Welch in a bikini featuring Welch's back, her shoulders so powerful Noel would've been certain they belonged to a man if the caption hadn't noted that Raquel needed those shoulders to flaunt her impressive bosom.

They entered an office at the back of the boutique, Chelsea gestur-ing to a chair for Noel, closing the door, rounding the desk, sitting. "So good of you to come. And to call. To let me know. I hadn't heard."

"His friends and family are very upset." Noel realized Chelsea's eyes glittered. "Was Sandro a good friend to you as well?"

Chelsea sniffed a small laugh. "He was affable and intelligent. He knew what he was doing. He'd known he wanted to for a long time. I liked him, yes. A great deal."

"How did you meet him?" Hmm. I'm calling him *him* and so is Chelsea.

She pointed toward the computer monitor on her desk. "The miracle machine." The moving curve of Chelsea's arm displayed the delicacy of a ballerina. The low neck of her dress and the open brocade vest over it revealed the upper sides of full breasts.

Noel nodded. "It brings people together."

"Yes." Chelsea sighed. "Tell me what happened."

Noel did, watching Chelsea as he spoke. The smooth skin of her forehead, delicate high cheekbones, together with full lips, framed a narrow yet finely rounded nose. She listened, her chin resting on her folded hands. Noel couldn't tell if she had an Adam's apple. "A friend hired us to find out if the whole story has been told."

Chelsea's eyes closed slightly. "The whole story. In what way?"

Noel chose his words with care. "Our client finds it hard to believe that Sandro killed himself, either with intent or accidentally."

"Then what's left? Except murder?"

"It's what we're beginning to think."

"My god." She quivered. "Someone actually killed him? Who? Why?"

"And that's what we're trying to find out."

"Well, of course, I'll help as much as I can, but—I mean, what can I tell you?" Chelsea suddenly looked flustered.

"Tell me about Sandro's life, the part you played." Noel saw Chelsea nod, perhaps as much to compose her face as in agreement. Her hands dropped to her lap and she sat up straight, like a good pupil ready to recite. No, no Adam's apple. "Whatever you can."

"As I said, we met on the Internet. My site, have you seen it?" Noel nodded. "Then you know I use it partly to advertise new styles, and partly to reach out to women-in-progress. It's something I feel I have to do. When I was outwardly becoming the woman I was inside, over fifteen years ago, there were a few people who helped me. Not many. People who'd been in my own situation. I hoped and guessed I had a lot of sisters out there. But it was hard to find them. Those who helped were wonderful. Well, some weren't so great, but I didn't have lots of trannies to talk with, I had to take whoever I found. But with the great machine," she smiled softly, once more collected, "people of all sorts can find me from wherever their homes are. And Sandro e-mailed me."

"And that was—?"

She thought back. "About two years ago. He wanted to know from a real person what was involved in making the change. He'd read a lot, but he said he wasn't ready yet. People have to move at their own pace, you know. But I could tell from his e-mails, he was already a woman-in-progress." She smiled, curiously gentle. "That's my phrase. I think a lot of men who are nearly ready find it soothing. I wrote back. He said he found what I said helpful."

"Did he say why he wasn't ready?"

"Money, in part. It's pricey, you know. But he inherited some and he found a great team of doctors. He liked them, and they were good to him." Noel nodded. "But those hormones cost like crazy. And then the surgery, that's not cheap either."

"I guess not."

"But he would've had enough." She suddenly giggled, and stroked her cheek. "You like my nose?"

Noel half-smiled. "Very elegant." This, talking with Chelsea, wasn't that hard.

"Damn well should be. Cost me as much as the surgery down below. That doctor I couldn't stand. But she did a good job."

"Very."

Chelsea grew serious again. "But I need it. This face. In the business. And," she shrugged, "it helps to be an attractive role model."

"How do you mean?"

"To a woman-in-progress like Sandro." Chelsea looked away suddenly. "I can't believe he's dead."

"I know."

"He was so happy. So pleased with his developing breasts. And the beard he'd always hated—his skin had gone smooth and lovely." Her little laugh returned. "The first time he came here— Oh, I was saying, my having to be attractive— I have teas here four times a year. On Sundays. We cover the windows with curtains so we're very private, and we push the racks to walls. I've got folding tables down-stairs."

"Your teas are—?"

Chelsea leaned forward, her arms on the desk helping to support her breasts. "They're for the about-to-bes. To meet each other and some of the new women, and there's support for the women-in-progress. I'd invited Sandro."

"Were they men or women?" Noel asked. "I mean, were they dressed as such? I mean, are they?" Out of his depth, for sure.

Chelsea smiled and Noel thought: my lifestyle is maybe as for-eign to her as hers is to me. He relaxed a bit.

Chelsea said, "People come in male clothing or unisex stuff, but more in women's clothing. If a woman-in-progress can't wear her frills here, where can she?"

"Right."

"Back to Sandro. That night I saw a man outside wearing a plaid shirt and jeans. He came to the door but didn't open it. I wondered if he was trouble. But no, only a tranny wannabe could know when and where we meet. I opened the door and invited him in. We'd exchanged a few e-mails by then so when we introduced ourselves we had a little hug. He was so gentle, my heart went right out to him. And he'd been cursed by the face of a macho man. Such a heavy beard, terrible."

"Yes." The beard. Suddenly it was Chelsea's context that brought Sandro's mother's shock and horror home to Noel. "Go on."

"He thanked me for inviting him. And then he said almost noth-ing else. Shy. But he stayed till the end, till only Charly and I were left. We talked for a couple of hours and he told me about himself. You know, there're some communities it's easier to come out of, and some a lot harder."

"His is a conservative world."

"Is it ever. But I could see he was going to make it—" She caught herself. "But he hasn't."

"Did you see him again?"

"Oh, four or five times. Mostly we wrote, maybe once a week, maybe more at the big moments. When he came here I always gave him some small article of clothing." She fingered her vest, brocaded in purple silk and brown satin. "He liked that. Made him happy like you wouldn't believe. His own stockings, his own blouse."

"And the last time you saw him was—?"

"Maybe a month ago. He drove down from Whidbey wearing a lovely chiffon blouse and a miniskirt. I said to him, 'Sandro, just because you're nearly a woman doesn't mean you can't wear pants, it's cold out there.' He smiled, sorta like he was keeping a secret."

"What did you talk about?"

"Oh, this and that. He was telling me how his doctors were saying he was nearly ready and they had a new procedure where for some people they could avoid surgery. He wasn't sure how they'd do it but he'd end up with a real vagina and it'd get wet like it should and— Sorry, Mr. Franklin, does this kind of talk bother you?"

"Oh no, not at all." He breathed deeply. "Well, just a little."

"You looked sort of—funny."

Noel waved the bother away. "I need to hear what you're telling me."

"Well, okay. He said maybe they could change him without cutting. And I said, to reassure him, because they have to cut, right? I said, 'They always cut, just a little,' but I couldn't convince him, he defended his doctors completely. Okay, good for him. You have to, right? If you can't trust your doctors you're going to be a total psychic mess and you better believe it." She stopped and gazed at Noel. "Mr. Franklin? Would you like a glass of water?"

"No, that's fine. Please, go on." Quickly. Please.

"Sandro left saying, 'I'll be completely Sandra when you see me next.' I call them by their male names until after the operation, almost always it works okay but I'm kinda superstitious. I don't like to project the new life in that kind of absolute way until it's really there. But wouldn't it be amazing if his doctors were telling him the truth and they wouldn't have to cut?"

"Amazing." Noel spoke quietly.

"Well," said Chelsea, "can I tell you anything else?"

Noel thought. "Did you ever know Sandro to use heroin?"

"No," said Chelsea.

"Or if he ever bought heroin for anyone, or where he might have gotten it from?"

"No. He wouldn't. He had to be in control of himself. As much as possible."

"Did he have any enemies? Did anyone hate him?"

"No, not that I know of. He disliked a lot of the members of his family, a couple of cousins. But he didn't hate them. He just sort of wished they didn't exist."

"Could any of them have wished Sandro didn't exist?"

"Why?"

"Because he was a woman-in-progress?"

Chelsea blinked. "I can't imagine anybody knew. He wouldn't have told them."

"Not even his mother?"

"Especially not her. And didn't you tell me she saw his face in the coffin and said it wasn't even Sandro?"

"Right." He glanced at his watch. "I've taken a lot of your time. Thank you."

"Thank you for letting me talk about him. It makes it easier." She got up and opened the door. "I appreciate it." She led him through the boutique, touching several items as she walked.

She stopped at a velveteen jacket, one of half a dozen, brocaded it seemed to Noel by the same hand as had made her vest. "Very attractive."

"Yes. I like this work." She turned to Noel and smiled. "Before my transformation, I was an upholsterer. I appreciate textures." She resumed walking. Noel noticed a rack of woven capes. Actually, quite beautiful.

Charly smiled at Noel as he followed Chelsea to the front door. He opened it. "Good luck with your teas. They seem important."

"Yes. They are."

The last he saw of Chelsea was the attractive balanced face, and the glittering eyes.

⸻

After dropping Noel off, Kyra had battled the traffic back to the Lake Washington area. The Cascade Building was an imposing twenty-storey edifice of glass and stone. A mural of assorted forms of transportation dominated the foyer. The eighteen-wheeler in the center bore the logo *Cascade Freightways*. Beside the mural, the directory.

Cascade Freightways itself occupied the ninth to fifteenth floors, executive offices on the fourteenth.

Kyra took the elevator and stepped out into a hall, then through a doorway to a reception area. The carpet, thickly underlaid maroon Berber, accentuated forest green walls on which hung half a dozen Currier and Ives prints of hunters and horses. More transportation.

A woman at a computer behind a desk looked up from under gold eyeshadow. Kyra introduced herself. "Ah yes, Mr. Vasiliadis is expecting you." She stood, and led Kyra toward a half-open door. Kyra followed her through. "Mr. Vasiliadis, Ms. Rachel." The woman faded.

"Yes, Ms. Rachel." Andrei rose from a comfortable chair, one of two looking out across Lake Washington, blue in the morning sun.

He walked toward her, appraising her. She met his stare and assessed him back. Six feet tall, maybe played fullback at college if he'd gone to college, iron gray hair neatly cut but not styled, face handsome if you like the older Clint Eastwood look. She'd bet his nose had been broken, tight lips, and flinty, dark, appraising eyes. Shirt, no tie, cardigan, casual slacks, loafers. Kyra said, "Good of you to see me."

He smiled and took her hand. "Come and sit, Ms. Rachel. We're informal on Saturdays."

"Thank you."

"You've learned something about my unfortunate nephew's death."

"Not a great deal, Mr. Vasiliadis." She took the chair he had indicated, across from an immense black walnut desk. He stepped behind the desk and sat. Kyra smiled inwardly. He'd placed her to his advantage, light from the two floor-to-ceiling windows illuminating her while his face was in the shadow of a glowing maple wall. "My associate and I are still asking questions."

"You told me you were off the case."

"We were hired by someone else."

"Who is that?"

"I'm not at liberty to say. As I wouldn't have divulged your sister's name when she was our client." Did she, Kyra, want to keep this session pleasant? "Tell me, why is it so important that nothing about Sandro's death, or life, be mentioned? Important enough to send your young persuader to threaten people?"

"Threaten?" A quizzical smile.

"You must have a lot to cover up regarding Sandro. What else is there?"

Vasiliadis' hands grasped the heavy arms of his chair. "What do you mean by that?"

Kyra sailed on. "It's possible Sandro's death was neither accident nor suicide. It's possible he was murdered. Your persuader's threats tell me he wants silence from everyone regarding Sandro. Just like silence from Sandro himself?"

He stood, a sudden bear of a man, dark against the buffed wood wall. His voice, a hiss: "If you can't be civil, Ms. Rachel, you will leave. Now."

Kyra played her trump. "The autopsy wasn't thorough. The police were too sure Sandro died by accident or committed suicide. They didn't much care which. So the coroner conducted only a rudimentary investigation. For your sake—for your family's sake—order another autopsy. If his death wasn't suicide, you can lay him to rest in sanctified ground."

Vasiliadis walked around his desk and opened the door. "Goodbye."

Kyra got up. "Goodbye." She anchored her purse on her shoulder and strode out. She nodded at the receptionist, opened the main door and pressed for the elevator. It was waiting. The door slid closed. Had she hooked him? She let out a long, quavery, relieved breath. Thank you, Bettina, for *sanctified cemeteries*.

A new cloud cover forewarned more rain for the soggy fields. Driving back to Bellingham, Kyra and Noel filled each other in about their interviews.

Kyra considered Noel's report. "Everything Chelsea said about clothing jibes with what we know from Ursula and Brady. So why sloppy clothes when he was found?"

"Yeah. And he'd been wearing a skirt and pantyhose that afternoon, according to Trevelyan." Noel thought. "Do we know the actual time of death?" He opened his laptop and searched. "No, just evening." He searched through their facts. "What points to someone else being involved are his mudless shoes and his attire, which don't sound like anything either Sandro or Sandra would have chosen."

"And the syringes."

"Except what motive?"

"Hiding a family disgrace?"

"Strong enough?" He sounded dubious.

"Some families don't care much for sex changes."

He closed up his laptop. "I'm hungry. Stop at the next hamburger, please."

Some miles down the highway they barreled out the Mount Vernon exit and found a joint with mushroom burgers and a decent local mini-brew. In half an hour they were back on the road. Forty minutes later they pulled into the underground garage.

Upstairs, Kyra collected her personal messages first: Jerome, checking in; her father, ditto; Sarah, a jugglers' meeting; and on the business line, the Whidbey coroner, Dr. Ferrero, sounding icy, returning Triple-I's call.

"Herewith," Kyra said, looking up his number, "continueth telephone tag." But it was not so; Dr. Ferrero himself answered.

Their identities out of the way, Kyra came to the point. "We believe a more detailed autopsy of Alessandro Vasiliadis is necessary."

"Oh you do? Why?" He spoke with a 1940s Western movie accent.

"We have reason to believe Sandro was murdered." Each time she said this, her conviction grew stronger.

"Oh, you do. What reason?"

"No mud on his shoes. In the rain, in early March? Syringes found in his house, as noted by a reliable observer. Planted between Wednesday and Friday. No indication Vasiliadis was either suicidal or a user. No indication of the amount or kind of toxic substance."

"Have you talked to the State Patrol? The sheriff?"

"Yes." Do not elaborate, Kyra.

"What you are asking, Miss, is impossible."

Noel came into the office and sat on the sofa. She turned her back to him. "One other thing. The family is Greek Orthodox. A suicide cannot be buried in hallowed ground." She softened her tone. "While the family wouldn't like Sandro being a murder victim, they do not want to think he killed himself." Tone firm again. "They're talking about a court order. So. A complete pharmacological analysis. It seems he took some Demerol around four."

"You expect me, on your say-so, to rewrite a report that's already satisfied—"

Kyra held the phone from her ear and swiveled to look at Noel. He smiled and shrugged.

"—see your license revoked!" Bang!

Blessed silence. Kyra quietly placed the receiver on its console.

"Good work, partner," Noel said.

Gary Haines let himself in through WISDOM's front door at 6:45 Saturday evening. So what if someone saw him at dinnertime on a non-workday, it was his damn clinic for god's sake. If the Vasiliadis file reached the wrong people it would be devastating. Gary had to modify it right away. Stock had reported that Terry said Richard had likely given up the idea of running to the cops. Gary didn't believe that.

Gary stepped behind the reception desk to the file cabinets. He found the $T-U-V$ drawer; pulled it open. Okay, here—Thompson, Turner, Ursell, Vaccinata, Vernon— What the hell? He shoved Vaccinata away from Vernon. Had Vasiliadis slipped down? Nothing. Misfiled? He searched the whole drawer. Nothing. He searched the $R-S$ drawer. Nothing. The $W-X-Y-Z$ drawer, practically nothing in there. Certainly no Vasiliadis file. Shit!

Maybe one of his partners pulled it? He didn't like poking around their offices, but he had no choice. Lorna's first. No obvious file, not unless she'd shoved it in some cabinet or drawer. Richard's office, piles of papers, could be anywhere, or not. No actual files, just loose papers. How could Richard work without subdividing his papers? Slob. Stockman's office, easy to tell the file wasn't here. Unless he'd stuck it in some hidey-hole. But there weren't a lot of these in Stockman's tight-assed space.

Okay. Think. He walked past the reception desk, down the hall, into his own office, sat at his desk. What to do. Obvious: wait till Dawn arrived on Monday, ask her where the file was. But he couldn't be obvious. Okay. Somebody took it. Five of us who could have. Not himself. Dawn made no sense. Lorna? What for? Moved it to the lab? Not according to WISDOM policy; patient files went no further than clinic offices. So: Stockman? He wanted to wipe his hands clean of Vasiliadis? Had he taken the file to destroy it? That'd be stupid.

The thing to do was change the notations, make it look like Sandro was going through a normal Sexual Reassignment. Stockman could scribble those changes in, he'd been handling sexual surgery cases for decades. He could even fake lab reports. Except Stockman wouldn't. Not even to save the clinic? Gary wasn't sure.

Richard? He could have taken the file, it'd be just like him. To give it to the police. Richard needed tangible evidence to show the cops. If he came in shouting Vasiliadis killed himself and it was the clinic's fault, they wouldn't take him seriously. He needed proof. Vasiliadis in the process of a fucked-up transformation. Richard Trevelyan, endocrinologist, taking the blame. WISDOM taking the blame. Makes sense. Likely Richard stole the file.

SIXTEEN

KYRA BEGAN RETURNING her phone calls. Sarah, the jugglers' meeting was set for two weeks Monday. Lucas, her father felt very well—his antique shop had just sold a finely carved early nineteenth-century walnut whatnot for a hefty sum. He reported her mother Trudy was back from eight months in Turkey—Canadian Literature, a huge new interest world-wide, put professors of English from Canada in high demand. Trudy would phone when she was unpacked and settled in with Fred, her Cadillac millionaire. Kyra sighed. Her divorced parents sometimes acted like children, hard to organize.

Then Jerome. Nelson the Dog snuffled in the background. Was Kyra free for dinner?

"Just a minute." Kyra covered the mouthpiece. Noel had opened his laptop. Dinner with Jerome, away from her swirling thoughts about the case—away from Noel?—would be relaxing. She'd be able to think differently tomorrow. "Noel?"

He glanced her way.

"If I go out for dinner, will you be okay?"

He blinked.

"There's food in the freezer and leftovers from the potluck—" God, how low could she get? He was her guest. No. Her business partner. Jerome was her theoretical love interest and he'd been on hold for days. Her eyebrows questioned.

"Oh sure," said Noel. "I'll do some research. And this place does have mod cons—bathtub and TV." He smiled. "Go."

She grinned back, and uncovered the phone. "Sure, dinner. Your place or out?"

Noel watched her head for her room. In fact he'd been hoping for a quiet evening with her. Till now, realizing she'd not be here, he'd not known how strong the hope had been. Okay, she needed a little time for her personal life, away from the case. Fair enough.

Dumping Sandro's clothes in that empty lot's pile of trash had been important, every shred of evidence gone. Andrei was pleased. Well, as much as he could be. And no need to talk with Miss Brady Adam, she'd have the keep-your-mouth-shut and get-rid-of-the-detectives messages by now from her lezzie partner. He'd catch up with her later. On a more personal basis. He'd never done a lez before, least not as far as he knew. He kind of looked forward to it.

The most important thing yesterday was burning those pictures. Bad enough Andrei needed to hear the whole story, if he'd had to see Sandro's boobs too, well shit. Vasily had looked for negatives, for pictures not in the album, found nothing. Maybe Sandro himself had burned the others, only kept the ones he liked. A weird fuck, his cousin.

Andrei hadn't needed Vasily today so he'd spent most of his time with Cynthia, upstairs, downstairs, all around the town. She didn't give him a hard time when he'd announced, an hour and a half ago, that he couldn't stay till morning, he had to go to work. He showered, put on the black sweatshirt, jeans and sneakers from his shoulder case. Packed his shoes in a plastic bag and put them in the case, then folded his shirt, sweater, and slacks and dropped them in. Kissing Cynthia combined great memory and many promises. He put on his black leather jacket and drove away.

No rush getting to Whidbey, he didn't have an appointment. He smirked. He'd decided against the ferry, little chance of anybody seeing him but always best to think ahead, don't take chances. He drove five miles over the speed limit. And then he'd seen the sign, Bellingham, 46 miles. Decision made in an instant—plenty of time. The detectives lived in Bellingham.

Kyra showered and dressed. At six-thirty Jerome buzzed from downstairs. Noel was reading. She waved a kiss in his direction. He waved her goodbye without looking up from his book.

Jerome, double-parked, stood beside the passenger door. He kissed her on the cheek. "Hi."

"Hi." She pecked him on the mouth. From the appreciation in his eyes, she figured she looked okay in the gray silk pantsuit Margery had made her buy before Christmas and also her silk blue and green batik scarf her mother had brought from Indonesia two years ago.

He looked good too—dark blue hand-knit Icelandic sweater

under a short black jacket above dark trousers. Also a subtle aftershave. Or just him?

"Where are we going?" Kyra asked as she foiled his attempt to open the door for her, then wished she'd let him.

"I made reservations at Sanding's. It's not too discovered yet, even on Saturday."

"Sounds great." The car smelled of Nelson. Kyra's father, Lucas, was a long-time devotee of Nelson, the British admiral who'd defeated the French navy of Napoleon. Kyra had grown up on that Nelson's exploits and his gruesome end, killed in battle and transported home in a barrel of alcohol. The Admiral's exploits were rapidly being erased by those of Nelson the Dog.

Jerome put the car in gear and eased away.

"Why did you call Nelson Nelson?"

He looked a bit sheepish. "I had a neighbor once who was a Nelson."

"I see." She didn't, of course.

"He was loud and ignored boundaries. Like your friend Bettina at the potluck."

"Hardly my friend."

"But Nelson the neighbor was affable. He'd do anything to keep us happy. Except for what he didn't notice."

"Violating boundaries." She got it.

"Mm. So we, the other neighbors, excused a lot of his behavior. And his wife kept apologizing."

Kyra laughed. "So you're cleanup detail. Wife to Nelson."

Jerome laughed too. "Essentially."

He parked close to the restaurant, and in the silence squeezed her hand. "No Nelson tonight. He's home with his rawhide chew bone."

Kyra squeezed back.

Sanding's was decorated in maroon and green. The colors jolted Kyra. Why? Of course: Andrei Vasiliadis' office in Seattle.

Nearly full. Clever Jerome had made a reservation. And he looked quite handsome talking with the hostess, amazing that thinning hair could be so attractive. They were seated immediately. Jerome consulted with the waiter about wine. Wild coho steamed on sorrel seeds was on special, and *filet mignon au poivre*. Jerome took the first, Kyra the second. And a vodka martini to start? Why not. She sat back and basked. Nice to be taken care of.

"So. Is there a new case?"

Kyra laughed. "Same one. The day after the potluck we got hired by someone else."

"Is that usual?"

"It can happen."

"What now? With this case?"

Kyra leaned forward confidingly. "Maybe you can tell us something." She dug in her bag for the slip of paper she'd written Sandro's medications on. "You know what these are?"

He took the paper, studied it. "Percocet is a powerful painkiller, the other's a sedative, Valium derivative actually."

Kyra nodded.

"But this?" He read, "Hipoperc?" and handed the paper back. "Never heard of it. Who's it for?"

"Sorry, can't tell you. You understand." She stuffed the paper into her purse.

"On second thought, give it back. There's someone I could ask. He knows a lot of specialized stuff."

Kyra passed the paper over again. Jerome studied it, folded it, put it in his shirt pocket.

"Don't wash your shirt first thing tomorrow," Kyra said.

Noel poured himself a glass of red wine and opened the refrigerator. Familiar leftovers from the potluck. Which somehow didn't appeal. Might have if Kyra and he were eating together. No, Roquefort and bread and a little butter would do him nicely. And some pickles. And a little paté. He found a plate, a knife, sipped some wine— The downstairs entry phone buzzed. He went to the hall. "Yes?"

A deep voice said, "Is this Islands Investigations?"

"Yes."

"It's the police, sir. We'd like to speak with you."

"What it's about?"

"Sandro Vasiliadis."

"Sure. Come on up." He buzzed the door open and set the phone down. Wouldn't you know, just at dinnertime. He set himself a place at the table, put the paté back in the fridge. Wouldn't hurt the cheese to stay out. A knock on the door. He opened it. A large man in a black leather jacket stepped in, far too quickly. You didn't ask for identification, Franklin you ass—

"You're Noel Franklin?"

"May I see ID?"

"Is the dame around?"

"Your ID—"

"Shut up."

"You're not police." Oh, so astute.

"You alone?" The man shoved the door closed so it locked. He caught Noel by the shoulder and twisted him around. "Sit down."

"Get out of here." Noel pulled away, headed for the office, that phone—

The man grabbed Noel's elbow and pulled him back. "I said, sit!"

"Let go!" Noel stood motionless. Trouble trouble. The man, who looked like the guy Ursula, Cora and Rudy had described, the Vasiliadis enforcer, dropped Noel's arm. "Leave it." He stood between Noel and any phone.

"What do you want?"

"Conversation." He pinched his fingers under Noel's clavicle and guided him down the hall by his shoulder, checking Kyra's bedroom and the office. Noel couldn't breathe through the pain. Back in the living room, the man shoved Noel on to the sofa. "Sit, asshole!"

Noel sprawled, gasped, and rubbed his collarbone.

The man, a menace in black, towered over him. "Leave the Vasiliadis case alone, fucker, or you'll be looking for your balls."

Noel, gulping breaths, rubbed his shoulder. He recognized this guy: *schoolyard bully*. No teacher to tell, no other kids to help.

"Hey, you hear me?" Black Jacket, still standing over him, raised his fist.

Noel wondered if his collarbone was cracked. He drew in enough breath to speak. "You want conversation? What about?"

"Let Sandro Vasiliadis rest in peace."

Now the immense man grabbed Noel by his sweater and pulled him up. His face inches from Noel's, he said, "You're done with Sandro or you're hamburger, got it? The dame too. Got it?"

"Got it."

With his right hand the man shoved Noel away, the left rose high and the flat of his palm swooped against the side of Noel's head, dropping him to the sofa again. The man leaned over Noel. "You're done. Both of you." He faux-grinned at Noel. "I'll see myself out."

— — —

Jerome picked up his martini, reached over to Kyra's glass, and they clinked. "To you," he said.

"And to you." Their eyes met. Jerome smiled first, then Kyra.

"You didn't order the coho."

"I love salmon," she said. "And steak."

"You don't get this wonderful wild salmon in Indiana where I grew up. You ever fish for salmon?"

The way he asked, it sounded as if more was implied. She laughed lightly. "Oh yes. It was Noel who taught me how."

"Oh?"

"For years Noel's parents owned a cabin on Bowen Island. That's a short ferry ride from Vancouver."

"Yes, I was there once."

"My family took the summer place next door. And that first summer Noel took me fishing. I was ten, I'd never caught a salmon. He was eighteen and he knew where they ran."

"Good to have a knowledgeable teacher," Jerome said.

"I still remember my very first one, flopping in the bottom of the boat. Noel showed me how to club the fish, right between the eyes." She put her finger in the middle of her forehead. "So it doesn't suffer. Then back at the cabin Noel made me gut the fish. I can still hear him saying, 'Never keep more than you can use.'" She smiled in memory.

For a moment Jerome said nothing. Then: "Sounds like a powerful moment."

"It really was." Suddenly their dinners arrived, a large slab of peppercorned T-bone for Kyra, a glorious coho filet for Jerome. Plus, thought Kyra, handsome aroundments. And an assorted greens salad for two. "Salad saves us from ourselves." She felt happy. She cut into her steak. Then she realized she'd been doing all the talking.

Jerome was strangely quiet. But she continued to talk through the meal, mainly stories from the lives of the people at the potluck. He'd liked most of them, he said. Except that strange Bettina.

Meal over, he drove her to her condo. She thought: Isn't he attracted to me? She didn't want to make the first move. At her door he said, "Could we get together tomorrow? I have to paint my living room. I'd like your advice on colors."

Colors! Mellow with steak, baked potato, good wine, and he wanted to know about colors?

She opened the door. "Sure. When?"

"Oh, mid-afternoon. If it's not raining, Nelson can stay outside. And I might have the answer to your pharmacological question."

"Goodnight, and thanks for dinner." Kyra kissed Jerome lightly on the cheek. "See you tomorrow." She went in and closed the door. She didn't understand Jerome. "Hi Noel" she said quietly in case he'd gone to bed.

But she found him on the couch, his head propped against cushions, holding a bag of ice cubes to his face. "What happened to you?"

"Visit from the enforcer."

"You're kidding! How did he get in?"

"Said he was the police about Vasiliadis. I just opened the door and in he leapt."

"And he beat you up?"

"He whapped me in the face." Noel lifted the ice cubes off his cheek so she could see. The mark was inflamed and swollen, but the skin was intact. He put the ice cubes back.

"I know what'll help." From a cupboard Kyra took the single malt out of hiding, poured him three fingers and two for herself.

"That'll definitely help." He tried to smile as he took the glass. "God—" He set his fingers lightly against the right side of his face. Another lefty, he thought.

"To you," Kyra toasted. Then, "Leave your face alone."

Noel put back the ice cubes, and sipped.

"I'm sorry I wasn't here. The two of us could've handled him."

"He'd have slapped you around too."

"And he told you to stop investigating?"

"Yeah."

"Do you want to?"

"No. And I'll be damned if I let myself be bullied."

Sitting at a rear table at Archie's behind a chilly pint of beer, Burt Vanderhoek watched Spike Ferrero head toward him. Quarter past ten, Spike was fifteen minutes late. The muted light brought out the dull yellow in Spike's hair and beard, making it shine. Buckskin, Brady called the color; he saw what she meant. Brady was smart, and with it. Too damn sexy for her own good. Lucky Brady swung her own way or one day long back Burt might've started something he maybe couldn't have finished. Least not so far as Liz was concerned. He'd been with Liz twenty-three years and she was good to and for him.

Spike sat across from Burt. "Evening."

"Yep," said Burt. "How you doing, Doc?"

"Just fine."

A waitress arrived, smiled at the coroner, "The usual?"

"Yep."

She nodded and left.

Spike Ferrero scowled. "Okay, what's so important it's got you barking louder'n your bitches when you starve 'em?"

"That damn corpse."

"The one that won't go away?"

"You got any more down there?"

"Nope. Just one that maybe is maybe ain't somebody's son."

Burt squinted lightly to see if Spike was pulling his leg. Spike, who came from L.A., liked to talk local construction slang here, Burt was never sure if maybe Spike was laughing at him and his buddies. "Every corpse is somebody's son."

No, right now Spike looked serious. "That Greek corpse."

"What about it?"

The sheriff sighed. "Lemme be upfront. How much of an autopsy did you do?"

The coroner stared at the sheriff. "You too?"

"Me too what?"

"Who started this? Those detectives?"

"What you talking about?"

"Those detectives, the ones the corpse's maybe-mother hired, they wanted to know how thorough my autopsy was. Hell, I didn't have to cut the guy up to see what killed him."

Burt Vanderhoek nodded. "Right." Not for the first time, though, did he wonder if Dr. Gregory "Spike" Ferrero had come from Los Angeles to Bellingham for some reason other than the fishing and hunting. "But, see, I'm a little worried about that corpse right now. 'Cause I want it to go away too, right? But I asked one of the boys down in Seattle to have a good look at the car we found at the cemetery, and—"

"The cemetery?" Ferrero smiled at the waitress as she set down his double bourbon.

"Where that kid found the body." Burt leaned forward, to speak more quietly. "So the Seattle print guy came up and dusted the car, and you want to know something weird? Lots of Vasiliadis prints, couple of others, no idea who. But on the steering wheel, no prints at all."

"So maybe he wore driving gloves."

"Yeah. Or somebody wiped the wheel clean."

"Mmm." Ferrero nodded lightly. "Maybe."

Burt leaned further forward. "You notice anything weird about the corpse?"

"Those needle marks?"

"His balls."

"Their size?" The coroner shrugged. "I've seen 'em big."

"That big?"

The coroner shrugged again.

"Look, Spike." Burt poured beer down his throat. "I think you ought to take another look."

Ferrero thought about that. "No prints, huh?"

"Nope."

Third shrug. "Sure, I can do that."

"Thanks."

Noel lay on the opened sofa bed, unable to sleep. He felt very tired. This was a quiet place, high above the street, no windows open. No ferry back and forth, unlike his place above the Gabriola Island berth, Nanaimo side. His face ached dully, despite Scotch and painkillers.

Good thing Kyra had been out. She probably would have fought back and made things worse. He rubbed his hand over the sofa's nubbly material behind his pillows, and remembered Chelsea's enthusiasm for fabric. From upholsterer of furniture to outfitter of the transgendered. The pleasure she took in that jacket, she was almost in lust with it. She was a real shiny lady.

But how does it happen? How did she reach that point? Those who get transgendered, penis metamorphosed into vagina, how do they feel? He lay his arms on his thighs, touched his crotch. He thought of sex, with Brendan, with those few others before Brendan. What was a vagina, anyway? Foreign territory. Damn it, sometimes you weren't meant to explore the Arctic, Patagonia, Nunavut. Sometimes you were meant to stay home with what you knew.

Sandro/Sandra was unknown territory. Noel noted that his legs were tightly crossed, his balls constricted. He loosened his legs and put his hands between them, took his testes in his hand and soothed them.

Sexual identity is in the brain: he'd read this and believed. So if you felt like you were one sex but had the other's equipment, you could change the equipment. But not your brain. Or?

It's not your problem, guy. Your problem is the side of your face and your shoulder. Your problem is, how did Sandro die, and why.

It took Noel a long while to fall asleep.

A March sun poured down from a fragile blue sky and cast a little early morning warmth over Richard Trevelyan. The air smelled washed and sweet. He felt a pleasure, an ease—though he often found the light grayness of a Whidbey drizzle comfortable too.

He'd guessed he'd feel better on the boat, clearer in his thinking—though without thoughts as yet. The engine purred along so sweetly that when it missed a single tiny beat it tingled in Richard's ear. He headed south to Baby Island; less to see in the water down there, but the less included fewer other divers. He searched the water ahead. Out at ten o'clock he saw a sailboat tacking, but that was it—nearly alone on the water. He set *Panacea* on automatic pilot, got out of his clothes, didn't feel cold, and pulled the wetsuit on. It had aired overnight but still felt clammy. *Panacea* skimmed the surface. Far out from Penn Cove now, and past Snakelum Point, a nice spit of land except when Navy planes flew in low overhead. He didn't see any but for a moment caught a whiff of something like aviation fuel. Then the air was clean again.

Last night, after Terry went back to the lab, Richard had leafed through early project notes looking for forgotten insights, anything to rethink possible hypotheses for Sandro's swollen testes. All they'd done right for Marcie Johnson and Stephanie Gustafson had gone the other way with Sandro Vasiliadis. Why? He read through his gloss of Terry and Lorna's work on *Thor manning*, found in tropical sea grass meadows. These pretty little fish divided into two sub-units. Half of any given population would be true hermaphrodites, male to female. The other group were what Terry called primary males; they never changed sex. And these males had substantially enlarged genitalia; "titans" was Terry's word for them. All very interesting, except they'd gone no further with *Thor*.

Panacea sped along. The engine again missed a beat, a second later another. It caught again and purred ahead. What was going on? The winter, the engine not running for so long, something dried up in there? After a $1780 tune-up? His memory scanned more notes from their research. Other fish had massively large testes; but, Richard knew, massive is a comparative notion. In certain kinds of Tilapia the testes would comprise only a tiny percentage of body mass— say 0.2–0.3 percent. In an everyday brown trout like those he'd seen taken from Cranberry Lake the testes made up 10 percent of body mass. But WISDOM had never worked with trout either.

The smell of fuel again. But he was way south of the airfield. From the boat's engine? He glanced ahead. Flat open water. Still on automatic, he came aft, unbolted the bulkhead latch cover and glanced in. Everything looked to be running smoothly. A tiny smell of gasoline, no big deal.

He reached under the section of wetsuit covering his hair to scratch an itch. He itched in his crotch as well. The thought from before came back, shouldn't have put on the wetsuit, it wasn't time, he wasn't ready—

Was it something like that? Maybe Sandro hadn't been ready for the injections. When surgery was still their primary procedure, they could tell immediately when a patient was set to go. But they'd never considered a readiness factor other than readiness for surgery. What if the body had differing kinds of readiness for receiving the hormones? What if something in Sandro had to commit itself to an equivalent of a black hamlet head-snap? But the other two males had turned into perfect females. Had WISDOM just been lucky? Or unlucky with Sandro? They'd run hundreds of tests with the mice and the rabbits.

In the clownfish the female partner had to die before the male took over the female role and that took four days. If Sandro had waited a period of time—four days, say—before starting the dose, would the hormones have run their natural course? Simply put, maybe Sandro wasn't physiologically ready? But that made no sense, with the others there'd been no question of readiness or a lack of it. Okay, maybe the others in fact were ready? Maybe, he thought, we're the ones who aren't ready.

Damn those detectives! And damn Sandro, leaving that hipoperc lying around. Or maybe Sandro hadn't been taking his hipoperc? They'd all made it so fucking clear: Sandro, after the hipophrine and percuprone injections, you have to follow up daily with the hipoperc, you absolutely have to. Now if Richard had spoken to the detectives about that— Which was ridiculous. You don't broadcast your research till it's finished, published, patented—

Damn damn damn! He'd just proven it to himself. His partners were right! What sense going to the police now? None! Finally, the project was grander than any of them.

He smiled to *Panacea*, to the rolling sea, to the bluing sky. Worthwhile coming out by himself. Ocean and air clear the brain. He would tell them Monday. The silly idea of talking with the police had disappeared.

He sped past Race Lagoon. Nearly halfway to Baby Island. Another missed beat from the engine. He'd definitely take it back in to Stan this afternoon. He'd just passed Glenwood Beach; good. He returned to the wheel and angled forty degrees to port, crossing Holmes Harbor inlet, making direct for Rocky Point. Baby Island lay just off the coast there—

A ping from the engine, then another. But it purred on, speed steady. Check it again? If he stopped and turned it off and it wouldn't start? He'd have to anyway when he dove, plenty of time then to see if it restarted. Anyway, he could limp back to Coupeville on the outboard.

Suddenly from under the bulkhead, a crackle, a wheeze, a squeal— A flash of flame. He rushed to the wheel, snapped into neutral and turned off the engine. More flame! He grabbed the fire extinguisher, plastered the bulkhead with foam, but the flames kept coming. He had to tear it open, blast it directly! He reached for the latch, couldn't grasp it, already too hot. Then a roar, the bulkhead popped open and eight-foot flames burst through. He turned the little extinguisher on the flames and a phrase came to him, pissing against the wind. This was mad— A blast from the flames and the sides of the bulkhead were tinder, the deck was aflame! To the stern, one foot over the rail— The final move was made for him. The engine blew, its impact flinging him into the sea.

Over breakfast—despite his mashed cheek and stiff shoulder, Noel was up first and had cut cantaloupe, made toast, and scrambled eggs in honor of Sunday—he said, "Remember when I looked up WISDOM? The psychiatrist, Haines, the one who seems to have been sexually venturesome with one of his patients?"

"What about him?" Kyra's fork paused momentarily.

"If he could do that, which indicates he's operating outside the accepted moral box, what else might he do?"

Kyra wrinkled her forehead. "Say more."

"I don't know what. But I flagged it."

"I did a bit of thinking outside our box too—god, I hate that phrase. In the clear light of morning, do you want to drop the case?"

Noel smiled. It hurt to smile. "No."

Kyra nodded, and forked up some egg. "What if Sandro was exploring being a woman and let himself get picked up in a bar, say, and the guy was pissed off he had male equipment? Like Cora, except she's a she."

Noel considered. "Not likely. Our Sandro seems to have been a careful guy. And more inclined to hang out with women." He finished his eggs and spread jam on his toast. "Okay, where are we? Not likely an accident, not likely suicide. More and more we have to consider

Sandro's death a murder. The most plausible explanation, right?" He looked at her.

Kyra cut the last of her egg and piled it on her toast. "If it's murder," she murmured, "my prime suspect is Andrei. And his thug, the guy trying to obliterate every detail about Sandro."

"Makes sense."

"They have motive and, I imagine, opportunity. We better find out where they both were the night he died."

Noel looked at her across the table, stolidly munching away. "And dinner with Jerome? With all that other stuff last night, you never said."

"Fine. Though I should have been here with you."

"He might've had a gun." He smiled, through pain. "Good restaurant?"

"Nice. No dog." She wrinkled her face. "His car sure smelled. He votes Democrat."

American politics weren't Noel's department. Better they vote than not, he supposed.

"His wife voted Republican so they had equal opportunity lawn signs. And he likes jazz better than classical."

"You think this relationship is going anywhere?" Noel grabbed the coffee pot and refilled.

Kyra shrugged. "I'm seeing him this afternoon, he wants an opinion on paint colors."

The downstairs entry phone buzzed. Kyra stood and picked it up. "Yes?"

Squawk, squawk. Kyra pressed nine, put the receiver down. "State Patrol."

Noel raised an eyebrow. "Let's make sure." They both quickly cleared the table.

A few minutes and the condo doorbell rang. Both of them went to the door. "Yes?"

A muffled voice said, "State Patrol, ma'am."

"What do you want?"

"Need to talk to you about your conversation with Dr. Ferrero."

Kyra said, "Can you show us some identification, please."

"You'll have to open the door, ma'am."

Noel pointed to the floor, and planted his foot against the door. Kyra set her foot in a line with Noel's, unlatched the door and opened it an inch. A police officer's face on a plastic card appeared. Kyra glanced through the opening. One man, more or less the same face as on the plastic. She opened the door. Tall, black-haired, in green uniform. Noel noted the gun at his hip.

"Ma'am. Sir. State Patrol. Sergeant Carl Assounian." He smiled. "May I come in?"

Kyra opened the door to its full width.

He said, "I was in the Bellingham area, thought I'd pop by, ask you in person."

What accent, Kyra was wondering, Kansas, Kentucky? "Come in."

He did, following Noel to the living room. Kyra closed the door and tailed the parade.

The State Patrol officer looked at the business card in his hand. "You represent Islands Investigations International?" He was addressing Kyra.

"We are Triple-I. I'm Kyra Rachel, this is Noel Franklin."

"Private detectives."

Investigators, thought Noel.

"You talked to the coroner, Dr. Ferrero."

"Is that a crime?"

"Ma'am."

She felt reproved by his smiling aggrieved look. "Would you care to sit down?" She did.

So did Assounian. "Why do you think another autopsy is necessary?"

"Nobody believes Sandro injected himself with heroin."

"Do you have information about an alleged crime the police don't?" *Po-lice.*

She listed the reasons for their doubts, as she had done for Ferrero.

"You didn't see any syringes on Wednesday."

"Definitely not. Friday we found them behind the cat food. The bag had to come out to feed the cats both days."

The officer drew out a notebook, a pen. "Anybody beside you two there?"

Noel leaned forward, arms on his thighs. "A woman named Ursula Bunche, in the X-ray department at the Coupeville Hospital. And Brady Adam, the sheriff's secretary."

"And what was their relation to Vasiliadis?"

"Friends."

Assounian smiled. "Good friends?"

Kyra glared at Assounian. "Advisors."

"Advising on?"

Flat: "Vasiliadis was in the process of a sex change."

Assounian's face tightened and his smile faltered. "How far along was he?"

Noel could all but see the image in Assounian's mind. "He still had his male genitals."

"I see." Assounian plastered his smile back on. "And was he—"

Kyra said, "Officer, what's happened that we managed to get your attention?"

Assounian put his notebook down. "Fair enough. Vasiliadis' body contained a large amount of an opiate—heroin, possibly morphine. Enough to kill someone whose body wasn't used to such a dose, not enough to kill an addict."

"His doctor gave him Demerol at four that afternoon. Some drug interaction?"

"We don't think so."

Assounian had a small pot-belly. If he didn't smile constantly, Noel thought, he'd be presentable.

"Will Ferrero do a more thorough autopsy?" Kyra asked.

"It's happening as we speak," Assounian allowed.

On Sunday! Kyra smiled. "He'll find out about the needle tracks."

Assounian stood. "Yes. He coulda been giving blood, a course. We get a lot of druggies try to sell their blood."

"He wasn't a druggie, you just said." Kyra stood too. "Uh, does this mean you've opened an investigation into the Vasiliadis death?"

"In a manner of speaking."

"Will you let us know what you find out?"

"Will do. And anything else you learn, you let Sheriff Vanderhoek or me know."

Noel followed Assounian to the door, opened it, watched him

stride down the hall. He locked, took a sip of his coffee, made a face and headed for the microwave.

"The State Patrol investigates, so our work's done," Kyra said. "They must think it's homicide. Should we let Ursula know?"

Noel looked at his watch; ten-thirty. "Go ahead."

She dialed. Ursula answered. Kyra reported the conversation with Assounian. "The coroner's doing another autopsy. Know him? Ferrero?"

"Oh sure. He's a pathologist."

"Ursula, we think we've done all we can. We don't need to be on your payroll any more. There's a police investigation now. It looks like homicide." She explained.

"Oh god." She sighed. "Thank you. A lot." More details, goodbyes, and they hung up.

Noel sipped his again cooling coffee. "I better worry about a flight to Nanaimo." He dug out the phone book, looked up the number, phoned. Taped recording, nothing till tomorrow morning, eight o'clock. "Okay, I'm hooped. You get to put up with me for another twenty-one hours."

"Excellent." She looked at him. She thought he looked pleased at not leaving yet. Good. "I'm supposed to give Jerome an opinion on paint color. Want to come along?"

"You don't have," Noel raised his eyebrows, "sexier plans for the afternoon?"

"If we do, there's the night." She raised her brows in mockery.

"Paint color, eh?"

"You'll just love Dog Nelson."

"On reconsideration, I think I'll stay here."

Would she prefer to have Noel along? Actually, no. She had to decide about Jerome.

Noel remembered he'd promised to phone Chelsea. "If there were any developments. And now we've convinced the cops that maybe Sandro was murdered. Chelsea should know."

Kyra should rinse the breakfast dishes. Kyra should do a load of laundry, it had piled up for ages. Laundry, the lesser of two evils.

Dr. Stockman Jones said goodbye to Terry Paquette, set the phone down, and stared into the fire. It warmed the room prettily but

Stockman shivered. Normally his living room gave him comfort, its shape and height, from the moment he'd first stepped into it—and even more so after Bonnie had given the space substance and beauty. This morning, though, it felt emptied out, brooding where it should embrace, dark where he needed light.

Poor Richard. On top of everything he'd suffered for Sandro's sake. Knowing Richard, he'd likely blame himself for his boat's explosion. But how lucky to be wearing a wetsuit, hypothermia could've done him in as easily as the accident. How can a boat catch fire, just like that? Dreadful. Stockman hoped against the superstition that bad luck comes in three parts. And Terry herself didn't sound great. A dreadful situation. Her husband had nearly died. But Terry would pull herself together. Richard had loved that boat so much, he must be extremely upset. Poor Richard.

The fire crackled but Jones didn't warm up. He reached for his coffee, gone cold from neglect, and sipped. He'd better call the others. He picked up the phone again, stared at it, some strange object he might never have seen before, and pressed Lorna's code. He told her about Richard's accident. Richard wouldn't be in the clinic tomorrow, he needed to pull himself together. Yes, Tuesday they'd all meet and talk. Lorna thanked Stockman and promised to call Terry. Poor Richard. Jones set the phone down and wondered why Terry hadn't called Lorna herself.

Next he phoned Gary Haines, not expecting to catch him in but there he was at the end of the line. Jones explained again and Gary sounded aghast, horrified even—what an awful thing. Gary thanked Stockman for calling.

Stockman stared at the flames, trying but failing to banish the darkness of the brooding room. Bonnie should be back soon. He'd suggest they go out for dinner this evening, somewhere bright and cheery, nice tablecloths, shiny cutlery. Terry's tone, even beyond her news, had caught him hard. Poor Richard. Stockman breathed a small prayer: Thank You for protecting the Jones household.

PART III

SEVENTEEN

"ISLANDS INVESTIGATIONS INTERNATIONAL, **Noel Franklin**."

"Noel, this is Chelsea again."

"Hi."

"I was so broken up by your news." Her voice still sounded thick. "It's as if Sandro died a second time."

"Yes, it does throw a different—"

"To have his life just taken away. Would you and your associate be willing to go on? Find out who did this? Whatever it takes. Send me the bill."

"I don't know. The police are on the case now."

"They have lots of cases but you're on top of this one. Please, stay with it."

"Can you hold just a minute?" Noel set the phone down and left the den. He said to Kyra, "Chelsea. She wants to hire us. Find out who did Sandro in."

Kyra shrugged, then nodded. "She can afford us."

Noel put a finger to his lips and returned to the phone. "Okay Chelsea, you're on."

"Great. And can you let me know—"

Kyra came into the room, gesturing her desire to speak. "Chelsea, I'm going to let you speak to my partner."

Kyra took the phone. "Hi, this is Kyra Rachel. A question. I'm wondering what you were thinking in the few minutes between Noel's call and your phoning back."

"Two things. First, how happy Sandro was. And then, something that's been nagging at me. Is it possible to be fully transgendered without at least some surgery? Sandro said his doctors said surgery might not be needed. Except I've never heard of anything like that. It stands out like a giant question mark."

"Worth asking. We'll follow up." Goodbyes. Kyra hung up. She shouted at Noel, who was tidying her kitchen, "Think three times is the record for getting hired on the same case?"

"So far."

The washing machine beeped, cycle over. She transferred its contents to the dryer.

Noel at his laptop entered Assounian's visit and the call from Chelsea. He moved his head around, testing. "Damn. My face aches."

"You got slapped good."

"I guess." He stared at his computer screen. "Okay, what do we know?"

Kyra sat beside him on the sofa and put her feet on the hassock. "If Sandro's dead he can't become a woman. So no family shame because you can't transgender a corpse. What if Andrei sicced the thug on Sandro. Ever get his name?"

"No." Noel scowled. "Let's back up. Everything I've read says surgery is necessary in transgendering. So what if this clinic doesn't cut?"

"Or maybe that was just Sandro? Maybe he was afraid of surgery so he pretended?"

Noel keyed in the idea.

"On the other hand, he died of an overdose of opiate. The coroner's original report assumed heroin. But if it was morphine, well, most doctors have access."

Noel looked up, raising an eyebrow. Which hurt his cheek. Shit. "Yeah, pharmacologically difficult to distinguish between opiates if you're not looking specifically." He stared at Kyra. "But would someone at the clinic want to off Sandro?"

"Where do you find your language, Noel?"

He smirked.

"It's true, I can't think of a motive for them. Sandro's family is much more obvious. The uncle and the thug have a clear motive. I reiterate, what were they doing that night?"

He typed. He looked up. Kyra's dark curls were wild this morning, and her cheeks held a bright flush.

"If Sandro was murdered. Hmmm. Let's start by hypothesizing it was done by someone close to him. Which gives us a few likely possibilities—someone with the clinic, or Sandro's family, or some other recreational heroin user, or his so-called friends."

"Brady or Ursula? Cora? Rudy? I doubt it. And if Sandro was using, they'd have known about it. And I don't think he used heroin with others. Not from what we know of him so far. No, I like the doctors better. Someone messed up his balls, remember. Or the family."

"We don't know enough about the clinic. But Mrs. Vasiliadis is right here in Bellingham, we could talk to her. Let's drop by on our way to Jerome's."

"I'm not going to Jerome's. Why talk to Mrs. V.?"

"See how she's doing, be friendly." She drummed her fingers on the sofa arm. "Maybe she'll tell me the thug's name."

"Let's divide the responsibilities. You go, I'll stay here."

"I thought you liked investigating together."

"Ordinarily I do. This case just seems to be dividing us up."

Kyra stood. "What you can do is find out more about the clinic. I think you should make an appointment. Say you want to be transgendered. Use a false name."

"Are you out of your mind?" He felt himself flushing. The bruise hurt again.

"They aren't going to tell us anything as *us*. Anyway they know me. You can fake it."

They stared at each other. She had a point, but—"The one on the boat, Trevelyan, he knows me."

"It was raining, it was dark, I did most of the talking and you had your anorak hood pulled up. Anyway, see the psychiatrist or Jones. Find out what their methods are. It'll be a hell of a lot safer than the thug last night. Phone the clinic."

"It's Sunday, sweetheart," said Noel. "I'll think. One of us should."

Kyra grabbed her purse and shoes. "Call the coroner or the police, see if the autopsy's finished and what they found."

Kyra pulled up in front of Maria Vasiliadis' house. Good, she thought, no other cars parked nearby, likely Mrs. V. was alone. She got out and locked.

Mrs. V. answered the door, her questioning look intensifying when she recognized Kyra.

Kyra smiled. "Hi. I just popped by to check on how you are. Is this a convenient time?"

"I suppose." Her tone was reluctant, but she opened the door wider.

Kyra entered. "The checkup call on ex-clients is a Triple-I special service—" She dribbled off as she realized humor was inappropriate; Maria was barely a week into her grief for Sandro. They reached the living room in silence. "I mean, how are you managing?"

Maria shrugged. She seemed more in control, probably how she usually looked, gray hair, mid-fifties wrinkles, her color better and her body straighter. She was wearing black slacks and a dark gray sweater, not particularly flattering. The desk in the corner between the living and dining rooms was piled with papers, Kyra noted. "I won't stay long, I'm sure you're busy. But could I ask you a couple more questions?"

Maria sat on the sofa, gestured for Kyra to sit also. "I thought you were done."

"Ah. Sandro has—had many friends. We've been rehired." Maybe she shouldn't have come. She was blundering. "There's a possibility he didn't die by accident."

The statement sank into Maria, wide eyes of surprise, a shiver of shock. "What do you mean?"

"The police are investigating."

Maria's eyes dampened. She wiped them. "How? Who?"

"The police may come to talk to you."

"But I don't know anything."

"Just answer any questions they have."

"Will they want to know about Sandro's—the changes he wanted?"

"They may." Kyra leaned forward. "How are you—I mean, about all that?" She smiled across the space from her chair.

Maria looked to the cluttered desk. She sighed and placed her hands between her thighs. "That, a change like that, it's minor compared—compared to this. I could have learned to live with a daughter. I'd rather have him—her—here. However it was to be."

"Does your brother-in-law agree?"

"He's all uproared about Sandro changing." Her face was sad and severe. "But he wouldn't have disowned him. Eventually. I don't think." She looked up. "And I wouldn't have! He—she was my child! What are you really asking?"

Kyra held herself in against Maria's sadness. "I'm very sorry for your pain, Mrs. Vasiliadis," Kyra said. "But we wonder if anybody in your family would be so distressed at Sandro's sex change that one of them might have killed him."

Mrs. Vasiliadis sat straight, legs together, hands linked on her lap. Kyra thought of elementary school. The silence in the room grew. A car passed by. A crow cawed. A clock ticked. Mrs. Vasiliadis said, "The Family would have been extremely upset at Sandro's choice. The Man is most admired in a Greek Family. And the Family, not just here in America, but there's Family in Greece," she started to tear up again and pulled a tissue from her pocket. "They would have ostracized him, maybe forever, maybe for a few years. But no one would have hurt him. They would have accepted her. Eventually."

"Mrs. Vasiliadis. There's someone in your family, a young guy, going around threatening Sandro's friends. He even visited my partner last night. Noel's face is not great today. The man could be charged with assault."

"Oh." Maria twisted her tissue. She tightened her lips.

"What's his name?"

She lowered her eyelids and shrugged. "Family's family." She stood.

Kyra got the message. "Thank you, Mrs. Vasiliadis." She stood and bowed her head. Maria acknowledged, a small bob. Kyra showed herself out.

—

Vasily turned off the I-5 and headed east along Iowa. He shouldn't have told Andrei about smacking the detective. The detective wasn't about to go to the cops and Andrei would never have known anything. Dumb. So he had his reward—messenger boy. At least the road was dry. The sky threatened again.

It'd been months since he'd seen Aunt Maria. He liked her well enough. Once when he was about ten he'd made some remark and Aunt Maria said to him, 'We're two of a kind.' He hadn't had to ask what way, he just grinned. Aunt Maria and Uncle Kostas had thumbed their noses at the family, not much but enough to piss off Andrei and the others, by leaving Seattle, and Vasily as a kid sometimes wanted to thumb his nose at them all too.

He angled left at Yew, then right on Alabama. Now, he under-stood Andrei was right, but then, he'd loved it when Aunt Maria told him they were two of a kind. So this errand wasn't all that terrible: taking her the packet of Sandro's papers. Andrei had collected the pile, wiping the record clean, like Sandro hadn't existed. Cancel heating and electricity and phone accounts. And all the stuff Maria had to sign as next of kin. Andrei had shown Vasily one piece of paper that could've caused problems, the change of name form on the bank account from Alessandro to Alessandra, filled out, but luckily not yet mailed in.

He turned left and skirted the northern shore of Lake Whatcom, its water a reflected gray. A left, a right onto Dulcey. The car coming toward him? He jerked his head left. Same damn Tracker he'd seen at Sandro's? Same damn woman detective driving! What the hell, talking to Maria? About? Ask Maria? No, ask the detective, damn it. He screeched into a driveway two houses from Maria's, backed out, saw the detective's car turn left and disappear.

———

Kyra had noticed the gray sedan change its mind about whatever business it had on Dulcey Lane. Now it drove a steady hundred feet behind her. Following? Test it out. At St. Clair she turned left, one block, then right on Texas, right again on Michigan. The gray sedan stayed with her. Okay, confrontation time. She crossed Alabama, a long block to Connecticut and right on Yew. Yep, still back there. On to the circle at the dead-end in front of Roosevelt Elementary School. She turned three-quarters of the way around the circle, slammed on her brakes, turned off the engine. The school's roof overhang covered this part of the circle. The gray car didn't follow her around. Instead it veered left and came to a stop angled, in front of her. Shit! For the first time in her detecting life she wished she carried a pistol. Hey, she had a purseful of Mace.

Okay, Kyra, confrontation time. She grabbed the purse and jumped down from the Tracker with all the aggression she could muster. The gray car door opened more slowly, and a man stepped out, cool and in control. Hell! The black leather jacket. Okay, Kyra, blast him. She walked toward him as he approached her. "You," she said.

"Listen, lady—"

At two feet they glared into each other's faces. Afterward she couldn't explain why she didn't grab the Mace and blind the guy.

Instead her arm swung back and before Leather Jacket could think or move she'd slammed the side of his face with the weight in her purse—Mace, cellphone, wallet.

"Hey!" He threw his left arm in front of his face for protection. "What the fuck you think you're doing!"

Kyra instantly realized he wasn't about to hit her back. "That's for the one you gave my partner yesterday."

Leather Jacket stepped back. "Listen to me, okay? I tried to tell the guy something and he wouldn't listen to me so I had to get his attention, okay? So just listen."

Kyra waited. He stared at her. "What?"

"What were you doing at Maria Vasiliadis' house? What're you bothering her about?"

The man looked worried. Hmm. "I dropped by to see how she was doing."

"Bullshit." He pointed a finger at her. "You're still sneaking around about Sandro. That nurse hired you to sneak and you won't stop, no matter how much you're upsetting the family."

Kyra gave him a bleak smile. "Triple-I is not working for any nurse."

"So you're working for her yourself, on the side."

"Nope. Not for ourselves either." A raise of her eyebrows. "Okay?"

Leather Jacket stared at her. "Why not?"

"Because we finished our job for that client."

"Yeah?"

"Yeah."

And suddenly he smiled. "Good. I knew you'd be sensible. What's your name?"

Kyra squinted at him. "Kyra Rachel."

"Hello, Kyra Rachel." He touched the side of his face. "No hard feelings." He reached out his hand, his smile now rueful. "Vasily Constantinides, Sandro's cousin. Can I buy you a coffee?"

Unbelievable. "I'm late for an appointment."

"Sure. Some other time, maybe. See ya." He turned, got into his car. He backed away, drove around the circle the wrong way, doing up his seatbelt, and down Yew.

Un-effing-believable.

She watched the gray sedan turn a corner. She shivered. She had hit him. Completely without thinking. She'd slugged a man who could have murdered Sandro. Out of anger, without planning. Stupid. Then she thought: but the Mace worked fine. In its way.

She reached the Tracker. She sat behind the wheel, closed the door. Turned on the engine. Pushed the heater to high. Truly stupid.

And if he'd been carrying a gun? Or if she had?

Noel, alone in the silence of Kyra's condo, paced. Friday's rain had washed in sunny early spring. When he paced past the windows he could see sunlight highlighting daffodils, magnolias and flowering cherries. He'd go for a walk, he thought. Later.

Okay, Kyra's theory. Maybe a family member had killed Sandro. And then there was Chelsea's surgery/no surgery question: what's that about? Maybe they had to talk with WISDOM.

Back in the den he looked up the coroner's number and dialed. An answering machine. He informed it who he was and asked if the autopsy had been completed. He pulled out the State Patrol's card and dialed that number. Another answering machine. Well, it was Sunday. He left the same message.

Maybe the coroner hadn't answered his phone because he was just finishing the autopsy. If Noel were there, he could get the report in person. But do autopsies get done on Sundays? Only one way to find out. A rental car. He dialed.

Andrei entered his study with the envelope he'd received from Vasily and locked the door behind him. He put another log on the fire, sat at his desk, took a file from the envelope, promised himself to be as open-minded as he could, and began to read.

After a half hour, no use going on. He understood well enough what they had done to Sandro. What Sandro had let them do. Andrei felt sick in his gut, and sick in his soul. God had given Sandro a human body, and Sandro together with these so-called doctors had mangled it. And then he'd taken his life. All that nonsense from the woman detective, that he might have been murdered. Sandro had killed himself, simple as that. So in all God's decency he couldn't ask that Sandro be buried in holy ground. But what would he tell Maria?

One act he needed to commit, and now. Sheet by sheet he fed the file to the flames.

———

This was a good idea, Noel said to himself after he'd dropped off the car rental guy and got the feel of the Neon gripping the pavement. When he was a child, his family had gone for Sunday drives, Dad at the wheel, Mum beside, he and Seth in back punching each other. The first car he remembered was a blue '58 Rambler, no seatbelts, no air bags, just car. Seth tickled him, tickled him, tickled him. He punched Seth, made his nose bleed, their mother shouting, 'Stop the car! Out, you two! Walk home!' They had, over a mile. Had he been about five, Seth nine? The last blocks, Seth had held his hand. Noel thought now, good for Mum, we must have been pests. For sure, Seth was. I was an angel. He smiled. We behaved in the car after that. More or less.

The bridge over Deception Pass. No ferry here. Whidbey, anchored to the rest of the state by this bridge, a spiderline between the chasmed precipices of the mainland where most people lived, a bridge hanging over churning whirlpools below. How had they built the bridge, with cables guiding the girders across? He drove on, ten miles per hour under the speed limit, gazing at the railings, his rental the only vehicle in sight.

He drove around Coupeville, the section between the WISDOM clinic and the town, to give himself a better sense of how one lives here. Some fine nineteenth-century captain's houses complete with widow-walks, a couple in rough shape, some well preserved. He slowed in front of an exceptional one, well back from the road and up a slope, all a warm orange, the windows trimmed in maroon and white. Someone had done a good job.

He drove back up the hill and stopped in front of the WISDOM clinic, a squat building surrounded by the requisite daffodils just about to bloom, some blue flowers and the omnipresent dusty junipers planted to hide the foundation.

The door. Locked, of course. Sunday, of course. Tomorrow he'd phone for an appointment, present himself as a potential trans. Use a pseudonym. Yes, Kyra's idea had logic. But he didn't like it.

He was hungry. That restaurant by the water, did it serve lunch?

EIGHTEEN

NOEL SAT IN his car and poked at numbers on his cell. Once more, answering machines for the sheriff, coroner and morgue. He drove to the hospital, parked, walked in and down the stairs. At the morgue he tried the door. Locked. What else to expect. He took the highway north, crossed the Deception Pass bridge, on to Bellingham. In Kyra's kitchen he checked the freezer, found a chicken chow mein— good, but later—and sat down with the TV guide. In an hour *The Thirty-nine Steps* would be on one of the obscure channels. That'd do just fine.

Question: What's dumber than leading a possible murderer and partner-basher down a dead-end street, then getting out of your car and confronting him without benefit of weapon other than a can of Mace that you don't even use?

Answer: Smacking him across the face with a purse and pissing him off and letting him think you were off the case even though you'd only bent the truth a little, but he'd misinterpret and figure you for a liar and come back and get you good, that's what.

So when she arrived at Jerome's at two-thirty, still shaken, Kyra made herself park half a block away, sit still for five full minutes, get out and walk ten houses in the wrong direction.

She had slammed the guy. He threw up his arm to protect himself. Well, that was normal. He had slammed Noel. Right side of Noel's face. With his left hand. Noel said the guy was a lefty. Like Sandro. She headed back to the car, sat down, needed to run her experiment, already knew what she'd learn. From her purse she took a pen. If a pen were a syringe— She held the pen between the index and middle finger of her right hand and brought the point to the inside of her left elbow. She pressed the top with her thumb and let the pen slide between her fingers. Okay, that worked. She shifted the pen to her left hand, and repeated the gesture. Well, she could do it, she supposed, but being a righty she had far greater control with her right hand. Would a lefty use his right hand to inject himself in his dominant arm? Not likely.

She drove forward and pulled over to the curb. Her Tracker was the sole car on the street so Jerome would have thought it weird her parking so far away.

Jerome's home, a two-storey yellow-shingled house built in the thirties, was the largest on this side of the street. She rang the bell and heard Nelson pounding to the door, his bark preceding. What did Jerome see in that animal? Just because it had been Bev's, given her by their son when she first got sick. Kyra understood why Jerome needed to keep it. But.

Jerome and Nelson opened the door, the man by turning the handle and the dog by forcing nose, then body, through the opening. Nelson glanced up and barked again. "Nelson! Quiet!" Remarkably, the barking stopped. To Kyra, Jerome said, "Sorry. Hello." He grabbed Nelson's collar, pulled him back from the door, and opened. "Come in."

"Hi." Kyra stepped into the hall. She had known one thing about the house before arriving: that Jerome had moved here five months ago because he couldn't continue to live in the house Bev had died in. And knew, as soon as she glanced to the living room, it needed lots of work. A solid stairwell and handsome banister led to the next floor, though the dull yellow was all wrong. Seemed like good bones, but shabby. Walls and wainscoting painted and rechipped too many times, ceilings graying, carpet worn. Painting wouldn't help till Jerome stripped the woodwork and tore up the carpeting. Right, a new carpet for Nelson.

"Your coat?"

Coat off, hung up. He led the way to the living room. The furniture was okay—large chair in a dark floral pattern with matching sofa, leather-teak lounger from the sixties with its own footstool, dark green leatherette armchair. Nelson, quarter German shepherd, quarter English setter, the other half a symphony of the streets, stood between her and Jerome and glared at her.

"Do sit down."

Kyra did, on the leatherette chair. "Comfortable."

"Thanks." He studied her face. "But you're not sure about the house, are you?"

"What do you mean?" Was she that transparent?

"It needs work, I know that." He smiled, a weariness around his eyes. "But when I think of what lies ahead—"

If he thinks painting isn't what it needs, why am I here? Hmm.

As if in answer, Nelson growled at her.

"Nelson! Stop it!"

Nelson barked twice.

"Okay, that's it." Jerome pulled Nelson toward the kitchen. A door opened, closed. Jerome came back. "I don't know what gets into him sometimes."

A mixture of German and English blood had gotten into Nelson, that's what. Forever warring in his veins. "So. Paint colors? Or larger changeover?"

"What do you think?"

Kyra stood, ran her hand along a door frame, rubbed her shoe over some badly worn carpet. "The place has great potential." Except it was closing in on her. "But it's going to cost. Hey! Maybe you'll win the lottery." The sense of reduced space shifted to sudden claustrophobia. "Why don't we head out and buy you a ticket. There's a bit of sun. We'll go for a walk."

"Nelson would like that." Jerome opened the kitchen door and the dog barreled in. He skidded to a stop when he saw Kyra was still there, and barked. "Nelson, stop!"

Why had she suggested this?

Nelson tugged Jerome along. Kyra walked fast, with some running steps, to keep up. At a corner store Kyra bought a lottery ticket while Jerome, outside, tried to prevent Nelson from tangling his leash around the lamp pole. Yes, she'd come here wondering about sex but felt very little draw from Jerome. She'd not had sex in months. You're being careful, right?

They walked back. They passed a small lounge. "Would you like a coffee? Some tea?"

"What about Nelson?"

"Oh. Right." He brightened. "We can have something at my place."

How could he forget about the dog? His arm must be practically out of its socket.

In the house, Nelson trotted into the living room and came back with a green tennis ball, which he dropped in front of Jerome, giving

Kyra an excellent view of his backside.

"No, Nelson." And to Kyra, "What can I offer? Coffee, tea? I have several." He smiled.

She needed more than tea. "How about a vodka martini?" She returned the smile.

From the kitchen she heard the rattle of ice cubes. Jerome returned, a tray, a shaker, two glasses, two toothpicked olives. Nelson with ball padded behind. Jerome poured, added olives. "Cheers."

They sat on the couch and sipped, looking at each other. A new charged energy between them. Let's see what happens.

He put his glass down. So did she. He put his hand on her upper arm. "Kyra." He bent to kiss her. She closed her eyes. Searching lips, mouths open, tongues flicked—

A growl, a flash of pain in her calf. "Yow!" She pulled away and opened her eyes. Nelson barked, ready to strike again. She kicked out at him. He flattened his ears.

Jerome grabbed his collar and dragged him to the door. "Out! Bad!" He returned. "He's never done that before. I'll take you to Emergency."

"No." She hiked her pant leg up. "Just get some antiseptic, please." She stanched the blood with a tissue. Jerome came back with a wad of cotton batten and a brown bottle. He knelt by her leg but she took the bottle from him. "His rabies shots are up-to-date?"

"Yes. I'm sorry—"

"So much trouble getting family approval." Dog as family, hmmm. The bite was shallow but she saw two distinct tooth-holes.

"I think we should go to Emergency."

"Dogs' mouths have fewer bacteria than humans'. It's not serious." Better to take the dog to be put down than take me to Emergency. "If you have a couple of Band-Aids?"

He returned with them. She pasted herself together, lowered her pant leg, picked up her martini glass and leaned back. The earlier mood had traveled far away.

Jerome sat on his sofa. "I'm sorry."

"Have you considered doggy boarding school?"

"He flunked obedience class."

"Forget it." Kyra's leg throbbed. She raised her glass. "Cheers, again."

Noel let the phone ring. If it was Kyra, he'd hear her voice and pick up. He waited.

"Hi beautiful, it's me, your one-time beloved. I was thinking, maybe we could have supper, just talk. We don't have to be completely apart, right? Call me, okay?"

Definitely not Kyra.

Kyra unlocked her front door and paused in the doorway. Noel was watching a grainy black and white movie. The sound was appalling.

"Hi." Noel clicked the remote and the TV went blank.

"You can watch."

"I know how it comes out. Have you eaten?"

"No."

Noel picked up his empty glass and raised an inquiring eyebrow. "Vodka tonic?"

"Sure." She hung up her jacket, slipped off her shoes and flopped onto the sofa.

Noel poured them both vodka tonics. "There's a message for you. Your private line."

Not very private. She sipped and listened to Sam's voice. She erased the message and returned to the living room.

"I was going to have your frozen chow mein."

"Let's order pizza." She handed him a takeout menu. "Choose intelligently."

He smiled to himself. In her request he heard her pleasant domestic bossiness taking all their years together as a given, shared, never spoken. He grabbed a pen and checked peppers, salami, mushrooms and anchovies.

She stared at him in fascination. "Noel, give me that pen."

"What? I chose brilliantly."

She took the pen from him. "Watch." She repeated her experiment from earlier, using her left hand and the pen as a syringe. "See how clumsy I am using my non-dominant hand?"

"Sandro the lefty, injecting himself in his left arm. Maybe not." He laughed. "Clever, Kyra. But so what?"

"File the notion for now."

"Okay." He sipped and told her about his driving to Coupeville.

"How did you get on? Other than your syringe experiment?"

She explained Maria's sense of the family's probable reaction to Sandro, or Sandra. "She wouldn't tell me who the young tough was but I found out anyway. Vasily Constantinides. I smacked him with my purse."

"You did what?"

"Paid him back for bashing you." Pride in her voice.

"And he didn't slug you back?"

"He offered to buy me coffee." She giggled. "I turned him down."

"Bashing him? Really stupid, Kyra."

"That's what I thought. But only afterwards." She handed her glass and his pen to Noel. "Toppings chosen?" She took the menu to the phone, ordered, put the phone down. "Another, please."

He took their glasses to the kitchen. "How'd it go with Jerome?"

"The dog bit my leg. It's better than a chastity belt."

Noel smiled. "How was the paint choosing?"

"Didn't get there. The place needs updating. Jerome offered me dinner. I said we needed to get organized for tomorrow."

Noel made a face. "I'm not looking forward to this trans masquerade."

"You'll see—no problem. Meanwhile I'll track down Sandro's ex-wife in Seattle."

"You know where she lives?"

"You've got her phone number, find her address on-line."

"What's she going to tell you?"

"Maybe an outside opinion on the Vasiliadis family? I could meet up with you in Coupeville. In fact, while we're there we should check out the doctor who runs the lab. If we knew where the lab was."

"Why?" Noel's tone was suspicious.

Kyra frowned. "No, the real question is, why do they need a lab in the first place? Do they have to conduct experiments in transgendering? And how would you experiment anyway? On whom? Did they experiment on Sandro and the experiment went wrong?"

The downstairs entry phone beeped. A voice said, "Pizza."

"Really fast." She got up to buzz it in.

I hope it really is pizza, thought Noel.

"Goodnight!" Kyra closed her bedroom door. Too much pizza. She opened the window and breathed in damp night air. It tasted good. She should have gone for a walk, she needed to move. She still could. No. She took her juggling balls from the closet. Her best exercise, physical and mental. Two balls. Jerome number one and— Oh dear, Sam number two. She threw Jerome into the air, caught him with the same hand. Sam likewise. Why Sam? Jerome up, Sam up, Jerome in hand, pass over, up again as Sam came down. She reached for a third ball, fumbled.

Kyra didn't feel like juggling Sam—or any men—any more.

—— • ——

"You said more men have sex changes than women. Of course it has to be you." She stood with her arms crossed, but her heart melted for him.

Noel sighed, and picked up the phone. He asked for an appointment for Neil Ferguson, who was the right sex in the wrong body. Two-thirty? Okay. He hung up. "Wasn't I lucky. Ordinarily appointments must be made weeks in advance but she'd just had a cancellation." His best wry-but-soulful glance.

"Don't brood all day. I'm heading off. Leave your phone on. I'll call before two-thirty. When I'm finished with Diana."

"What time are you seeing her?"

"No appointment." She collected her jacket and shoes, and her purse.

"She might not be there." Noel sat slumped on the edge of the den pullout bed.

"I'll track her down. With a kid in school she won't be far." Noel had found McRae, on King Terrace. In the car she consulted the Seattle street map. King was in the northeast sector; good, she didn't have to drive through the city. She organized a selection of CDs and headed off.

Increasing sun, greening grass, early flowers. Only ten days till equinox, then spring. When this case was over she'd go to Vancouver, check in on her parents, maybe go across and visit Noel's parents in Qualicum. She'd always been fond of them. With Jerome? He needed some time off, Kyra decided. Put Nelson in a kennel.

Jerome. What did she want with him? Before they committed themselves to a trip they'd better go to bed. Didn't want to be cooped up in a car all those days with a non-compatible man. Pachelbel's *Canon* swelled out of the speakers.

Diana McRae's house, pseudo-colonial, stood on a street of other mildly stately houses. A maroon BMW was parked in the driveway. The boulevard trees showed a young gangliness. Kyra stopped under one, crossed the sidewalk and followed a curved path of interlocking paving stones to the front door. She rang the bell. The door opened. A pretty woman, thirtyish, short dark hair, glasses, beige shirt and pullover, tight-cut jeans. "Ms. McRae?"

"Yes?"

Kyra handed her a Triple-I card. "I understand you used to be married to Sandro Vasiliadis. I'm looking into his death. May I ask you some questions, please?"

Diana McRae opened the door farther. Kyra entered a marble-tiled foyer, living room to the right. Its cathedral ceiling revealed a railed corridor across the second floor. A design Kyra loathed.

"In here." Ms. McRae led her into a sitting room, floral chintz sofa and armchairs, a desk, entertainment center. Still not Kyra's style, but comfortable. "How can I help you?"

"We have reason to believe Mr. Vasiliadis' death may not have been an accident."

"What do you mean?" Diana McRae sat.

"Could anyone have wanted to harm Sandro?"

"Harm? Why would anyone want to?"

Kyra took a chair. "Is it possible someone could prefer him dead?"

Ms. McRae took off her glasses and studied them. Her face took on a look Kyra recognized: What should I say? "I don't know, I can't imagine—"

"Everyone we've talked to agrees he wasn't a drug addict. Everyone agrees he was excited about his prospects. Did you know Sandro was undergoing a transgendering procedure?"

A small smile. "He told me. I was shocked then. But yes, it made sense. Especially of our marriage." The woman replaced her glasses.

"Yes?"

"Would you like coffee?" she asked. "The pot's on."

"That would be nice." Kyra followed her into the kitchen. A sunny yellow room, modern fixtures, a green granite counter. "Black, please."

They sat on stools at the breakfast island and sipped from mugs. "We had an uncomfortable marriage. I didn't know why. We got divorced. We both felt better. We became friends." She smiled. "His family disapproved of both our marriage and the divorce."

"They didn't know about his transgendering plans?"

"No. He wouldn't have told them."

"What do you imagine their response would have been?"

"*Not* pleased. That's why he moved to Whidbey. That and the clinic, of course."

"There's a cousin of Sandro's, Vasily—"

A grim smile from Diana. "An asshole. Whenever he found me alone he came on to me, like, paw!" Kyra nodded. "I didn't want strife. But finally I told Sandro and he had it out with Vasily. That was years ago. Carla was maybe a year old then."

"They fought?"

"Probably not. Sandro was in his tough phase, but Vasily still would've won. Sandro was better with words. And tough as he sounded, he hated fighting. The others in the family were nice enough. Maria's always been good to me, though she and Kostas didn't like Sandro and me marrying. We were too young, they said, and she was mad I'd got pregnant. She's devoted to Carla, and Carla loves her grandmother. I never had much to do with Andrei. Sandro was a nice guy, he'd have made a nice girl. And we tried to figure out what to say to Carla one day. He gave me a copy of his will, everything in trust for her."

We tried to figure, Kyra filed. This was a terrific woman. They sipped their coffee as in silent memorial to Sandro. Outside, a robin practiced its spring song. They looked at each other, and smiled.

Diana said, "Sandro was happy about how it was all going."

"Did he tell you much about the procedure? The hormones, the surgery?"

"Not in detail. He liked the doctors and the clinic. Mainly we talked about Carla." Diana looked off into the distance, and frowned. "I've been trying to remember. About three days before he died he called. He was really mad about something. It wasn't like him, he's always been pretty even-tempered. Something had happened, he didn't tell me. He talked a lot about hormones, and hermaphrodites, and changing sex."

"Was he upset?"

"Scared." They listened to the robin's trill. She turned to face Kyra. "If you find out anything, will you let me know? One day, for Carla's sake."

"Of course." Kyra stood. "And Triple-I's numbers are on the card, if anything more occurs to you. Thank you."

Diana stood too. She showed Kyra to the door. A new and different picture of Sandro.

NINETEEN

COULD DIANA AND Sandra have become friends? What would Carla have thought of two mothers? Or would Sandra still have been her father? The glimpses into people's lives while looking for the pattern. This glimpse made Kyra sad. Or was she sad in a larger way, about the futility of marriage? Her own three, and Sandro's. One huge fact, that *he* wanted to be *she*, had screwed up his, and Diana's.

Check out the woman doctor. Hormones and hermaphrodites. Exactly what was WISDOM's research?

On the Mukilteo ferry, Kyra phoned Noel's cell. No answer. She phoned their business line. He picked up. "It's twelve-thirty. I thought you'd be on the road!"

"It's only an hour to there. Did you talk to the ex-wife?"

"Yeah. Really nice woman. She said Sandro was upset about something his last week, maybe his treatment. She has his will, everything left to their daughter. I'm on the ferry. At the clinic, ask to see their lab."

"I'll see how it goes." His tone was flat.

"Have we heard from the coroner?"

"Yep. Morphine killed him, definite."

"He's sure? Even with embalming fluid in there?"

"That's what he said. Diluted, but morphine. No way to tell how much, our coroner friend said, but it must've killed him since he's dead."

"A real scientist, that feller."

"Yep."

"Did he confirm which arm?"

"Left."

Kyra sighed out a long breath. Left arm, and not a street drug. "Phone me when you're through with the interview."

"Mmrph."

She disconnected. She didn't envy Noel.

The ferry docked, cars drove off onto Whidbey Island, finally she did too. Hungry. Nearly one, no wonder. Highway 525 began, or ended depending on your direction, at the Clinton ferry wharf. She followed the cars and shortly spied a Mexican restaurant. She wheeled into the lot. The place had takeout service. Chimichanga in napkin, many napkins over her sweater, pants and Gore-Tex, limeade in the coffee holder, and she started forth again. Pretty good. Better if she'd loaded on more green salsa. Another place worth filing under Emergency.

She drove past the turn-off to Sandro's house. In the last week Sandro had shifted from a corpse to someone she might've known, even liked. Chelsea had brought him alive for Noel, and through Noel to her. Diana cemented the connection. Unfair when a life ends abruptly. But then she and Noel got to be the snoops.

Why do you do it? she asked.

Because I love it, she answered.

Does it make a better world?

A tiny bit, maybe. I sure as hell hope so.

Noel had no desire to be driving down the road to Coupeville. Nor any desire to walk through the door to WISDOM.

One-forty-five. Noel would be here soon. Kyra sat for a minute in WISDOM's parking lot looking wistfully at the building, then got out of her car. WISDOM looked only one storey, but from this angle, the side, the ground sloped down to the back. A whole other floor. She'd like to know what was in the basement: walk around, a quick twist of her lock picks— Except it's broad daylight, Kyra, lots of windows. Explain she was here to fix the furnace? Right.

Inside, a cheery Dawn Deane glanced up from her computer. Kyra gave her her toothiest smile. "I'd like to see Dr. Lorna Albright, please."

Dawn Deane seemed devastated. "I'm so sorry, Dr. Albright doesn't see patients on Mondays. In fact, on Mondays she isn't here." Her look said she hoped Kyra wouldn't faint at this message of doom. She held out a hopeful solution: "Would you like an appointment? You could see her a week Thursday."

"Where does she work on Mondays?"

"At the Mary Teeseborough House."

"Maybe I could see her there."

"I doubt it." More bad news. She lowered her voice and looked around the empty waiting room. "The clinic deals with women's issues. It's heavily guarded."

Abortion clinic. "Do you know her hours? If I could catch her leaving—"

Dawn looked dubious. "I'm not sure, probably nine to five."

"Where is it?"

"Oak Harbor. I can't remember the street."

Poor woman, so much regretful news to deliver. "Thank you. If I don't have any luck, I'll take your appointment." Kyra's smile reassured Dawn Deane her news wasn't a four molar extraction, only a minor cavity.

Kyra drove to the nearest gas station, filled the Tracker. Two cents a gallon more than Bellingham. In the junk food store she paid and asked for the phone book: Mary Teeseborough House, S.E. Fourth in Oak Harbor; Albright, an L.B. on Summit Loop.

Back in the car again, she checked her map. Fourth Ave was close to Skagit Valley College. Summit Loop looped off N.E. Pennington Loop which looped off Pennington Loop. Loopy.

Two-thirty-two. Noel would be at the interview. Go for it, Noel! Now find Albright.

Damn paperwork. Terry sat back. She should be home with Richard, should have called in sick. Lorna would've understood well enough. Terry'd called him twice in the morning and he hadn't been able to talk till just before noon, the Coast Guard was still with him. They'd answered a good Samaritan SOS call and pulled him from the water, now were back. And she'd talked with him after lunch—not that she'd had lunch, all appetite gone. She glanced at her watch: 2:35. She'd phone in twenty minutes, leave right after.

In fairness, Richard seemed controlled. Or was it a superficial coolness he'd put on this morning, like a clean shirt? Lorna had said it sounded like she, Terry, was the upset one. Lorna had talked to Richard; he'd seemed fine despite the shock. Just a boat, he'd said, and Lorna said, You can always buy a new boat. He'd told Lorna staying home had turned into a good idea except for how much time he had to spend with the Coast Guard guys, every detail over and over again; but he probably would put in his time in the evening at the hospice. Her phone rang. "Hello?"

Silence for a moment, then a voice said, "Terry?"

"Yes?" More silence. "Hello?"

"Hi. It's Gary."

"Oh. Hi." His voice came through so low she hadn't recognized it. "What's up?"

"Just calling to see how Richard is."

"Fine, I think. I haven't seen him all day."

"I didn't want to call the house."

"He's sounding pretty okay."

A pause on Gary's end. "That's good."

Terry waited, but Gary said nothing more. "He'd be glad to talk to you. He'll be alone now."

"Alone?"

"The Coast Guard were there this morning, asking questions about the *Panacea*."

A second before Gary said, "Oh."

"But go ahead, phone."

"Yeah. Okay." Another pause. "Will he be at the clinic tomorrow?"

"I'm pretty sure." Gary sounded strange, somehow more worried—about what?—than Richard. "He's going to the hospice tonight, carrying on as usual."

"Good. That's good."

"Gary? You okay?"

"Yeah. Fine."

"I was about to leave"

"Sure. See you. Take care."

The phone clicked dead before Terry could say goodbye. She scooped up a file of printouts relating to the anemone that hosted the black percula clownfish. She stuffed the package into her case, picked up the phone and pressed Automatic, then 1. The home line was busy. Likely Richard talking to Gary.

———

Behind a counter sat a blonde woman about Kyra's age, a bright smile for Noel as the door closed behind him. "Hello. You must be Mr. Ferguson." A nameplate made her out to be Dawn Deane.

"Yes. Neil Ferguson." The name tasted strange.

"Dr. Haines will be with you shortly." She slid a clipboard holding a form across the counter. "Please fill this out while you're waiting. And we did tell you there'll be a one-hundred-dollar fee for the consultation, payable beforehand?"

"Yes." From his wallet—no credit card or check for this, Neil Ferguson had neither—he produced two fifty-dollar bills.

"I'll get you a receipt."

He took the clipboard and sat down in a tan armchair. In fact, despite the upcoming interview, the whole space made him feel relaxed. Kyra had commented on this. He glanced at the form. Contact details, some vital stats, and an explanation of their fee scale. He had to sign to say he understood it though signing didn't commit him to paying, not right now. Basic fee, genital surgery only, $10,000. Additional skin grafting could cost between $1,000 and $2,000, dependent on how much was necessary. Skin grafting? Yeaghgh ... Preliminary psychiatric evaluations, according to fees charged. Final psychiatric evaluation at WISDOM, $600. Half a dozen items that he didn't understand. Good, he couldn't sign the document because he'd not understood it.

"Mr. Ferguson? This way."

Noel stood, took the receipt from her, handed her the clipboard, let her lead him along a hallway to the left. She knocked on a door with Dr. G. Haines stenciled on the wood, opened it and stepped in. Noel followed.

Gary Haines' office felt chilly, its white walls draining any softness from the air. A water cooler stood in the corner. A curious light, sweet smell in here. Haines remained seated behind his desk, a man not much older than Noel, hair gone gray at the temples, a good sharp face. His shirt was pearl gray, his necktie brightly red-flowered, his braces black. "Thank you, Ms. Deane. Mr. Ferguson, please have a seat."

Noel did, in a leather easy chair. Also very comfortable. If you pay enough for a chair, is it always easy? "Thanks." Dawn Deane had disappeared.

"So. We have half an hour. First, why don't you tell me about yourself. And then I'll tell you about WISDOM."

Noel did, as he and Kyra had agreed—stick as close to the truth as possible; except for recent truths. He explained to Haines how he'd thought when he reached puberty that he was gay, except when he tried out the gay world, it didn't fit him. He'd become a journalist, worked nearly twelve years for several newspapers, resigned a few years ago to write a book. In the meantime he'd been struggling over his sexuality. Increasingly he knew he felt like how a woman must sense herself to be. It was an agony, being captured in the wrong body, the woman—maybe Nelly—inside him. And so on. Without Sandro, Noel would have nothing to tell this doctor; even a week ago he couldn't have talked like this. He'd done a lot of reading, he told Haines, books and the Internet. He'd met a couple of transgendered people, he figured he knew the route he needed to take and had finally worked up the courage to make this preliminary appointment at WISDOM.

Haines sat back and smiled. "I'm glad you said transgendered people, not transsexuals."

"Yes, I understand the difference." A good thing to say, but did he truly? He'd read somewhere on the Transgender Café that some trans people figure the thing that's wrong with them isn't their gender, it's their sexuality, the physical part of it all. In that sense, Sandro was in fact being transexualized. It was all too complicated.

"Good. Then let me tell you what we can do for you."

Noel leaned forward, as if for greater intimacy. The chilly room seemed even cooler. "May I take notes?"

For a moment Haines said nothing. Then he smiled. "Still the journalist, are you?"

Noel forced his own smile. "Old habits die hard. I remember best when I have a pen in hand." He took out notebook and ballpoint. The stare from Haines seemed less than friendly.

"Very well. Have you consulted with or had any treatments from another transgendering clinic?"

"I'm at the beginning of all this."

"Good, good. First, it'll be necessary for you to have two psychiatric evaluations over a period of four to six months. We'll need consensus in the reports to go ahead with a sexual reassignment procedure. We can suggest several excellent people. You'll choose among them."

"The evaluation lasts that long? Why?"

"It's a complex path you're starting on, Mr. Ferguson. SRP is irreversible. We can't have you changing your mind once it's too late."

"Of course," said Noel in a tiny voice.

"So if the psychiatrists agree you're an appropriate candidate, we'll begin the hormones. You're not HIV positive, are you? Or have any venereal diseases?"

"No no, nothing."

"That's good. We can't perform SRP on anyone like that." He glanced at Noel. "And you're not overweight, good good. For your height, we'd have a hard time if you weighed over a hundred ninety pounds. Weight?"

"About a hundred sixty."

"Good good."

"Oh, I remember. I've read there are choices."

"Right. Much depends on how deep you want your new vagina to be. Which partly depends on the length of your penis, since one gets transformed into the other."

Haines' smile asked Noel how long his penis was without actually putting this into words; fine, since there'd be no word response either.

Haines waited a moment and went on. "We try to make sure the new vagina is at least between six and eight inches deep. The longer your penis, the more material we have to build you a deeper vagina, right?" Now he didn't pause for an answer. "If you've got a little fella and you want a deeper entryway, we graft. We can take skin from your abdomen, or your scrotum. Abdomen grafts leave little scars, but it's good thick skin. Scrotum grafts are thinner but there's no scarring and you won't be needing your scrotum anyway."

Noel was sure he'd forgotten how to breathe.

"If you want to have sex in your new vagina, we recommend a deep one, and that'll mean grafting. And then there's building a clitoris, and your new urethral opening, as well as labioplasty for the full female look. But usually we do that last bit in the second stage, a few months down the line." He squinted at Noel. "Would you like a glass of water?"

Noel nodded. The word *Yes* would not come.

Haines brought Noel a paper cup of water from the cooler. "If I may say so, Mr. Ferguson, you look uncomfortable."

"No no, I'm fine." He took a small sip.

"Actually, I suspect you really haven't thought this through very well."

Shit. "No, honestly, I'm just very nervous, I often am." Damn, all his investigative reporting skills had fallen apart. Damn!

"Very well then. Our aim is to be as clear as possible, so you can come to terms with all of it. As I said, after the operation there's no going back. So. What else can I tell you?"

Something different had happened with Sandro. Chelsea's question. Both of them must have gone through this, god! "I'm not sure."

"Good, good. And you understand our fee structure?"

"I think so. Now—"

"Unfortunately we will need to receive full payment in advance. In the early days we had a couple of unfortunate circumstances."

"Oh?"

"Procedure completed, but the client could not or would not pay. All very messy."

"I see." Come on, Noel, just ask. "Uh, Dr. Haines—"

Haines glanced at his watch again. "Yes?"

"I know I want to become Nelly Ferguson, more than anything I've ever wanted. But it all sounds so gruesome. Isn't there another way?"

"Another way?" Haines flexed his fingers against each other. "How do you mean?"

"I mean, all that cutting. If Nelly's already inside me, can't you bring her out without the cutting, and blood?" Come on, Noel, pull yourself into the detective inside you, that's what you're here for. "I mean, one of the transgendered people I talked to had a friend, he was going through this process. Here, I think. And I heard, the friend said he was being transgendered without all the cutting?"

For at least half a minute Haines studied Noel in a silence that chilled Noel further. Then he sighed, shook his head, sighed again. "With some men there are the beginnings of certain medical procedures." Another head shake.

Careful, Noel. "Uh, medical?"

"It demands a specific kind of chemistry. For some men—" He shrugged.

"Would I—?"

Another squint from Haines, looking Noel over with profound medical scrutiny. "It's hard to know, Mr. Ferguson. Very hard. There'd have to be a whole other series of tests, and even then— It's hard to know."

"But—possible?"

"Many things are possible." Haines stared into a middle distance somewhere beyond Noel's right ear. "And many aren't."

"I see. And, how do we proceed?"

"You'll have to consider what I've told you, Mr. Ferguson. And when you're ready, just give us a call."

"I see." Noel nodded. Time to go. Suddenly he felt a whole lot better. "I call you."

"When you've considered."

"Yes." He breathed deeply. The scented air clung to his palate. His taste buds cringed. "I'll consider." He pushed his palms against the leather arms of the chair, and stood.

"Would you like my receptionist—?"

Noel forced another smile. "Thank you. I'm fine." He took a test step. Only a little rubbery. "I'll call." He took five steps, grabbed the door handle and turned to Haines. "Thank you."

"Of course." Haines made no attempt to stand.

"Goodbye." Noel stepped into the hall and pulled the door closed. His armpits dripped. He rubbed his chin, then his brow. Chilly, both. At least the air here didn't have that sweet rancid smell. So there was another way to do a sexual reassignment. The rubber in his legs had hardened. He walked to the lobby, the front door, and out. He just barely heard Dawn Deane calling, he hadn't signed the form!

Mary Teeseborough House was literally a house, two-storey brown clapboard. Kyra parked, strode up the stairs. A man in a security company uniform lounged by the front door. He looked her over, and decided she was harmless; maybe. "Howdy, ma'am."

Kyra, trying to look helpless, gave him a faint lip twitch. He held open the door.

Inside was a receptionist, about sixty, gray hair pulled into a chignon. "May I help you?"

"I'm here to see Dr. Albright, please."

"Do you have an appointment?"

"Yes," lied Kyra.

The woman looked at her computer screen. "You must be Concordia Lopez."

"Yes."

"Concordia Lopez is seventy years old and has only one eye. I don't think so."

Damn. Kyra smiled, she hoped ingratiatingly. "You win." She hauled out a Triple-I card. "I'm a detective. It's important I see Dr. Albright about a case I'm on."

Chignon looked up at Kyra. "It's important Dr. Albright see the rest of her appointments. These women need medical care. However, she's leaving at four."

Kyra consulted her watch. Just after three. She looked at the overflowing waiting room; not everyone was here for an abortion. Women in advanced pregnancy, women with toddlers, older women, teenagers. "Thank you," she said with the chagrin she felt. "I'll catch her elsewhere." Kyra slunk out.

"Bye, ma'am," the security guard said.

Kyra drove away. And, a block later, stopped. Was she being bull-headed in wanting to talk to Albright? No, she needed to. Noel's information said this was the gynecologist who headed the research team. Their research for Bendwell, precisely what was it?

Before any waiting, pee. She drove to a Taco Time/Pizza Hut, used the washroom and bought a large coffee. Back at Teeseborough House she sussed out the parking lot. How would she know Albright? Leaving at four was her only clue.

Promptly at four a short plumpish woman in a drab brown suit and high heels clicked from around the back of the clinic into the parking lot. Kyra belted up. The woman got into a blue Acura and headed off, direction Coupeville. Going home? But she zipped by the turn-off and continued. And continued. The Acura slowed, turned left through a gateway in a wire fence topped with barbed wire. Kyra followed. Behind the fence was a long, low building. The Acura parked, Kyra parked next to it. The woman got out and locked. Kyra got out. The woman headed to the building—

"May I have a moment, Dr. Albright," Kyra said.

The woman stopped, startled. She looked Kyra up and down. "Yes?"

Kyra thrust a Triple-I card at her. "Kyra Rachel. Detective. My partner and I are looking into the Sandro Vasiliadis case. I'd like to ask a few questions about WISDOM's research."

"This is extremely unusual."

"But important."

"Who are you working for?"

"I'm not at liberty to say. You understand." Kyra smiled, again toothily. "I've heard that WISDOM has received a grant from Bendwell Pharmaceuticals to follow up some research. What research is that?"

"I don't talk about research."

"Is this your lab?"

"What business is it of yours?" Dr. Albright's eyes sparked. "Excuse me." She turned on her heel, marched across the gravel parking lot and let herself in a door. It slammed behind her.

Noel needed to speak with the coroner, get some clarification on the drug analysis, but once again the morgue was shut tight. Still, the talk with Haines behind him, he felt strong again—just leaving that interview gave him back his control. He took out his cell and called Kyra. They agreed to meet for an early dinner. Samson's? Sure. Then Noel drove to Coupeville's library and with the help of a generous young librarian searched newspapers for any information about WISDOM. He found nothing. A discreet organization.

At five-thirty, menus open, Kyra told him about Albright's refusal to talk. "And you?"

His eyes, stern, fell on her. "I am happy in the body I was born into." He watched her elaborately unfold her napkin. "The description of the surgery was difficult. However, when I pushed, Haines didn't say it had to be surgery. He was unforthcoming with details. But," Noel picked up his menu, "he hinted."

The more her partner understated, the more upset he must have been. Maybe still was. "How could it happen?"

"Damned if I know."

"We'll find out." She smiled, "I discovered where the lab is."

"Lab?"

"Their research, remember? Bendwell Pharmaceuticals. Money."

"Oh. Yeah."

The server arrived. They buried themselves in the menus. He stood patiently. Not many diners on a Monday night.

"The T-bone steak," said Noel. "Medium rare."

"The sole, please. And a bottle of—no, a half bottle."

Noel looked at her. "Merlot," he finished. The waiter left. "A half bottle? After this afternoon, a bottle apiece."

"We still have work to do."

"What work?"

"We need to find out what's going on in that laboratory. What they're working on."

"I'll get back on-line and—"

"It won't be there. Too new. Unpublished."

"Then how? You said that researcher-doctor wouldn't talk to you."

"I know. So we take a look in the lab, right? See if something there connects with what they were doing to Sandro."

"What, just walk in?"

"Nope." She smiled.

"Oh no, Kyra. No way. No no no."

"It's okay, I'll do it. You'll stand guard. We'll take your rental and leave the Tracker here."

"You're not breaking in. Please, Kyra."

"One of us has to. And you won't."

"And not you either."

"No choice."

"But what are you looking for?"

"If they're manufacturing a transgendering drug, the lab's the only place that'll tell us."

"We could work through the pharmaceutical company."

"Get serious."

"Can't we do this without—?"

"No way I can think of. Can you?"

He had nothing to say.

Their wine arrived, and was poured. "To a hard day, not yet over," Kyra toasted. They sipped. "We'll have more wine at home."

While they ate, Kyra described the outside of the lab, the gate in the fence, the building.

"There'll be a security alarm," Noel said.

"So? Mike told me a couple of things about them."

"I think you're crazy."

"If this is where they manufacture the drugs, we'll find out what they are."

Noel cut a tiny slice of steak, chewed, swallowed; his appetite had dissipated.

"I'll keep my phone on. If there's trouble outside, warn me."

Noel swallowed. "You can't be long."

"Long as it takes." They sat back. She'd inhaled her meal, no lingering tonight. Most of his remained on the plate. Good food, Kyra realized in retrospect. They paid and left. Six-thirty. Dusk.

TWENTY

SANDMAN LODGE, HALF a block from the sea, had been named neither for the sleepiness of the farm compound three miles south of Anacortes nor for the beach down the dirt road where Richard could hear waves lapping, but for Cornelius Sandman, whose family had summered here in the twenties and thirties. For most of the nineties the Lodge had remained abandoned. Then some civic-minded residents applied for and, remarkably, received, federal and state money to turn it into a hospice for nine individuals with AIDS who could live in their own community.

Four years ago Dr. Trevelyan had offered his services. He had since spent most Monday evenings here, 5:00 to 8:00 PM, seeing three of the nine residents. Today he'd given an hour each to two patients, advising them about things medical, their choices and options, and letting them talk out their states of mind. He felt he was doing them some good. Or at least no harm. His third patient for the evening didn't want to talk. So Richard spent half an hour on paperwork. He could leave early.

He called Terry at the lab, home in twenty minutes. She'd be there in fifteen, she'd get the martinis ready. No question, he felt better. WISDOM's work had to go on. Stock, Lorna, Gary—yes, they had it right, the research and its application were paramount. Taking calculated risks, that's the nature of medicine, and when you see the breakthrough approaching— The greater the risk overcome, the finer the satisfaction.

A risk becomes dangerous only when you don't know you're taking it. Like *Panacea*. Who'd have thought a fuel line could split, an aberrant spark set off a fire, just like that? Richard had explained to the Coast Guard everything had been checked. No, after talking to the guys at the marina Richard could report the hoses weren't replaced, they'd weathered the winter and were in fine shape. The Coast Guard people were unimpressed. Didn't sound right. Tomorrow they'd send a dive team down, take a look, the boat lay in only forty-five feet of water. Did Richard plan to salvage it?

The rain had stopped. Gary Haines drove into the Sandman Lodge parking lot. He stopped his beet-red Lexus, shut off the engine and waited for a moment in the dark. Richard's Prius still sat silent near the walkway. Good. The car clock said 7:40. He got out and strolled across the line of grass demarcating the end of the parking lot and the beginning of the beach. Little waves nibbled at wet sand. Richard would be out in twenty minutes. They'd have a long talk. Richard would understand why it was wrong to take the Vasiliadis file to the police. Gary felt lopsided; three extra pounds in his right coat pocket.

Richard said goodbye to Alex, combination Sandman guard and house father. He walked out onto the dark veranda, down the steps, and along the path to his car. He got in, started the engine, and drove away.

Gary heard an engine and whirled around. The Prius! Damn! He ran to his car, leapt in, fumbled with the key. He roared after Richard's disappearing tail lights. Heading home? Not so good as here.

Richard pulled into his driveway, triggering the motion detector light. He stopped the car and got out. Terry's car not here yet? On the road he heard the squeal of brakes, and turned. Headlights coming toward him. Terry? The car pulled in beside his. Not Terry. A Lexus? Gary's? As if in answer, Gary got out.

"Richard!"

"What're you doing here?"

"We need to talk." A pause. "It's important."

Richard sensed worry in Gary's voice. "I'll be in at the clinic tomorrow. We could have lunch."

"No, no, now."

"I'm tired, Terry'll be home any minute."

"Just a few minutes." Gary took Richard's arm. "It's been a long day for me too, Richard."

"What's up?"

"You've got to return the Vasiliadis file."

"What?"

"You want to show it to the cops, right?"

"You mean the file's gone?"

"Of course. You know that!"

Richard squinted at Gary. "How could I know that?"

"Don't be coy."

"What the hell are you talking about?"

"The file's gone because you took it."

"You're crazy."

"I'm not crazy! I want it. I have to change it."

"Change it?"

"So anyone who reads it will assume Sandro was being prepared for surgery."

"But we were doing hipop and percuprone on him—"

"I need that file, Richard."

"I don't have it. It's at the clinic."

"Don't lie. Just give it to me."

"You're nuts." He shook Gary's hand off his arm and walked toward his front door.

"Richard!"

His name had fear in it, and a threat. He turned. In Gary's hand, an object flashed dull silver in the dim light.

"You will not give that file to the police. You'll give it to me. Or to no one." He walked toward Richard.

Maybe not crazy. Desperate. And—was that a pistol? No one had ever pointed a pistol at Richard before. "Look. When I was out on *Panacea* I decided not to talk to the cops about Sandro, okay?"

"Really. Not to talk to the cops." A small laugh. "Did you decide that before the boat exploded, or while it was exploding, or after it exploded?"

Oh, Jesus. Richard felt a deep shudder. That Coast Guard guy had said— "Gary. You fucked up the engine?"

"We don't want you talking to the cops. Not you or Terry. Get it?"

"You killed *Panacea*, you son of a bitch!" He lunged at Gary, grabbing for the pistol. But the pistol fired first.

A dark night, thick clouds. A single light illuminated the parking lot behind the wire fence. Noel stopped his rental on the other side of the road. The gate across the drive to the laboratory's lot, closed tight, didn't surprise Kyra. But no car where Lorna Albright had parked. In fact no cars at all. Excellent.

Noel had deep reservations. He'd checked the Internet. Both Bendwell and WISDOM were super-legitimate. The grant was too, and the research had FDA approval. So how could anything illegal be going on? Except Haines had implied another way of transgendering. Chelsea and Ursula were dubious there could be. Diana described Sandro as furious and scared the last week of his life. For the third time since leaving the restaurant Noel said, "I hate this."

She said only, "Stop it."

"I'm worried, you in there alone."

"Come with me."

"No way." The lab looked like a bunker, a concrete block of a building, one storey. "You really want to do this?"

"Yes."

He grabbed her hand, she squeezed. "Be careful, Kyra."

"Okay." She would be. She could handle the locks. Mike her B and E teacher had told her, never try to figure an alarm under the pressure of the situation. A cut-off code is easy for the guy who uses it every day, spell out his mother's or his boa constrictor's name, but if you don't know the guy from Eve you'll never figure it. If it doesn't go off soon as you get in there's a delay, thirty seconds, couple of minutes. So go for the jugular—locate the breaker box, cut the system's juices, then get on with your business. Even if there's no alarm, find the box and kill the power. If it goes off while you're inside, get the hell out fast as you can.

Terry was late because she'd stopped for olives. She turned into their driveway. The motion detector light came on, illuminating the Prius. Good, Richard was home. She got out clutching her purse and the olives, and headed for the front door. On the path—? She ran— "Richard!" The olives crashed to the gravel as she fumbled for the cellphone and punched in 911. "My husband—blood on his chest—" She gave their address. She knelt. "Richard! Richard! Can you hear me?" No answer. "Oh god!" She knelt, searched for a pulse, fingers trembling. Nothing. She reached into his mouth to assure his airway wasn't blocked, pinched his nose and brought her mouth to his.

When the paramedics found them Terry's mouth was still tight on Richard's.

———

Kyra and Noel waited in the car for minutes, tense inactivity. No traffic this evening. Normal on Monday night on a rural road on a small island. "Okay. I'm going in."

"Just be careful," Noel whispered.

She took his wrist. "Anything happens out here, you call. Press 1. I'll be there."

"Of course."

She slipped on thin leather gloves, slung her purse over her shoulder. "See you soon." She got out and crossed the road. Enough light, dim blue at the side of the building, wouldn't need her flash. The padlock was no big deal, a Therrien, two-tumbler model, holding a thick chain tight where the doors met. Like going back to elementary school; a couple of her lessons with Mike had been on Therriens. From her purse came the lock picks; a six-seventeen combination popped the lock open. Chain off, push door, in, close, chain on, set in place but not snapped to, and she waved to Noel.

Noel waved back.

It took Kyra half a minute to the front entry. She played her flash beam across the door. A small sign said, WIRED. Uh-oh. And then she figured it out, or most of it—like WISDOM, Whidbey Island Research and something else. She shone the light on the handle, and the lock. Unbelievable—a Noble double. Like a Crackerjack box. With a two and seven the door sesame'd before her eyes. In, and close.

———

A cold wave of relief swept Noel, chilling his sweat. So far, so good. He couldn't handle thinking about Kyra inside so he looked the other way. A blip of noise? Oh for god's sake, headlights! A car, stopping. What to do? Instinct told him to bolt. No, can't leave Kyra. One of the doctors? A researcher? What the hell? He grabbed his cellphone, turned it on, pressed Kyra's code. Bright flashing blue and red lights now—no, no! A man got out, uniform, hat on his head, hand on his holster.

Doubleshit.

———

A small vestibule, a locked double door beyond. On the wall, a metal box. She opened it. Yep, the alarm system, blipping little red and green lights. The second lock, a single Noble, opened with just the four and seven. In. Take the chance? Yes: lights on. A room full of fish tanks! Mice! Rabbits! And other stuff— Find the breaker box! She went down on her knees, under the tanks and cages, nothing obvious. Offices past the lab? She glanced in each. No. Back to the foyer. There, stupid, side of the door where you come in, the switch handle practically beckoning! Flash still in hand she loped toward it— A screeching wail hit her eardrums.

She reached up, grabbed the handle, pulled it down. Silence, and complete darkness. How long had it blared? Maybe half a second. Was she safe? Hard to know. No call from Noel, nothing happening outside.

She clicked on her flashlight. In the same instant a small whining roar, and new lights. Now what? She stared through the door window to the lab. The fish tanks, all illuminated! Must be a generator, tanks would need water circulating. Stupid, Kyra, you could've killed the fish. She glanced into a tank to the right, labeled *Midshipmen*. Hard to spot them in the bad light. Well, this trip didn't involve watching pretty fish. Better note down the names, fish were clearly central to whatever was going on here. She read labels: *Sixspot gobies*. *Caridean shrimp*, might be yummy cooked in beer. *Saddleback wrasses*. *Percula clownfish*, handsome orange and black and white stripes.

"Howdy," the policeman said.

Noel tried to smile. "Good evening."

"This isn't a good place for parking."

Noel asked, "Oh, I'm just trying to—to clear a bit of confusion." A shake to his voice.

"License and registration, please."

Noel gave him both. The cop went back to the patrol car. Noel waited. He wanted Kyra out of there. But not just yet!

Four minutes and the cop came back, returning Noel's documents. "Please get out of the car, Noel."

Noel did.

"See that yellow line?" The cop shone his flash beam along the road divider. "I want you to walk it."

Noel did. Nice and straight, even though he felt mighty shaky. Luckily just a glass of wine.

"Okay, Noel. Get in, move along. Don't want to see you here when I come around again."

He would drive away slowly. Make the cop pass him. Turn. Get back.

He painstakingly put away his license, his registration. The cop drove off. Noel waited.

Enough with fish. She wished she knew what she was searching for. Maybe in those offices? The first held two desks, chairs, a large-screened computer and very little else. On the desks, a few sheets of paper. She picked up the top sheet. A scientific paper, with a note attached: For your input. She flicked through it, four pages. Latin words, some vaguely familiar from her oceanography degree, a series of chemical formulae. She glanced at the title: "*Amphiprion percula* and *Hypoplectrus nigricans* in the Production of Hipophrine and Percuprone as Transform Mechanisms in Sexual Definition Management." Right.

She checked the offices across the hall, Lorna Albright's, with a sofa. Terry Paquette's. Nothing seemed of significance. But how would she know? Better get out, anyway. The only factor, each desk, except Albright's, had a copy of that paper, each with a note requesting input. Albright's name appeared under the title in large caps, then the names of the other three physicians from the clinic in smaller print.

One more door, another lab. She glanced about. Vials and beakers and tubes, a couple of sinks, computers, paper and more paper. She read headings. The words *hipophrine* and *percuprone* appeared and reappeared, with formulae and lists of other unknown words juxtaposed. None of it made sense. But they were in fact brewing something here.

Noel breathed deeply, and pressed 1 on his phone.

"Yes?"

"Police just came by. They check here regularly."

"You okay?"

"Just barely."

"Hang in, I'm nearly done. Out in a minute."

He closed his phone, stuffed it into his pocket and grabbed the steering wheel tightly.

A quick thought: take a copy of the paper. She grabbed one from the most cluttered desk. She stared again at the title. In fact she did know the meaning of most of those words. Except hipophrine and percuprone. Hipophrine. Percuprone. Hormones? Hipo— Perc— Holy shit!

Okay, outa here. Electricity back on. Would the alarm scream at her again when she threw the switch back? Had to be done. She checked her escape route. Both inner and outer doors open, ready for her to stampede away. Her cellphone rang. Shit. Noel's voice: "Kyra, can you hear me?"

"Yes. What?"

"Come on out. The cop'll be back. We've got to get out of here."

"I'm coming. Two minutes." She shoved the phone into her purse, glanced about once more, and ran her eyes across the fish tanks. Where had she seen fish tanks recently? She pulled the switch. Lights on. No screaming wail. Get out before it comes on. She heard the generator's whine die. All lights out. Picks into lock, inner door closed. Outer door, out, picks, locked. Down the walk, the fence, chain open, gate, chain on, lock in place. Click. Only Noel's rental over there. She heard the engine start. She walked quickly, did not run, to the passenger door. In. "Let's go!" Kyra gave Noel a brilliant smile. He caught the gleam of her teeth in dim light. "Drive! I found something, maybe research results."

He pulled out, one eye on the rear-view mirror. God he felt drained. And she was hyped. She flicked on her flashlight and read him the title. "Those pills in Sandro's medicine cabinet, weren't they called hipoperc?"

"I don't remember. Didn't you give the name to Jerome?"

"Yeah. Maybe he's heard something from his friend." She glanced back at the paper. "Let's drop by. He may understand the report." She flipped through it. Way too complicated. She switched off the flash.

"What was in there?"

"Tanks of fish. Shrimp. White mice and rabbits in cages. Computers. Three offices and two labs."

"How about security?"

"I had to flip the breaker. Did you hear an alarm go off?"

"No."

"Good."

Noel drove in silence. His fear, turned to relief, left him with nothing to say. Ten minutes later he pulled up beside the Tracker in front of Samson's.

"I'll call Jerome, make sure he's there." She pressed numbers, and explained. "We have a document we need translated out of scientific-ese. Great, within the hour, we won't stay— Thanks."

They drove in tandem up-island, off-island, to, and up, the I-5.

TWENTY-ONE

NOT YET TIME for bed but she could get ready. Lorna Albright flicked off the sit-com halfway through. A long day coming tomorrow and something would go wrong, she felt it. Something worse than Richard's desire for confession. Terry had confirmed Richard's change of mind; he too wanted only for the work to go on. Richard had stopped being an issue.

She headed upstairs. Clothes off, pajamas on. No report reading tonight, a novel to take her mind off— The doorbell rang. She glanced at her watch. 9:12. Who? She could pretend to be in the bathroom, shower running. It rang again, longer, more insistent. Hell, she wasn't at the beck and call of any doorbell. If the phone rang now, she'd be damned if she'd answer. Another blast on the bell. She pulled on a bathrobe and walked down the stairs. Make damn sure you know who's out there before opening. A thin curtain covered the face-high window, hard to see in, easier looking out. She slowly glanced through. Gary. What the hell? The bell razzed again, right by her ear. She opened the door. "Enough, Gary!"

"Oh, thank god." He brushed past her. He walked down the hall, turned. "Lorna—" He stared into the living room, strode over to the liquor cabinet, found a bottle of Scotch, a glass, poured it half-full and drank a quarter of it.

Lorna followed. Gary had gone questing after the bottle as if it were a grail. "What's up?"

He set the glass down and put his hands in his pockets. "Richard's dead."

"What!"

"Take my word for it. Dead."

She tried to say, How? But her throat had gone so tight she couldn't speak. Oh, poor Terry! She forced her voice to whisper, "How? What?"

"Listen carefully." Gary's voice was steady. "This evening we had supper together. Here. I was with you from seven o'clock on."

"What? Why? You—?"

"He attacked me. We fought. The pistol went off, he fell. I checked him. He was dead. I grabbed his wallet. Nobody saw me. It's okay."

Okay? What did that mean? "But—you fought? Why?"

"He was going to open up all that Vasiliadis shit." On Gary's lips, a half smile. "I think Richard knew."

"No. Not possible."

"Quite possible. But it doesn't matter. He's not going to tell anybody. That episode is over." Gary drank more Scotch. "So okay, I was here with you, right? Seven o'clock, you cooked—?"

"I was at the lab till about six-thirty. Then I went to Stockman's place. Bonnie's away, visiting one of the kids. I had dinner with Stockman tonight."

Gary stared at her. "Shit," he said.

"You've got to go to the police, you have to tell them—"

"Don't be stupid! Not the police!"

"You tell them what you just said to me, it was an accident."

"Get this through your head. We have to keep this as far from the clinic as possible."

"As far? For god's sake! Richard *is* a quarter of the clinic. Was. Oh, goddamn it!" The first real sense of his death hit her, her throat trembled, she sat. "You-have-to-explain-to-the—"

"Don't be ridiculous."

"Then I'll tell them."

"Will you try to understand what I'm saying? You're involved in this as much as I am."

"I didn't kill Richard."

He smiled at her, a cold, flat smile. "No. Not Richard."

She shivered. "I didn't kill anybody."

Gary's smile stayed in place. "No. Not in that sense."

"I wasn't even there."

Gary took another tumbler and poured more Scotch. He studied the liquid, then poured again as much. "You agreed." He handed her the glass.

She took it with two hands, brought it to her lips, sipped. Her eyes filled with tears, and her nose ran. She sniffed. "I wasn't there."

"We all understood what had to be done."

She blotted her eyes with her bathrobe tie. "Richard wouldn't have thought so."

"Exactly. We were right not to include him. You must see that."

In her mind's eye all she saw was Richard and Terry, the lab, the clinic, their patients, Stockman, Gary, Dawn, everything she knew and cared about, falling from the heavens, so much dissolving sleet. Flat, still puddles. She set the glass on the shelf and hugged herself, as if she were the only thing still possible to hold on to. "Oh god oh god oh god—"

"So." Gary sounded filled with cheer. "What did Stockman cook for you and me this evening?"

"What?"

"Let's go for a drive."

Noel pulled in behind the Tracker. In the streetlight he saw Jerome's house. Yes, it needed more than paint. The days renovating an old Nanaimo house with Brendan were gone, but his eye hadn't changed. He followed Kyra to the door. Jerome opened, his hand on Nelson's collar. The dog bellowed ferociously.

"He sure doesn't like me." Kyra glared at Nelson.

"How's your leg?"

"Tender but not throbbing. No infection. I'll survive."

Jerome leaned over and kissed her cheek. "Hello," he said to Noel. He transferred Nelson's collar to his left hand and stuck out his right. Noel shook it.

They entered. Jerome shut the door and let go the collar. Nelson sent a low growl in Kyra's direction, bounded to the living room and returned with a ball. He dropped it at Noel's feet, looked up and panted in anticipation.

"Better you than me." Kyra said.

"No ball games in the house," Jerome told Nelson, but in a non-authoritarian tone. "Let me take your coats. Some coffee? A drink?"

If no games in the house how come a ball was lying around? Kyra shrugged out of her jacket, tossed it on the newel post— Jerome hung both coats in the closet.

They entered the living room. "A drink would be great," Noel said.

"Me too," added Kyra.

"Scotch? Gin? Drambuie?"

Kyra said, "I could handle a Scotch."

"Fine." Noel sat in the leatherette chair.

Jerome disappeared. Nelson picked up his ball, padded across the carpet, again dropped it in front of Noel. The dog crouched, looking from Noel to the ball.

"I get the idea Nelson does not like girls." Kyra sat on the sofa.

Jerome returned with a tray and three glasses. He passed them around, took his, and sat beside Kyra.

She handed him the paper. "Here it is."

Noel took two good sips and put his feet on the hassock. Nelson lay down, head between paws, still checking out Noel. Jerome speed-read the paper. Noel tried to imagine Kyra living here with Jerome. Something out of whack there. Which part, Kyra living here, or living with Jerome? If Jerome knocked out that wall, combined the space here with the dining room he saw through the door, and modernized the kitchen, he'd have a presentable downstairs. Space under the stairs would likely accommodate a powder room.

Jerome said, "I don't know the biochemistry here. But it deals with enzymes derived from hermaphroditic fish and crustaceans. From what I understand the researchers have injected them into mice, and the mice have changed from males to females." He got up and fetched a green tome, a pharmacopeia, from the bookshelf and searched the index.

Noel considered the living room for several minutes. Yes, he'd replace that old cracked fireplace with a wood stove. Were wood stoves legal in urban Bellingham?

Jerome said, "Neither of these has been approved. The two in the title are likely the active agents in this hipoperc. I emailed my friend but I haven't heard. I'll phone him in the morning."

"Thanks." Kyra took back the paper. "What do you make of it?"

"Looks like early research. Not stuff I'd invest in yet. Still your transgendered guy?"

"Yeah."

"I'd guess at a process where the biochemistry is central to the changes."

"That's what we were getting to," Kyra said. Noel nodded.

Nelson picked up his ball, dropped it closer to Noel's feet, let out a yowl and wagged his tail. "Be a good dog," Jerome said. "Noel isn't going to play."

Kyra finished her drink. "We better be heading off." She stood.

Noel drained his glass and stood. "Sorry, Nelson."

"It's okay, I'll take him out before bed. And I'll phone you when I hear something."

"Thanks," said Kyra.

Jerome squeezed her hand, then brought their jackets.

Noel glanced into the dining room. Maybe wainscoting. "Kyra said you want to redecorate. The place has neat possibilities."

"You think so?"

"My partner and I renovated a house like this in Nanaimo. You need an architect who specializes in renos. Ask around. That's what we did."

Jerome looked surprised, and grateful. "Okay. Thanks."

"Thanks for your help with the paper. And the drink."

Jerome kissed Kyra's cheek. "I'll be in touch."

Nelson, carrying his ball, gave Noel a look of betrayal. The door closed.

Noel got in the Tracker beside Kyra. Jerome had taken her hand, Jerome had kissed her cheek. No response from Kyra. Hmm.

"Going to leave your car here?"

"Kyra," he took her forearm, "they're using drugs on people that haven't been approved yet for animals."

"On one person we know of."

"One is plenty." Noel squeezed, let go. "They could all lose the right to practice medicine."

"Yeah."

"Something went wrong with that one person. If he complained about his condition beyond the clinic, they could all lose their licenses. Someone had to make sure Sandro never spoke about their work."

"And maybe killed him."

Noel opened the Tracker door, "Meet you back at your place," and got into his rental.

Stockman Jones opened his door wearing a red silk smoking jacket, a glare dominating his face. "What?"

Gary said, "Aren't you going to ask us in?"

Stockman swung the door open wider. Lorna followed Gary through the entryway. Stockman swung the door shut. "You could at least have called."

"Always better not to leave a phone record, right?"

"What're you talking about?"

Gary took off his jacket. "We need to talk."

"What can't wait till tomorrow?"

"Lots. We should sit down."

Stockman shrugged, and led them to the living room.

"Yes thanks," said Gary, "I'll have a Scotch."

Stockman glanced at him. "Lorna? You too?"

"No thank you."

"No ice," said Gary.

Stockman opened a cabinet, took out a bottle and a crystal goblet, and poured. He handed Gary the glass. They all sat. "What's this all about?"

Gary told him. The color faded from Stockman's face. When Gary finished, Stockman said nothing. He stared at neither of his colleagues but between them, as if a third person sat there. So it ends, he thought. So it ends.

"Lorna thinks the honey chicken with rice and asparagus you made for us was delicious," Gary said. "I agree."

"What?"

Lorna said, "His alibi."

"You want me—?"

"Yes, I want that. We need that."

"But how can I—"

"Stockman. Cool. I know how to handle this. With a little help from each other, we can all handle it."

"But if you—"

"It's going to be just fine. You want it to be fine, and I want it to be fine. So does Lorna." He turned to her. "Right, Lorna?"

She met his gaze, but said nothing.

"Right. Richard was killed this evening by a person or by persons unknown."

"What—" Lorna looked away then, "what happened to the pistol?"

"I got rid of it."

"Where?"

"We're on an island. There's water all around."

"But—where?"

"You don't need to know. All you need to know, and you'll know it when you see it on TV, is the motive was robbery. Richard put up a fight. He died."

Stockman sighed heavily. "The poor man."

Lorna stared at him. Had it taken so little for him to accept Gary's story as truth?

"What kind of wine did we drink, Stockman? A Liebfraumilch?"

"Too sweet with honey chicken. A Chardonnay. One of our fine Washington state wines."

"I don't like Chardonnay. Let's say, a Pinot Gris."

A chill crept down the marrow of Lorna's bones. She needed some time to consider all this— Gary had gotten up. She thought she heard an echo of his words, that he needed a bathroom. She saw Gary walking away as through a mesh, a receding figure, vague and dim. She heard Stockman say her name. "Huh?"

"Are you okay?"

"Okay?" What an incredible question. "No. No. He killed Richard. While we were having dinner. Just like that."

"I know." Stockman rubbed the back of his neck. "It's all over."

"Maybe not. But we have to make him go to the police. It's not a good route but the only possible one I can think of."

"He's out of control, Lorna." Stockman thought about an uncontrollable Gary. "Again."

Lorna thought back to the night Sandro Vasiliadis died. Till now their most worrying moment ever, brought on by Gary's lack of restraint. "In Seattle."

Stockman nodded. "That woman."

The story had nearly gotten into the news, a local reporter. Gary had convinced the others he should be allowed to engage in sexual intercourse with certain patients for whom such therapy would be helpful. And just before the act, a patient decided she didn't want his help. Gary insisted. The woman went to the police and tried to bring charges. After interviewing Gary and his colleagues the cops decided she'd brought the incident on herself. So she laid the story out for that damn reporter. Gary just about lost it. A quiet fury, but extreme. He told the woman to withdraw the story. She refused. Gary made it clear what could happen if she continued: the incident would bring shame to herself, to her family, and especially to her twelve-year-old daughter, the girl would be laughed at, maybe beaten up, possibly sexually attacked, who could tell with a mother like that. The woman and her daughter left Seattle. Gary had made all the danger go away.

Lorna said, "I will have a bit of Scotch."

Stockman found a glass, poured, brought it to her.

Gary returned. "It'll all be fine. You'll see. Just like it was with Vasiliadis."

Stockman glared at him. "We agreed to never mention it again!"

Gary laughed. "Very well for you not to mention it. Just like you didn't want to do anything about it. Who had to drive us there? Who had to convince the guy? Who had to administer the morphine? Not you, Stockman. You didn't want to mention it. Who had to hide those syringes? Not you, Lorna. Sometimes I can't stand either of you." He crossed to the Scotch bottle, poured. "Any of that honey chicken left? I haven't had time to eat."

"Yes," said Stockman. "There is."

"Come on, you guys. You'll see. It'll be fine."

Lorna didn't believe him. Not this time.

<hr />

No clean underwear. One pair of socks, Kyra's least favorite. The contents of both bureau and closet seemed unreasonably skimpy. Ah, the dryer! Where they'd been since Sunday morning. The other way to store clothes. She dumped everything into the laundry basket and carried it to her bedroom. The other way? For five minutes she organized, piled, hung up clothes. She started the coffee. The other way. She pulled on underwear, jeans, a shirt. She knocked on Noel's door.

"Mm?" He lay in bed, half-awake.

"Remember what Ursula said Sandro said: 'This is what I get for trying to go the other way?' About his swollen balls?"

"Mm?"

"We've been understanding 'the other way' to mean becoming a woman. What if he meant he knew he'd get transgendered without surgery?" She stared at him. "What if he was telling her that?"

Noel sat up. "That they were using the fish stuff on him. Without his actually saying it?"

"Because they'd warned him against talking to anyone beyond the clinic. Because he was involved in an unapproved experiment. Because—" The phone rang, her personal line. She picked it up and turned her back to Noel, to give him privacy. "Hello?"

Noel swung his legs out and pulled on his trousers. He went into the bathroom.

Kyra sat on the end of the bed. "That's great, Jerome, thanks so much . . . Good, *sans* Nelson . . . Depends on the case . . . I'll let you know."

Noel returned after she'd hung up. "Jerome's FDA friend had checked into the WISDOM experiments. Jerome was right, early-stage research in transgendering by hormones alone. They have approval to use animals. But not human subjects."

"That drug in Sandro's cabinet?"

"Derived from hermaphroditic fish species." Kyra headed for the kitchen to check the coffee maker. "Okay. What we know. Transgendering via drugs is successful on the mice. They try the hormones on humans. Something goes wrong with Sandro—"

"And one of them killed him?"

"We don't know that. Had they tried the hormones on anybody else?"

"Maybe Sandro was the first." Noel spoke slowly. "Nobody knew about anybody else. Wouldn't Chelsea have heard if there'd been a non-surgical success?"

"Maybe not. It all must be pretty secretive."

"These guys are in deep shit."

"We need to see their files." Kyra poured the coffee. "Tonight—?"

"No. We go to the police." Noel spoke firmly. "We tell them enough to interest them. They seize the files."

"Does doctor-patient confidentiality override a search warrant?"

"There's a lot of legal dispute about that. At least in Canada." He took the mug Kyra handed him. "Thanks."

"We could confront the other doctors. The smug ones, Jones and Haines."

"No. Let the police—" The business line rang. Noel headed for the study and took it.

Kyra turned on the radio and sipped her coffee. More alleged terrorists jailed for interrogation, a small plane crash. Local morning news, "A Whidbey Island physician was shot at close range yesterday evening." Kyra turned up the volume. "Dr. Richard Trevelyan, an endocrinologist at the WISDOM clinic in Coupeville, was found in front of his home. He is in critical condition. The State Patrol suspects robbery. The same Dr. Trevelyan was also in the news on Saturday when he was plucked from the water by the Coast Guard ship *Neptune* after an explosion aboard his pleasure yacht. In other news—" Kyra turned the radio off.

Noel returned. "That was Chelsea wanting an update. I filled— Kyra, you're white—"

"The doctor, that endocrinologist? He was shot last night. Trevelyan."

"The one whose boat exploded?" Kyra nodded. "Is he dead?"

"No, but critical."

"How?"

She told him what she'd heard.

"The cops have to, have to, confront the other doctors."

"We've got suspicions, that's all. That sheriff won't give a damn."

"Maybe that State Patrol cop."

"We need more information. I'd prefer to break in, go through the files ourselves."

"No, Kyra. Period." He picked up his mug. "We tell Assounian what we've figured out about the clinic. Then we talk to Trevelyan's wife. Before anybody else dies. Or gets hurt."

"I bet she's with him at that hospital in Coupeville," Kyra said. "Can you find the number?"

He did. Kyra picked up the phone. "You have Richard Trevelyan there? . . . ICU? . . . What's his status? . . . Thanks." She hung up. "Still critical," she told Noel. "Let's go."

"I'll return the rental on the way."

Just three of them at the conference table this Tuesday morning. The only good thing for Lorna, Gary wasn't doused with aftershave.

Stockman said, "You told us he was dead."

"He will be soon. No one could live through that much trauma."

"So far he has," Lorna said. "He was still in a coma when I stopped by at the hospital."

"So we have to rethink," said Stockman. "If Richard dies and no suspicion falls on you, we won't give you away. Right, Lorna?"

Lorna nodded, reluctantly. "But if he lives, he'll name you. And we won't, at least I won't, cover for you." She looked at Stockman, who nodded also.

"He won't live," Gary repeated. "He won't regain consciousness." He smiled. "It'll be fine."

———

Kyra followed Noel to the car rental. He climbed into her Tracker. They drove in silence. As she slowed for the Anacortes turnoff, she said, "Do you think she'll even talk to us?"

"We should have called." He took his cellphone from his pocket. "We still can."

"I'd rather just arrive."

"If I were her, I wouldn't see us."

They crossed the bridge onto Whidbey Island, through Oak Harbor, into Coupeville and parked at the hospital. At the desk they asked for directions to the ICU. "But no one's allowed in," said the receptionist.

Kyra said, "Is Ursula Bunche on duty today?"

The receptionist picked up her phone and asked for Bunche. "Thank you." She set the phone down. "She's here but she's terribly busy."

"Richard Trevelyan's in ICU, he's my cousin," Kyra pleaded "We're pretty sure his wife's there, she'll want to talk with us. Ursula could go in and ask her to come out."

"There's a phone by the ICU door. You can talk to the nursing station. They can tell you," she raised an eyebrow, "if your cousin's wife is there."

"Thank you." They followed the receptionist's directions and found the phone. Was Richard Trevelyan's wife with her husband?

She looked at Noel. "The nurse'll see if she's available." Noel watched Kyra shuffle until she said, "Thank you," and put the phone down. "She'll be right out."

A woman, her blouse rumpled, came through the doorway. "Yes?" The skin around her eyes, red in the whites, was puffy and bruised.

Kyra said, "Mrs. Trevelyan?"

The woman nodded. "Terry Paquette. Mrs. Richard Trevelyan."

"This must be a terrible time for you, and we apologize for intruding."

She glanced from one to the other. "What do you want?"

"We talked with your husband Saturday morning, before he went out in his boat. About Sandro Vasiliadis."

"Oh. Yes." She sat on a naugahyde divan.

"First," Noel said, handing her a Triple-I card, "here's who we are. Please tell us how your husband is."

"He's not regained consciousness, but they're hopeful." She looked at the card, and at them. "Who are you?"

"As my partner said, we've been investigating the Vasiliadis death. We won't take much of your time."

She stared at her hands. "I've got plenty of that. Ask away."

Kyra sat on the divan beside Terry. Noel took a chair. Kyra said, "We are very sorry about your husband. It's awful."

Terry's eyes watered. "I just don't understand."

"We don't either, Mrs. Trevelyan. But we think—"

"Paquette. Terry. Richard's my husband. I never took his name."

Noel said, "We think there may be more to the shooting than mugging and robbery."

Terry stared at him. "What do you mean?"

"Have you spoken with anyone from the police?"

"Two State Patrol officers came by last night. And Sheriff Vanderhoek was here a couple of hours ago. Why did you say that—more than robbery?"

"He almost died on Saturday, didn't he? At sea?"

"Yes, but—I mean, that was an accident, *Panacea* burnt and sank."

"Ms. Paquette, can we back up a minute? Your husband was in charge of Sandro Vasiliadis at WISDOM, right? For transgendering."

"Yes. The clinic was. All the doctors are involved in all the cases."

"Would it be fair to say that something went wrong with Sandro's treatment?"

Terry paused for a moment. "Well, not all clients react similarly. Everybody's chemistry is slightly different, and—"

"But Sandro's treatment was experimental, isn't that correct?"

Terry shrugged.

"We know it was, Ms. Paquette. His medications included a combination of hormones, something called hipophrine, and something else called percuprone, to produce non-surgical transgendering. Isn't that right?"

Terry stared at them. "Why are you here?"

Noel glanced at Kyra. She began gently. "Ms. Paquette, WISDOM didn't have FDA approval to test these hormones on a human subject, did they?"

She said nothing.

"These two drugs were being tested on mice and rabbits. But a human?"

Terry interrupted with a whisper. "I don't know where you have your information from. But if you insist on making these accusations, at least be accurate. The animal tests were successful. And sufficient. Two trials on patients at the clinic were successful. Yes, something did go wrong with Vasiliadis. But we would have solved that problem, too." She rubbed her forehead.

"Two other patients?"

Terry looked at them. "Two successes."

Kyra glanced at Noel. He nodded. Kyra said, "We think it likely a member of the WISDOM team injected Vasiliadis with an overdose of morphine."

Terry shut her eyes and covered her mouth with crossed hands. "Richard feared that was—possible."

"Did he mention this to any of the other doctors?"

"I doubt it. He told me yesterday. Before he went to the hospice. He always tries his ideas on me first."

"Could someone have overheard him?"

"He was calling from home. He was by himself."

"Who could have known he was going to the hospice?"

"Anybody." She shrugged. "That's where he went on Monday evenings."

"Even on a Monday after he'd nearly died on the boat?"

"Richard is devoted to his hospice work."

Noel leaned forward. "Do you agree with your husband? That one of his colleagues might have brought on Sandro's death?"

"I know them all. They wouldn't—couldn't—they're physicians!"

"And yet?"

"Their purpose is to improve lives, not take them away. That's been the whole importance of WISDOM. To give new life to certain kinds of people. We all sacrificed ourselves to that ideal. We'd all do anything to safeguard WISDOM."

"Anything?" Noel asked gently.

"Oh god," said Terry.

———

The Tracker drove out of the hospital parking lot. Noel said, "We need to report this to the State Patrol. The hormones, the other patients." He took his cellphone from his pocket. "Shall I?"

"Yes."

TWENTY-TWO

DAWN DEANE KNOCKED on Dr. Stockman Jones' door. She heard his usual interrogative, "Yes?" turned the handle, and entered. He beamed up at her from his desk chair. Then he saw her face. The smile disappeared. "Are you all right?"

"There're two men here." She spoke quietly. The State Patrol, and the FDA."

"What do they want?"

"To speak to someone with authority."

"Send them in." Did they already know about Gary and Richard? Oh dear oh dear.

Dawn left. Stockman breathed deeply. He rubbed damp palms on his trousers. The police and the Food and Drug Administration. Maybe a routine check. Except they'd not had a routine check before so how could this be routine? Should he have legal counsel present? Bob Melman was a phone call away. Ridiculous. He could handle it. A sharp knock on the door. "Yes?"

The door opened. A man in uniform entered, followed by another man, tall and thin. Carl Assounian introduced himself as the sergeant in charge of the Sandro Vasiliadis investigation, the other man as Joe Turndeck of the Seattle branch, FDA. Turndeck wore a dark suit and tie, and an open raincoat. He carried a briefcase. Stockman asked them to sit. Turndeck did, setting the case on his lap.

Assounian remained standing. "I understand your colleague Dr. Trevelyan's in the hospital. Have you heard how he is?"

Stockman sighed. "He's still in Intensive Care."

"Had a run of bad luck, hasn't he?"

"Yes." Damn him, why didn't he sit.

Turndeck said, "About Sandro Vasiliadis."

"Vasiliadis? The man who killed himself?"

"Was Vasiliadis your patient, Dr. Jones?"

"A patient of the clinic, yes. We look after the patients according to our specialties."

"You were treating him? Specifically for a sex-change procedure?"

"Yes. That's one of the treatments we do here. I am one of the team."

Assounian glanced at Turndeck long enough to make it impossible for Jones not to notice. Assounian said, "Were you treating Vasiliadis in any way different from your other patients?"

Should he bristle? Placate? "Each of our patients is unique, Sergeant. They're all handled differently."

Turndeck, his voice low in his throat, said, "Dr. Jones, were the procedures you were trying on Vasiliadis different from those used on others?"

Stockman smiled. "Not at all. Quite similar, in fact." How easy to tell the truth.

Turndeck opened his briefcase. "You and your colleagues have a long-standing research contract with Bendwell Pharmaceuticals, is that correct?"

"Absolutely. We've been working with them for seven years." Bad bad.

"And the nature of this research is?"

Stockman hated it when somebody asked him a question while all the time knowing the answer. Sneaky. "We're trying to develop," be technical, or speak to the cop? To the cop: "to develop a drug or drugs which will abet the transgendering process with as little surgical intrusion as possible."

"I see." Turndeck took a file from his case, closed the lid, set the file on top and opened it. "You've been successful, right, with both mice and rabbits?"

"That is correct." As well as nearly public knowledge, Stockman almost declared, but decided they might think he was taunting them.

"Have you experimented with monkeys?"

"No."

"Do you plan to?"

"No." But Stockman could hear the next series of questions.

"Have you experimented with humans?"

"It would be the logical next step." Maybe now was the time to call Melman? But they knew everything already.

Assounian took over. "Were you transgendering Sandro Vasiliadis with the same drugs that had been successful with mice and rabbits?"

Stockman closed his eyes. He massaged his brow. Hard.

"Dr. Jones?"

"Yes." Barely audible, but he knew they'd heard. And anyway, they knew.

"But with Sandro Vasiliadis, you weren't successful."

"We were." He looked up. "Nearly. We would have been, if—if he hadn't killed himself."

"You would have been? How do you know?"

"Because—because—"

"Because you'd achieved success with two other patients?"

Oh My Dear God help me here. Stockman Jones crossed his arms over his chest and tried to breath deep into his diaphragm.

"Dr. Jones, we'd like to see your file for Sandro Vasiliadis. And the two others."

"No. You can't. Files are confidential. Vasiliadis is—was—a patient here." Stockman stood, pushing himself up with his hands on the chair arms.

Turndeck stood also, grasping his case. "You can show the files to us, which will suggest you want to help in the investigation. Or we'll get a search warrant. Your choice."

"Very well. Follow me." He led them, on legs firmer than he'd feared, out the door to Dawn Deane's reception counter. He gestured to the cabinets behind her. "Dawn, would you pull the Vasiliadis file, please."

She stared at Stockman.

He nodded. "It's all right." It wasn't. But he had no choice.

She shrugged, circled her chair around, pulled open the $T-U-V$ cabinet, bent over it, ran her fingers forward along the files. Ran them back. Separated several files. Turned. "It's not here."

Turndeck glanced at Assounian, then asked Dawn, "Could someone have it out?"

"I don't think so. When I give out a file—"

To Jones, Assounian said, "The other two files as well, please."

Jones frowned. "I don't think— I mean, that's not— There's a difference, these women are alive, they have their lives."

"The same principle, Doctor. We can see them voluntarily, or—"

Stockman's eyes felt like they'd filmed over. "Dawn, bring the files for Johnson and Gustafson."

A new voice: "What's going on, Dawn? Stock?" Gary Haines glared at Assounian and Turndeck. "Who are these guys?"

Stockman introduced them. Dawn explained what they wanted.

Gary grabbed Stockman by the arm and drew him a few feet up the corridor. "Are you crazy?" he whispered. "They've got no right to ask, and you've no right to show those files to anyone!"

"They said we could cooperate. Or they'd get a search warrant."

"No judge in this state is going to give them a warrant to poke around in the files of one of our patients!"

"They said—"

"I don't care what they said! Did you call Melman?"

Stockman shook his head.

"This is why he's on retainer!" Gary whirled and strode to the counter. "Dawn, call Melman. And nobody gets to see confidential files."

Dawn reached for the phone. She looked up at Gary. "The Vasiliadis file seems to be missing."

Gary sighed through his teeth, a deep dramatic breath. "And what else is going wrong?" He squinted at Assounian and Turndeck. "You gentlemen better leave. Now."

Turndeck looked at Assounian. Assounian nodded. He said, "See you soon."

⁓

Stockman turned up his driveway. He knew the pitch and shift of the gravel surface as well as he understood the disaster facing him, but his concentration hadn't been on driving since he'd left WISDOM. He parked the Jaguar in the redone barn, beside the Pathfinder. Bonnie was back. Good. He knew what he had to do next.

After the two men had left the clinic, Gary had berated him for ten minutes, first in front of Dawn, and when Stockman wouldn't listen and marched back to his office, Gary followed and rebuked him some more. Gary couldn't figure which was Stockman's worst offense, talking to those guys in the first place instead of bringing the attorney in, or saying he'd show them Sandro's file. A good thing it was missing. To even think of letting them see the other files! The castigation had stopped only because Stockman refused to respond. Gary strode out.

Stockman left the barn door open and walked toward the house. Some nerve, Gary, upbraiding me when I'm protecting you! The hilltop lay in deep fog, the mock fascia and crenellation blurred. The whole house felt soggy. The knob turned with a squeak. In the kitchen he called, "Bonnie!" She'd only spent one night at Franny's, checking out the house their daughter had made an offer on. It felt like a week since he'd seen her. "You there?"

A voice came to him from around a couple of corners. "In my office!"

He found her behind the computer, working on a kitchen design. "Hi." He stood in the doorway. Sheets of house plans covered the long work table, her overnight case unopened on the loveseat.

She turned and smiled. "Give me a moment to save." She returned to the screen, clicked several times. "There." She stood and hugged him. He hugged her back limply. "Not much of a greeting."

"Not much, no." He hugged her hard.

"That's better." She stepped back and looked at his face. "What's wrong?"

One thing at a time. "You haven't heard?"

She shook her head, a small fear batting her eyelids.

"Richard, last night, he was mugged. Shot, he's in ICU."

"Oh dear God." She hugged him again, and held him. "Oh, poor Terry—"

"It's awful." He pulled away. "But there's worse."

"What could be—"

He led her to the loveseat, picked up her case, set it on the carpet and sat down.

She sat beside him, and took his left hand in both hers.

He covered her fingers with his right and squeezed. "It's all over. We're all done."

Her face said she didn't understand. "What's over?" She pulled away. "God! Us?"

He gave her a weak smile. "No, not in that way." He hugged her to him. "I'll love you beyond death." He drew back. "The work. The clinic."

"What's happened?"

He sighed. "Sandro Vasiliadis."

"But you had that under control, didn't you?"

"It came out of control. We had a visit today from the State Patrol and the FDA."

"Oh. Oh dear. That's what you were worried about."

"Partly. The human trials, yes—"

"But your successes, Stock, they should be worth a great deal."

"It might have been worth everything. But then we had the Sandro—mishap."

"Sure, he killed himself, but that shouldn't—"

"Bonnie. He didn't kill himself."

She squinted at him. "Then it really was an acci— Oh my God." She leaned close to him and took his forearm. "What?"

He couldn't look at her. "We were all responsible. Except Richard, I mean. He wasn't around, we couldn't find him. In truth, we didn't want him around. If only he had been."

"But—what did you do?"

"Gary and Lorna and I talked about it, we had to quiet Sandro down, we had to silence him till—till—I don't think we knew till what. We agreed, we'd do whatever it took. We were in my office. We'd go to Sandro's home that Friday evening and—deal with him. We all agreed, we'd do whatever it took. The work of the clinic was too important to let him mess it up. We drove to his house. Down near Clinton. Not Lorna, she had to be at Teeseborough. Or so she said. But she agreed, Gary and I to do what was necessary."

Bonnie said, "Necessary?"

"Sandro was in such pain when we arrived. He nearly didn't let us in. He was wearing a housecoat and he looked like a hag with streaked makeup. We tried to talk to him but he only screamed, he called us quacks and torturers, and then he pulled the housecoat open to show what the hormones had done to his testes. 'Here!' he shouted, 'Look! See what you've done!' and— It was a disaster. They were huge, like they might burst."

"Oh, Stock, the poor guy."

"Gary had his bag, we got Vasiliadis onto the bed, we said we'd help him, but he didn't trust us, he fought us so I had to hold him down and Gary shot his arm with morphine, a substantial dose, but it only quieted Sandro down a little so Gary grabbed another syringe and shot more morphine into him but it still didn't put him out, he was still moaning, I said 'Gary! Enough!' but Gary took another syringe and—"

"Another? Three?"

"Yes."

"Oh God."

"I know, yes I know."

"And you held him?"

"I didn't have to then, not any more."

"Gary had the syringes ready? Prepared? Three of them?"

Stockman nodded.

"Please God." She pulled her hands from Stockman's and cupped her brow, eyes, nose. "This didn't happen."

"Sandro was dead in minutes." Stockman breathed deeply. "I panicked. Gary stayed cool. We had to make it look like he overdosed. We washed the makeup from his face and dressed him in sweatpants and a shirt, the only men's clothing in his closet. Except for bowling clothes but Gary didn't think he'd overdose before or after bowling and we couldn't find any men's underwear."

Bonnie turned to face him. "I can't believe this."

He looked squarely at her. "It's what happened."

"And you took Sandro? You drove his body?"

"Yes. Gary took Sandro's car, with the body. I followed. To the cemetery. I wasn't thinking, I was so scared, going on automatic. The cemetery's usually deserted enough but people would pass by. Gary told me he'd spent the drive thinking if we should leave a syringe with the body, and he finally decided not to, make it look as if Sandro had shot up somewhere else, driven there and died."

"Oh Stock, Stock." Tears washed her cheeks.

He took her hand again. "It doesn't end yet, Bonnie."

"Oh my God."

"Richard. He was so upset about Sandro, he'd been responsible for Sandro's dosages, so upset about what WISDOM had done, he wanted to confess. To the police. We tried to calm him. He went out on his boat, and it burned."

"But he was rescued. But—do you mean—?"

Stockman nodded. "Gary decided to deal with it. This time we didn't talk. Gary rigged the gas line to leak and bared a piece of wiring

284

so when everything in the engine housing vibrated enough, a spark would touch some gas and make the whole thing blow. But Richard escaped. Then last night Gary shot Richard. He thought he was dead. He came to Lorna to give him an alibi, but Lorna and I had supper together yesterday so Gary needed me for the alibi too."

"And you said—?"

"I told him yes, of course. He was acting so crazy, he might've killed Lorna and me right there. But I can't cover for him. I said I would, but I can't. He killed Richard." Stockman looked at Bonnie. She was blurred through his tears, his pain. "When he did that, he destroyed WISDOM. We're done."

Bonnie wiped her face with the heel of her hands. "Gary brought the syringes, you say."

"Yes—"

"He had three with him, loaded with morphine."

"Yes."

"He injected Sandro not once, or twice, but three times."

Stockman nodded.

"You tried to stop him, the second time. And the third."

"I think—"

"Listen to me. You tried to stop him. The second time, the third time. You just told me that."

"I—" He breathed, shallow. "Yes. I tried to stop him, after the first shot. But I couldn't."

"We have to go to the police. The State Patrol. I'm going with you. Call Melman, we'll stop there first. He should be with us when you speak to the police."

"It won't work."

"We have to try." She stood. "Come on." Stockman stayed seated. She reached for his hand and tugged.

He looked up at her. "I've destroyed it all. The respect of the community. Our private life. All of it. I've defiled myself in the face of God."

"We'll rescue what we can."

A small sigh from Stockman.

"Get up."

He pushed himself up. "Okay."

"There's a way through this."

"Okay," he said again. "We'll go to the police. I'll call Melman." He stared at her for a moment, but didn't see her. "First I want to go to the clinic."

"Why?"

"Something I forgot to do."

"The sooner we—"

"I need to do this."

She stared at him, her face drawn. "I'll go with you."

"No, Bonnie."

"I'll wait. Read a magazine."

"I'll just be a short while."

"What if one of your patients comes by?"

"I don't see patients on Tuesday."

"I'm coming with you. You do what you have to, I'll call Melman's office and say we'll be there in an hour."

"What if he's busy?"

"Lawyers are available for emergencies. They get paid enough."

As Stockman and Bonnie drove down the hill, the fog thinned out, and patches of actual sunlight poked through. He parked the Jag in his assigned space and marched up to the front door, Bonnie falling in behind. He felt better. In charge again. WISDOM usually did this for him. He greeted Dawn with a smile and a cheery, "Hi, I'm back."

Her brow furrowed. "Are you okay?"

"Everything's under control. All okay here?"

She shook her head slowly. "Not with Richard shot."

Stockman let the solemnity of the moment take him. "Of course. It's dreadful."

"I'd— Would it be okay if—if I went home early?" She noted Bonnie. "Hi."

"Yes," Stockman said. "We should close the office. Anyone else coming in?"

She glanced at the appointments book. "Tiomkin in forty minutes. For Gary."

"Oh." Stockman laughed lightly. "Gary's here then. And Lorna?"

"She went to the lab. Since Terry's not there—"

He frowned. "Do you mind waiting till Tiomkin arrives? I'll take it from there."

"Thank you."

Bonnie sat down. Stockman strode to his office, sat at his desk, glanced about the room. The thick books on their shelves, he'd never need to consult them again. The garden outside the window would have to take care of itself. A thin shaft of sun made a triangle on the window. Ah well. From his desk drawer he took a hand-held tape recorder and began speaking. When he finished, fifteen minutes later, he set the machine on the middle of his desk, and stared at it. He looked about the office. The center of his working universe. He left his office, passed behind the reception counter, said to Dawn and Bonnie, "I need to check some old files," opened the door, flicked on the lights and walked down the steps. Bonnie stepped outside to phone the lawyer.

Stockman stood in front of the metal cabinets, brought out keys, unlocked the middle one. He found rubber tubing, the syringe he needed, and three vials. He drew morphine from a large bottle. He stared at the three full vials. So it must be. So he must transfuse himself, so he must purify WISDOM. He relocked the cabinet. If in minutes he would meet his Maker, he must arrive cleansed. Though Heaven for him wasn't very likely. For a moment he thought of Bonnie, would she think him unfair, to leave her behind? But she wasn't ready to leave yet. He felt a preparedness in his soul.

In the operating room he flicked the light switch and sat on a straight-backed chair. Not a sterile situation, this; but the subsequent cleanliness of his spirit would compensate. He took off his jacket, rolled up his left shirt sleeve, with his right hand and teeth he tied the tubing on his forearm. He sat upright, leaning slightly backward. He must not slump over.

Dawn glanced at her watch. Fifteen minutes till Tiomkin's appointment. She heard the door open, and glanced up. A man and a woman. Dawn recognized the woman detective from a few days ago. And the man, he'd been in for an appointment recently.

They stood in front of the counter. The woman said, "Hi. Kyra Rachel again. And Noel Franklin. I was in last week. About Sandro

Vasiliadis. We need to talk to Dr. Jones, Dr. Haines, and Dr. Albright. It's a matter of great urgency."

Dawn disliked this woman. And his last time here the man had had a different name. But her only role here was to receive people and pass them through. Or not. "You don't understand. You need appointments for each one." She glanced at her book. "You can see Dr. Jones next—"

Franklin said, "No. You don't understand. We have to see them now."

"No need to be dramatic, sir. You'll just have—" But Franklin and Rachel were marching down the corridor toward the Jones and Albright offices. "Wait! You can't—" Franklin opened Stockman's door, glanced about, stepped in. Rachel opened Lorna's door and looked inside. They both reappeared as Dawn rushed down the corridor after them. "This is intrusive. I'm calling the police."

They pushed past her, past the reception desk, down the opposite corridor. "Stop! You can't do that." They did stop. At Richard's office, glancing down to Gary's office. The man grabbed the handle and pushed the door open.

⸻

Not exactly breaking and entering, Noel realized, but they had reached the rim of disturbing the peace. This doctor was in. "Dr. Haines. My colleague and I need a word with you."

The receptionist pushed in from behind. "I'm sorry, I tried to stop them."

"It's okay, Dawn," said Haines, seated, his desk a barrier protecting him from this little fracas. "I'll speak with them."

"You have," she glanced at her watch, "just a few minutes before your next patient."

"Buzz me when he arrives. I'm sure we'll be done by then."

The receptionist closed the door behind her. Haines said, "Yes?"

Noel said, "It's again about Sandro Vasiliadis."

Haines swept his arm before him. "Have a seat. Mr.—Ferguson, was it? Are you here to speak about transgendering options? Or is it your business," he turned to Kyra, "the two of you have come for, Ms.—?"

"Rachel. The latter. But it connects to the former. How did your transgendering of Sandro Vasiliadis go awry, Dr. Haines?"

"But it didn't, Ms. Rachel. Sandro was evolving properly."

"Do your procedures include torture?"

Haines laughed. "Don't be ridiculous. Sandro was overcoming every one of the difficulties normally understood to be part of the procedure."

"Then you've had several patients who've undergone this procedure?"

"Of course. That's what the clinic does."

"The revolutionary new procedure. That some men might be suited for."

Haines leaned forward, his face puzzled. "The new procedure?"

Kyra leaned forward, underlining her mockery. "The new purely medical procedure. Which you've evolved for Bendwell Pharmaceuticals."

"Oh. Well. That." The telephone buzzed twice. He pressed a button. "Yes?" The receptionist's voice, saying Mr. Tiomkin had arrived. "Tell him I'll be just a few minutes." He turned back to Noel and Kyra. "You have to leave now."

"As soon as you tell us about the new procedure."

"We've still got a long way to go before that's approved. Our mice have been—"

"But in the meantime you've tested it out, to see how it works on humans."

"Hardly, Ms. Rachel."

"The research paper authored by the four of you, regarding hipophrine and percuprone?"

"I beg your pardon?" He squinted at her. "How did you have access to documents produced by WISDOM?"

"Professional journals can be leaky places, Dr. Haines. As is the FDA bureaucracy."

"We've been working on several hormones that—"

"Sandro Vasiliadis was taking precisely those two hormones. The bottle of hipoperc was in his medicine cabinet when he died."

For a moment Haines said nothing. The squint faded from his eyes. He stood. "I know nothing of that. Now if you'll excuse me. As you heard—" He walked to the door and opened it. "Leave. Now."

Kyra and Noel remained seated. Then something outside the door caught Haines' attention and in a moment Dawn Deane, horror in her eyes, had collapsed against him. "What, Dawn? What?" He slid his arm around her waist.

Dawn, her breath pulsing out, whispered that Stockman Jones was unconscious down in the operating room. Kyra and Noel looked at each other, then sprinted out and downstairs. Haines followed them more slowly. At the commotion, Bonnie joined the charge. Stockman, sleeve rolled up, a blue tinge to his skin, eyes wide open, barely breathing, tiny pupils, two empty vials at his side, the syringe still sticking out of his inner arm.

Noel pulled out his cellphone, punched in 911 and shouted at Haines, "For god's sake, do something!"

Kyra found a tissue in her purse, grabbed the syringe in it and pulled it out.

A fearful peace took Gary Haines. Stock lay as Vasiliadis had. It was just. Stock had fought against finishing off Sandro, Stock was too weak in that, as in everything. He had turned away as Gary punched the needle into the man's arm again. And even ran out as Gary punched it in again, again four-five-six times for good measure, making it clear the guy was an addicted pincushion. Stockman would have approved less than necessary. He would get less than necessary now.

Bonnie leaned over her husband, her mouth to his, breathing out, was this the right treatment but what else to do, air in, press chest, air in, press chest, a dozen times—

She looked exhausted. Noel pulled her away, took over, she stood back. Haines stared at Jones, not moving.

"Do something for him!" Kyra shouted. "For god's sake, you're a physician!" She put her arm around Bonnie, who collapsed onto her shoulder.

Haines remained frozen for interminable seconds, then turned toward the women, his face void of information. "Nothing to be done. He'll be fine."

"Is what they're doing wrong?" Kyra practically spat in his face.

"No."

Kyra found herself, while supporting Bonnie, breathing in symmetry with the CPR.

Two state patrolmen arrived at WISDOM within minutes of Noel's call. The police secured the basement and commanded everyone upstairs. An ambulance arrived and carted away the still unconscious Stockman Jones and his wife.

Sheriff Burt Vanderhoek showed up half an hour later, then Carl Assounian and his partner, a woman in her thirties, a couple of minutes after that. They disappeared downstairs. Noel, Kyra, the white-faced receptionist and the totally silent Dr. Haines waited. A forensics unit arrived, heavy with equipment. They found the recording machine on Jones' desk, a tape in place. They listened: a confession from Stockman Jones, that he had participated in killing Sandro Vasiliadis in order, as he believed at the time, to rescue WISDOM's reputation; that Gary Haines had admitted to Jones and to Dr. Lorna Albright, in demanding an alibi of them, he had shot Dr. Richard Trevelyan and previously tampered with his boat; that Dr. Jones had already detailed all this to his wife, Bonnie O'Hara; that she tried to convince him to take the full story to the police, where he would repeat it with his lawyer present; but that Stockman Jones felt it best to conclude the whole dreadful business in this present manner.

Assounian and his partner took Dawn and Gary to separate offices and questioned them. They each made statements regarding the afternoon, and signed them. Dawn was allowed to go. Gary Haines explained he had an appointment in Seattle that evening, but Assounian assigned two patrolmen to take him to the sheriff's office for further interrogation. And to bring in Dr. Albright as well.

Assounian questioned Kyra and Noel again, verification of the information so far before him. He thanked them for providing the link between the Vasiliadis death and the new drugs the clinic had been experimenting with. Kyra and Noel requested permission to be present at the interrogation of Albright and Haines. Assounian couldn't allow that, but if they called later in the evening he would tell them anything he could as long as it didn't jeopardize his investigation. They were free to go. From the front door they saw, behind the police tape, a TV station truck.

TWENTY-THREE

KYRA AND NOEL drove back to Bellingham in almost complete silence. They stopped at a fast food joint for late refueling. Kyra finished her fishburger first, with Noel close behind.

At Kyra's they waited impatiently till 8:30 PM when they couldn't stand waiting any longer. Kyra called Assounian. He told her:

Richard Trevelyan had regained consciousness and barring any setbacks would live; his wife's instant intervention had likely saved him with the kiss of life; she said his heart had stopped when she found him.

Stockman Jones was alive but it was too early to know the extent of the damage he had done to himself.

Bonnie O'Hara had corroborated her husband's story about his role in the Vasiliadis death, clarifying responsibility by underlining the fact that Haines was the primary perpetrator, Stockman having attempted to stop the administration of the second and third dose of morphine, her husband wanting only to calm Vasiliadis down and reduce his pain. She also corroborated the part Stockman claimed Lorna Albright played, again repeating what Stockman had told her.

Albright, with lawyer present—Melman couldn't act for her, he was Jones' lawyer—denied she was involved with the Vasiliadis death, but did admit she and Stockman had agreed to provide Haines with an alibi for his admitted killing of Richard Trevelyan. Why did they agree? They were afraid of Haines. He had previously threatened people with violence and was capable of killing either or both of them.

Haines, a lawyer at his side—Melman couldn't act for him either—denied he had killed or harmed anyone, and on the lawyer's advice refused to speak further.

Assounian had dispatched a Bellingham patrol car to inform Maria Vasiliadis that her son had been murdered, and that they had the alleged murderer or murderers in custody.

Kyra hung up. "We should tell all this to Chelsea. Before she hears about it on TV."

"I'll call her."

"Or wait till morning?"

"Now is better." He found her number and picked up the phone. And Kyra had better call Jerome.

A deeper voice than Noel remembered said, "Hello?"

"Hi. Chelsea? Noel Franklin. Reporting in."

"Oh how are you? What's happening?"

"You were right to keep us on the case." He told her about WISDOM's new medical transgendering procedures, how they'd failed with Sandro, and Jones' confession and attempted suicide.

Chelsea remained silent for a few seconds. "It must have been so awful for him. But I'm glad it wasn't Sandro who gave up." Her voice caught in her throat. "They gave up on him."

"Yes."

"Will he be buried now?"

"I imagine so. You planning on coming?" The image of her at the funeral lifted his eyebrows. They said goodbye.

When he arrived back at the table, Kyra said, "Jerome invited us for supper Thursday evening."

Noel could still make tomorrow morning's flight to Nanaimo. But he had a strong sense that Kyra wanted, maybe even needed, him there. "Okay." Anyway, what was waiting for him at home? Two more days with Kyra, preferably quiet days, would be pleasant. And the plants on the balcony could take care of themselves. Or not.

"What did Chelsea say?"

"She seemed upset. We should have been there when we spoke to her."

"Getting the story from TV would've been worse— Oh god!" She rubbed her brow. "Maria Vasiliadis."

"Assounian said he sent someone to tell her."

———

Terry rattled around her house. They'd insisted she get some sleep. But she was still too wound up. In the dining room Richard's navy cardigan, flung off the other day, lay as it had draped. In the bathroom she smelled his aftershave, in the bedroom his tossed pajamas on the bed. Hairbrush and coins on the bureau, he'd pulled them from his pocket Sunday night, dropped a quarter, looked for it, didn't find—

Three nights ago. His study, full of him. Thank heaven he'd opened his eyes and breathed, Hi. She'd never want anything more than that in her whole life. What if this hadn't been the outcome. She wouldn't think that. She had to go back to the hospital.

Was eleven too late to call Chelsea back? She'd want to know the time and place of Sandro's funeral. Noel would phone in the morning once he had that information.

Maria Vasiliadis had very much appreciated Kyra's call. After speaking with Andrei she'd called Kyra back, to say the funeral was set, day after tomorrow, 2:00 PM.

Bonnie watched as Stockman was wheeled from Emergency to Intensive Care. She paused to use the washroom. She checked the messages on her cellphone. Lorna. She called back. "It's Bonnie."

"Oh Bonnie, it's so awful."

"You can't know." Condolences, and shock, and how could Stockman, and soon both women were in tears again. Till Bonnie heard the drift of Lorna's comments, trying to learn what Stock had told Bonnie; if anything. So Bonnie, less kindly, told Lorna.

"Bonnie, you have to believe me, I only concurred with the idea of sedation," she responded weakly. "I didn't want Vasiliadis to die."

"Your research, Lorna. The center of the universe, right? He had to die, didn't he? For—" WISDOM? She found she couldn't say the word. She closed her phone.

Terry left the hospital again about 4:00 AM. Richard was sleeping, sedated. She'd go to the lab and see to her kiddies. What an adolescent word for them. WISDOM and WIRED, all done. Bendwell shares would take a big hit.

Start looking after yourself, Paquette.

In the meantime, she had to look after the fish.

She opened the gate and drove in. No other cars. She parked, got out, closed the gate, unlocked the door, deactivated the alarm system.

In the lab she switched on the lights. The white mice squeaked; she represented food. The males were now female, but sterile. They'd be getting new females— Stupid thought. No more experiments. No more research, no more research.

———

Lorna had tossed and turned all night, half expecting the doorbell to ring, State Patrol officers again, this time with a warrant. They'd been by around 8:00 PM. They'd asked questions. They hadn't been rude. Just insistent. The only thing she'd learned from them that she hadn't already known, they'd asked if she had taken the Sandro Vasiliadis file. Of course not. So the file was missing. The police told her not to leave Coupeville. What a total mess—a collapsed card house, a toppled row of dominoes. At 6:33 by the backlit numbers on her clock she got up. She would comb through the WIRED records, try to construct a defense. Thank god she'd had an emergency meeting at Teeseborough House that night. She dressed, ate a cinnamon bun, and drove to the lab. She noted Terry's car in the parking lot. Maybe they could figure something out together.

———

Terry heard the front door open and glanced toward the hall: Lorna. She felt an upwelling of rage, retreated to the caridean shrimp tank and stared into it. She hadn't thought much about Lorna during the night. Gary should have shot Lorna instead. Shit, even angrier than she'd realized. Not just their work, which was her life, but physical lives destroyed, and all because—

Lorna opened the inner door. "Hi. Didn't expect to find you here."

"Well, I'm here."

"I see. The Vasiliadis file is missing. Could Richard have taken it?"

Terry turned. Her rage welled. "My husband is barely alive. Bonnie's husband is in Intensive Care too. Your remaining partner is arrested for murder and attempted murder. You knew how Vasiliadis died. All you can think about is a missing file?"

Lorna, struck by the blast, backed up. "I knew they were going to sedate him—"

"You knew way more than that."

"I didn't! The two of them—"

"The three of you agreed. Stock told Bonnie. And left it all on the tape recorder." Terry crossed her arms, the heat of anger replaced by ice. "If you and Stock and Gary hadn't pushed so hard with the hormones, Richard wouldn't have been shot."

"I had nothing to do with that!"

"Little by little, everything moved toward Gary shooting Richard."

"You didn't try real hard to stop us moving to humans. Neither did Richard."

"I objected, but I just run the lab, remember? I'm not a full team partner, remember? Richard objected, and you three overruled him."

"It was a democratic decision. Like all—"

"Murder isn't democratic!" Terry felt her heart pounding, her face flushed. "If you hadn't killed Sandro none of this would have happened!"

"I didn't kill Sandro." Quietly she added, "He was a failed experiment."

Terry saw a pudgy woman in too-tight slacks and a thick Aran cardigan, lipsticked mouth twisted in desperation. Desperation only for herself. Lorna, once a close friend. Gone, all gone. "Lorna." Her words were crystals of quartz. "Maybe you'll wiggle out of the murder charge. But you'll never practice medicine again. Get out of here. Leave! Leave!"

Maria Vasiliadis spent the morning driving around the parts of Seattle that had once been central to her life—the old neighborhood, her parents' house, the homes of uncles and aunts; and the area around St. Demetrius where, on Sunday mornings long ago, she and her friends had walked and giggled and gossiped while escaping their parents still inside the church. Here, tomorrow, she'd see her son one last time. Then that too would end. At least he'd be properly buried.

She arrived at the Poseidon at precisely noon, as Andrei had requested on the phone last night. She joined him at a table by the window. Greetings and chat. They ordered. Family stories over the food. With coffee Andrei said, "Have you thought further?"

"All night. All morning. I've been here since ten."

"And?"

"It's too late for me to come back."

"For some things, it's never too late."

"All right then, perhaps too soon. I haven't left Bellingham yet."

"But Bellingham has left you."

"I'm sorry?"

He touched her wrist with two fingers. "Kostas, Sandro."

"But I am still there. And you see, Andrei, I am not here. There I have my house, and my life. I have no life here."

"You have us."

Andrei speaks with such certainty, she thought. Such a sense of: this is the way things are, they cannot be different. It drove Kostas from the old neighborhood. It made Sandro wait over thirty years to become himself. "Yes," she said, "that's true."

"I think you would be happier, Maria, if you came home."

"Perhaps," she said.

"At any rate, please think of it much more. And seriously."

"I will." But she knew she wouldn't. At least not seriously.

———

At ten AM Noel began writing his report to Chelsea. By eleven he knew it made little sense unless he preceded it by the work they did when Ursula had hired them. By noon clarity demanded that he move yet further back and include their investigation for Maria and Andrei. So the pleasant day he had hoped for with Kyra didn't begin until mid-afternoon.

At which time they took an agreeable walk along the sunny shore and refused to talk further about the Sandro Vasiliadis case. At one point Kyra said, "Jerome. What do you think?"

"Well, he's different from what you've told me about Vance and Simon. And hugely different from Sam."

"Noel! I'm not thinking about marrying Jerome, for god's sake!"

"Well that's good." Kyra's three previous marriages and their bad ends. "Then what are you asking? Jerome does seem to be a fine person."

"Fine. Yes, I think so. I've never been with a fine person. Someone who was simply a nice man."

"True. But would you want to be, some day?"

She said nothing for a minute or two. A breeze had come up and they'd lost the sun. Would a nice man ever bash her around? Would a nice man kill himself? Would a nice man get irritated because she was off on a stakeout? Wasn't there someone partway between beating, suicide, jealousy on the one hand, niceness on the other? "I honestly don't know."

They'd understood Greek Orthodox funerals tended toward heavy ceremony and a long service, so on Thursday Kyra and Noel arrived an hour after starting time. They were there primarily to pay condolences and to respect Sandro's last moments, not to watch a performance.

On the drive to St. Demetrius Noel had remarked, "There's a loose end."

"Only one?" Kyra pulled out and passed a truck.

"Lorna Albright. With a good lawyer she's going to walk. Scot free."

"Not that free. The clinic's finished, her career as a researcher is over, and she'll probably lose her license."

"But she should pay in some more active way."

"I agree. But how?"

They drove in silence for three or four miles. The day had turned gray, neither rainy nor sunny, an unbroken grim sky, neither hot nor cold. The Pacific Northwest Coast in March.

Noel said finally, "I can't find or even create any kind of hold over her."

"Best I can think is putting her on cleaning duty in that women's health clinic she works at. Swab the floors. But I don't know how to set that up. It'd be a waste of her training."

Noel stared at a field of cows. "Some kind of alternative justice."

"I'd love it but I don't see it." Kyra's sarcastic tone. "I think society's bumpy punishing wheel will have to grind on."

"And I'm sure Dr. Haines will have a clever lawyer too."

"At least we did manage to stop him."

"And Jones stopped himself."

They had learned this morning from Assounian that the surgeon would have major brain damage. Oxygen deprivation. If Dawn Deane had found him a few minutes earlier, if he'd injected less morphine, if he'd been simply lying down so that his heart didn't have to fight an uphill battle to get oxygen to his brain— Most important, even then someone who knew, a doctor, could have administered naloxone. It was right there in the closet.

"What's naloxone?"

"An antagonist," Assounian had explained. "It competes with opioids for their receptor sites. It would have competed with the morphine and likely he'd have started breathing normally."

"His wife did CPR."

"Too late."

"But Haines was right there."

"We know," said Assounian.

"Jones will live?"

"We'll know more if he lasts the week. But Trevelyan is out of ICU."

Kyra parked the Tracker three blocks from the church and walked past attractive suburban houses with green lawns and flower beds about to burst with spring blooms. A hearse and half a dozen funeral-parlor limos waited in front of red brick walls that surrounded the church property. The sides of the octagonal church, red brick as well, rose to a semi-cupola, which formed a multiple arch. The roof, gliding down to where one arch touched another, shone pristine white. From the middle of the roof rose a narrow ten-foot lantern, also eight-sided, each wall built of glass frames in reds, greens, blues, purples.

Kyra and Noel entered the courtyard. Several men stood about talking. Half a dozen children, two on scooters, played a game that involved a lot of running. The door of the church stood open; sounds of chanting poured out. Inside, a wide vestibule separated the entry-way from the sanctuary, but the open glass doors created a unified space. Men wearing dark jackets and ties and deep in conversation milled about in the vestibule, and behind the pews, women in black sat with children, youngsters, and more men. On a table at the head of the central aisle, below the altar, rested the coffin. A priest waved a golden censer. Incense smoke poured from it, adding to the clouds above the coffin, the altar, the first rows of pews. Four boys in white cloaks with red cowls followed the priest.

Kyra and Noel sat in the next-to-last row on the far right aisle. A woman smiled at them, the only recognition of their arrival. The chanting continued, rose to a high pitch, became softer. Fifteen minutes later the ceremony ended with the pallbearers—they both recognized

Andrei Vasiliadis and that damn Vasily—carrying Sandro's coffin down the center aisle and out to the waiting hearse. The coffin was preceded by a gowned priest and his acolytes. Behind the coffin came Maria Vasiliadis on the arm of a man they didn't recognize, but who looked a bit like Andrei, and a group of men and women in black.

Kyra and Noel lingered in the vestibule as the mourners milled past. On the right, Maria, surrounded by other mourners, received condolences. Kyra saw Diana, Sandro's ex-wife, holding the hand of a pretty, leggy young girl, indubitably her daughter, Carla.

A voice behind them: "Hello." Noel and Kyra turned. Rudy Longelli, Sandro's bowling friend. "How you doing?"

They exchanged sad words about Sandro. Rudy said, "It's like his death was the tip of the iceberg."

"Yes," said Kyra.

"I mean, can you imagine, those doctors killing him? Crazy."

Kyra and Noel agreed. "Are you going to the cemetery?" Noel asked.

"No, I took a few hours off but I got to work tonight." He said goodbye, and left.

Brady and Ursula came out. Brady dabbed her eyes with a tissue, then spotted Noel and Kyra. "Hi," she said in a small voice. "I think she's resting quietly, don't you?"

It took Kyra a moment to understand. "I think she is, yes."

"Jeez, I just about cried my eyes out. Again." Brady smiled bravely. Ursula said they would go to the cemetery and bid a final goodbye to Sandra. "Thank you." They hugged, and she led Brady out.

Noel spotted Garth Schultz in the slowly exiting group; he hadn't noticed Kyra or Noel. Fifteen or so people behind Garth, the incongruous green-haired figure of Cora Lipton-Norton ambled past. No one paid her particular attention, and she seemed oblivious.

The crowd around Maria and the man who looked like Andrei led her to the door. Kyra and Noel headed toward them. Kyra said, "Mrs. Vasiliadis, we just came to present our condolences."

Noel said, "And wish you great strength for the future."

Maria Vasiliadis took a moment to recognize them. "Oh. Yes. Thank you very much."

Kyra said, "It's very sad."

"No. Truly. It's—it's better like this. Now I know that Sandro—that Sandro—"

"Maria. Come along." Andrei Vasiliadis had appeared at her side. "The limousine is waiting." He glanced at Kyra. "Oh. You. You have no place here." He took Maria's arm. "Come."

"Mrs. Vasiliadis?" A deep voice, behind Noel.

"Yes?" said Maria.

"My name is Chelsea."

Noel and Kyra turned.

"I was a friend of Sandro's. And an advisor." She reached out her hand to Maria. She stood three inches taller than Noel. Her makeup had been applied with a fine hand. She wore a straight black wool dress with a black sateen jacket over, and a string of pearls.

Maria took the offered hand and studied Chelsea's face. "You were a friend."

"Yes. I believe I helped Sandro in the last year of his life."

Noel would have sworn Chelsea had lowered her voice. Contradiction between an elegant woman and her baritone. Noel believed he could see that Maria Vasiliadis had heard what Chelsea was telling her.

Andrei stood at her side. "Maria, we really have to go now, the cemetery—"

"I'm glad you were able to help," said Maria to Chelsea, smiling sadly.

"In ways he wanted to be helped."

"Maria, really, we—"

Chelsea faced him. "Mr. Vasiliadis, I'm sorry for your loss. But Sandro's life would have been far easier if you'd tried to understand him better."

"What right do you—"

"Very little. But it's important for me to tell you that. And for you to hear it." She turned and strode out the door, a tall elegant woman, and disappeared around the corner.

"Goodbye, Mrs. Vasiliadis," said Noel. Kyra nodded at her, a small smile, and they left.

A NOTE:
This novel deals in part with transgendered sexual identity and sexual reassignment procedures. Trans experiences vary widely from person to person, and the story would like to honor that reality. The limited incidents and issues included here are not meant to represent any full spectrum of the trans community, nor should they be construed as a full understanding of what it means to be trans. This, therefore, is an apology for any offense that might be taken, for none is intended.

ACKNOWLEDGEMENTS

The authors would like to thank a number of people who have given us considerable insight into the complex subcultures that play a role in *Always Kiss the Corpse*. Barrie Humphrey guided us as we tried to clarify much of the science produced by the doctors of the WISDOM Clinic. Dorothy and Alex Ludwick were our first informants regarding the social and cultural side of Whidbey Island. Demetra Peters answered many of our questions about Greek Orthodoxy. And David Szanto shared with us his knowledge about queer identity. We appreciate all we learned from all of you. Any errors in the text are our own, either accidental or intentional to further the story.

Much of Whidbey as we have represented it is drawn from our research on the island. But don't go looking for the clinic. You'll have a hard time locating it.

SANDY FRANCES DUNCAN is the author of ten award-winning books for children and adults. Her short fiction and non-fiction articles have appeared in numerous literary journals, magazines and newspapers. Sandy's most recent historical fiction is *Gold Rush Orphan*, which was shortlisted for the BC Book Prize.

A National Magazine Award recipient and winner of the Hugh MacLennan Prize for fiction, GEORGE SZANTO is the author of half a dozen novels, the most recent being his Mexican trilogy, *The Underside of Stones, Second Sight* and *The Condesa of M.*, as well as several books of essays. He is a Fellow of the Royal Society of Canada. Please visit www.georgeszanto.com.

Duncan and Szanto's previous collaboration is the Islands Investigations International series is *Never Sleep With a Suspect on Gabriola Island.*

Never Sleep with a Suspect
on Gabriola Island

978-1-894898-89-8
$14.95, softcover

The first in the Island Investigations International Mystery series by
power-duo Sandy Frances Duncan and George Szanto

Noel and Kyra are on Gabriola Island to investigate the murder of an
art gallery groundskeeper. The vicious rumors surrounding the case
take several sinister turns, leading them into grave personal danger.
Kyra and Noel discover that even charming island communities can
keep deadly secrets

"Very sophisticated and great fun."—Shelagh Rogers, *The Next Chapter*